...is nothing new for the multitalented author,
but here she also brings in an intensity of political history
that is both fascinating and detailed."
—*RT Book Reviews* on *Seduction*

"Joyce excels at creating twists and turns
in her characters' personal lives."
—*Publishers Weekly*

"Another first-rate Regency, featuring multidimensional
protagonists and sweeping drama...Joyce's tight plot and
vivid cast combine for a romance that's just about perfect."
—*Publishers Weekly* on *The Perfect Bride* (starred review)

"Truly a stirring story with wonderfully etched characters,
Joyce's latest is Regency romance at its best."
—*Booklist* on *The Perfect Bride*

"Romance veteran Joyce brings her keen sense of humor
and storytelling prowess to bear on her witty,
fully formed characters."
—*Publishers Weekly* on *A Lady at Last*

"Joyce's characters carry considerable emotional weight,
which keeps this hefty entry absorbing,
and her fast-paced story keeps the pages turning."
—*Publishers Weekly* on *The Stolen Bride*

BRENDA JOYCE

Surrender

HARLEQUIN®
entertain, enrich, inspire™

Recycling programs
for this product may
not exist in your area.

ISBN-13: 978-0-373-77729-7

SURRENDER

This one's for Tracer and Tricia Gilson—
thanks for making my world of horses such a great place!

Surrender

PROLOGUE

Brest, France
August 5, 1791

HER DAUGHTER WOULD not stop crying. Evelyn held her, silently begging her to be quiet, as their carriage raced through the darkness. The road was rough, especially at their frantic pace, and the constant lurching and jostling did not help. If only Aimee would sleep! Evelyn feared they had been followed; she was also afraid that her daughter's cries would cause suspicion and bring undue attention to them even if they had successfully escaped Paris.

But Aimee was frightened—because her mother was frightened. Children could sense such things. But Evelyn was afraid because Aimee was the most important thing in her life, and she would die to keep her safe.

And what if Henri died?

Evelyn D'Orsay hugged her daughter, who had recently turned four, harder. She was seated in the front of the carriage with the driver, Laurent, her husband's valet, now turned jack-of-all-trades. Her husband was slumped in the backseat, unconscious, seated between Laurent's wife, Adelaide, and her own ladies' maid, Bette. She glanced back now, her heart lurching with alarm. Henri remained deathly white.

His health had begun to fail him sometime after Aimee

had been born. He had also become consumptive. Was his heart failing him now? Could he survive this mad, frightening dash through the night? Would he survive the Channel crossing? Evelyn knew he needed a doctor, desperately, just as she knew this wild carriage ride could not be helpful to him.

But if they could make it out of France, if they could make it to Britain, they would be safe.

"How far are we?" she whispered. Luckily Aimee had stopped crying; in fact, she had fallen asleep.

"I think we are almost there," Laurent said. They were speaking French. Evelyn was an Englishwoman, but she had been fluent in French even before she had met the Count D'Orsay, becoming his child bride almost overnight.

The horses were lathered and blowing hard. Fortunately, they did not have much farther to go—or so Laurent thought. And it would soon be dawn. At dawn, they were to disembark with a Belgian smuggler, who was awaiting them even now.

"Will we be late?" she asked, keeping her tone low, which was a bit absurd, as the coach rattled and groaned with the horses' every stride.

"I think we will have an hour to spare," Laurent said, "but not much more than that." He glanced briefly at her, his look a significant one.

She knew what he was thinking now—they were all thinking it. It had been so hard to escape Paris. There would be no going back, not even to their country home in the Loire Valley. They must leave France if they were to survive. Their lives were at stake.

Aimee was sound asleep. Evelyn stroked her soft, dark hair and fought her own need to weep with fear and desperation.

She glanced back at her elderly husband again. Since meeting and marrying Henri, her life had felt so much like a fairy tale. She had been a penniless orphan, subsisting on the charity of her aunt and uncle; now, she was the Countess D'Orsay. He was her dearest friend, and the father of her daughter. She was so grateful to him for all that he had done for her, and all he meant to do for Aimee.

She was so afraid for him now. His chest had been bothering him all day. But he had survived their flight from Paris, and Henri had insisted that they must not delay. Their neighbor had been imprisoned last month for crimes against the state. The Vicomte LeClerc had not committed any crimes—she was sure of it. But he was an aristocrat....

Their usual residence was Henri's family estate in the Loire Valley. But every spring Henri would pack up the family and they would go to Paris for a few months of theater, shopping and dining. Evelyn had fallen in love with Paris the very first time she had set foot in the city, before the revolution. But the city she had once loved no longer existed, and had they realized how dangerous Paris had become, they wouldn't have gone for another visit.

In spite of the revolution, Paris remained flooded with unemployed workers, laborers and farmers, who roamed the streets seeking revenge upon anyone who had anything, unless they were striking or rioting. Taking a stroll down the Champs-Élysées was no longer pleasant, nor was riding in the park. There were no more interesting supper parties, no more scintillating operas. Shops catering to the nobility had long since closed their doors.

The fact that her husband, the comte, was a relation of the queen had never been a secret. But the moment a hatmaker had realized the connection, their lives had suddenly and truly changed. Shopkeepers, bakers, prostitutes, sansculottes and even National Guardsmen had kept watch upon her and her family at their townhome. Every time her door was opened, sentinels could be seen standing outside. Every time she left the flat she had been followed. It had become too frightening to venture outside of the apartment. It was as if they were suspected of crimes against the state. And then LeClerc had been arrested.

"Your time will come." A passerby had leered at her the day their neighbor was taken away in shackles.

And Evelyn had become afraid to go out. She had ceased doing so. From that moment, they had become actual prisoners of the people. She had begun to believe that they would not be allowed to leave the city, if they tried. And then a pair of French officers had called on Henri. Evelyn had been terrified that they were about to arrest him. Instead, they had warned him that he must not leave the city until given permission to do so and that Aimee must remain in Paris with them. And the fact that they had said so—that they even knew about Aimee— had triggered them as nothing else could. They had immediately begun planning their escape.

And it was Henri who had suggested they follow in the wake of the thousands of émigrés now fleeing France for Great Britain. Evelyn had been born and raised in Cornwall, and once she had realized that they were going home, she had been thrilled. She had missed the rocky beaches of Cornwall, the desolate moors, the winter storms, the blunt, outspoken women and the hardworking men. She missed taking tea at the nearby village inn, and the wild celebrations that ensued when a smuggler arrived with his precious cargo. Life in Cornwall could be difficult and harsh, but it had its softer moments. Of course, they would probably reside in London, but she also loved the city. She couldn't imagine a better—safer—country in which to raise her daughter.

Aimee deserved so much more. And she did not deserve to become another innocent victim of this terrible revolution!

But first they had to get from Brest to the smuggler's ship, and then they had to get across the Channel. And Henri had to survive.

She felt the surge of panic and she trembled. Henri needed a doctor, and she was tempted to delay their flight to attend him. She could not imagine what she would do if he died. But she also knew he wanted her and Aimee safely out of the country. In the end, she would put her daughter first.

"Has he shown any signs of reviving?" she cried, glancing over her shoulder.

"*Non,* Comtesse," Adelaide whispered. "*Le comte* needs a physician soon!"

If they delayed, in order to attend Henri, they would remain in Brest for another day or perhaps even more. Within hours, or at least by this evening, their disappearance would be noticed. Would they be pursued? It was impossible to know, except that the officials had warned them not to leave the city and they had defied that edict. If there was pursuit, there were two obvious ports to search—Brest and Le Havre were the most frequently used ports of departure.

There was no choice to make. Evelyn clenched her fists, filled with determination. She was not accustomed to making decisions, and especially not important ones, but in another hour they would be safely at sea, and out of reach of their French pursuers, if they did not delay.

They had reached the outskirts of Brest, and were pass-

ing many small houses now. She and Laurent exchanged
dark, determined looks.

A few moments later, salt tinged the air. Laurent drove
the team into the graveled courtyard of an inn that was
just three blocks from the docks. The night was now filled
with scudding clouds, at times in darkness, at other times,
brightened by the moon. As Evelyn handed her daughter
down to Bette, her tension intensified. The inn seemed
busy—loud voices could be heard coming from the public room. Perhaps that was better—it was so crowded, no
one would pay attention to them now.

Or perhaps they would.

Evelyn waited with Aimee, asleep in her arms, while
Laurent went inside to get help for her husband. She was
clothed in one of Bette's dresses and a dark, hooded man-
tle that had been worn by another servant. Henri was also
dressed as a commoner.

And finally Laurent and the innkeeper appeared. Evelyn slipped up her hood as he approached—her looks
were too remarkable to go unnoticed—and cast her eyes
down. The two men lifted Henri from the carriage and
carried him inside, using a side entrance. Holding Aimee
Evelyn followed with Adelaide and Bette. They quickly
went upstairs.

Evelyn closed the door behind her two women servants, daring to breathe with some relief, but not yet daring to remove her hood. She signaled Adelaide with her
eyes, not wanting her to light more than one candle.

If their disappearance had been noted, the French authorities might have put out warrants for their arrests.
Descriptions would accompany those warrants and their
pursuers would be looking for a little girl of four with
dark hair and blue eyes, a sickly and frail older nobleman
of medium height with gray hair and a young woman of

twenty-one, dark-haired, blue-eyed and fair-skinned, one remarkably beautiful in appearance.

Evelyn feared that she was too distinct in her appearance. She was too recognizable, and not just because she was so much younger than her husband. When she had first come to Paris, as a bride of sixteen, she had been acclaimed the city's most beautiful woman. She hardly thought that, but she knew her looks were striking and hard to miss.

Henri had been made comfortable in one bed, and Aimee in another. Laurent and the innkeeper had stepped aside, and were speaking in hushed tones. Evelyn thought that they were both grim, but there was urgency in the situation. She smiled at Bette, who was tearful and so clearly frightened. Bette had been given the choice of going home to her family in Le Loire. She had chosen instead to come with them, fearing being hunted down and interrogated if she did not.

"It will be all right," Evelyn said softly, hoping to reassure her. They were the same age, but suddenly Evelyn felt years older. "In a matter of moments, we will be on a ship, bound for England."

"Thank you, my lady," Bette whispered, sitting down beside Aimee.

Evelyn smiled again, then walked over to Henri. She took his hand and kissed his temple. He remained terrifyingly pale. She would not be able to bear it if he died. She could not imagine losing such a dear friend. And she knew just how dependent she was on him.

She was not certain that her aunt and uncle would welcome her back into their home, if need be. But that would be a last recourse, anyway.

The innkeeper left and Evelyn quickly hurried over to

Laurent, who seemed stricken. "What has happened?" she asked, with another curdling sensation.

"Captain Holstatter has left Brest."

"What?" she cried, aghast. "You must be mistaken. It is August the fifth. We are on time. It is almost dawn. In another hour, he is taking us to Falmouth—he has been paid half of his fee in advance!"

Laurent was starkly white. "He happened upon a very valuable cargo, and he left."

She was in shock. They had no means of crossing the Channel! And they could not linger in Brest—it was too dangerous!

"There are three British smugglers in the harbor," Laurent said, interrupting her thoughts.

There was a reason they had chosen a Belgian to take them to England. "British smugglers are usually French spies," she cried.

"If we are going to leave immediately, the only choice is to seek out one of them, or wait here, until we can make other arrangements."

Her head ached again. How was it that she was making the most important decision of their lives? Henri always made all of the decisions! And the way Laurent was looking at her, she knew he was thinking the same thing she was—that remaining in town was not safe. She turned and glanced at Aimee. Her heart lurched. "We will leave at dawn, as planned," she decided abruptly, her heart slamming. "I will make certain of it!"

Trembling, she turned and went to a valise that was beside the bed. They had fled the city with a great number of valuables. She took a pile of assignats from it, the currency of the revolution, and then, instinctively, took out a magnificent ruby-and-diamond necklace. It had been in her husband's family for years. She tucked both within the bodice of her corset.

Laurent said, "If you will use one of the Englishmen, Monsieur Gigot, the innkeeper, said to look for a ship named the *Sea Wolf*."

She choked on hysterical laughter, turning. Was she really going alone to meet a dangerous smuggler—at dawn and in the dark, in a strange city, with her husband near death—to beg for his help?

"His ship is the swiftest, and they say he can outrun both navies at once. It is fifty tons, black sails—the largest of the smuggling vessels in the harbor."

She shuddered, nodding grimly. The *Sea Wolf*...black sails... "How do I get to the docks?"

"They are three blocks from the inn," Laurent told her. "I think I should come with you."

She was tempted to agree. But what if someone discovered them while she was gone—what if someone realized who Henri was? "I want you to stay here and guard *le comte* and Aimee with your life. Please," she added, consumed with another intense wave of desperation.

Laurent nodded and walked her to the door. "The smuggler's name is Jack Greystone."

She wanted to cry. Of course, she would do no such thing. She pulled up her hood and gave her sleeping daughter one last look.

Evelyn knew she would find Greystone, and convince him to transport them across the Channel, because Aimee's future depended on it.

She hurried from the room, and waited to hear Laurent slide the bolt on the door's other side, before she rushed down the narrow, dark corridor. One taper burned from a wall sconce at the far end of the hall, above the stairs.

She stumbled down the single flight, thinking of Aimee, of Henri and a smuggler with a ship named the *Sea Wolf.*

The landing below let onto the inn's foyer, and just to her right was the public room. A dozen men were within, drinking spirits, the conversation boisterous. She rushed outside, hoping no one had noticed her.

Clouds raced across the moon, allowing some illumination. One torch lamp was lit on the street. Evelyn ran down the block, but saw no one ahead and no one lurking in the shadows. Relieved, she glanced back over her shoulder. Her heart seemed to stop.

Two dark figures were behind her now.

She began to run, seeing several masts in the sky ahead, pale canvas furled tightly against them. Another glance over her shoulder showed her that the men were also running—they were most definitely following her.

"Arrêtez-vous!" one of the men called, laughing. "Are we frightening you? We only wish to speak with you!"

Fear slammed through her. Evelyn lifted her skirts and ran toward the docks, which were now in front of her. And she instantly saw that cargo was being loaded onto one of the vessels—a cask the size of several men had been winched up and was being directed toward the deck of a large cutter with a black hull and black sails. Five men stood on the deck, reaching for the cask as it was lowered toward them.

She had found the *Sea Wolf.*

She halted, panting and out of breath. Two men were operating the winch. A third stood a bit apart, watching the activity. Moonlight played over his pale hair.

And she was seized from behind.

"Nous voulons seulement vous parler." We only want to speak to you.

Evelyn whirled to face the two men who had been following her. They were her own age, dirty, unkempt and poorly clothed—they were probably farmworkers and thugs. *"Libérez-moi,"* she responded in perfect French.

"A lady! A lady dressed as a maid!" the first man said, but he did not speak with relish now. He spoke with suspicion.

Too late, she knew she was in more danger than the threat of being accosted—she was about to be unmasked as a noblewoman and, perhaps, as the Countess D'Orsay. But before she could respond, a stranger said, very quietly, in English, "Do as the lady has asked."

The farmers turned, as did Evelyn. The clouds chose that moment to pass completely by the moon, and the night became momentarily brighter. Evelyn looked into a pair of ice-cold gray eyes and she froze.

This man was dangerous.

His stare was cold and hard. He was tall, his hair golden. He wore both a dagger and a pistol. Clearly, he was not a man to be crossed.

His cool glance left her and focused on the two men. He repeated his edict, this time in French. *"Faites comme la dame a demandé."*

She was instantly released, and both men whirled and hurried off. Evelyn inhaled, stunned, and turned to the tall Englishman again. He might be dangerous, but he had just rescued her—and he might be Jack Greystone. "Thank you."

His direct gaze did not waver. It was a moment before he said, "It was my pleasure. You're English."

She wet her lips, aware that their gazes were locked. "Yes. I am looking for Jack Greystone."

His eyes never changed. "If he is in port, I am not aware of it. What do you want of him?"

Her heart sank with dismay—for surely, this imposing

man, with his air of authority and casual power, was the smuggler. Who else would be watching the black ship as it was being loaded? "He has come recommended to me. I am desperate, sir."

His mouth curled, but there was no humor in his eyes. "Are you attempting to return home?"

She nodded, still staring at him. "We had arrangements to leave at dawn. But those plans have fallen by the wayside. I was told Greystone is here. I was told to seek him out. I cannot linger in town, sir."

"We?"

She hugged herself now, still helplessly gazing into his stare. "My husband and my daughter, sir, and three friends."

"And who gave you such information?"

"Monsieur Gigot—of the Abelard Inn."

"Come with me," he said abruptly, turning.

Evelyn hesitated as he started toward the ship. Her mind raced wildly. She did not know if the stranger was Greystone, and she wasn't certain it was safe to go with him now. But he was heading for the ship with black sails.

He glanced back at her, without pausing. And he shrugged, clearly indifferent as to whether she came or not.

There was no choice. Either he was Greystone, or he was taking her to him. Evelyn ran after him, following him up the gangplank. He didn't look at her, crossing the deck rapidly, and Evelyn rushed to fall into step behind him. The five men who were loading the cask all turned to stare openly at her.

Her hood had slipped. She pulled it up more tightly as he went to a cabin door. He opened it and vanished inside. She faltered. She had just noticed the guns lining the sides of the ship. She had seen smuggling ships as a child; this ship seemed ready to do battle.

She was even more dismayed and full of dread, but she had made her decision. Evelyn followed him inside.

He was lighting lanterns. Not looking up, he said, "Close the door."

It crossed her mind that she was very much alone with a complete stranger now. Shoving her trepidation aside, she did as he asked. Very breathless now, she slowly faced him.

He was standing at a large desk covered with charts. For one moment, all she saw was a tall, broad-shouldered man with golden hair tied carelessly in a queue, a pistol clipped to his shoulder belt, a dagger sheathed on his belt.

Then she realized that he was also staring at her.

She inhaled, trembling. He was shockingly attractive, she now realized, in both a masculine and a beautiful way. His eyes were gray, his features even, his cheekbones high and cutting. A gold cross winked from the widely open neck of his white lawn shirt. He was wearing doeskin breeches and high boots, and now she realized how powerful and lean his tall, muscular build was. His shirt clung to his broad chest and flat torso, and his breeches fit like a second skin. He did not have an ounce of fat on his hard frame.

She wasn't certain she had ever come into contact with such an inherently masculine man—and it was unnerving somehow.

She was also the object of intense scrutiny. He was leaning his hip against the desk and staring back at her, as openly as she was regarding him. Evelyn felt herself flush. He was, she thought, trying to see her features, which were partially concealed by her hood.

She now saw the small, narrow bed on the opposite

wall. She realized that this was where he slept. There was a handsome rug on the planked floor, a handful of books on a small table. Otherwise, the cabin was sparsely appointed and completely utilitarian.

"Do you have a name?"

She jerked, realizing that her heart was racing. How should she answer? For she knew she must never reveal who she was. "Will you help me?"

"I haven't decided. My services are expensive, and you are a large group."

"I am desperate to return home. And my husband is in desperate need of a physician."

"So the plot thickens. How ill is he?"

"Does it matter?"

"Can he reach my ship?"

She hesitated. "Not without help."

"I see."

He did not seem moved by her plight. How could she convince him to help them? "Please," she whispered, stepping away from the door. "I have a four-year-old daughter. I must get her to Britain."

He suddenly launched himself off the desk and strode slowly—indolently—toward her. "Just how desperate are you?" His tone was flat.

He had paused before her, inches separating them. She froze, but her heart thundered. What was he suggesting? Because while his tone was brisk, there was a speculative gleam in his eyes. Or was she imagining it?

She realized that she was mesmerized, and unbalanced. "I could not be more desperate," she managed, with a stutter.

He suddenly reached for her hood and tugged it down before she knew what he meant to do. His eyes immediately widened.

Her tension knew no bounds. She meant to protest. If she had wanted to reveal her face, she would have done so! As his gaze moved over her features, very slowly, one by one, her resistance died.

"Now I understand," he said softly, "why you would hide your features."

Her heart slammed. Was he complimenting her? Did he think her attractive—or even beautiful? "Obviously we are in some jeopardy," she whispered. "I'm afraid of being recognized."

"Obviously. Is your husband French?"

"Yes," she said, "and I have never been as afraid."

He studied her. "I take it you were followed?"

"I don't know—perhaps."

Suddenly he reached toward her. Evelyn lost her ability to breathe as he tucked a strand of dark hair behind her ear. Her heart went wild. His fingers had grazed her cheek—and she almost wanted to leap into his arms. How could he do such a thing? They were strangers.

"Was your husband accused of crimes against the state?"

She flinched. "No...but we were told not to leave Paris."

He stared.

She wet her lips, wishing she could decipher his thoughts, but his expression was bland. "Sir—will you help us—please?"

She could not believe how plaintive she sounded. But he was still crowding her. Worse, she now realized she could feel his body's warmth and heat. And while she was a woman of medium height, he made her feel small and fragile.

"I am considering it." He finally paced slowly away. Evelyn gulped air, ignoring the wild urge she had to fan herself with the closest object at hand. Was he going to reject her plea?

"Sir! We must leave the country—immediately. I am afraid for my daughter!" she cried.

He glanced at her, apparently unmoved. Evelyn had no idea what he was thinking, as an odd silence ensued. He finally said, "I will need to know who I am transporting."

She bit her lip. She hated deception, but she had no choice. "The Vicomte LeClerc," she lied.

His gaze moved over her face another time. "I will take payment in advance. My fee is a thousand pounds for each passenger."

Evelyn cried out. "Sir! I hardly have six thousand pounds!"

He studied her. "If you have been followed, there will be trouble."

"And if we haven't been followed?"

"My fee is six thousand pounds, madam."

She closed her eyes briefly, then reached into her bodice and handed him the assignats.

He made a disparaging sound. "That is worthless to me." But he laid them on his desk.

Evelyn grimly reached into her bodice. He did not look away, and she flushed as she removed the diamond-and-ruby necklace. His impassive expression did not change. Evelyn walked over to him and handed him the necklace.

He took the necklace, carried it to his desk and sat down there. She watched him take a jeweler's glass from a drawer and inspect the gems. "It is real," she managed. "That is the most I can offer you, sir, and it is not worth six thousand pounds."

He gave her a skeptical glance, his gaze suddenly sliding to her mouth, before he continued to study the rubies with great care. Her tension was impossible now.

He finally set the necklace and glass down. "We have a bargain, Vicomtesse. Although it is against my better judgment."

She was so relieved she gasped. Tears formed. "Thank you! I cannot thank you enough!"

He gave her another odd look. "I imagine you could, if you wished to." Abruptly he stood. "Tell me where your husband is and I will get him and your daughter and the others. We will disembark at dawn."

Evelyn had no idea what that strange comment had meant—or, she hoped she did not. And she could not believe it—he was going to help them flee the country, even if he did not seem overly enthused about it.

Relief began. Somehow, she felt certain that this man would get them safely out of France and across the Channel. "They are at the Abelard Inn. But I am coming with you."

"Oh, ho!" His gaze hardened. "You are hardly coming, as God only knows what might arise between the docks and the inn. You can wait here."

She breathed hard. "I have already been separated from my daughter for an hour! I cannot remain apart from her. It is too dangerous." And she was worried that, if someone discovered her party, they might take Henri prisoner—and Aimee, as well.

"You will wait here. I am not escorting you back to that inn, and if you do not do as I say, you may take back your necklace, and we will cancel our agreement."

His gaze had become as sharp as knives. Evelyn was taken aback.

"Madam, I will guard your daughter with my life, and I intend to be back on my ship in a matter of minutes."

She inhaled. Oddly, she trusted him, and clearly, he was not going to allow her to come.

Aware of her surrender, he opened a drawer and removed a small pistol and a bag of powder with a flint box. He closed the drawer and his stare was piercing. "The odds are that you will not need this, but keep it with you until I return." He walked around the desk and held the gun out to her.

Evelyn took the gun. His eyes had become chilling. But he was about to aid and abet traitors to the revolution. If he was caught, he would hang—or worse.

He strode to the door. "Bolt it," he said, not looking back.

Her heart slammed in unison with the door. Then she ran to it and threw the bolt, but not before she saw him striding across the ship's deck, two armed sailors falling into step with him.

She hugged herself, shivering. And then she prayed for Aimee, and for Henri. There was a small bronze clock on the desk; it was five-twenty now. She went and sat down in his chair.

His masculinity seemed to rise up and engulf her. If only he had let her join him to retrieve her daughter and husband. She leaped up from his chair and paced. She could not bear sitting in his chair, and she wasn't about to sit on his bed.

At a quarter to six, she heard a sharp knock on the cabin door. Evelyn rushed to it as he said, "It is I."

She threw the bolt and opened the door. The first thing she saw was Aimee, yawning—she was in the smuggler's arms. Tears began. He stepped into the cabin and handed Aimee to her. Evelyn hugged her, hard, but her gaze met that of the captain's. "Thank you."

His glance held hers as he stepped aside.

"Evelyn."

She froze at the sound of Henri's voice. Then, incred-

ulous, she saw him being held upright by two seamen.
Laurent, Adelaide and Bette were behind them. "Henri!
You have awakened!" she cried, thrilled.

And as the seamen brought him inside, she set Aimee
down and rushed to him, putting her arm around him to
help him stand.

"You are not going to England without me," he said
weakly.

Tears fell now. Henri had awoken, and he was determined to be with them as they started a new life in England. She helped him to the bed, where he sat down,
still weak and exhausted. Laurent and the women began
bringing in their baggage as the two seamen left.

Evelyn continued to clasp her husband's hands, but
she turned.

The Englishman was staring at her. "We are hoisting
sail," he said abruptly.

Evelyn stood, their stares locked. His was so serious.
"It seems that I must thank you another time."

It was a moment before he spoke. "You can thank me
when we reach Britain." He turned to go.

It was as if there was an innuendo in his words. And
somehow, she knew what that innuendo was. But surely
she was mistaken. Evelyn did not think twice. She ran
to him—and in front of him. "Sir! I am deeply in your
debt. But to whom do I owe the lives of my daughter and
my husband?"

"You owe Jack Greystone," he said.

CHAPTER ONE

Roselynd on the Bodmin Moor, Cornwall
February 25, 1795

"THE COUNT WAS a beloved father, a beloved husband, and he will be sorely missed." The parson paused, gazing out on the crowd of mourners. "May he rest eternally in peace. Amen."

"Amen," the mourners murmured.

Pain stabbed through Evelyn's heart. It was a bright sunny day, but frigidly cold, and she could not stop shivering. She stared straight ahead, holding her daughter's hand, watching as the casket was being lowered into the rocky ground. The small cemetery was behind the parish church.

She was confused by the crowd. She hadn't expected a crowd. She barely knew the village innkeeper, the dressmaker or the cooper. She was as vaguely acquainted with their two closest neighbors, who were not all that close, as the house they had bought two years ago sat in solitary splendor on the Bodmin Moor, and was a good hour from everyone and anyone. In the past two years, since retreating from London to the moors of eastern Cornwall, they had kept to themselves. But then, Henri had been so ill. She had been preoccupied with caring for him and raising their daughter. There had not been time for social calls, for teas, for supper parties.

How could he leave them this way?

Had she ever felt so alone?

Grief clawed at her; so did fear.

What were they going to do?

Thump. Thump. Thump.

She watched the clods of dirt hitting the casket as they were shoveled from the ground into the grave. Her heart ached terribly; she could not stand it. She already missed Henri. How would they survive? There was almost nothing left!

Thump. Thump. Thump.

Aimee whimpered.

Evelyn's eyes suddenly flew open. She was staring at the gold starburst plaster on the white ceiling above her head; she was lying in bed with Aimee, cuddling her daughter tightly as they slept.

She had been dreaming, but Henri was truly dead.

Henri was dead.

He had died three days ago and they had just come from the funeral. She hadn't meant to take a nap, but she had lain down, just for a moment, beyond exhaustion, and Aimee had crawled into bed with her. They had cuddled, and suddenly, she had fallen asleep....

Grief stabbed through her chest. Henri was gone. He had been in constant pain these past few months. The consumption had become so severe, he could barely breathe or walk, and these past weeks, he had been confined to his bed. Come Christmastime, they had both known he was dying.

And she knew he was at peace now, but that did not ease her suffering, even if it eased his. And what of Aimee? She had loved her father. And she had yet to shed a tear. But then, she was still just eight years old, and his death probably did not seem real.

Evelyn fought tears—which she had thus far refused to shed. She knew she must be strong for Aimee, and for those who were dependent on her—Laurent, Adelaide and Bette. She looked down at her daughter and softened instantly. Aimee was fair, dark-haired and beautiful. But she was also highly intelligent, with a kind nature and a sweet disposition. No mother could be as fortunate, Evelyn thought, overcome with the power of her emotions.

Then she sobered, aware of the voices she could just barely hear, coming from the salon below her bedroom. She had guests. Her neighbors and the villagers had come to pay their respects. Her aunt, uncle and her cousins had attended the funeral, of course, even though they had only called on her and Henri twice since they had moved to Roselynd. She would have to greet them, too, somehow, even though their relationship remained unpleasant and strained. She must find her composure, her strength and go downstairs. There was no avoiding her responsibility.

But what were they going to do now?

Dread was like a fist in her chest, sucking all the air out of her lungs. It turned her stomach over. And if she allowed it, there would be panic.

Carefully, not wanting to awaken her child, Evelyn D'Orsay slid from the bed. As she got up slowly, tucking her dark hair back into place while smoothing down her black velvet skirts, she was acutely aware that the bedroom was barely furnished—most of Roselynd's furnishings had been pawned off.

She knew she should not worry about the future or their finances now. But she could not help herself. As it turned out, Henri had not been able to transfer a great deal of his wealth to Britain before they had fled France almost four years earlier. By the time they had left London, they had run down his bank accounts so badly that they had finally settled on this house, in the middle of the stark moors, as it had been offered at a surprisingly cheap price and it was all they could afford.

She reminded herself that at least Aimee had a roof over her head. The property had come with a tin mine, which was not doing well, but she intended to investigate that. Henri had never allowed her to do anything other than run his household and raise their daughter, so she was completely ignorant when it came to his finances, or the lack thereof. But she had overheard him speaking with Laurent. The war had caused the price of most metals to go sky-high, and tin was no exception. Surely there was a way to make the mine profitable, and the mine had been one reason Henri had decided upon this house.

She had but a handful of jewels left to pawn.

But there was always the gold.

Evelyn walked slowly across the bedroom, which was bare except for the four-poster bed she had just vacated, and one red-and-white-print chaise, the upholstery faded and torn. The beautiful Aubusson rug that had once covered the wood floors was gone, as were the Chippendale tables, the sofa and the beautiful mahogany secretary. A Venetian mirror was still hanging on the wall where once there had been a handsome rosewood bureau. She paused before it and stared.

She might have been considered an exceptional beauty as a young woman, but she was hardly beautiful now. Her features hadn't changed, but she had become haggard. She was very fair, with vivid blue eyes, lush dark lashes and nearly black hair. Her eyes were almond-shaped, her cheekbones high, her nose small and slightly tilted. Her mouth was a perfect rosebud. None of that mattered. She looked tired and worn, beyond her years. She appeared to be forty—she would be twenty-five in March.

But she didn't care if she looked old, exhausted and perhaps even ill. This past year had drained her. Henri had declined with such alarming rapidity. This past month, he hadn't been able to do anything for himself, and he hadn't left his bed, not a single time.

Tears arose. She brushed them aside. He had been so dashing when they had first met. She had not expected his attentions! Mutual acquaintances had directed him to her uncle's home, and the visit of a French count had put the household in an uproar. He had fallen in love with her at first sight. She had, at first, been overwhelmed by his courtship, but she had been an orphan of fifteen. She could not recall anyone treating her with the deference, respect and admiration that he had showered upon her; it had been so easy to fall in love.

She missed him so much. Her husband had been her best friend, her confidant, her safe harbor. She had been left on her uncle's doorstep when she was five years old by her father, her mother having just passed away, and she had never been accepted by her aunt, uncle or her cousins as anything other than the penniless relation they must raise. Her lonely childhood had been made worse by taunts and insults. Her clothes had been hand-me-downs. Her chores had included tasks no gentlewoman would ever perform. Her aunt Enid had constantly reminded her of what a burden she was, and what a sacrifice her aunt was making. Evelyn was a gentlewoman by birth, yet she had spent as much time with the servants, preparing meals and changing beds, as she had spent with her cousins. She was a part of the family, yet she was only allowed to reside on its fringes.

Henri had taken her away from all of that, and he had made her feel like a princess. But in fact, he had made her his countess.

He might have been twenty-four years older than she was, but he had died well before his time. Evelyn tried to remind herself that he was finally at peace—in more ways than one.

While he had loved her and adored their daughter, he hadn't been happy, not since leaving France.

He had left his friends, his family and his home behind. Both of his sons from a previous marriage had been victims of Le Razor. The revolution had also taken his brother, his nieces and nephews, and his many cousins, too. Adding to his heartache had been the fact that he had never truly accepted their move to Britain; he had left his beloved country behind, as well.

Every passing day in London had made him a bit angrier. But perhaps it was the move to Cornwall that had truly changed him. He hated the Bodmin Moor, hated their home, Roselynd. He had finally told her that he hated Britain. And then he had wept for everything and everyone that he had lost.

Evelyn trembled. Henri had changed so much in the past four years, but she refused to be completely honest with herself. If she was, she might admit that the man she had loved had died a long time ago. Leaving France had destroyed his soul.

Caring for him and their daughter, in such circumstances, had been exhausting enough, and when his illness had become so severe, it had been even worse. She was exhausted now. She wondered if she would ever feel young and strong again, if she would ever feel pretty.

She stared at her reflection more intensely. If the tin mine could not be turned around, the day would come where she would not be able to feed or clothe her daughter. And she must never let that happen....

Evelyn inhaled. A month ago, when it had become

clear that the end was near, Henri had told her that he had buried a small fortune in gold bullion in the backyard of their home in Nantes. Evelyn had been incredulous. But he had insisted, right down to the details of where he had buried the fortune. And she had believed him.

If she dared, a fortune awaited her and Aimee in France. And that fortune was her daughter's birthright. It was her future. Evelyn was never going to leave her daughter destitute, the way her own father had left her.

She ignored a new, terrible pang. She must do whatever she had to for Aimee. But how on earth could she retrieve it? How could she possibly return to France, to recover the gold? She would need an escort; she would need a protector, and he would have to be someone she could trust.

To whom could she turn as an escort? Whom could she possibly trust?

Evelyn stared at the mirror, as if the looking glass might provide an answer. She could still hear her guests in conversation in the salon downstairs. Tired and grief stricken, she was not going to find any answers tonight, she decided. Yet she was almost certain that she knew the answer, that it was right there in front of her; she simply could not see it.

And as she turned, a soft knock sounded on her door. Evelyn went to her daughter, kissed her as she slept and pulled up a blanket. Then she crossed the room to the door.

LAURENT WAS WAITING for her in the hall, and he was stricken with worry. He was a slim, dark man with dark eyes, which widened upon seeing her. "*Mon Dieu!* I was beginning to think that you meant to ignore your guests.

Everyone is wondering where you are, Comtesse, and they are preparing to leave!"

"I fell asleep," she said softly.

"And you are exhausted, it is obvious. Still, you must greet everyone before they leave." He shook his head. "Black is too severe, Comtesse, you should wear gray. I think I will burn that dress."

"You are not burning this dress, as it was very costly," Evelyn said, ushering him out and closing the door gently. "When you see Bette, would you send her up to sit with Aimee?" They started down the hall. "I don't want her to awaken, alone, with her father having just been buried."

"Bien sûr." Laurent glanced worriedly at her. "You need to eat something, madame, before you fall down."

Evelyn halted on the landing above the stairs, very aware of the crowd awaiting her downstairs. Trepidation coursed through her. "I can't eat. I did not expect such attendance at the funeral, Laurent. I am overcome by how many strangers came to pay their respects."

"Neither did I, Comtesse. But it is a good thing, *non?* If they did not come today to pay their respects, when would they come?" Evelyn smiled tightly and started down the stairs. Laurent followed. *"Madame?* There is something you must know."

"What is that?" she asked, over her shoulder, pausing as they reached the marble ground floor.

"Lady Faraday and her daughter, Lady Harold, have been taking an inventory of this house. I actually saw them go into every room, ignoring the closed doors. I then saw them inspecting the draperies in the library, madame, and I was confused so I eavesdropped."

Evelyn could imagine what was coming next, as the draperies were very old and needed to be replaced. "Let me guess. They were determining the extent of my fall into poverty."

"They seem amused to find the draperies moth-eaten." Laurent scowled. "I then heard them speaking, about your very unfortunate circumstances, and they were extremely pleased."

Evelyn felt a new tension arise. She did not want to recall her childhood now. "My aunt was never kindly disposed toward me, Laurent, and she was furious I made such a good match with Henri, when her daughter was far more eligible. She dared to say so, several times, directly to me—when I had nothing to do with Henri's suit. I am not surprised that they inspected this house. Nor am I surprised that they are happy I am currently impoverished." She shrugged. "The past is passed, and I intend to be a gracious hostess."

But Evelyn bit her lip, as memories of her childhood tried to rush up and engulf her. She suddenly recalled spending the day pressing her cousin Lucille's gowns, her fingers burned from the hot iron, her stomach so empty it was aching. She couldn't recall what mischief she had been accused of committing, but Lucille had habitually fabricated attacks upon her, causing her aunt to find some suitable punishment.

She hadn't seen her cousin, now married to a squire, since her wedding, and she hoped Lucille had matured, and had better things to do than amuse herself at Evelyn's expense. But clearly, her aunt remained inclined against her. It was so petty.

"Then you must remember that she is merely a gentlewoman, while you are the Comtesse D'Orsay," Laurent said firmly.

Evelyn did smile at him. But she had no intention of throwing her title in anyone's face, especially not when her finances were so strained. She hesitated on the threshold of the salon, which was as threadbare as her bedroom. The walls were painted a pleasing yellow, and the wainscoting and woodwork were very fine, but only a striped gold-and-white sofa and two cream-colored chairs remained in the room, surrounding a lonely marble-topped table. And everyone she had seen at the funeral was now crowded into the room.

Evelyn entered the salon and turned immediately to her closest guests. A big, bluff man with dark hair bowed awkwardly over her hand, his tiny wife at his side. Evelyn fought to identify him.

"John Trim, my lady, of the Black Briar Inn. I saw your husband once or twice, when he was on the road to London and he stopped for a drink and eats. My wife baked you scones. And we have brought you some very fine Darjeeling tea."

"I am Mrs. Trim." A tiny, dark-haired woman stepped forward. "Oh, you poor dear, I can't imagine what you are going through! And your daughter is so pretty—just like you! She will love the scones, I am certain. The tea, of course, is for you."

Evelyn was speechless.

"Come down to the inn when you can. We have some very fine teas, my lady, and you will enjoy them." She was firm. "We take care of our own, we do."

Evelyn realized that this Cornishwoman considered her a neighbor, still, never mind that she had spent five years living in France, and that she had married a Frenchman. Now she regretted never stopping by the Black Briar Inn for tea since moving to Roselynd. If she had, she would know these good, kind people.

And as she began greeting the villagers, she realized that everyone seemed genuinely sympathetic and that most of the women present had brought her pies, muffins, dried preserves or some other kind of edible gift. Evelyn was so moved. She knew she was going to become undone by all of the compassion her neighbors were evincing.

The villagers finally drifted away, leaving for their homes. Evelyn now saw her aunt and uncle, as only her family remained in the room.

Aunt Enid stood with her two daughters by the marble mantel above the fireplace. Enid Faraday was a stout woman in a beautiful gray-satin gown and pearls. Her eldest daughter, Lucille—the initiator of so many of Evelyn's childhood woes—also wore pearls and an expensive and fashionable dark blue velvet gown. She was now pleasantly plump, but she was still a pretty blonde.

Evelyn glanced at Annabelle, her other cousin, who remained unwed. She wore gray silk, had brownish-blond hair, and while once fat, she was now very slim and very pretty. Annabelle had always followed Lucille's lead and had been very submissive to her mother. Evelyn wondered if she had learned how to think for herself. She certainly hoped so.

Her aunt and cousins had seen her, as well. They all stared, brows raised.

Evelyn managed a slight smile; none of her female relations smiled back.

Evelyn turned to her uncle, who was approaching her. Robert Faraday was a tall, portly man with a rather distinguished air. Her father's older brother, he had inherited the estate, while her father had taken his annual pension and gone gaming in Europe's infamous brothels and halls. In appearance, Robert hadn't changed.

"I am terribly sorry for your loss, Evelyn," Robert said gravely. He took both of her hands in his and kissed her on the cheek, surprising her. "I liked Henri, very much."

Evelyn knew he meant it. Robert had become friendly with her husband when he had first come to stay at Faraday Hall. When Henri wasn't courting Evelyn, he and Robert had been hacking, hunting or taking brandy together in the library. He had attended the wedding in Paris, and unlike Enid, he had enjoyed himself extremely. But then, he had never shared his wife's antipathy toward Evelyn. If anything, he had been somewhat absent and indifferent.

"It is a damned shame," her uncle continued. "I so liked the fellow and he has been good to you. I remember when he first laid eyes on you. His mouth dropped open and he turned as red as a beet." Robert smiled. "By the time supper was over, you were strolling in the garden with him."

Evelyn smiled sadly. "It is a beautiful memory. I will cherish it forever."

"Of course you will." He remained grave, his gaze direct. "You will get through, Evelyn. You were a strong child and you have obviously become a strong woman. And you are a very young woman, still, so in time, you will recover from this tragedy. Let me know what I can do to help."

She thought about the tin mine. "I wouldn't mind asking you for some advice."

"Anytime," he said firmly. He turned.

Enid Faraday stepped forward, smiling. "I am so sorry about the count, Evelyn."

Evelyn managed to smile in return. "Thank you. I am consoling myself by remembering that he is at peace now. He suffered greatly in the end."

"You know we wish to help you in any way that we can." She smiled, but her gaze was on Evelyn's expensive black velvet gown and the pearls she wore with them. Di-

amonds encrusted the clasp, which she wore on the side
of her neck. "You must only ask."

"I am sure I will be fine," Evelyn said firmly. "But
thank you for coming today."

"How could I fail to attend the funeral? The count was
the catch of your lifetime," Enid responded. "You know
how happy I was for you. Lucille? Annabelle? Come, give
your cousin your condolences."

Evelyn was too tired to decipher the innuendo, if there
was one, or to dispute her version of the past. Now she
hoped to end the conversation as quickly as possible, as
most of her guests were gone and she wished to retire.
Lucille presented herself. As she stiffly embraced her,
Evelyn saw that her eyes glittered with malice, as if the
past decade hadn't happened. "Hello, Evelyn. I am so
sorry for your loss."

Evelyn simply nodded. "Thank you for attending the
funeral, Lucille. I appreciate it."

"Of course I would come—we are family!" She smiled.
"And this is my husband, Lord Harold. I don't believe
you have met."

Evelyn somehow smiled at the plump young man who
nodded at her.

"It is so tragic, really, to be reunited under such circumstances," Lucille cried, jostling in front of her husband, who stepped backward to accommodate her. "It
feels like yesterday that we were at that magnificent
church in Paris. Do you remember? You were sixteen,
and I was a year older. And I do believe D'Orsay had a
hundred guests, everyone in rubies and emeralds."

Evelyn wondered what Lucille was doing—certain that
a barb was coming. "I doubt that everyone was in jewels."
But unfortunately, her description of the wedding was
more accurate than not; before the revolution, the French

aristocracy was prone to terribly lavish displays of wealth. And Henri had spent a fortune on the affair—as if there were no tomorrow. A pang of regret went through her—but neither one of them could have foreseen the future.

"I had never seen so many wealthy aristocrats. But now, most of them must be as poor as paupers—or even dead!" Lucille stared, seemingly rather innocently.

But Evelyn could hardly breathe. Of course Lucille wished to point out how impoverished Evelyn now was. "That is a terrible remark to make." It was rude and cruel—Evelyn would never say such a thing.

"You berate me?" Lucille was incredulous.

"I am not trying to berate anyone," Evelyn said, instantly retreating. She was tired, and she had no interest in fanning the flames of any old wars.

"Lucille," Robert interjected with disapproval. "The French are our friends—and they have suffered greatly—unjustly."

"And apparently, so has Evelyn." Lucille finally smirked. "Look at this house! It is threadbare! And, Papa, I am not retracting a single word! We gave her a roof over her head, and the first thing she did was to ensnare the count the moment he stepped in our door." She glared.

Evelyn fought to keep her temper, no easy task when she was so unbearably tired. She would ignore the dig that she was a fortune hunter. "What has happened to my husband's family and his countrymen is a tragedy," Evelyn said tersely.

"I hardly said it was not!" Lucille was annoyed. "We all hate the republicans, Evelyn, surely you know that! But now, you are here, a widow of almost twenty-five, a *countess,* and where is your furniture?"

Lucille hated her even now, Evelyn thought. And while

she knew she did not have to respond, she said, "We fled France—to keep our heads. A great deal was left behind."

Lucille made a mocking sound as her father took her elbow. "It is time for us to go, Lucille, and you have a long drive home. Lady Faraday," Robert said decisively to his wife. He nodded at Evelyn and began guiding Enid and Lucille out, Harold following with Annabelle.

Evelyn slumped in relief. But Annabelle looked back at her, offering a tentative and commiserating smile. Evelyn straightened, surprised. Then Annabelle, along with her family, disappeared into the front hall.

Evelyn turned, relieved. But the feeling vanished as she was instantly faced with two young gentlemen.

Her cousin John smiled hesitantly at her. "Hello, Evelyn."

Evelyn hadn't seen John since her wedding. He was tall and attractive, taking after his father both physically and in character. And he had been her one somewhat secret ally, during those difficult years of her childhood. He had been her friend, even if he had chosen not to engage his sisters directly.

Evelyn leaped into his arms. "I am so glad to see you! Why haven't you called? Oh, you have become so handsome!"

He pulled back, blushing. "I am a solicitor now, Evelyn, and my offices are in Falmouth. And…I wasn't sure I would be welcome—not after all you endured at the hands of my family. I am sorry that Lucille is still so hatefully disposed toward you."

"But you are my friend," she cried, meaning it. She had glanced at the dark handsome man standing with him, and recognized him instantly. Shocked, she felt her smile vanish.

He grinned a bit at her, but no mirth entered his dark eyes. "She is jealous," he said softly.

"Trev?" she asked.

Edward Trevelyan stepped forward. "Lady D'Orsay. I am flattered that you remember me."

"You haven't changed that much," she said slowly, still surprised. Trevelyan had evinced a strong interest in her before Henri had swept into her life. The heir to a large estate with several mines and a great tenant farm, it had almost seemed that he meant to seriously court her—until her aunt had forbidden Evelyn from accepting his calls. She hadn't seen him since she was fifteen years old. He had been handsome and titled then; he was handsome and commanding now.

"Neither have you. You remain the most beautiful woman I have ever seen."

She knew she blushed. "That is certainly an exaggeration—so you are still the ladies' man?"

"Hardly. I merely wish to flatter an old and dear friend—truthfully." He bowed. Then, he said, "My wife died last year. I am a widower, my lady."

Without thinking, she said, "Evelyn. We can hardly stand on formality, can we? And I am sorry to hear that."

He smiled at her, but his gaze was filled with speculation.

John stepped in. "And I am affianced. We are to wed in June. I wish for you to meet Matilda, Evelyn. You will like her very much."

She took his hand impulsively. "I am so happy for you."

Evelyn realized that she was now standing alone with the two gentlemen—everyone else had left. Her salon mostly empty, she became aware of just how exhausted she was—and that, as happy as she was to see both John and Trev, she desperately needed to lie down and rest.

"You seem tired," John said. "We will take our leave."

She walked them to the front door. "I am so glad you called. Give me a few days—I can't wait to meet your fiancée."

John hugged her, rather inappropriately. "Of course."

Trev was more formal. "I know this is a terrible time for you, Evelyn. If I can help, in any way, I would love to do so."

"I doubt that anyone can help. My heart, Trev, is sorely broken."

He studied her for a moment, and then both men stepped outside.

Evelyn saw their mounts tied to the railing as she closed the door—and that was the last thing she saw. Instantly, blackness claimed her and she collapsed.

"You are so exhausted that you fainted!"

Evelyn shoved the smelling salts with their sickly odor from her nostrils. She was seated on the cold, hard marble floor, a pillow between her and the front door. Laurent and his wife knelt beside her, both extremely concerned.

And she was still light-headed. "Is everyone gone?"

"Yes, everyone has left—and you swooned the moment the last guest was gone," Laurent accused. "I should have never allowed the guests to stay as long as they did."

"Aimee?"

"She is still asleep," Adelaide said. She stood. "I am going to get you something to eat."

Evelyn saw from the look on her face that protesting that she was not hungry would not dissuade her. Adelaide walked away, and she looked at Laurent. "This has been the longest day of my life." God, the tears threatened her again. Damn it. She would not cry!

"It is over," he soothed.

She gave him her hand and he helped her to stand up. As she did, a terrible migraine began. And with it came the now-familiar surging of panic and fear. "What are we going to do now?" she whispered.

He had become her confidant in these past few years, and she did not have to elaborate. "You can worry about Aimee's future tomorrow."

"I cannot think about anything else!"

He sighed. "*Madame,* you just fainted. We do not need to discuss finances tonight."

"There are hardly any finances to discuss. But I intend to start going over the estate ledgers and my accounts tomorrow."

"And how will you read them? They befuddled the count. I tried to help him, but I could not understand the numbers myself."

She studied him. "I heard you and Henri discussing the arrival of a new foreman. Did the previous foreman leave?"

Laurent was grim. "He was dismissed, madame."

"Why?"

"We have suspected theft, Lady D'Orsay, for some time. When *le comte* purchased this estate, the mine was doing handsomely. Now, there is nothing."

So there was hope, she thought, staring at the dapper Frenchman.

"I am afraid to ask what you are thinking," he said.

"Laurent, I am thinking that I have very little left to pawn."

"And?"

He knew her so well, she thought. And he knew almost everything there was to know about her, Henri and their affairs. But did he know about the gold? "Two weeks ago,

Henri told me that he had buried a chest filled with gold
at the château in Nantes."

Laurent simply met her gaze.

"You know!" she exclaimed, surprised.

"Of course I know—I was there—I helped him bury
the chest."

Evelyn started. "So it's true. He did not leave us penniless. He left a fortune for us."

"It's true." They stared at each other. "What are you
going to do?" he said unhappily.

"It has been quiet in France, since the fall of Robespierre."

He inhaled. "Please do not tell me that you are considering retrieving the gold!"

"No, I am not considering it—I have made up my
mind." And she was resolved. Her decision was made. "I
am going to find someone to take me to France, and I am
bringing that gold back—not for myself—but for Aimee."

"And who could you possibly trust with such a fortune?" he cried, paling.

But even as he spoke, the image came to her mind of a
tall, powerful man standing on the deck of a ship racing
the sea with unfurled black sails, his golden hair blowing in the wind....

She could not breathe or move. She hadn't thought
about the smuggler who had helped her and her family
escape France in years.

My services are expensive.

Thank me when we reach Britain.

Evelyn looked up at Laurent, stunned.

"Whom could you possibly trust with your life?" he
added desperately.

She wet her lips. "Jack Greystone," she said.

CHAPTER TWO

EVELYN STARED OUT of her bedroom window, still in her nightclothes, her hair braided. She was hugging herself.

She had just awoken. But she had slept fitfully, and her rest had been interrupted with terrible dreams. Oddly, she had been dreaming of her childhood. Of going to bed without supper, and being so lonely she had cried herself to sleep. And she had dreamed of Lucille and Enid, both of them mocking her for her airs, and declaring that she had gotten just what she deserved.

But then her dreams had changed, and she had dreamed that she was running through the night, being chased by evil. The night had become familiar, and she realized she wasn't on foot—she was in a carriage, and Aimee was crying in her arms. But they were being pursued. The gendarmerie were after them, and if they did not escape, Henri might be arrested and executed. She was terrified. The hand of evil was right behind them, ready to snatch them back....

She had awoken in a sweat, shivering with fear, her stomach in knots, tears upon her cheeks. It had taken her a second to return to reality and recall that she was not in the midst of fleeing France on that particular summer night. Henri had been buried yesterday, at the local parish church. She wasn't in France; she was at Roselynd.

Her chest seemed to tighten.

The sight of Jack Greystone standing at the helm of his

black ship, all sails unfurled, his legs braced against the sea, his tawny hair whipped by the wind, assaulted her. The image was one of power and command.

She suddenly found it hard to breathe.

She hadn't thought about Greystone in years—not until yesterday.

Was she really going to approach him and ask him for his services—again?

Did she have any other choice? Henri was dead, and she had to recover the gold he had left for them.

She trembled, because Henri's death still felt unreal— as if a part of her dream. Grief rose up instantly, choking her. So did fear, and even the feeling of abandonment. God, she was so alone, so overwhelmed, and frightened.

If only Henri had retrieved the gold before his death. But he had left that monumental task up to her, Evelyn. She prayed she was up to it.

Aimee would never find herself in the straits that Evelyn had been left in as a child, she vowed. Evelyn's father had loved her, or so she believed, but he had failed in his responsibility to her. He had been right to leave her with Robert, as he was too reckless and irresponsible to care for her, but it had been wrong to leave her penniless. She, Evelyn, must never fail her daughter.

"Mama? Are you crying?"

Aimee's small, frightened voice cut through her thoughts. Evelyn realized she was battling rising tears, but some of them were due to the great strain she was under. She faced her daughter, but not before wiping her eyes quickly with her fingertips. "Darling! Have I overslept?" She swept her close, into a big embrace.

"You never sleep in," Aimee whispered. "Are you tired today?"

"I was very tired, darling, but I am back to being myself now." Evelyn kissed her. "I will always miss your father," Evelyn said softly. "He was a good man, a good husband, a good father." But why hadn't he retrieved the gold in the past five years? Why had he left her with such a daunting task? When he hadn't allowed her any duties except those of being a mother and a wife, when he was still alive? If she had been allowed more independence, she might not feel so overwhelmed now.

She stepped back from Aimee, knowing she must find the kind of courage she never had before.

"Is Papa watching us from Heaven?" Aimee asked.

Evelyn wet her lips and somehow smiled. "Papa is certainly still with us—he will always be with us, even when he goes further into Heaven, he will be in our hearts and in our memories."

But suddenly she didn't understand why he hadn't at the very least made arrangements to have that gold brought from France to them. He had been of sound mind until the very end.

Was she actually *angry* with Henri now? She was incredulous. He had just passed, and she must not be angry with him! He had been so ill, he had loved her and Aimee, and if he could have recovered that gold for them, he would have done so!

And if Henri hadn't been able to retrieve the gold, was she mad to think that she could do so now, when she was just a woman, and a somewhat pampered noblewoman, at that?

But she would not go to France alone. She hoped to go there with Jack Greystone, and he was certainly capable of achieving anything he set his mind to.

His image assailed her again, as he stood at his ship's helm, the wind buffeting his shirt against his body, his hair streaming in it, as his cutter raced the wind.

Aimee stared solemnly at her. "I want Papa to be happy now."

Evelyn quickly hugged her. Aimee had seen how bitter and dark her father had become over the past few years. Children could not be fooled. She had sensed his anguish, his pain and his anger. "Your papa is certainly at peace now, Aimee, because he is in heaven with angels," she said softly. Aimee nodded solemnly. "Can he see us, Mama? From heaven?"

"I think he can." She smiled. "And that is how he will always watch over us. Now, can you leave me while I get dressed? And then we can take *le petit déjeuner* together."

And as Aimee nodded, smiling, Evelyn watched her leave the room. The moment her daughter was gone, she let Jack Greystone fill her thoughts. Her chest seemed to tighten again. And she most certainly knew why—but she hadn't expected to have such a silly reaction to the mere idea of him, not after all of these years.

Carefully, she sorted through her memories.

Henri had slept through most of the Channel crossing, and Bette had read to Aimee until the sea had lulled her back to sleep. Evelyn had stood by the porthole, watching the sunrise as it turned the sea pink and gold, marveling at the experience of crossing the Channel on a swift sloop with black sails. But she had been impatient. She hadn't wanted to remain in his cabin—while he was on deck.

And as soon as Aimee was asleep, with the sun barely in the sky, she had gone up on deck.

The sight of Jack Greystone standing at the helm of his ship was one she would never forget. She had watched him for a moment, noting his wide stance, his strong powerful build, as he braced against the wind. His hair had come loose, and it was whipped by the wind. Then he had turned and seen her.

Evelyn remembered his gaze being searing, even across the distance of the deck. However, she was probably imagining that. He had seemed to accept her presence, turning back to face the prow, and she had stood by the cabin, watching him command the vessel for a long time.

Eventually he had left the helm, crossing the deck to her. "There's a ship on the horizon. We're only an hour from Dover—you should go below."

She had trembled, their gazes locked. "Are we being pursued?"

"I don't know yet, and if we are, there is no way they can catch us before we reach land. However, we could encounter other vessels, this close to Britain. Go below, Lady LeClerc."

It wasn't a question. Silently, she had retreated to his cabin.

And there had been no chance to thank him when they had reached their berth, just south of London. Two of his sailors, in striped boatnecked tunics and scarves about their heads, had escorted her and her family to land in a small rowboat. Somehow he had arranged a wagon for them, in which they had been transported to the city. As they got into the vehicle, she had seen him in the distance, astride a black horse, watching them. She had wanted to thank him and she had wanted to wave; she hadn't done either.

As she got dressed now, choosing her dove-gray satin, she was reflective. He had haunted her for several days, and perhaps even several weeks. She had even written him a letter, thanking him for his help. But she hadn't known where to send it, and in the end, she had tucked it away.

She was older and wiser now. He had rescued her, her

husband and her daughter, and she had been somewhat smitten with him—not because he was undeniably attractive, but out of gratitude. Although she had paid him for his services—even if it was less than he had initially asked for—she owed him for the lives of her and her family. That cast him as a hero.

Trembling, she fastened the clasp of her pearl necklace, regarding herself in the mirror, surprised that she did not look half as haggard as she had yesterday. Her eyes held a new light, one that was almost a sparkle, and her cheeks were flushed.

Well, she certainly had her work cut out for her. She had no idea how to locate Jack Greystone, but now that she had thought about it, she was resolved. She trusted him with her life and she even trusted him, perhaps foolishly, with Henri's gold. He was the man for the task at hand.

Before there had been fear and panic. Now, there was hope.

EVERYONE KNEW THAT the road between Bodmin and London was heavily used by smugglers to transport their cargoes north to the towns just outside of the city, where the black market thrived. Having been raised at Faraday Hall, just outside of Fowey, Evelyn certainly knew it, too. Smuggling was a way of life in Cornwall. Her uncle had been "investing" in local smuggling ventures ever since she could recall. As a child, she had thrilled when the call went out that the smugglers were about to drop anchor, often in the cove just below the house. As long as the revenue men were not nearby, the smugglers would boldly berth in plain sight and in broad daylight, and everyone from the parish would turn out to help them unload their valuable cargo.

Farmers would loan their horses and donkeys to help move the goods inland; young tubsmen would pack ankers from the beach to the waiting wagons, huffing and puffing with their load; batsmen would be spread about, bats held high, just in case the preventive men appeared....

Children would cling to their mother's skirts. Casks of beer would be opened. There would be music, dancing, drinking and a great celebration, for the free trade was profitable for everyone.

Now, in hindsight, Evelyn knew what had brought Henri to Cornwall and her uncle's home in the first place. He had been investing in the free trade, as well, as so many merchants and noblemen were wont to do. It wasn't always easy making a profit, but when profits were made, they were vast.

She suddenly recalled standing with Henri in his wine cellars, in their château in Nantes, perhaps a year after giving birth to Aimee. He had insisted she come down to the cellar with him. His mood had been jovial, she now recalled, and she had been in that first flush of motherhood.

"Do you see this, my darling?" Still dashing and handsome, exquisitely dressed in a satin coat and breeches with white stockings, he had swept his hand across the rows of barrels lining his cellar. "You are looking at a fortune, my dear."

She had been puzzled, but pleased to find him in such good spirits. "What is in the barrels? They look like the barrels the smugglers in Fowey used."

He had laughed. "How clever you are!" Henri had explained that they were the very same kinds of casks used by smugglers everywhere, and that they were filled with liquid gold. He had untapped a barrel and poured clear liquid into the glass he held. She now knew that the liquid was unfiltered, undiluted, one-hundred-proof alcohol, which in no way resembled the brandy he drank every night, and had been drinking a moment ago.

"You can't drink it this way," he had explained. "It will truly kill you."

She hadn't understood. He had explained that after it arrived at its final destination in England, it would be colored with caramel and diluted.

And he had hugged her. "I intend to keep you in your silks, satins and diamonds, always," he had said. "You will never lack for anything, my dear."

Like her uncle, and a great many of her neighbors, Henri had financed and invested in various smugglers, both before and after their marriage. She knew he had stopped those investments when they had left France. There hadn't been enough in their coffers for him to finance those ventures anymore; he had become averse to taking risks.

He had intended to make certain that she had the resources with which to raise her daughter in luxury, but he had failed. Instead, she was the one fighting for enough funds to raise Aimee. She was the one seated in a carriage now, about to enter the kind of establishment no lady should ever enter alone, because she had to locate a smuggler, in order to provide for her daughter.

The Black Briar Inn was just ahead on the road, and Evelyn stared. Her heart skipped. She had taken the single horse curricle by herself, ignoring Laurent's protestations. If she was going to locate Jack Greystone, she would have to begin making inquiries somewhere, and the inn seemed like the most logical starting point. Surely John Trim knew Greystone—or knew of him. Surely Greystone had, at some time or another, used the coves in and around Fowey to land his cargoes. If he had, they would have had to traverse this road in order to reach London's black markets.

There was no other dwelling in sight. The inn sat upon the Bodmin Moor and the road to London in absolute isolation—a two-storied whitewashed building, with a slate-gray roof, a white brick stable adjacent. Two saddled horses and three wagons were parked in the stone courtyard. Trim had customers.

Evelyn braked her gig and slowly got out, tying her mare to the railing in front of the inn. As she patted the mare, a young boy of eleven or twelve came running out of the adjacent stables. Evelyn told him she wouldn't be long, and asked him to water the mare for her.

Evelyn pulled her black wool cloak closed, while removing her hood. As she crossed the front steps of the inn, she pulled off her gloves. She could hear men speaking in casual conversation as she pushed open the front door.

There was some tension as she stepped directly inside the inn's taproom. She realized she hadn't been inside an inn's public rooms in years—not since she had briefly paused with her family in Brest, before fleeing France.

Eight men were seated at one of the long trestle tables in the room, and all conversation ceased the moment she shut the front door behind her. One of the men was John Trim, the proprietor, and he leaped to his feet instantly.

Her heart raced. She felt terribly out of place in the common room. "Mr. Trim?"

"Lady D'Orsay?" His shock vanished as he came forward, beaming. "This is a surprise! Come, do sit down, and let me get the missus." He guided her toward a small table with four chairs.

"Thank you. Mr. Trim, I was hoping for a private word, if possible." She was aware now of the silence in the room, that all eyes were trained upon them, and that every word she uttered was being heeded.

Trim's dark brows rose, and he nodded. He led her into a small private dining room. "Please, have a seat, and I will be back in one minute," he said, and rushed out.

Evelyn sat down, rather ruefully, certain he was racing to his wife to tell her that she had called. She laid her gloves down on the dining table, glancing around the simple room. A brick fireplace was on one wall, several paintings of the sea on the others. He had left the door open, and she could see into the common room if she wished to do so.

She had no intention of explaining to Trim why she wished to engage a smuggler, and a specific smuggler at that. But she did not expect him to press her.

Trim returned, smiling. "The missus is bringing tea."

"That is so kind of you." Evelyn smiled as he took a seat, now clutching her reticule tightly. "Mr. Trim, I was wondering if you are acquainted with Jack Greystone."

Trim was so taken aback that his eyes widened and his brows shot up, and Evelyn knew his answer was yes. "Everyone knows of Greystone, Lady D'Orsay. He is the greatest smuggler Cornwall has ever seen."

She was aware of her heart racing. "Do you know him personally, sir? Has he passed through this inn?"

His expression of surprise was as comical as before. "My lady, I mean no disrespect, by why do you ask?"

He was wary, but of course he was—smugglers were hardly free men. "I must locate him. I cannot explain why, exactly, but I am in need of his services."

Trim blinked.

She smiled grimly. "Greystone got my family out of France, almost four years ago. I prefer not to say why I must speak with him now, but it is an urgent matter."

"And it isn't my concern, of course," Trim said. "Yes, Lady D'Orsay, he has passed through my inn, once or twice. But I will be honest with you—I haven't seen him in several years."

Her disappointment was immediate. "Do you know how I can find him?"

"No, I do not. The rumor is that Greystone lives in an abandoned castle on a deserted island, in the utmost secrecy."

"That is hardly helpful," Evelyn mused. "I must find him, sir."

"I don't know if you can. There's been a bounty on his head, which would explain why he lives on that island. He is wanted by the British authorities, Lady D'Orsay."

Evelyn was slightly amused. "Aren't all free traders wanted by the preventive men?" Smuggling had been a capital offense for as long as Evelyn could recall. Bounties were hardly uncommon. However, a great many smugglers got off scot-free, once they agreed to serve in His Majesty's navy, or find a few friends to do so in their stead. A smuggler might be able to plead down his case, as well, if he had the right solicitor. Many smugglers were deported, but they often returned, illicitly, of course. No smuggler took a bounty very seriously.

Trim shook his head grimly. "You don't understand. He has been running the British blockade. If His Majesty's men catch him, he will hang—not for smuggling, but for treason."

Evelyn froze. He was running King George's blockade of France? He was supplying the French in a time of war? Suddenly she was cold. "I don't believe it."

"Oh, he's running the blockade, Lady D'Orsay—they say he brags often and openly about it. And that is treason."

Evelyn was shaken. "Is he a spy, then, too?"

"I wouldn't know."

She stared, but rather than seeing Trim before her, she saw Jack Greystone at the helm of his ship. So many Cornish smugglers were spies for the French. But he had helped them escape France. Surely a French spy would not have done that.

She did not know why she was so dismayed. "I must speak with him, Mr. Trim, and if you can help me, I will forever appreciate it."

"I will do my best. I will make some inquiries on your behalf. But my understanding is that he lies very low, to avoid His Majesty's Men. If he is not at sea, he is on his island. I do know that, once in a while, he has been seen in Fowey. You might try the White Hart Inn."

Faraday Hall was just outside Fowey. Was it possible that her uncle might know, or know of, Greystone?

"You might also go to London," Trim said as his wife entered the room with a tray filled with tea and refreshments. "His two sisters live there, and so does his brother, or so I have heard."

EVELYN STARED AT the letter she was trying to write.

Dear Lady Paget,

I hope I am not offending you by writing to you now. We have never met, and you may find my request presumptuous, but it has come to my attention that you are Jack Greystone's sister. I was briefly acquainted with him several years ago, and am currently trying to contact him. If you could help me do so, I would be greatly in your debt.

Sincerely,
Lady Evelyn D'Orsay

It did not seem right—it seemed terribly forward and bold. Evelyn laid her quill down and tore the parchment into shreds.

Any woman receiving such a missive would instantly dismiss it. If she received such a letter, she would assume that some lovesick woman was pursuing her brother! Yet Evelyn could not state why she wished to locate Greystone, and therein lay the problem.

She might have to go to London, and boldly call on either the Countess of Bedford or the Countess of St Just, Evelyn thought grimly. As she did not know either woman, the notion was daunting. However, she had learned that Lady Paget was married to a man with French relations, so she might be able to use that as some kind of entrée. But before she took such a trip, which would require some expenses and take several days, she would leave no stone unturned in Cornwall.

She felt some despair. Having already spent the past week unearthing a great many Cornish stones she did not have very many left to turn over.

Greystone had a bounty on his head. If caught, there would be no pleading down the charges of smuggling, no simple transportation. If caught, he could be imprisoned indefinitely—habeas corpus had been suspended last May—or he could hang, as John Trim had said. And that meant…Jack Greystone was in hiding.

Of course he was. She happened to know firsthand how clever, resourceful and adept he was. She had no doubt that he was also an extremely wary man. A few days ago, she had been so hopeful, and so certain, that she would be able to find him and convince him to aid her in recovering the gold in France. Now she was filled with doubt. It almost felt as though she was looking for a needle in a

haystack. If he did not wish to be found, would she ever
be able to locate him?

She had spent the past week asking everyone she
thought could be even remotely helpful about him. She
had gone to the various shopkeepers in the local village,
one by one, but while everyone knew of him, no one knew
him personally. He was most definitely notorious, and
held in the highest esteem by the local Cornish people.

Then she had turned her attention to Fowey. She had
spoken to the owner of the White Hart Inn, as John Trim
had suggested, but he had been purposefully unhelpful.

She had spent two days in town, speaking with the
shopkeepers and merchants there, but to no avail. She was
beginning to think that there were very few stones left to
turn. Of course, there did remain one—and it was a rock.

She was going to have to call on her uncle.

EVELYN STARED AT the imposing front entrance of her aunt
and uncle's home. A tall square stone house, the front entrance was in the style of a temple, with large columns
supporting a pediment. She inhaled. She had not been
back to Faraday Hall since her marriage, almost nine
years ago.

As she slowly got out of the gig, she thought about her
childhood: her aunt's constant harping, Lucille's cruelty,
and spending most of her time by herself, doing various
chores. A wave of loneliness swept over her. It was accompanied by a wave of grief. How had she survived such
a lonely childhood? Her husband had changed all of that,
by taking her away from this place, by giving her Aimee.
But in that moment, as she stood there looking at the entrance of the house, she felt just as lonely as she had as
a child. In that moment, she missed Henri, and realized
how alone she was, even though she was a mother, and

Laurent, Adelaide and Bette were as loyal and beloved as family.

It was foolish nonsense, she decided, shaking herself free of such despondency.

Evelyn rapped on the front door, using the brass-ring knocker. A moment passed before Thomas answered. The butler, whom she had known for years, took one look at her and gasped. "Miss Evelyn?" he asked.

She smiled at the short, bald manservant. "Yes, Thomas, it is I—Evelyn."

He flushed and bowed. "I beg your pardon, Countess!"

She smiled, and in doing so, shook off the last vestiges of her past. "You must not bow to me," she said.

She meant it. The staff had always been kind to her— far kinder than her own family.

A few moments later, she was escorted in to see her uncle, and she was relieved that her aunt was not at home. Robert greeted her warmly, surprising her. "I am so glad you have called. I have been meaning to send Enid to do so, to see how you are faring," he said. "But you look well, Evelyn, considering what you are going through."

She wondered if she had misjudged her uncle, if his indifference had been nothing more than that. "We are managing, and do not put Aunt Enid out, please, not on my account. I have decided to ask you for help, if your offer stands."

He gestured for her to sit in one of the two chairs before his desk. A tall window was behind it, and through it, she could see the gardens behind the house, and the sea, just above the treetops. He turned to the butler, asking for tea and cakes. Then he sat down behind his desk. "I would love to help you if I can."

"Will you keep what I am about to tell you in confidence?" she asked. "I am in an unusual position, and I hardly wish to have anyone know—not even my aunt."

His smile was amused. "I keep a great many confidences from my wife, Evelyn, and I hardly failed to notice that she did not care for you greatly when you were a child." He sighed. "I have never understood the ladies."

She had no comment to make on that sore subject. "I am sure you have noticed that I am currently somewhat short on funds. However, Henri left a fortune for me and Aimee—at our home in France. The time has come for me to find a way to retrieve the family heirlooms he has left us, and I have decided to hire someone to do so." She had decided not to tell her uncle that she meant to go with Greystone to France to retrieve the fortune there.

"I am relieved to hear that D'Orsay left something for you, but by God, how will you ever convince anyone to go to France now to retrieve the valuables? And are you sure that whatever Henri left for you, it is worth the risk?"

"It is quieter in France now than when we left, isn't it?"

"It is hardly quiet! The countryside remains up in arms over the secularization of the clergy. Mobs continually attack the priests who have taken the new oaths required of them while opposing mobs attack the priests who have refused to do so. Vigilantes hunt down the terrorists, or what remains of them. The need for revenge remains as strong as ever—it is just directed at different groups. How will you find someone capable of getting to France— and then getting to your country home there? And again, what if nothing remains of the heirlooms? There has been a great deal of looting and theft in the great châteaus."

He made her plan sound daunting and difficult, indeed. God, what if the gold was gone? "I have to attempt to retrieve it, Uncle. Henri said he left us a chest of gold," she finally confessed.

His eyes widened. "That would be a good fortune, indeed! But then you have the problem of finding someone you can trust!"

How perfect his cue. "Have you ever heard of Jack Greystone? He smuggled us from France, and I was impressed with his courage and his skill. I have been trying to locate him since the funeral."

Robert stared, flushing a little. "Of course I have heard of him, Evelyn. He is rather famous. Or should I say infamous? I didn't know Greystone got you out of the country. Well, I am not surprised you think he is the man for the mission. I suppose, if anyone could retrieve that gold, it is he. And I would even trust him to do so, in this case—he is rather fond of beautiful women. Or so they say!"

Was he suggesting that Jack Greystone would help her because she was beautiful? "I am prepared to pay him well," she added. "Once he retrieves the fortune."

"I do not know if I can ferret him out," he quickly said with another flush.

Evelyn was dismayed, but trying to decipher Robert's somewhat odd behavior. She sensed he was withholding something. "Is there something I should know?" she asked.

"Of course not. I will begin making a few inquiries for you, immediately," he said. "How is your daughter managing, Evelyn?"

She tried to hide her disappointment, wondering if she was engaging in more futile action. Briefly, they discussed Aimee, and Evelyn assured him that Aimee was doing well.

She was about to leave when she heard the front door open. Evelyn grimaced as she thanked her uncle and left the study, leaving him immersed in his papers.

But her aunt was not in the front hall; Annabelle was

there, and so was Trevelyan. She was handing off her cloak, as he was his coat, and when she saw Evelyn, Annabelle faltered. Trev instantly came forward, smiling. "This is a delightful surprise," he said with a brief bow.

The gesture was not affected—it was casual and elegant. Evelyn was as surprised to see them—and especially to see them together, but of course, they had all been friends since childhood. She smiled and came forward. "Hello, Trev. Have you been escorting my cousin about?"

"Actually, I was calling on Robert, and I bumped into her in the drive. How are you, Evelyn? You are looking very well today."

"I am doing better, thank you," she said, having briefly wondered if a romance might be brewing between Trev and her cousin. She turned to Annabelle. "We did not have a chance to speak the other day. You have become a beautiful young woman, Annabelle."

Annabelle blushed. "Hello, Evelyn, I mean, Countess. Thank you. I am sorry I could not greet you properly the other day." She stopped. She glanced at Trev. "I am also sorry it became a bit awkward. Lucille still has her temper."

Evelyn thanked Thomas as he handed her cloak to her. "It is difficult, I suppose, after so many years have passed, to be reunited as we have. But we all have different lives now and a great deal has changed."

"You are being patient and kind," Annabelle said.

"Is there a point in being impatient and cruel?" Evelyn smiled.

Trev looked at them both. "Lucille has more than a temper, and she has always been jealous of Evelyn, for obvious reasons. She is now a married woman, so one would think bygones were just that. But there is no reason that the two of you cannot patch things up and become friends."

While Evelyn looked at him in some surprise, Annabelle looked at him with obvious admiration. Evelyn said, "You are right, I think. When you feel like it, Annabelle, please call. You are Aimee's cousin and she would love to meet you."

Annabelle nodded. "I will try to come by next week."

Trev took Evelyn's cloak from her and draped it over her shoulders. "And may I come by, as well? Strictly as a family friend, of course?"

She started, wondering at his choice of words—wondering if he had a romantic inclination toward her. Surely, she was mistaken. "Of course you can call." She stared closely at him. Trev's father had always been as actively involved in the free trade as her uncle had been. She happened to have heard, in the past weeks, that he remained in good health, being about seventy years of age now, but that he had given Trev control of the estate and its affairs. Perhaps he had the information Evelyn sought. "Can I speak with you for a moment?"

Annabelle flushed again. "I must go anyway. It was nice seeing you, Evelyn. Good day, Trev." She quickly left.

He smiled at her. "Hmm, should I be flattered?"

"Surely you are not flirting with me?"

"Of course I am flirting. You are impossibly attractive." A dimple joined his smile.

She couldn't help it—she smiled back. "I had forgotten how charming you are."

"I do not believe it. I think you have been pining away for me for years."

She laughed for the first time since Henri had died. It felt rather good. Then she became serious. "Can you help me locate Jack Greystone?"

His smile vanished. "Why?" His tone was sharp.

She was not about to tell Trevelyan her reasons. "He helped us flee France, Trev, but other than that, I cannot tell you why I am looking for him. It is a business matter."

"Are you thinking of getting into the trade?" He was incredulous.

She did not want to lie, but misleading him was not lying, so she said, "Maybe."

"You are a woman—a lady!"

She laid her hand on his arm, surprising them both. "I am sure you have noticed that I am in very strained circumstances. I need to speak with Greystone, Trev, and frankly, I am rather desperate."

He was grim. "You could lose everything, Evelyn."

"I know the risks."

She stared back at him, releasing his arm. He looked about to curse. "I will think about what you have asked."

"Does that mean you know how to reach him?"

"It means, I will think about what you have asked."

IT HAD BEGUN TO DRIZZLE, and as Evelyn looked up at the dark, cloudy sky, she knew it would soon rain. She shivered as the wind picked up, but she had just reached the iron front gates at the head of Roselynd's drive.

Ahead, Roselynd was a three-story square house, statuesque in impression, and very current in design. Cast of pale, nearly white stone, it stood out eerily in the darkness. All the windows were dark except for one on an upper floor, which she happened to know was Laurent and Adelaide's room.

It was later than she had thought, and her poor mare was tired—it had been a long difficult week for her, with all the traipsing about that Evelyn had done. The mare had hardly been used in the months prior.

She felt a pang, thinking of Henri, and a stirring of anger as she thought about the predicament she was in. Very firmly, she told herself that he had not left her destitute by choice; the revolution had done that.

She halted the mare before the barn, and as she did so, she heard Laurent calling to her. She smiled as she slipped from the gig, and Laurent approached from the house. "I was becoming very worried about you, madame."

"I am fine. I had a very good conversation with my uncle, Laurent, and if I am fortunate, he will locate Greystone for me." She was too tired to tell him about Trevelyan, and decided she would do so tomorrow. "It is later than I thought. Is Aimee awake?"

"She is asleep, and Adelaide has left a covered tray in your rooms. I will put the mare away."

She thanked him, as the drizzle turned abruptly into a pounding rain. They both cried out, Laurent hurrying the mare into the stables, as Evelyn pulled up her skirts and ran for the house.

Inside, she slammed the front door closed, breathing hard. The front hall was in darkness, which pleased her—why waste candles to light the entry when she was the only one expected? Evelyn removed her soaking cloak. The rest of her clothes remained dry, but her shoes and stockings were wet.

Her cloak over her arm, Evelyn went upstairs in the darkness, going directly to Aimee's room. As Laurent had said, she was soundly asleep. Evelyn pulled the covers up, kissing her forehead, the rain now pounding on the windows and the roof above their heads.

In her own bedroom she lit a single taper, hung up her cloak and removed her wet shoes and stockings. Thunder boomed. Just after it did, she heard Laurent entering the house, the front door closing. She felt a moment of relief, for, like a child, she disliked fierce storms. But now, the mare was settled and fed for the night, Laurent was on his way upstairs and the house was securely locked.

She removed the pins from her hair, which always made her head ache at this time of the day, letting it down. As she shook her hair out, she realized that she was exhausted. Undressing would be a chore, but she somehow removed her gown and underclothes, donning her white cotton nightgown. In France, the loose but luxurious garment with its puffed sleeves and lace trim was called a *robe innocente.*

She was just about to uncover the tray Adelaide had left for her and try to eat a morsel or two when she heard a movement downstairs. She stiffened, alarmed, until she realized that it was the sound of a shutter banging against the side of the house.

She was going to have to close those shutters—she would never sleep with all of that banging. Evelyn took the taper she had lit and hurried down the hall. Then she hesitated, and as the wind ceased, the rain became a quiet steady pitter-patter and the shutter was silent.

Thunder boomed.

She jumped, her heart skipping, and scolded herself for being a fool. Now she heard nothing but the gentle steady rhythmic rain.

She was about to turn and go back to her room when a light went on below her.

She froze, incredulous.

And then, as she inched closer to the top of the stairs, she realized that a taper had been lit in the salon.

Her heart thundered with alarm.

She stared down the stairs, across the entry hall and into the salon, which was in shadow, but clearly, a single light shone within.

Someone was in her salon.

She almost called out, hoping it was Laurent, but he had gone up to the room he shared with Adelaide—she was certain.

She needed a gun. She had a pistol under the mattress of her bed. Should she seize it, or should she get Laurent? And as she debated what to do she saw a man cross the salon.

Evelyn froze again.

His stride had been unrushed, indolent—familiar.

Every hair on her nape had risen. Now her heart slammed.

He came to the doorway of the salon, holding a drink in his hand, and looked up at her.

And even in the shadows, even as their gazes locked, there was no mistaking who he was.

"I hear you are looking for me," Jack Greystone said.

CHAPTER THREE

HE WASN'T SMILING as he spoke.

Evelyn seized the banister to remain upright. For an entire moment, one that felt like an eternity, she could not speak. She had found Jack Greystone—or, he had found her.

And he hadn't changed. He remained so unbearably attractive. He was tall and powerfully built, clad now in a rather wet riding coat, fashionable lace cuffs spilling from the sleeves, a darker vest beneath. He also wore doeskin breeches and high black boots with spurs, now splattered with mud.

And his golden hair was pulled casually back, some of it escaping from its queue. But that only made his high cheekbones seem sharper, his jaw seem stronger. And his gray gaze was intent upon her.

Evelyn's heart slammed another time—he was regarding her attire, rather thoroughly.

She knew she flushed. But she was dressed for bed, not for entertaining. "You have scared me witless, sir!"

"I apologize," he said, and she could not decide if he meant it. "But I rarely go anywhere in broad daylight, and I never use the front door."

Their gazes were now locked. She continued to reel, remaining stunned by his appearance in her home. He was referring now to the bounty on his head. "Of course not," she managed.

He said wryly, as calm as she was not, "I have not mis-heard, have I? Half a dozen of my acquaintances have alerted me to the inquiries you have been, rather reck-lessly, making. You *are* looking for me, Lady D'Orsay?"

"Yes," she said, suddenly very aware that he had just identified her as the Countess D'Orsay, not the Vicom-tesse LeClerc. She had never corrected the misinfor-mation she had deliberately given him—when they had parted company, four years ago, upon landing just south of London, he had still believed her to be Lady LaSalle, Vicomtesse LeClerc. "I am desperate to have a word with you, sir." As she spoke, she recalled their first meeting, four years ago. She had been desperate then, and she had said so.

But his gaze never flickered; his expression did not change. It occurred to her that he did not recall that meeting—and that he did not recognize her.

But how could he fail to recognize her? Was it even possible?

His stare was prolonged. It was a moment before he said, "That is an attractive nightgown, Countess."

He did not recognize her, she was now certain. It was shocking! She had remarkable features—everyone said so. She might be tired and pale, but she was still an at-tractive woman. Trevelyan had thought so.

She was flushing, uncertain of what he meant, and whether there had been mockery in his tone. She did not know how to respond to such a remark—or what to do about his failure to recognize her. "I was hardly expecting to find a visitor, within my home, at this hour."

"Obviously." He was wry. "If it eases you, I have two sisters, and I have seen a great many female garments."

She felt certain he was laughing at her now. It crossed

her mind that a great many of those female garments had not belonged to his sisters. "Yes, I had heard."

"You have heard that I am accustomed to the sight of women in their nightclothes?"

"You know that is not what I meant." But of course, it was probably very true! "I am going to get a robe—I will be right back!"

He seemed amused as he sipped his wine, looking up the stairs at her. Evelyn turned and fled, her disbelief growing. In her chamber, she threw on a cotton robe that matched her nightgown. Maybe he would recognize her once she stepped fully into the light. But just then, she was feeling oddly insulted.

Didn't he think her attractive?

She forced herself to a calmer pace and returned downstairs. He was in the salon—he had lit several tapers, and he watched her as she entered. "How do you know about my sisters?" His tone remained bland. "Have you made inquiries about them, too?"

She was trembling, and her pulse was racing but she stiffened, instantly sensing that she was venturing into dangerous territory. He was, she thought, displeased. "No, of course not. But they were mentioned in the course of a conversation."

"About me?" His stare was relentless.

She shivered. "About you, sir."

"And with whom did you have this enlightening conversation?"

"John Trim." Was he worried about betrayal? "He admires you greatly. We all do."

His gray gaze flickered. "I suppose I should be flattered. Are you cold?"

Her pulse was rioting but she was hardly cold—she was unnerved, undone, at a loss! She had forgotten how manly he was, and how his presence teased the senses. "It is raining."

There was a wool throw on the back of the sofa and, very casually, he retrieved it. She tensed as he approached. "If you are not cold," he said softly, "then you are very nervous—but then, you are also very *desperate*."

For an instant, she thought he had inflected upon the final word—and that he recalled their first meeting, when she had been so desperate, after all. But his expression never changed as he laid the wool about her shoulders and she realized that he did not remember her, not at all. "I am unused to entertaining at this hour," she finally said. "We are strangers and we are alone."

"It is half past nine, Countess, and you asked for this rendezvous."

It felt like midnight, she thought. And clearly, he was not shaken by their encounter, not at all.

"Have I somehow distressed you?" he asked.

"No!" She quickly, falsely, smiled. "I am thrilled that you have called."

He eyed her, askance. Thunder cracked overhead and the shutter slammed against the house. Evelyn jumped.

He had just raised his glass and now he set it down. "It is incredible, that you live in this house with but one manservant. I will close the shutter." He left.

And when he was gone, she seized the back of the sofa, trembling wildly. How did he know that she lived alone with Laurent, her only manservant? Obviously he had made some inquiries about her.

But he did not recognize her. It was unbelievable, that she hadn't made any impression on him.

He returned to the salon, smiling slightly, and shutting both doors behind them. Evelyn clutched the throw more tightly across her chest as their gazes met.

He walked past the sofa, which remained between them, and picked up his glass of wine. "I would prefer that no one here is aware of my presence tonight, other than yourself."

"Everyone in this house is utterly trustworthy," she managed, standing on the other side of the couch.

"I prefer to choose when to take risks—and which risks to take. And I rarely trust anyone—and never *strangers.*" His smile was cool. There was that odd, derisive, inflection again. "It shall be our little *secret,* Countess."

"Of course I will do as you ask. And I am very sorry if my asking about you, so openly, has caused you any alarm."

He took a sip of the red wine he was drinking. "I am accustomed to evading the authorities. You are not. What will you say to them when they come knocking at your door?"

She stared, dismayed, as she had not considered this possibility.

"You will tell them that you haven't seen me, Lady D'Orsay," he said softly.

"Should I expect a visit from the authorities?"

"I think so. They will advise you to contact them the moment you have seen me. And those are games best left to those who wish to play in very high stakes." He paced past the sofa. "Do you want me to light a fire? You are shivering, still."

She was trying to absorb what he had said, and she faced him, distracted. She wasn't shivering, she thought, she was trembling. "You have obviously just come in out of the rain, so, yes, I imagine you would enjoy a fire. And I would, too."

He shrugged off his damp wool coat. "I assume you do not mind? As the attire is so casual tonight?"

Was she blushing yet again? Was he mocking her again? Somehow she walked to him and took the jacket. The wool was very fine, and she suspected the coat had Italian origins. "Hopefully this will dry before you leave," she said, although the rain was pounding the house again.

He eyed her, then removed a tinderbox from his waistcoat, knelt and started a fire. The kindling quickly took. He poked the logs with the iron poker until the wood was burning. Standing, he closed the grate.

Evelyn stepped beside him, holding his coat up in front of the warm fire. He glanced down at her. As they were standing so closely now, she saw a somewhat intent gleam in his eyes. It seemed suggestive and it felt seductive—like a raw male appraisal.

"Would you care for a glass of wine?" he asked, softly. "I so dislike drinking alone. That Bordeaux is excellent. And I hope you do not mind, I helped myself."

His tone had become soft, raising goose bumps on her skin. "Of course I do not mind. It is the least I can offer you. But, no, thank you. I cannot imbibe on an empty stomach," she said truthfully.

He turned and moved one of the salon's two chairs to the front of the fire. Then he took the coat from her and hung it on the back of the chair. "I remain curious about your desire to speak with me. I have not been able to imagine what the Countess D'Orsay wishes of me." His stride unhurried, he walked to the bar cart and retrieved his glass of wine.

She watched him, knowing she must not be distracted by his tone, his proximity, not when she had to make her case. "I have a proposition, Mr. Greystone."

He stared over the rim of his glass. "A proposition… I am even more intrigued."

Had he just looked through her robe and nightgown?

Evelyn walked over to the sofa and sat down, still unnerved. She reminded herself that the cotton was far too
tightly woven for him to be able to look through it, but
she felt as if he had just taken a quick glance at her naked
body.

"Countess?"

"It has come to my attention, Mr. Greystone, that you
are probably the best free trader in Cornwall."

His dark brows lifted. "Actually, I am the best smuggler in all of Great Britain—and I have the accounts to
prove it."

She smiled a little; she found his arrogance attractive, his confidence reassuring. "Some might be put off
by your bravado, Mr. Greystone, but bravado is exactly
what I require now."

"I am now entirely intrigued," he said.

She met his probing gray gaze and wondered if he was
intrigued with her, as a woman. "I wish to hire a smuggler,
and not just any smuggler, but someone who is skilled
and courageous, to retrieve family heirlooms from my
husband's château in France."

He set his glass down and said slowly, "Did I just hear
you correctly?"

"My husband died recently, and those heirlooms are
terribly important to me and my daughter."

"I am sorry for your loss," he said, without seeming to
mean it. Then, he said, "That is quite the task."

"Yes, I imagine it is, but that is why I have been seeking to locate you, Mr. Greystone, as surely you are the
man capable of accomplishing such a mission."

He stared for a long time, and she was becoming accustomed to being unable to discern even a hint of his
thoughts or emotions. "Crossing the Channel is dangerous. Traveling within France now is madness, as it re-

mains in the midst of a bloody revolution, Countess. You are asking me to risk my life for your family heirlooms."

"Those heirlooms were left to me and my daughter by my recently deceased husband, and it was his greatest wish that I retrieve them," she said firmly. When his expression did not change, she added, "I must recover them, and your reputation is outstanding!"

"I am certain they are important to you. I am certain your husband wished for you to have them. However, my services are quite expensive."

She wasn't sure what his stare meant—but he had said the exact same thing to her four years ago. Intending to offer him a share of the gold once it was in her possession, she said carefully, "The heirlooms are valuable, sir." She did not think it wise to tell him that Henri had left her a chest of gold.

"Of course they are…. This isn't about nostalgia, or sentiment, obviously." He nodded at the barely furnished room.

"We have fallen into very strained circumstances, sir. I am desperate and I am determined."

"And I am neither desperate nor determined. I prefer to preserve my life, and would only risk it for a great cause." His gaze was piercing. "One with just compensation."

"This is a great cause!" she gasped.

"That is a matter of opinion." He was final.

He was going to refuse her? "I have hardly finished making my case," she said swiftly.

"But haven't you? My services are very costly. I do not mean to be rude, but it is obvious that you cannot afford them. I would need a great incentive to risk my life for you." His stare locked with hers. "You are hardly the only impoverished widow in Cornwall. You will surely find a way into a better fortune."

She wet her lips, shaken by the realization that their discussion would soon be over—and she would not have achieved his help. "But those heirlooms are very valuable, and I am prepared to offer you a very fair share," she said quickly.

"A share?" He laughed. "I am always paid in advance, Countess. And how would you do that?" His smile vanished. His stare hardened. It slipped down her robe and nightgown. Then he turned away, his expression grim. His head down, he began to pace, wine in hand.

She trembled, watching him. She must focus now. When they had fled France, she had paid him with rubies—in advance. Now, she had very little jewelry left. She could not imagine using her last pieces now.

"Clearly, you are in some financial straits," he said, finally looking at her. "Unfortunately, it is a common practice to take payment in advance—and it is good business. I am not interested in 'fair shares,' after the fact."

She stared, dismayed. Of course he wanted an advance payment—what if he went to France and failed to retrieve the gold? Or was hurt during the voyage? So much could go wrong, preventing him from attaining a successful conclusion.

But she could not pay him in advance. So now what was she to do? The only thing that Evelyn was certain of was that she could not give up.

"Can you not make an exception?" Evelyn finally asked slowly. "For me and my daughter? We have fallen on terrible times, which you can see. I am desperate—because I am a mother! If all went well, you would be handsomely rewarded, just not in advance, and I am vowing it!"

He slowly turned and looked at her, his gray eyes dark. "I am not prepared to risk my life for you, Countess."

Her mind raced frantically, as he was denying her—denying Aimee. "But I can promise you that there will be just compensation—I give you my word! Surely you have the heart to make an exception now, not for me, but for my daughter!"

He lifted his wine and finished it. "Do not try to use your daughter to play me," he warned.

She didn't mean to do any such thing—but he was about to walk out her door—she simply knew it! She was desperate, and impulsively, she moved to stand in front of him—to bar his way. "Please, do not dismiss my proposal. How can I convince you to at least consider it?"

He looked very directly at her now. "I have considered it."

She trembled, taken aback as never before. A terrible silence fell. It was thick with tension—and his relentless stare never wavered.

Couldn't she convince him to help her? Men were always rushing to her side, to help her across the street, to open doors for her, to see her into her carriage. She had never paid much attention to her power as a beautiful woman before, but she was not a fool—Henri had fallen in love with her because of her beauty. It was only after he had become further acquainted with her that he had loved her for her character and temperament.

Greystone hadn't recognized her, but she was certain of his interest. When he looked at her directly, it was a glance any woman would recognize.

Her heart lurched. Henri was surely turning over in his grave now! Going into this man's arms would be the last recourse! "Mr. Greystone, I am desperate," she said softly. "I am begging you to reconsider. My daughter's future is at stake."

"When I set sail, I not only risk my own life, I risk those of my men," he spoke, now seeming impatient.

She could barely breathe. "I am a widow in great need, without protection, or means. You are a gentleman. Surely—"

"No, I am not." He was abrupt and final. "And I am not in the habit of generously rescuing damsels in distress."

Did she have any other choices? Aimee's future was at stake, and he did not seem about to bend. She had to get that gold; she had to secure a bright future for her daughter! Evelyn lifted her hand; somehow, she touched his jaw.

His eyes widened.

"I am in mourning," she whispered, "and if France is as dangerous as you claim, then I am asking you to risk your life for me."

His thick, dark lashes lowered. She could not see his eyes, and another silence fell. Evelyn dropped her hand; it was trembling. He slowly lifted his lashes and looked at her.

"Aren't you curious, Countess? Don't you want to know why I came here?" he asked very softly.

She felt her heart slam. "Why?"

"You have a reputation, too."

"What does that mean? What reputation could I possibly have?"

"I have heard it said, often enough, that the Countess D'Orsay is the most beautiful woman in all of England."

It was suddenly so silent, that she could hear the rain, not just pounding over their heads, but running from the gutters on the roof. She could hear the logs and kindling, crackling in the hearth. And she could hear her own deafening heartbeat.

"And we both know that is absurdly false," she said thickly.

"Is it?"

Evelyn wet her lips, oddly dazed. "Surely you agree… Such a claim is absurd."

He slowly smiled. "No, I do not agree. How modest you are."

Evelyn did not know what to do, and she couldn't think clearly now. She had never been in any man's arms except for Henri's—and he hadn't been young or good-looking or sensual. Her heart raced more wildly. There was alarm and confusion, there was even some dismay, but mostly, there was excitement.

She hesitated. "I was sixteen when I married my husband."

He started. "What does that have to do with anything?"

She had been trying to tell him that she wasn't really experienced, but now, it didn't seem to matter. Jack Greystone was the most attractive man she had ever come across, and not just because he was so handsome. He was so utterly masculine, so brazen and confident, and so powerful. Her knees were buckling. Her heart was thundering. Her skin prickled.

She had never felt this way before.

Evelyn stood up on her tiptoes and as she prepared to kiss him, their gazes locked. His was wide, incredulous. But then it blazed.

Her insides hollowed in response and she brushed her mouth once upon his. And the moment their lips met, a shocking sensation of pleasure went through her.

Standing there with her mouth open was like being on fire!

He gripped her shoulders and kissed her. Evelyn gasped, because his mouth was very firm and even more demanding; he began kissing her with a stunning ferocity.

And Evelyn kissed him back.

Somehow, she was in his arms. Her entire body was pressed against his, enveloped by his, her breasts crushed by his chest. For the first time in her life, she realized she was in the throes of desire. It was maddening—senseless.

And then he stepped back and pushed her away from him.

"What are you doing?" she gasped.

He looked at her, breathing hard—his gray gaze on fire.

Evelyn clutched her robe to her body. She reached for the sofa so she could continue to stand upright. Had she just been in his *arms?* The arms of a veritable stranger? And since when did anyone kiss that way—with such hunger, such intensity?

"You are trouble, Countess," he said harshly.

"What?" Evelyn cried. Some sensibility was returning, and she could not believe what she had just done!

"I am sorry you are desperate, Countess. I am sorry you are destitute. But one night in your bed isn't enough to entice me to France on your behalf." His eyes blazed with desire, but she saw anger, too.

Evelyn started. She had kissed him—she hadn't suggested an affair. "I do need your help," she heard herself cry.

"You are a dangerous woman. Most men are fools. I am not." Giving her a grim look, he strode past her. At the door he paused. "I am certain you will find someone else to do your bidding. Good night."

Evelyn was so bewildered that she could not move, not until she heard the front door slam. She collapsed upon the sofa. She had found Jack Greystone. She had dared to kiss him, and he had kissed her back, with fervor. And then he had refused her pleas and walked out on her!

She told herself that she was crying for Aimee—and not because Jack Greystone had had her in his arms only to reject her.

JACK WAS STILL IN A VERY foul mood. The sun now high, he slid from his mount, tied it to the rail in front of the inn and patted its rump. He had just dropped anchor on one of the beaches below the village of Bexhill, and as it was half past noon, he was late.

The Gray Goose Inn was a dilapidated white stucco building with a shingled roof, a dusty courtyard, and a great many suspicious patrons. Just north of Hastings, set in rolling green meadows, it was his preferred meeting place because he did not wish to pass through the Strait of Dover, just in case he was boxed in there by his enemies. He could outrun a naval destroyer and a revenue cutter, and he had, but there was not a great deal of room to maneuver in the Straits.

He sighed as he entered the dark, somewhat malodorous and smoky public room. It had stopped raining well before dawn, when he had been hoisting sail and leaving the cove near Fowey, but he was somewhat chilled from the entire damp, cold night. At least it was warm inside the inn, but it was a far cry from his uncle's home on Cavendish Square in London, where he would greatly prefer to be now.

The bounty on his head had begun to truly restrict his movements. He had been amused when he had first learned of its existence a year and a half ago. But instead of meeting his brother and uncle in the comfort of the Cavendish Square townhome, he was confined to a clandestine meeting in the cramped back room of a foul, roadside inn. It wasn't as amusing now.

Jack had been engaged with smugglers since he was

a boy of five years old, when he had insisted on standing watch with the village elders, on the lookout for the preventive men. Nothing had pleased him more than to watch the smugglers drop anchor in Sennen Cove and begin to unload their wares, except when the night was lit up with the torches carried by the revenue men as they rushed down the cliffs and invaded the beach, guns blazing. Casks would be dragged into secret caves, while others were left behind for the authorities. Some smugglers would turn tail and flee, others would fire back at the customs agents. He would join in the fighting—until an adult would espy him and drag him, protesting, away.

At seven, he had been dragging ankers filled with brandy across the beaches at Sennen Cove, as he was too small to carry them upon his shoulders. At ten, he had put out to sea with Ed Lewes as a cabin boy, at the time one of the most notorious and successful Cornish free traders. At twelve he had been a rigger, at fourteen, first mate. At seventeen he had become captain of his own ship, a fore and aft rigged sloop. Now, he captained the *Sea Wolf II,* an eighty-gallon frigate built just for the trade, her hull so skillfully carved that she cut the water like a dolphin. He'd yet to be caught when challenged.

He had spent most of his life outwitting and outrunning the revenue men, the customs agents and now, the British navy. He was accustomed to the danger and pursuit, and he was thrilled by both. He especially loved being hunted, and then tacking across the wind and becoming the hunter. How he loved chasing his enemies and driving them aground—he enjoyed nothing more.

He was also used to lying low, or going into hiding. He had no intention of going to prison, being transported, or now hanging for the acts of treason he was charged with committing.

He did not think his life would have changed as much, if it were only for the bounty. But both of his sisters had married into the highest echelon of British society, marrying the earls of Bedford and St Just, respectively. And he had become a subject of fascination for the ton.

Gentlemen admired him at their dinner tables, while ladies swooned over tales of his exploits on their shopping expeditions. There was gossip, rampant speculation and even some idolatry. There were a dozen debutantes calling upon his sisters, in the hopes of soliciting his attentions!

As such, the authorities had placed him squarely in their targets. He was, without a doubt, the one smuggler the Admiralty most wished to catch and hang.

He hadn't been to London in at least six months. His brother, Lucas, was staying at the Cavendish Square flat, and the house was frequently watched. Apparently lookouts were occasionally stationed at Bedford House and Lambert Hall. A few years ago, he could come and go in broad daylight, he could shop on Pall Mall, he could attend supper parties and balls. Even a year ago, he could enter London to visit his sisters, as long as there was no fanfare. Not anymore.

He had a niece and nephew he never saw. But he was hardly a family man.

He had to exercise the utmost caution wherever he went. In fact, he had been as careful when he had ventured to Roselynd last night. He had considered the countess's inquiries a possible trap. But he had not been followed, and no one had shown up at her door to arrest him while they spoke.

He paused on the threshold of the public room, trying to peer through the smoke, a very dark, partly sexual, tension within him. The Countess D'Orsay was as beautiful as claimed. Curiosity had compelled him to meet her. He had wanted to see if she was such a great beauty—which she was—and he had also wanted to see if she was setting a trap for him—which she was not. But he hadn't expected her to be the woman he had rescued in France, four years earlier.

And the moment he had recognized her, it had been like receiving a stunning blow to the chest.

He had realized, instantly, that she was the woman who had claimed to be the Vicomtesse LeClerc. He had been stunned, but he had hidden it.

He could easily forgive her that deceit. He did not blame her for hiding her identity from him, although he would have never revealed it had he known.

But he hadn't ever really forgotten her. She had haunted him day and night for days and even weeks after that Channel crossing.

And now, that old man she had married was dead.

And for one moment, he did not see the dozen men within the tavern he'd stepped into. He could only see Evelyn D'Orsay, with her dark hair and vivid blue eyes, so tiny and petite.

He lived a dangerous life, and his survival depended upon his instincts. They were finely honed from years of outrunning the revenue men, and now, two navies. Every instinct he currently had warned him to stay far from Evelyn D'Orsay.

It wasn't just that he had found her terribly beautiful four years ago, so beautiful he almost felt smitten at first sight. But when she'd looked at him with her big blue eyes, imploring him to rescue her, she awoke the strongest, most unfamiliar urges in him—urges to defend and protect. It was as if she had endured a lifetime of suffering and hurt, which he must somehow ease. He had been highly affected by her desperation back then. But he had hidden it, taking her rubies as payment for his services. He had remained as indifferent and aloof as possible.

Last night, he had steeled himself against her again.

It hadn't been easy. He had forgotten how striking she was—how tiny. And the shadows in her eyes remained. When she looked at him, her eyes filled with desperation, he had those same consuming urges as before—urges to protect her from life's ills. Urges to rescue her. Urges even to hold her tight.

It was absurd.

So while she might be destitute now, he reminded himself that she had hardly had a life of misery—she had married one of France's premier titles. She had been wealthy for many years. The odd urges he had when she looked at him were senseless. The raging attraction, well, that he could certainly justify—and dismiss.

But the truth was that he had helped several families flee France without receiving any kind of compensation from them at all. These Frenchmen and women had left everything they had behind; he hadn't considered turning them away. But with the Countess D'Orsay, it was different. He knew he must never come to her rescue in a personal way. Their relationship must remain a strictly impersonal one—he was sure of it.

She was simply too enticing and too intriguing. She stirred up too many feelings, and he could very easily become attached. And he had no use for attachments outside of those to his family. He was a rogue, a smuggler and a spy—and he liked his life exactly as it was—he liked living outside society, he liked being on the run.

As for the kiss they had shared, he had to stop thinking about it. Thus far, that had proven impossible. He could not recall ever being so aroused, but when he had

kissed her, it had also felt as if he were holding an innocent debutante in his arms.

Yet he knew better—she was a countess, a grown
woman, a widow and a mother. She was not innocent
and inexperienced. And if he believed, even for a moment, that he could enjoy her bed without becoming en-
tangled with her, he would do so immediately. But he did
not think it would be easy to leave her after a single night,
so he would stay away—far away.

Therefore, no matter what she offered, no matter how
she offered it, he was not going to France for her. He had
never been more resolved.

"You have made it—and you are in one piece," his
brother said, cutting into his dark thoughts. He was embraced, hard, by a tall golden-haired man, more politely
dressed than Jack was. No one could mistake them for
anything other than what they were—brothers. "We are
in the back," Lucas added unnecessarily.

Jack was thrilled to see his older brother. Their father
had been an irresponsible rogue, and he had abandoned
their mother when Jack was six years old. Lucas had been
almost ten at the time. Their uncle, Sebastian Warlock,
had managed the estate for them for several years, mostly
from afar, as an absentee landlord. Lucas had stepped into
the breach by the age of twelve or so, taking over the reins
at an early age. Now the brothers were as close as brothers
could be, although as different in nature as night and day.

For Lucas managed not just the estate, but the family. Jack knew that a great burden had been lifted from
his brother's shoulders when their sisters had fallen in
love and married. Now Lucas spent most of his time in
London—or on the continent.

"How are you?" Lucas asked.

Jack smiled. "Do you need to even ask?"

"Now that is the brother I know so well. Why were you glowering at the crowd?" Lucas led him across the room and into a private back room.

Jack debated telling him a bit about the Countess D'Orsay, but then he saw Sebastian Warlock standing facing the fireplace, his back to them. As usual, their uncle wore a black velvet coat and dark brown breeches. As Lucas closed the door, the prime minister's spymaster turned. "You are rarely late." His glance was skewering.

"Yes, I am fine, thank you for asking," Jack returned.

"I imagine that he is late because it is difficult traveling about the country with a bounty on one's head," Lucas said, pulling out a chair from the table, which seated four. A fire blazed in the hearth. Bread, cheese, ale and whiskey were on the table.

"Your brother harps like a woman when he is concerned," Warlock said. "And he is always concerned about you. However, that bounty is the perfect cover."

"It is the perfect cover," Jack agreed. Lucas specialized in extracting émigrés and agents from the enemy's hands and lands. He was a patriot and a Tory, so his having become involved in the war was perfectly natural and Warlock had known it when he recruited him.

Jack had been a different story. For while Jack occasionally moved such human cargo for his brother or another one of Warlock's agents, Warlock was more interested in receiving the information Jack ferried across the Channel. A great many smugglers moved information along with their cargo across the Channel. Most Cornish smugglers were French spies, however. Jack found it amusing to play such games, and he knew Warlock had known he would think so when he had first approached him some years ago.

"I may have been briefly deluded by such an argument

nine or ten months ago," Lucas said, "but I am not deluded now. It is a very dangerous game. I do not like it. Sebastian, you are going to get my brother killed."

"You know I did not place that bounty on his head. However, my first rule is to exploit opportunity, and that bounty has provided us with vast opportunity. Were you delayed?" Warlock asked Jack.

Jack took the proffered seat. "I was delayed—but not by the bounty." He decided to smirk, as if he had spent the night in Evelyn's arms. And he sobered. He could have seduced her, and maybe, he should have done so. But then he would probably be halfway to France as her errand boy.

Lucas rolled his eyes and poured Jack a scotch before sitting down with him. Warlock smiled and took a seat. He was an attractive man, but unlike his nephews, he was dark, with a somewhat brooding air. In his late thirties or early forties, he had the reputation of being a recluse. The world thought him a rather impoverished and boorish nobleman. It was wrong. In spite of his reputation, he did not lack for the ladies' attentions.

"What do you have for me?" Warlock asked bluntly.

"I have it on very good authority that Spain intends to leave the Coalition," Jack said.

A shocked silence greeted his words. But the war had not been going well for Britain and her Allies; France had recently conquered Amsterdam and annexed the Netherlands. Holland was now the Batavian Republic. There had been a number of French victories since the Allies' terrible defeat at Fleurus, last June.

"You are confirming a rumor that I have already heard," Warlock said grimly. "Now Pitt will have to seriously press Spain, before we lose her."

Jack shrugged. He was not interested in the politics of war.

"What of La Vendée?" Lucas asked.

Jack looked at Lucas, meeting his glance. Their sister Julianne had married the Earl of Bedford in 1793. He had been a royalist supporter, and actively involved in the La Vendée uprising against the revolution. Unfortunately, the rebels had been crushed that summer, but fortunately, Dominic Paget had made his way home to Julianne, surviving a great massacre. But La Vendée had been rising again. The Loire countryside was filled with peasants, clergy and noblemen who remained furious over the execution of the king, and the forced secularization of the church.

In the Loire, the rebels were led by a young aristocrat, Georges Cadoudal. "He claims he now has twelve thousand troops, and that there will be more by summer. And once again, his question is, when? When will Britain invade Brittanny?" Jack said calmly. But as he spoke, he recalled Cadoudal's desperation and fury.

"Windham has yet to finalize the plans," Warlock said. "We only have a thousand émigré troops amassed for an invasion of Brittany, but someone has suggested we use our French prisoners of war, and if we do, we will have about four thousand troops in sum."

"At least we know they can fight," Jack joked.

Lucas smiled a little, the tension inherent in such a discussion relieved.

"There must be a timeline, Sebastian," Lucas said. "We all know that General Hoche has already sent a great number of rebels into hiding. We lost La Vendée once. Surely we will not fail the rebels there again." Lucas was grim.

Jack knew he was thinking of their sister Julianne. When La Vendée had gone down in flames, her husband had lost his mother's family estates. His heart had been broken—and so had hers.

"There are many issues, but I am trying to convince Windham and Pitt to invade Quiberon Bay in June," Warlock said. "And you may relay that to Cadoudal."

Jack was glad he had some news to convey, and news that might reassure the rebel. Warlock stood and looked at Lucas. "I assume you wish to spend a few more moments with your brother. I must get back to London."

"I do not mind riding back the way I came," Lucas said.

"Keep me apprised," Warlock said to Jack before leaving.

Lucas leaned forward. "How difficult was it for you to contact Cadoudal?"

"Hoche's interest in La Vendée has made it more difficult than it was," Jack said. "But we have a prearranged means of communication—and it is in code. You worry like a mother hen."

"If I don't worry about you, who will?" Lucas said darkly. "And I wasn't jesting—I am damned tired of that bounty. Every day, your life is at risk. And the risk is even greater when you are at sea." He leaned forward. "Captain Barrow is gunning for you. He was bragging the other night at an affair at Penrose's home."

Barrow had quite the reputation, but Jack was amused, and he shrugged. "I welcome the gauntlet."

"Will you ever take life seriously?" Lucas demanded. "Everyone misses you—everyone is worried about you—it isn't just I."

Jack felt himself soften. The truth was, he missed his sisters, very much.

"Amelia is about to have her first child."

"The babe is due in May."

"That's right," Lucas said. "But she looks like she is about to have the child at any time. You have to see her,

Jack." Then he smiled. "She is so happy. She is a wonder-ful mother and she is so in love with Grenville."

Jack laughed, but he was thrilled for his sister, whom he had assumed would remain a spinster, but who was not just married, but a stepmother to three children, with her own on the way. "As long as he is loyal and true."

"He remains besotted," Lucas said, and both brothers finally laughed. Their sister was such a serious woman, and Grenville had been a catch. It was inexplicable, really.

Jack realized he looked forward to a long-overdue fam-ily reunion. "Tell Amelia I will come to see her as soon as I can." He almost wished that he could simply ride back to London with his brother, and call on Amelia now. But the war had changed everyone's life, including his. These were dark, dangerous times.

Evelyn D'Orsay's pale, beautiful image came to mind. He tensed. Damn it, why couldn't he dismiss her from his thoughts?

"What's wrong?" Lucas asked.

"You will be pleased to know that I have turned down a beautiful damsel in distress—that I have decided not to risk my life for a woman seeking to reclaim her family's fortune." And he was careful to sound mocking, when he did not quite feel that way.

"Oh, ho. Have you been rejected?" Lucas was incredu-lous. "You sound very put out."

"I have never been rejected!" he exclaimed. "It is in-credible that her wealthy husband left her so destitute, but I have no time now to play the knight in shining armor to save her."

Lucas laughed, standing. "You are in a twist because of a woman! This is rich! Are you certain she did not reject you? And whom, pray tell, are we discussing?"

"I rejected her," Jack said firmly. But suddenly he re-

called the way he had left Roselynd—and how shocked
and hurt she had been. "We are discussing the Countess D'Orsay. And Lucas? I am not interested in becoming ensnared." He added, "No matter how beautiful and
desperate she is."

"Since when have you ever been ensnared by a
woman?" Lucas asked, surprised.

Jack looked grimly at him. Maybe it was time to be honest, not with his brother, but with himself. "I got her out of
France four years ago, with her husband and her daughter.
And the problem is that I could not forget her then, and I
am afraid I cannot forget her now."

CHAPTER FOUR

THE BLACK BRIAR Inn was very busy; every table was full.
It was Friday afternoon, so apparently a great many of
the nearby village men had stopped by for a mug of ale.
The conversation was loud and raucous. Tobacco wafted
in the air.

Evelyn shifted uncomfortably in her seat. She did not
care for this crowd, or the man she had come to meet. He
was a very big, dark man in a striped jersey, a vest over
that. The vest revealed the pistol he wore, as well as the
dagger. His black trousers were tucked into a seaman's
boots. He was unshaven, wore a cuff earring in one ear,
and one of his front teeth was black.

He also smelled, and not of the sea. She did not think
he had bathed in a month.

Several days had passed since her heated encounter
with Jack Greystone. She was still in some disbelief—
both over her having kissed him, and his having refused
her. What had she been thinking? How had she acted as
she had, when she was in mourning? How could he have
been so uncaring? So indifferent to her cause? And he
had accused her of being dangerous! She would never
understand what he had meant by that.

And to think that, for all these years, she had secretly
thought of Greystone as a hero!

But she was hurt by his rejection, just as she was hurt

by how he had judged her. It did not seem fair, yet she knew, firsthand, that life was so rarely fair.

Determined to move on, as she must do for her daughter's sake, she had since toured the tin mine. And she had been shocked to see how run-down the mine and warehouse were. The new manager wanted to discuss repairing the facilities. He believed they were not shipping enough ore because they were not extracting enough tin. She did not even have to ask to know that repairing anything would be costly, too costly, as far as she was concerned. And when she had asked the previous manager's opinion, he did not agree that there had been any kind of theft in the mining operations.

How could she be in this position now? She should be with her daughter, teaching her to read and write, to dance, play the piano and sew. But they did not even own a piano now, and instead, she was at the Black Briar Inn, about to discuss a very dangerous proposition with yet another smuggler—this one frightening in appearance.

She had gone to Henri's grave every day, bringing fresh flowers. Instead of missing him, she was angry.

But she was even angrier with Greystone.

Her pondering was interrupted. "So ye wish for me to run to France and bring back yer husband's chest," Ed Whyte said, grinning. He seemed to like the idea.

Evelyn inhaled and focused on the man she was seated with. It hadn't taken her very long to decide to find another smuggler to hire—the fact that she could not count on the mine for revenues had made the choice for her—and John Trim had given her several names. But Trim hadn't been thrilled to suggest either Whyte or his associates. "They're a rough bunch, my lady," he had said. "And no great lady should consort with the likes of Whyte and his cronies."

Evelyn hadn't explained why she needed to interview smugglers other than Greystone, nor had she explained that she had no choice. But now, she was almost regretting her decision. Whyte was so scurrilous in appearance, with his blackened teeth, foul odor and lewd gaze, that he made Greystone seem like a knight in shining armor in comparison.

Whyte had a very untrustworthy appearance, she thought grimly. He reminded her of a horse trader, or a weasel. And to make matters even worse, he kept staring through her veil, which was transparent, and he kept looking at her bust, even though the neckline of her dress was so high, she could not wear her pearls. He made her terribly uncomfortable. When Greystone had given her a male appraisal, it hadn't been frightening like this.

"I realize it is a dangerous mission," Evelyn said, adjusting the veil she wore attached to her hat. "But I am prepared to offer you a very fair share of my husband's valuable heirlooms. And I am desperate." But she kept her tone level. She could not plead with Whyte as she had pleaded her case with Greystone.

Whyte grinned at her. "An' what is that fair share, lady?"

"Fifteen percent," she said.

Evelyn looked down at her gloved hands, which she clasped tightly in her lap. She might still be hurt by Greystone's rejection, never mind that she should not care, but she still had a problem—she was haunted by the kisses they had shared.

She had to forget her kiss—and his. Hers was humiliating. His was disturbing her at night. It was disturbing her during the day. It was disturbing her even now. It made her body hum with a fervor that was shameful.

She hadn't even imagined that a man could kiss a

woman with such intensity, such passion, or so thoroughly.

It was time to forget him. He was not a hero. She had been mistaken.

"An' how much is fifteen percent?"

She looked up at Whyte. "I'm not certain."

He laughed. "Is this a jest, my lady?" He stood, preparing to leave. "If you want me to go to France for ye, you'll have to pay me very well—and not with some fair share."

She leaped to her feet. "Please don't go." Her heart pounded. This had been the point in the negotiation when she had begun to think of using her female charms on Greystone. But fortunately, while Whyte kept leering, he seemed entirely interested in money.

Whyte sat down. "Fer such a job, I'd need a thousand pounds—in advance."

Evelyn sat, inhaling. But she had come to this negotiation prepared. She laid her beaded black velvet purse on the table and opened it. She withdrew a wad of tissue, and unwrapped her sapphire-and-diamond ear bobs.

She had so little left to bargain with. There was the matching sapphire necklace, a sapphire ring, her pearls, a cameo and her magnificent diamond engagement ring.

His eyes widened and he seized the earrings, inspecting them. She winced when he bit into one. "What else do you have for me?"

She choked. "Those ear bobs were costly."

"They didn't cost you a thousand pounds. I don't think they even cost you a penny." He grinned, his black tooth making her look away.

He was right, if rude—the earrings hadn't cost her a penny. "They were a gift from my beloved husband," she whispered.

"An' now yer in hard times. Yeah, I heard—everyone's

heard. So he must have left ye something valuable in that chest in France. But if ye want it, ye'll have to pay with more than ear bobs."

She felt like crying. Evelyn took the matching ring from her purse and laid it on the table. It was a five-carat sapphire, flanked by diamonds.

He took it and shoved everything into the tissue, and into his hip pocket. He stood and smiled. "I'll be back in a week or two. We can speak some more then."

Evelyn jumped up. "Wait a minute, Mr. Whyte, I'm expecting you to go to France—immediately."

But he was sauntering away. He turned and grinned, saluting her with one finger to his temple. Incredulous, Evelyn seized the table as he walked through the crowd—and out the door.

He was leaving—with her jewels! Evelyn ran through the public room, comprehension hitting her—she had just given her sapphires to a stranger, a very untrustworthy stranger—but when she reached the inn's front door, Ed Whyte was already galloping away.

She collapsed against the frame. Had he just stolen her jewels? Was he actually going to come back and plan the trip to France with her? Oh, she did not think so!

And suddenly she realized how utterly naive she had been, to give him payment in advance. It was one thing to have paid Greystone in advance for escorting her out of France—she had already been on his ship! And she still trusted Greystone, even if he had kissed her and refused her and walked out on her, he could be trusted with payment in advance, because he was, by birth and by nature, a gentleman. He would never steal from her—he would undertake the mission. But Whyte was a smuggler, an outlaw and now, a damned thief.

Damn it!

Evelyn quickly left the inn, before Trim might ask her in to a luncheon with his wife. Tears burned her eyes. Somehow, she must find a way to retrieve those sapphires, she thought, but even as determination filled her, the wiser part of her knew it was a lost cause. She had been taken, robbed.

And now what? She could not afford to lose those jewels; she had so little left. And Jack Greystone's image loomed in her mind. She cursed, picking up the reins of her mare. This was his fault, she decided furiously. Evelyn knew she remained exhausted, not from lack of sleep, but from the fear over her daughter's future, which gnawed at her constantly. She fought tears of sheer fatigue. She could not succumb to her desire to cry—she had to find the strength to solve this crisis.

An hour later, her mare trotted into Roselynd, gravel crunching beneath her hooves. Evelyn was grim. She intended to confront Whyte, one way or the other, and make him return her sapphires. She might even enlist Trim to help her. Perhaps, if a group of the villagers barraged him, he would return the sapphires.

She was not hopeful. As she parked the gig in front of the stables, Laurent came out of the house and hurried over to her.

He took one look at her and said, "What happened?"

Evelyn climbed down from the curricle and patted the mare. "I have been taken."

Laurent groaned. "I knew you should not deal with common smugglers!"

"I gave Ed Whyte my sapphire ear bobs and the ring, and I have the terrible certainty I will never see him again."

"Ahh, I knew you should have tried to approach

Greystone again! He would not steal from you—he might be a smuggler, but he is a nobleman!"

She began to unhitch the mare from the traces. Laurent was right—he would never steal from her. But if only he knew what had really transpired, she thought. "Laurent, I told you that he refused me in no uncertain terms—after I begged and pleaded with him."

Laurent led the mare into the barn, turning her into a box stall. She watched him as he latched the stall door and walked back outside. "But you are beautiful, you are a woman and you are in distress. No man could remain indifferent."

She trembled, recalling their tense and then heated exchange—recalling his final indictment of her. "But he did walk away," she said, aware that her cheeks were hot and probably red.

"*Madame,* what really happened? You have been miserable for days!"

Evelyn stared. If there was anyone she could confide in, it was Laurent. "I didn't tell you everything. He mentioned that he found me very beautiful—but he was still about to refuse me. And…I kissed him."

Laurent started. "You kissed him?"

She blushed, her heart racing wildly, as she waited for Laurent to point out that she had behaved most improperly. "I don't know what overcame me, and then he kissed me back." She laughed mirthlessly. "It was quite the kiss, but he refused me anyway."

Laurent came to life. "That is odd!"

She didn't want to reveal every detail, so she shrugged. "I regret the kiss—of course I do, as I am in mourning," she said. Then, she said, "He seemed angry when he left."

"You must be wrong! You are a sweet, kind woman, and so beautiful, you steal a man's breath away!" Laurent said firmly. "He is the man for this mission, Countess. We both know how courageous he is—and how skilled. And we are not talking about a few family heirlooms. We are talking about Aimee's future. Therefore, it is time for you to mend fences—and approach him again."

She choked. "I beg your pardon?"

"Do you want to raise Aimee in splendor? Or in poverty?" he asked.

Evelyn sat down hard on the wood bench in front of the stables. "So I am to approach him again, without any pride? Beg him again? And then what?" She flushed instantly—imagining another heated encounter.

"Well, we both know you are not a wanton woman." Laurent sat down beside her, taking her hands. "You should write him a very sincere note of apology. In it, you must also tell him he is welcome here, anytime."

Evelyn looked at him carefully. "I may have kissed him, but he did kiss me back." But should she apologize to him all the same? Would it make a difference? What if he accepted such an apology—so they could discuss matters?

"So? Men can be such fools—I happen to know." Laurent smiled then. "I cannot tell you exactly what to write, as I was not there for your encounter. But we are a conceited lot, and we like it when we are right. Tell him you are so sorry if you offended him. It was hardly your intention. He will be pleased, Countess. And welcome him back to Roselynd."

She stared. Could she actually write such a note of apology? A part of her was loath to do so, but she had behaved inappropriately. Still, so had he.

"Who else can you ask to go to France for you?"

She trembled. Damn it. Laurent was right. She needed Jack Greystone.

"You could point out that you are terribly confused

right now—you have just lost your husband. *Madame,* I am certain you will find the right words to appeal to his male vanity. You could even tell him that he was right to refuse such an absurd advance on your part. He will love being told that!"

She wondered if Laurent was right. Most men would probably be enticed by such an apology, but she didn't think Greystone was at all like most of his peers. However, she remained desperate. If he would not respond heroically, then she had no choice, really, but to attempt to manipulate him.

"And when he calls—and he will call—you won't mention what you want of him. Trust me. He will quickly want to know why you aren't begging him for his aid. You must play an opposite role—you are desolate, inconsolable. It has become hopeless."

Evelyn stared, because the scenario Laurent was describing was starting to sound somewhat viable. "And maybe I could tell him I have given up. That it is too dangerous to go to Nantes, to my old home, to find an old chest—that no one could accomplish such a feat. And I must be resigned to my new circumstance."

"Now you are being very clever," Laurent said, kissing her on both cheeks in succession.

But would he insist that he could retrieve the chest? How would she know if she did not try? She thoroughly disliked the idea of playing games with Greystone, but she was desperate.

"I will write him," she said, thinking carefully now. "And I will send the letter to one of his sisters."

"You must deliver the letter yourself, so you can meet his sisters and befriend them," Laurent said. "Lady Paget is married to the son of a great Frenchwoman—the Dowager Countess of Bedford was a friend of Henri's, many years ago."

Evelyn hadn't known. "You have been making inquiries?"

"Of course I have. Aimee is like a daughter to me."

Impulsively, Evelyn hugged him. "I am feeling just a bit better," she whispered, meaning it. She was even excited—she hadn't been to London in two years, and a trip from the moors suddenly seemed terribly overdue. And surely Lady Paget would be able to locate her brother. But she wasn't about to allow herself to be hopeful. Instead, she felt a vast trepidation.

"And you may be even happier to know that you had a caller earlier—a gentleman caller—a very dashing one." Laurent smiled. "He left a note."

Evelyn started. "Who was it?"

"Lord Trevelyan," Laurent said.

HIS SHIP SECURELY at anchor in the cove, Jack leaped out of the dinghy two of his men had been rowing to the shore. He was accustomed to such a maneuver, and he landed on the damp sand, without getting even the toes of his boots wet. "Go up to the tower and keep watch," he ordered. "I will not be long."

His men dragged the boat onto the sand, both of them scowling. He did not blame them. They had left Roscoff, France, at dawn, and they were looking forward to a reunion with their families. Most of his men lived in the small village of Looe, or its outskirts. They had been bound for Jack's home on Looe Island, but he had abruptly decided to detour.

As his men vanished up a trail in the cliffs, Jack started up the wood steps leading to the house just above the cove. He had dropped anchor in this cove a hundred times, and even in the early evening darkness, he had no trouble making his way up the rough steps and the rocky path to Faraday Hall. Robert Faraday had been investing in his activities since Jack had had command of his first ship, eight years ago.

He had first met Faraday eight years earlier, in an inn in Bodmin. There, he had convinced the nobleman that the return on his investment would be well worth his while—and it had. Faraday was one of his most important patrons. He would be excited to learn about the high-quality Chinese silk in the Roscoff warehouses, which Jack intended to purchase on his next run. He knew Robert would want a piece of that pie.

And he told himself that that was the only reason he was trudging up to the back door of the house now. He did not give a damn that Evelyn D'Orsay had been raised at Faraday Hall. He had learned that she was Robert's niece last week. When she had been driving all about Cornwall, making inquiries about him, he had made a few inquiries of his own.

Talk about life's little coincidences! he thought grimly.

Of course, when he had first dropped anchor in this cove, Evelyn hadn't been in residence at Faraday Hall—she had been a bride in Paris. Or perhaps she had been a newlywed in the Loire countryside. It did not matter.

She had been sixteen when she had married; he recalled her telling him that, very clearly.

Their paths might have crossed far sooner, had she not married the French comte.

He supposed that was a coincidence, too—or was it an irony?

He did not know why the idea bothered him. He did not know why she remained implanted so firmly in his thoughts. He had just had a very successful run to France.

He had brought the French Republicans a shipload of woolens and metal grommets; he had then met one of Cadoudal's lieutenants, relaying the information given him by Warlock, while also relaying ten dozen carbines, five dozen pistols and enough powder for three times as many weapons. Warlock had also arranged the weapons transfer.

He knocked on the kitchen doors in the back, wondering if he was a fool. Right now, he could be at his island home, a good scotch whiskey in one hand, a pretty village wench in his arms.

Except, he wasn't exactly in the mood for a pretty village girl. Kicking at a rock, he waited rather impatiently, until a kitchen maid let him in. Redheaded and freckled, she blushed when she realized who he was. "Captain Greystone!" she breathed. "No one is expecting ye!"

Because he was annoyed, he gave her his fullest, most seductive smile. "Is Lord Faraday in?" He could not recall her name.

"He's in the library, sir." She smiled back, lashes lowered.

He was accustomed to good fortune, and hardly surprised that his host was within. He gestured and she led him through the house. He knew the way, but he followed her.

The mansion had been built twenty years earlier by Robert's father, David Faraday. It was a fine home, built in the early Georgian style, with beige marble floors in the entry, and parquet floors throughout. Works of art covered the walls, and while not masterpieces, they were pleasant enough. Bronze busts graced pedestals in the hallway. The house was not overly furnished, but the salon had a large, beautiful coral-and-blue rug from Persia, and other fine rugs graced the floors in the music room and library.

Most of the furniture was custom-made. Gilded chandeliers hung from the ceilings. Robert had clearly amassed a small fortune over the years.

He thought about Evelyn, living in a mostly unfurnished house, desperate to hire him to go to France to retrieve some family heirlooms. Obviously she meant to sell them. How could her husband have left her and their daughter in such straits? It was truly a dereliction of duty—and not his affair. He sighed as the maid knocked on Robert's door.

Faraday beamed when he saw him. "This is a pleasant surprise," he exclaimed, coming forward. He was casually clad in a smoking jacket, and a cigar was burning in an ashtray, a glass of French brandy beside it.

Jack turned to thank the maid, and when she retreated, he closed the door behind him. The library was a large room with one wall of books, several seating areas and a large desk, behind which was a window looking out onto the cove. Facing Robert, Jack shook his hand. "I have just come from Roscoff. I decided to stop by on my way home, as I have just seen a warehouse filled with the kind of silk we haven't glimpsed since before the war."

Robert's eyes brightened as he turned and poured Jack a glass of very fine French brandy—the kind Jack did not smuggle unless it was for himself. He then offered him a cheroot, which Jack accepted. These days, some of the best tobacco came from Virginia or the Carolinas, but when he inhaled, smiling with pleasure, he recognized it as being from somewhere else. "Is this Cuban?" he exclaimed.

"Yes, it is. You know I will participate." Robert grinned. "I imagine we will have that silk sold before you even touch down on the beaches here."

"I will make certain of it," Jack said, exhaling. He began

to relax, for there was nothing like a good cigar and brandy after a run across the Channel.

"Sit down, my boy," Robert said, pulling up a big up-holstered chair. Jack took it, stretching out his breeches and boot-clad legs, taking a sip of the brandy. It was old, French and excellent. Robert sat in the facing chair. "I have a small favor to ask of you."

Jack was mildly curious and he smiled, puffing on the cigar. "Feel free."

Robert exhaled a large cloud of smoke. "You have not yet met my niece, Evelyn D'Orsay. She has been recently widowed and lives with her young child on the Bodmin Moor."

His tension was immediate. "Actually, I have met her." And he suspected what would come next—Evelyn had lobbied her uncle to speak up on her behalf.

Robert seemed surprised, and then relieved. "It seems that her husband, who was a friend of mine, left her in rather dire straits. I cannot understand it, but of course, they are émigrés, so they left a great deal behind when they fled France. Still, she has a child to raise." He appeared disapproving.

Jack couldn't help it—he disapproved, too—and Robert had just echoed his very own thoughts.

"Evelyn believes that her husband has left her some valuables in France at their country home. She is determined to retrieve them—and she has asked me about you."

Jack smiled stiffly. Was his heart racing? "She has asked a great many Cornishmen about me, Robert. She has been trekking about the countryside, making inquiries about me, and indicating that she wishes to speak with me. A dozen cronies have alerted me to the fact."

"She believes that you could retrieve those heirlooms, Jack," Faraday said. And he lifted a thick gray brow.

Jack grimaced. "Robert, what she wishes is madness."

"She is grieving, and I cannot blame her if she is not thinking clearly. She was very fond of D'Orsay."

He almost choked on the sip of brandy he was taking. Had she loved that old man? Was it even possible? And why the hell should he care? He had assumed it to be an arranged and loveless marriage. "He was old enough to be her father."

"Yes, he was, and maybe that was the attraction—her own father was a rogue, as irresponsible as they come. And he abandoned her. She was left in our care when she was five years old. Why wouldn't Evelyn fall for Henri? He was everything my brother was not—solid, dependable and respectable—and he offered her a wonderful life. Besides, he fell in love with her at first sight." Robert smiled. "I know. I was there…. I witnessed it myself."

Jack felt like pointing out that it would be easy to fall in love with a beauty like Evelyn; she, undoubtedly, had fallen in love with D'Orsay's fortune. But Jack had heard Robert's every word—he hadn't realized her father had abandoned her. As it turned out, they actually had something in common.

"You are glowering," Robert said.

"Well, that is because I agree with you—D'Orsay should have provided for his wife and daughter." Jack hadn't thought about his own rakehell father in years—he could not recall what John Greystone had even looked like—but he thought about him now. His father had chosen the game halls of Paris and Antwerp over his own family. His mother had never been the same after he left, and a few years later she had begun her retreat from reality. To this day, she was often addled and incoherent, and entirely incognizant of her surroundings. She now lived with Amelia and Grenville.

"But he did provide for them, although not in a usual way. There is a small fortune in that chest," Robert said.

Jack took a puff of his cheroot. "She did not seem to know its value," he finally said.

"A chest filled with gold is either a small fortune or a large one. Did you agree to retrieve the chest for her?"

He almost coughed on the tobacco now, hearing for the first time that the chest was filled with gold rather than family heirlooms. As he attempted to compose himself, a light knock sounded on the door and Enid poked her head in. "Hello, Mr. Greystone. I heard you were here. I do not wish to interrupt. I merely wanted to greet you and see if you had had supper."

Jack was already on his feet, and bowing over her hand. "Lady Faraday, forgive my poor manners. But thank you for asking, and I have already dined."

She lifted a disapproving eyebrow at Robert, perhaps for all the smoke in the room. "You should open a window," she said.

Robert ignored that. "We were actually discussing Evelyn D'Orsay," he said. "Have you called on her yet?"

Enid stared, a bit coolly. "I have been intending to, all week. I will do so as soon as I can. Why on earth would you and Mr. Greystone discuss Evelyn?"

"She is recently widowed, and she is in a bad way— Jack agrees with me."

Enid smiled at Jack. "I did not realize that you were acquainted with Evelyn."

Jack smiled. "I have recently made her acquaintance." But he was still stunned by Robert's revelation. So she was chasing a pot of gold? He should have known! And wouldn't that solve a great deal of her problems? Not that it was his affair.

Enid seemed bewildered and Robert said, "She is in a difficult circumstance, and I was hoping Jack could be of help."

"Well, she has certainly come down in the world," Enid remarked. "But I would be careful if I were you. She is a fantastic coquette. Most gentlemen are taken with her, and leap to do her bidding—hoping to receive her favors."

"Enid," Robert reproved.

"Rest assured, I am not in need of any favors." Jack smiled, speaking mildly, but he did not care for Enid's condescension. Of course, he recalled how desperately he had wished to bed Evelyn the other night.

"Good." Enid approved. "Besides, after having married D'Orsay, I am sure she will seek to remarry some kind of title, with a fortune, of course. I imagine she will be married before the year is out. Her next husband will certainly restore her finances."

"You are probably right," Jack said, remaining outwardly indifferent. But that was what widows like Evelyn D'Orsay did. It would not be unusual for her to remarry as soon as was socially acceptable. And then she would not need him to run to France to retrieve a chest of gold. He should, in fact, be relieved.

"Trevelyan was quite fond of her when they were children," Robert remarked. "And he is now a widower."

"He is a great catch for most of us, but he will only inherit the title of a baron, dear, when Lord Trevelyan passes. I doubt Evelyn would marry so low."

Jack stared at them both. Having been friends with Ed Trevelyan since childhood, he knew Trev had been a rogue before his marriage, with an eye for beautiful women, and his family had been involved in smuggling for generations. If he wished, he could captain his own ship and he had the means to hire any smuggler he chose.

"I happen to recall that Evelyn also liked Trevelyan," Robert remarked.

Enid scowled. "Really? And what about Annabelle? She is about to become a spinster—she is twenty-two."

Robert sighed while Jack absorbed this news—that Evelyn had returned Trev's interest. Before he could ask when this old romance had occurred, Enid faced him. "So how can you possibly help Evelyn?"

"The countess is considering making an attempt to retrieve some family valuables that were left behind in France," Jack said, knowing better than to reveal full details.

Enid started. "That sounds dangerous, even for you. Are you going to help her?"

"I haven't thought about it," he lied.

"Well, she is clever and beautiful, and if she wishes for you to help her, I am sure you will be doing so, in no time whatsoever," Enid said rather disparagingly.

Jack simply smiled. Enid Faraday thoroughly disliked Evelyn, and he was somewhat affronted by her hostility. Of course, a beautiful woman like Evelyn would naturally use her allure to gain friends and allies, and he could not really fault her for that. But he hardly thought her a clever, scheming seductress—as Enid apparently did.

"Be careful where she is concerned," Enid said before she left.

Faraday clasped his shoulder. "Ignore her. She has always felt threatened by Evelyn, as if Lucille had to compete with her, which she did not. Women!" He sighed. "I hope there is a fortune in that chest. She has had a difficult life, and now she has a daughter to raise."

Jack ground out his cigar. "I doubt we will ever learn

how much is in that chest. Enid is correct. She will re-marry sooner, not later, and she will forget all about the pot of gold D'Orsay left for her in France." Or she could beseech her old flame Trevelyan.

Robert stared in disbelief. "You will not help her?"

"It is far too dangerous."

Robert was incredulous. "Everything you do is dangerous. You thrive on danger! And you adore beautiful women…."

Jack felt very much like a hypocrite. "It is too danger-ous," he repeated firmly.

"I am stunned," Robert said. "I was certain you would jump at the chance to throw yourself into such a fray, to outrace our navy, to elude the French army, to recover a chest of gold for a woman like Evelyn."

Jack folded his arms and stared. "Are you asking me to reconsider?"

Robert was blunt. "Yes, I am."

Jack kept his expression impassive, but inwardly, he felt like a small boy in the classroom, sitting in the cor-ner, squirming.

"We go back eight years—and it has been a good eight years, for us both," Robert said.

"So I am in your debt?" Jack asked slowly. He was stiff with tension now. "Or is that a threat?"

"We are friends," Robert said flatly. "I would never threaten you. Nor would I suggest that you owe me any-thing, as we have both prospered through our associa-tion. No. I am asking you as a friend to help her, Jack. I am asking you because I know you are a gentleman, and a man of honor."

"Touché," Jack said, scowling.

CHAPTER FIVE

EVELYN HANDED HER coat to a liveried servant, glancing around at the vast entry hall she had just been let into. The floors were marble, the ceilings high, with a huge crystal chandelier overhead. Red velvet chairs lined the circular chamber. Works of art—clearly masterpieces— hung on the walls.

It was an imposing house, and she was not surprised. Since deciding to come to London and present her letter for Jack Greystone directly to his sister, Evelyn had famil- iarized herself a bit with the Paget family. Dominic Paget was a well-known figure in the ton. The son of a French noblewoman, he was an outspoken Tory, both vehemently opposed to the French revolution and as passionately sup- portive of Britain's war against the new French repub- lic. Considered one of the wealthiest peers in the land, he moved in society's highest circles—and was close to Pitt and the governing elites. Although opinionated, his reputation was outstanding—he was considered a patriot and a man of honor.

There was even a rumor floating about that he had been a part of the La Vendée uprising in France. There were whispers that he had been one of Pitt's secret agents.

Evelyn had dismissed that gossip. But interestingly, Paget had married far beneath him. For Evelyn had also investigated the Greystone family. While the Greystones could claim an ancient lineage that went back to the days of the Conquest—their ancestors had been Norman aristocrats—they had been seriously impoverished for many generations. The estate relied exclusively upon a mine and a quarry for its subsistence. The manor, located close to Land's End in Cornwall on its most southern tip, had been closed up for several years. The Greystone patriarch had lost his title a century or so ago when on the wrong side of a rebellion.

Paget could have married a Hapsburg princess; he married Julianne Greystone instead.

It sounded rather romantic, but Evelyn was too experienced to believe that it had been a love match. Surely, a great many factors had gone into Dominic Paget's choice of a bride, even if she had heard some strange gossip about her, as well—that she was an eccentric, and that she was somewhat radical. Lady Paget was rumored to have once been imprisoned in the Tower—for her Jacobin sympathies! Since the Earl of Bedford was a Tory, close to Pitt and attached to the war effort, Evelyn doubted very much that he had married a radical of any kind.

As Evelyn waited to be received, her curiosity was piqued. No matter how skeptical she was of the gossip she had heard, she was intrigued, and very curious to meet Julianne Paget.

But she was also terribly nervous, as she must convince Lady Paget to forward her letter to her brother, and Evelyn had no clue as to how the countess would be inclined.

Another manservant appeared at the hall's far end, wearing the identical royal-blue-and-gold livery as the doorman, and the same powdered wig. His gray brows lifted rather imperiously as he approached. Evelyn quickly smiled, knowing that she did not look as destitute as she truly was—appearances now meant everything! She was clad in her finest black velvet gown, and she was wearing both her pearls and her diamond engagement ring. She had removed her gloves so her ring would be obvious, and now she held out her calling card. "Sir, I was hoping to call upon the Countess of Bedford, if she is in."

His brows shot up impossibly higher.

Evelyn knew she was not following the proper etiquette, which required that she leave her card, and return only when her call had been accepted. She continued to smile, and said, "I have spent the past two days and nights speeding across the country in coaches, and the matter I wish to broach is a fairly urgent one. I have yet to even acquire a hotel room." That was the truth. She was, in fact, exhausted from the madcap trip, just as she was exhausted from the events of the past month.

The butler placed her card on his tray and glanced at it. He looked up quickly, bowing. "Countess, I will tell Lady Paget that you have just arrived in town." His tone was vastly respectful.

Evelyn thanked him, her heart leaping with exultation—he could have sent her away. She had felt certain that Lady Paget would see her sooner or later, but she did not want to linger in town, far from Aimee, with every passing day adding to her hotel bill and depleting her small purse.

She followed the butler into a stunning gold salon with a dozen seating arrangements, and sat down to wait. Her heart continued to thunder. Sitting seemed impossible, so Evelyn stood and paced.

The letter she had written Greystone was tucked into her purse.

Dear Mr. Greystone,

My dear sir, I am writing to you to apologize. But I also must make a confession. Four years ago, you helped me, my husband, my daughter and our three servants flee France. I realize you do not remember the event, but I also hid my true identity from you, and wore a hood as a disguise. I was and remain vastly indebted to you, for saving the lives of my husband, my daughter and myself.

I will always be in your debt and I will never forget what you did for me and my family. The last thing I ever wished to do was impose upon you. Too late, I realize now that my having asked you for your aid, yet again, was a vast and reckless imposition.

And it put you in the position of having to refuse me. I understand now that my proposition was beyond folly, it was sheer madness. For you were very right. Returning to France now is far too dangerous for any one man. Of course you had to refuse.

Since then, I have had a great deal of time to reconsider. No family heirlooms are worth risking your life. I regret the misunderstanding we have had. I also beg you to accept this apology.

I want you to know that you are always welcome at my home. If I can ever entertain you in the future, please, do not hesitate. It is the least I can do for you, after all you have done for my family.

Sincerely,
Lady Evelyn, the Countess D'Orsay

Evelyn trembled, recalling her every word perfectly. She had thoroughly disliked writing such a dishonest letter, even if she had little choice—because Aimee's future was at stake. Of course, she would always be in his debt, and that much was very true. Still, she had yet to fully recover from their encounter. Not only did she remain hurt, she could not dismiss it.

How would Greystone react when he finally read her letter? Would he believe what she had written? Would he call on her at Roselynd, as Laurent thought? She had come to London with the gold in mind, but now, she genuinely wished to end the strife that had arisen between them. Maybe then, Greystone would cease to haunt her.

She heard soft, rapid footsteps—the clicking of feminine heels—and she tensed, turning.

A tall, slender red-haired woman in emerald-green satin and a matching headdress paused on the threshold of the salon. She was very beautiful, and close to Evelyn in age. Although her hair was curled beneath the headdress, she wore it loose to her waist, without a wig. As their gazes met, she smiled. "Hello, Countess D'Orsay. I am Lady Julianne Paget." Her expression was curious, not imperious, and her tone was rather friendly.

Evelyn was instantly relieved, as she was accustomed to pretensions. "Thank you for seeing me, Lady Paget. I realize this is rather improper, but I have decided to take my chances." She smiled warmly, hoping her anxiety did not show.

Julianne Paget came into the room, smiling in return. "I am not wedded to propriety, and anyone who knows me would say so," she said, laughing.

Evelyn wondered what was so amusing, as she recalled the odd gossip about Lady Paget being rather eccentric and having been a prisoner in the Tower.

Lady Paget said, "I have ordered tea for us. You are not French."

"No, but my husband was a Frenchman from Le Loire. He is deceased," she added.

"I am sorry," Julianne Paget exclaimed softly.

Evelyn smiled. "Thank you. He was a wonderful father, and a good husband. But he was a great deal older than myself, and he was ill for many years. His death was not unexpected. But I will always miss him." She hesitated. "I believe he was a friend of the Dowager Countess, your mother-in-law."

"That may very well be," Julianne Paget said. "Please, do sit." She sat down on one long gold sofa, and Evelyn sat down, as well. "The Dowager Countess was from Le Loire, and my husband had an ancestral home there." She sobered. "Of course, it is charred and ruined now."

Evelyn inhaled. They had so much common ground, she thought. "I do not know the state of our home, Lady Paget—we fled France four years ago. Friends did tell us it remained intact, but that was before Robespierre."

Lady Paget looked utterly sympathetic now—Evelyn had been attempting to curry favor. "I will pray that your home still stands. How can I help you, Countess? Gerard said that the matter that brought you here is an urgent one."

Evelyn smiled pleasantly, though inwardly, she was on pins and needles. Deception had never been a part of her life, and lying was not in her nature. She preferred to stay as close to the truth as possible. "I am in a bind," she said softly. "I was hoping you could relay a letter for me."

Lady Paget started. "Who is the letter for?"

Evelyn took the sealed letter from her purse, her heart skipping. "Your brother."

Lady Paget's eyes widened. It was a moment before she asked, "Which brother, may I ask?"

"Mr. Jack Greystone." And Evelyn knew she was now blushing, ever so slightly, for her cheeks were warm. She knew she must be careful. She did not want Lady Paget to suspect that there was anything untoward between the two of them.

Julianne was now staring closely, and with surprise. "You have a letter for Jack?" She fell silent and Evelyn knew her mind was racing. Then she said, "How do you know my brother, Lady D'Orsay? What do you want with him?"

Evelyn had expected the question. "He helped me, my husband and our daughter flee France, four years ago. We had arranged for a Belgian seaman to evacuate us, but he simply failed to wait for us to arrive on the day we had scheduled for our departure. Mr. Greystone happened to be in the harbor that night. Our contact sent us to him, and he agreed to transport us. I am in his debt, of course."

Her brows high, her eyes wide, Julianne said, "I see. But that was quite some time ago. Are you trying to repay that debt?"

Evelyn smiled. The rest of her explanation was difficult. "Not exactly. Actually, Mr. Greystone doesn't recall helping me and my family flee France."

Julianne's brows lifted. "Really?"

Evelyn thought her color might be higher. "I am a Cornishwoman, Lady Paget. I understand that you were born and raised in Cornwall, as well. I have been around the free trade since I was a child, and recently, with my husband's passing, I have decided I need the services of a smuggler."

Julianne simply stared, a slight smile on her face, and Evelyn knew she was trying to decipher what was truly going on.

"My husband left some terribly sentimental family heirlooms at our home in France. Now that he is gone I must retrieve them. I had hoped your brother would do so for me."

Julianne stood up, still smiling politely. "I am sorry—I am rather lost. You are sending my brother a letter to ask for his help—but it sounds as if you have already spoken with him, as you said he does not recall you."

Evelyn also stood, her heart racing. "I have actually already asked him for his aid. He refused me."

Julianne's smile vanished. Her eyes were wide. "Really?" she said again—oddly.

"I believe we had a misunderstanding," Evelyn said swiftly. "And of course, being as I am so indebted to him for saving our lives, it is bothering me immensely."

Julianne stared for another awkward moment. "Lady D'Orsay," she finally said, "my brother would never forget a woman as remarkable as you."

Evelyn stiffened.

"I'm sorry—I do not mean to dispute your tale. But I know Jack. We are very close. He is most definitely a ladies' man—with a terribly appreciative eye for beauty. If he evacuated you from France, he would never forget it." She was firm.

Evelyn was rigid with tension. "He did forget," she whispered truthfully. "He failed to recognize me."

Julianne kept staring intently. "No," she said now. "I am sorry. I do not believe it for a second."

Was she about to have a dispute with her hostess over her brother's character and memory? Evelyn quickly said, "Maybe I am mistaken, then. But in any case, I have been terribly unsettled since that encounter. Because I am in his debt. My letter is actually one of apology."

"So now you must apologize? For what?"

Evelyn knew what to say—she had expected such a question. Trembling, she walked away from Julianne, glancing outside at the gardens. "I am apologizing because I am in his debt, he is right—it is too dangerous in

France now—and I do not like misunderstandings." She was as firm as possible.

"I am confused," Lady Paget declared. "Jack would *love* to help a woman like yourself! He would love to be your hero!"

Evelyn had to turn and look at her. She seemed incredulous. "My brother adores danger. He cannot live without it," Julianne continued. "It does not make sense that he would tell you that such a quest was too dangerous! I almost feel that we are discussing two very different men."

Evelyn realized that her hostess was very suspicious now. "I'm sorry," Evelyn whispered in a strained voice. "But that is exactly what he said, that it was far too dangerous, and not worth the risk! That is why he refused—and he is right, of course!"

"Is he?" Julianne's red brows lifted. "It was far more dangerous to be in France four years ago—when he helped you and your family flee. As you know, my husband is half-French, and we follow the events in France very closely. I'm sorry, but I am so curious now. You are defending Jack, strangely, or so it seems to me."

Very uncomfortable now, not wanting to argue, Evelyn said, "It was a misunderstanding, my lady. It is actually as simple as that."

Julianne studied her, clearly trying to decide what to believe.

"Will you deliver this letter to him?" Evelyn finally asked, hoping she did not appear anxious. "I do not mind if you even wish to read it."

She started. "I would never do such a thing!" Then, she said, "When was the last time that you saw Jack?"

Evelyn was startled. Why would Lady Paget ask such a question? "I saw him last week," she replied.

Julianne Paget's gaze widened. "I see. I hope it does

not seem as if I am prying, Countess, but I am also wondering, was that the only time you have seen him since you left France?"

My God—what was Lady Paget thinking! That they were having a love affair? What else could she be thinking! "Yes," she managed. "Lady Paget, I am in mourning."

"My questions were rude, and I apologize. But you must admit, this entire story is a bit bizarre. I am sensing that there is more here than you are revealing. And I am not accusing you of deceit, my dear. It is just that I know Jack so well, and I only wish to help." To make her point, she patted Evelyn's arm.

"So you will forward my letter, then?"

Lady Paget stared closely. When she did not speak, Evelyn felt her tension increase. Julianne said softly, "Jack made advances, didn't he?"

Evelyn choked.

Julianne now sighed. "My brother undoubtedly owes you the apology. I know him so well, Lady D'Orsay." She took Evelyn's hand. "He is a gentleman when he wishes to be one, and he would know better than to pursue you when you are in mourning, but he probably was undone by your appearance! You surely set him back on his ear—and of course, he must have left in some anger." She sighed again. "Now, this entire misunderstanding makes sense. He simply has a weakness for women. I am certain he will apologize to you profusely when he next sees you." She smiled then—as if she intended to make certain of it.

Evelyn knew she was in dangerous waters now. Her mind raced frantically. This was a terrible conclusion for her hostess to draw. If Jack Greystone heard of it, he would certainly become angry. "He did not make advances, Lady Paget. He was—" she hesitated, breathing hard "—the perfect gentleman."

Julianne squeezed her hand. "You are being so lenient, so kind. How old is your daughter, my dear?"

Evelyn started. "She is eight."

"My daughter will be two years old in March. She is such a joy for both me and my husband."

Evelyn could not believe it—but Lady Paget was changing the subject! "I feel the same way about Aimee. She is the best thing that has ever happened to me," she managed, relieved.

"She must miss her father," Lady Paget said.

"Of course she does," Evelyn said.

"Why are you so worried?" Lady Paget asked sympathetically. "Why are you dismayed?"

Evelyn took a deep breath. "Your brother does not owe me an apology. Please. You have drawn the wrong conclusion!"

Lady Paget stared, very skeptically. "I take it you do not wish for me to interfere?"

"No, I do not. I wish to make amends, and I believe my letter might do so."

"Are you defending him because you still have a desire for him to go to France and retrieve your husband's possessions?"

This woman was so clever! "If he said it was too dangerous—" Evelyn began, but Lady Paget interrupted her.

"It is not too dangerous. It would be easy enough for Jack to sail to Nantes—or Quiberon Bay—and journey inland. How far is your home from the beachhead at Nantes?"

Evelyn started. "It is a forty-five-minute carriage ride, if the roads are good."

"As I said, this would not be a difficult mission for him—not that there isn't danger, of course. I think he will come around, Lady D'Orsay. As I said, he is very appreciative of the ladies…. You must send your letter, bide your time and then approach him again."

Evelyn could not believe that Julianne had seen through her plan—or that she was so optimistic. And was she on Evelyn's side? "You have been so kind."

"I am kind by nature," Lady Paget said. "And although we have only just become acquainted, your story is intriguing—and I like you already. My dear, when you are ready for a confidante, I am here."

"Thank you," Evelyn said. "But there really isn't much more to say."

Julianne smiled, her gaze openly skeptical. "Somehow, I doubt that." She went to a silver bell and rang it.

Lady Paget obviously knew that there was more to the affair than Evelyn was letting on. "Will you get my letter to him?"

Julianne smiled. "Of course I will. Now, Gerard said you have just arrived in town. Where are you staying?"

"I have yet to take an accommodation," Evelyn said, relieved that Julianne would deliver her letter to Jack and that she had survived the strenuous interview—for that was precisely what it had been.

Julianne sat down beside her and patted her hand. "How perfect! For you must stay here at Bedford House, so we can become better acquainted."

Evelyn started. "That is even kinder," she began. "But I cannot possibly impose."

"Nonsense. For Jack makes surprise visits—and don't you want to be here when he does so next?"

EVELYN LAY IN the luxurious four-poster bed, staring up at the pink pleats in the canopy over her head, as bright morning sunlight spilled into her bedroom. She could

barely believe she was awakening in the Earl of Bedford's home.

As she huddled under the down covers, she thought
about how Julianne Paget had invited her into her home.
Now that she was a guest, Lady Paget had been nothing
but kind, and she hadn't mentioned her brother or Evelyn's letter again. It was as if the awkward interview of
the day before had never taken place. But Evelyn knew
better than to fool herself. Lady Paget was very interested
in Evelyn's relationship with Jack, and she would probably continue to pry.

But last night had been so pleasant. She had taken such
an elegant supper with Lady Paget, her husband and the
Dowager Countess. A fantastic table had been laid out for
the four of them, and half a dozen delicious courses had
been served. Lady Paget had been resplendent in crimson
satin, and the Dowager Countess had worn dark green
silk with emeralds. A large staff had danced attendance
upon them. The conversation had ranged from the comings and goings amongst the ton, an impending engagement, a recent political appointment, to the war.

And no one had seemed the least surprised by her sudden appearance in town—or at Bedford House. Her relationship with Jack had not been discussed, and Evelyn
did not even know if Julianne had mentioned it to her
husband or her mother-in-law. She had been welcomed
at every turn. And, as it turned out, the Dowager Countess had known Henri very well, once upon a time. She
spoke of him fondly, wished she had been able to attend
the wedding, which a friend had described in great detail, and was distraught to have learned of his passing.

Dominic Paget had been more reserved, though ex-
ceedingly polite, and by the time supper had ended, Evelyn realized that her host and hostess were madly in love

with one another. It was not just the shared glances and smiles. It was the absolute ease with which they coexisted, as if they were of the same heart, soul and mind.

It had most definitely been a love match, Evelyn thought, intrigued.

She sighed, reluctant to get out of the warm bed. If she were at Roselynd, Aimee would be waking her up as she crawled into bed with her. A pang went through her. She missed her daughter terribly. She could not linger in town.

But what if Jack showed up at Bedford House? She became aware of so much tension within her. How would they ever have a chance to discuss her letter—how would she apologize—without alarming and alerting Julianne? They would need some privacy if she was to successfully persuade Jack to help her now. And she hoped that Julianne had not written to Jack—accusing him of impropriety and inflaming the situation!

A knock sounded on her door. Evelyn quickly got up, putting on a wrapper, and went to answer it. A maid stood there with a breakfast tray, and Julianne Paget was behind her.

"Good morning," Lady Paget said. "You have slept in, and I imagine you were exhausted. Did you sleep well?"

As the maid deposited the tray on a beautiful rosewood table, Evelyn smiled. "I confess that I fell asleep the moment I lay down. I doubt I moved even once the entire night. Lady Paget, do come in." She wondered at the intrusion.

Julianne smiled. "You may call me Julianne, if you wish, but then I will call you Evelyn, so be forewarned."

Evelyn smiled as Julianne thanked the maid and poured two cups of tea. "Besides," she said, "I am an early riser, and I have been hoping to spend some more time with you." She handed her a cup.

Evelyn accepted it with some apprehension. She felt certain another interview was about to occur. However, she sipped the tea and sighed—the brew was strong and delicious. "I can't thank you enough for welcoming me into your home as you have."

"It is my pleasure," Julianne said, taking a seat at the table. "You should spend a few days in town, now that you are here. I can introduce you around."

Evelyn sat down across from her. "I really can't linger, although I so appreciate the invitation," she said. "It has been a difficult month, with Henri so recently passing. I miss Aimee and I am not comfortable leaving her alone."

"I cannot imagine what you are going through," Julianne said. "I love Dominic so. If he passed, I would not survive."

Evelyn met her gray gaze and thought about how she was adjusting to Henri's death. But she had not had the kind of relationship that Julianne and her husband apparently had. Otherwise, she would have never allowed—and enjoyed—Jack Greystone's kiss. "Henri was a good husband—and he was my friend," she said. "But now, I must think of my daughter and her future."

"You are a very strong woman. There was a time when I was afraid I would never see Dom again. He was in France during the first La Vendée rebellion. But thank God, he came home."

Evelyn started, realizing that some of the rumors she had heard were, apparently, true. And she did not know why she confided in her, but she did. "Henri was a wonderful man, and I was so fortunate to be his wife. But he was ailing for the past few years, even before we left France." She hesitated. "He was a great deal older than

I was. He would have been fifty, this July, had he lived. I have known since the fall that he was dying. It was not a surprise."

Julianne's gaze was wide. "I am so sorry. But you mentioned this somewhat, yesterday. How difficult this past year must have been."

Evelyn nodded. "Now I am imposing upon you."

"You are not imposing, and it is obvious that you cared a great deal for your husband."

"I was an orphan when we met. My aunt and uncle raised me—somewhat reluctantly. I had no future to look forward to, not really—I had no dowry. But Henri gave me every opportunity when he gave me his name. I was so very fortunate, and then he gave me Aimee."

"He loved you," Julianne said, and it was not a question. "I imagine he loved you very much."

Evelyn nodded. "He loved me very much."

"I am sorry for your loss, but you are young, and you have your daughter to care for, as you have said." Julianne smiled, but her regard was searching. "You must bring her, the next time you come to London. She can meet Jacquelyn, my daughter, and maybe my sister will have had her child by the time you return. She is due in May."

Evelyn smiled and sipped her tea, realizing that she liked Julianne Paget—she seemed like a genuinely kind woman. It would be so lovely to bring Aimee to London with her for another visit. But an image of Jack Greystone invaded her mind. He had to agree to help her, otherwise, she would not be able to care for her daughter, much less take an expensive trip to town. "How exciting for your sister."

"She wishes to meet you," Julianne said. "I sent her a note yesterday."

Evelyn was alarmed.

Julianne set her teacup down. "My dear, I am hoping to become friends. You appear so worried. You will like Amelia, I am certain."

"You are being so kind again," Evelyn said, not wanting to reopen the debate of yesterday. "Yet you know I am in the midst of a vast misunderstanding with your brother."

"I imagine it will soon be resolved. I sent your letter by messenger yesterday, Evelyn. Jack should receive it tonight—if he is at home."

Her heart exploded. Evelyn took a lump of sugar that she did not need and put it in her tea. As she stirred it, she said, very casually, "I heard he lives on an island."

"Yes, he does."

Evelyn looked up, setting her spoon down. "And if he is not in residence?"

"Then I imagine he will receive your letter within the next few days, as he cannot stay at sea indefinitely." Julianne stood up. "He is rarely gone for more than a week at a time."

Evelyn stared. "You are being even kinder than you were yesterday."

"I wasn't all that kind yesterday. I was rather rude. However, that is all in the past, and I do hope we are truly friends now."

"Thank you," Evelyn managed. Julianne seemed entirely sincere. Did it really matter why she was being so kind? Jack was going to receive her letter any day now. "I hope so, too," she said.

"You must get dressed, Evelyn. Amelia is joining us for lunch. You will adore her. But be forewarned. She will be as curious as I am about your interest in Jack."

Evelyn straightened. Julianne was smiling, but it was

too serene—and too knowing. "But I already explained," she began.

"Of course you did. But the more I think about it, the more I think that you must have made a lasting impression upon my brother." She started for the door, smiling as if she knew a secret. There, she paused. "I feel confident that you will hear from Jack very soon, knowing him as I do."

Evelyn filled with tension as Julianne smiled and left.

CHAPTER SIX

EVELYN CAREFULLY FOLDED her undergarments and placed them in the valise that was open upon her bed. She added her nightgown and wrapper, oddly reluctant to leave Bedford House. She had so enjoyed her time in London, and she had become so very fond of Julianne and Amelia. She had spent three entire days in town, rather frivolously. There had been teas and luncheons, strolls in Hyde Park amongst other gentlewomen and browsing the extravagant shops on Oxford Street. She had enjoyed another magnificent supper at Bedford House, this time with Amelia's husband St Just joining them, and she had even attended the opera with her hosts. But she missed Aimee terribly. It was time to go home.

And there had been no word from Jack.

Julianne had been right. Amelia had been curious about their relationship—and she had asked far too many questions. A small, no-nonsense woman, she had seemed as pleased as her sister by the fact that Evelyn wished to engage Jack's services as a smuggler. Evelyn could not comprehend it.

By now, Jack had surely received her letter. Was he ignoring it? Or had he received it after all? Earlier that morning Julianne had pointed out that once in a while, his affairs might truly delay him. Evelyn could sense that she was a bit worried about him. After all, there was a bounty on his head.

Her heart lurched—as if she, Evelyn, were also worried about him.

There was another possibility, of course. Jack might ignore her missive, no matter how she wished to apologize, no matter how she tried to ingratiate herself.

Evelyn feared that might be the case. Julianne still believed that Jack had made improper advances, and that was the cause of their argument. Evelyn had no intention of telling her what had actually happened, even if she needed a confidante. But Jack might be so set against her, especially if Julianne had interfered, that perhaps he had dismissed her apology outright.

She was rather grim. If Jack meant to ignore her, so be it—there wasn't anything more she could do.

As she began to close the valise, a knock sounded on her door. Certain a maid was bringing up refreshments before she set out on the long journey back to Cornwall, Evelyn hurried to the door.

Jack Greystone stood there. "Hello, Countess."

Her shock was immediate.

His gray gaze seared hers. And before she could breathe—before she could even comprehend that he was at her door—he smiled ever so slightly and moved past her into the bedroom. Evelyn jumped, still shocked. He smiled again, this time as he shoved the door closed behind them. "You are certainly determined, Countess," he said. "And I am uncertain whether I admire such a stubborn bent, or not."

She gasped as their gazes held. And her heart thrilled, against all better judgment. He had come to London. Did that mean he had read her letter and that her apology had been accepted? Did that mean that they could forget their previous encounter, and start over?

Somehow, she had forgotten how magnificent he was.

Her pulse rioting now, she took a good long look at him.
He had clearly just come from his ship. She could smell
the salt from the sea on his clothes. His jacket was un-
buttoned, revealing the dagger at his waist and the pistol
hanging from the shoulder strap, at his hip—he would
hardly walk about town with such arms. The sight of
them made her shiver. His hair was coming loose from its
queue, and there was a bit of growth on his jaw, a shade
darker than his tawny hair. It only made him appear more
dangerous and disreputable. His lawn shirt was open at
the neck, revealing the gold cross he wore, with its ruby
stones. His breeches seemed damp, straining across his
powerful thighs. There was dirt on his high boots and
on his iron spurs.

He was a fatally attractive man. "You have given me
a fright," she managed.

He smiled slowly at her. "But you did expect me to
come rushing to your aid?"

Evelyn clutched her hands and backed up against the
bedroom door. "I was praying for a response to my letter. I was uncertain as to what that response might be."

"Apparently, your prayers have been answered."

His stare was unwavering, and Evelyn realized she
did not want to look away. She had truly forgotten how
dangerously handsome and terribly masculine he was,
how small and petite she felt, standing beside him—and
how utterly feminine he made her feel. But mostly, she
had forgotten the dangerous urge to leap into his arms.

She swallowed. "I did not expect you to come to London," she whispered. "Never mind that Julianne thought I
would hear from you. Forgive me—I am in some shock."

"Then we are even—as I was in some shock to learn
that you were at Bedford House with *Julianne*."

She trembled, wondering at his wry tone, and now

aware of another fact. He was in her *bedroom*. They were behind closed doors. "Mr. Greystone—we should go downstairs. We cannot possibly converse here." His mouth curled. His glance strayed to her mouth. "Of course we can, Countess."

She tensed—instantly recalling the torrid kiss they had shared—and certain he was recalling it, too. "I cannot entertain you here." She managed to think of Julianne, who was already suspicious of their relationship.

"Why not?" He seemed amused. "You did not mind entertaining me alone in your salon at the midnight hour. Our actions then were far more damning."

She knew she flushed. "It wasn't midnight," she exclaimed, searching his gaze, "and I did mind! I had no choice—as you simply showed up there with no warning—as you have done now."

"I am not going downstairs."

She started as his meaning struck her. "You fear being apprehended—in your own sister's home?" she cried.

"I must avoid scrutiny—even here. From time to time this house is watched." He walked over to a window and glanced outside at the gardens below. His movements were so casual, belying the danger he might be in. Then he faced her. "And while I did not notice any soldiers lurking about today, Julianne and Paget have a large staff. I have no intention of openly coming and going—I trust no one."

She hugged herself, finding it difficult to breathe normally. She hoped that she was not included in the circle of those he would not trust, but she was fairly certain that might be the case. And he could not even move freely in his sister's own home. Compassion arose. How could he live with such a bounty on his head? In constant fear of discovery—of arrest? She found herself staring closely at him, for some sign of vulnerability, but he instantly looked away.

If he was fearful of discovery, she could find no sign. "I am sorry," she heard herself whisper. And she meant it—yet she had to remind herself that he was running the British blockade. He was aiding her enemies. Yet he had saved her family by evacuating them from France. She would never indict him casually.

He lifted a brow. "So you are feeling sorry for *me,* Countess? I thought this was *your* tragedy."

She bit her lip, confused by his odd statement. Was he mocking her? "I am sorry you must remain in hiding. It must be terribly difficult, having to stay away from one's family. It is possible," she added, "to have sympathy for someone else's plight."

His expression tightened. "I do not need your sympathy. I am not in any plight. I suggest that you save your compassion for someone else. We have matters to discuss."

She trembled, taken aback by the hard look in his eyes. She had mistaken his mood. It wasn't light, not at all. He was grim, but then, he feared discovery and arrest. "Does your presence mean that you have read my letter…and can you accept my apology?"

His thick lashes lowered. "It means—" he paused, glancing up through them "—that you are in my *sister's* house."

She studied him, alarmed. He was distinctly unhappy that she had called on Julianne. "I was invited," she began.

He cut her off. "I have read your letter," he said flatly. "And I have also read Julianne's."

Julianne had written him. What had she said? "She has been very kind. She invited me to stay when I called, asking her to forward my letter to you."

His stare was sharp and searching. "I told you that I was not interested in your proposition. Yet you write me a letter—to attract my attention. And now, I find you at my sister's, her cherished houseguest."

"I pray you are not accusing me of manipulating your sister!" Evelyn cried, meaning it.

"Your prayers may be falling on deaf ears," he said bluntly. "What else am I to think?"

"Do you not know your own sister, sir?" Evelyn cried. "She is a very strong and intelligent woman. She can hardly be bandied about."

He stepped forward—Evelyn shrank. "I happen to know my sister very well. She is hopelessly naive. She believes in saving every lost soul. Undoubtedly she would even believe in saving yours."

"My soul isn't lost," she managed, pressing against the spiny bedpost. He almost loomed over her.

His large hands found his slim hips. "I can imagine the encounter now. You appeared on her doorstep, looking for me, with your tale of woe—while on the verge of destitution. Of course she offered to let you stay here." His gray gaze flashed, but it dropped to her mouth.

He *was* angry, she thought with dread. He did not like her new friendship with Julianne! "I did not expect her to invite me into her home."

"Somehow I doubt that!"

"It was more economical for me to stay here—and await your reply." She gave him a hard look. "And she does not have a clue that I am destitute."

"Is that true?" His hands relaxed.

She lifted her hand, showing him her large and expensive diamond ring. "I came here only to ask her to forward my letter to you, and I believe I must appear to be in ordinary straits. As you can see, I am wearing my finest clothes—and my only diamond ring."

He stared closely at her now, and it was a moment before he spoke. He said, softly, "Another man might feel as if he is being hunted, Countess—or pursued, rather boldly."

She realized his meaning and felt herself blush. "If you are suggesting that I am pursuing you for personal reasons, you are wrong!"

"Am I? Perhaps you cannot forget a scorching kiss."

She knew her color increased wildly—she felt the fire in her cheeks. "Did we kiss?" she managed. "I have forgotten!"

He laughed. "You damn well know we kissed, Countess. I doubt you have forgotten it! But I am relieved that you are not pursuing me for personal reasons." He was definitely mocking.

She trembled, absolutely breathless. "I am in mourning!"

"Of course you are." He studied her. Evelyn wished she could stop flushing. She hadn't behaved like a widow in mourning that night in her salon and they both knew it. "So tell me. What did you say to her? How did you get her to rally to your cause?"

She fought for composure. It was a moment before she could gather her wits and return to the subject of Julianne. "I told her that the letter I wished for her to forward was one of apology. I explained how I knew you, and I told her that we had had a misunderstanding, one I wished to resolve."

He continued to stare at her. "Did we have a misunderstanding?" He was wry.

Damn it, she felt certain he was referring to that kiss! "I believe so," she said, tilting up her chin. "I explained that I needed to hire a smuggler, and that as you had helped me escape France four years ago, I wished to hire you. She was very interested in my efforts to attain your services. She asked me a great many questions. I was stunned when she finally invited me to stay here."

"Stunned—or delighted?"

"I was pleased to stay here for matters of economy— which I imagine you must know. We have become friends, Mr. Greystone. Genuinely so."

"I do not like your involving my sister in your affairs," he said harshly, turning aside slightly. This was her cue, so she slipped away from the bedpost and past him, rushing to the window. She had felt trapped by the bed, but now, she felt trapped by the window.

He turned to gaze at her. "I was stunned to receive your letter, but not as stunned as I was to receive Julianne's." He made a mirthless sound. "But nothing has surprised me as much as learning that my sister thinks I have mistreated you!"

She shrank. "Is that what she said?" she asked carefully.

He slowly smiled and approached. Evelyn gasped and backed into the windowsill. "I think you know exactly what she wrote."

"She guessed what happened! Yet I told her, several times, that you did not make improper advances," she said quickly. "I defended you! I claimed you need not apologize to me!"

His gaze widened with utter surprise. Too late, Evelyn realized that Julianne hadn't told him her theory that she believed Jack owed Evelyn the apology, and not the other way around. "She thinks I made advances?" He flushed. "Of course she does! And you are the tragic heroine in all of this. While I am the villain!"

She stiffened. "I told her, several times, that you were the perfect gentleman!"

He laughed. "And did she finally believe you?"

"No."

He came close and leaned over her. Evelyn went still. He looked at her mouth again, and this time, he did not look away. Her heart thundered. Was he going to kiss her now? Like this?

But he jerked away. "You have courage, I will give you that. For a tiny woman, you have enough courage for a dozen men."

She shook her head. "I am not all that brave."

He started. "I don't believe it."

"I am afraid—I am afraid of the future, and what it holds for Aimee."

He stared. "Of course you are." He moved away and began to slowly pace. "My sister is now your champion. She thinks that, as a man of honor, I must rush to your aid."

Evelyn was afraid to move even if the windowsill was digging into her hip. "I don't know why she wishes for you to help me," she said truthfully. "I did not try to persuade her to my cause."

"Didn't you?"

"She is intrigued by our relationship."

His silver gaze shot to hers. "Of course she is. Julianne is a romantic, from the top of her head to the tips of her toes."

What on earth did that mean? She wondered, watching him. What did her romantic nature have to do with any of this?

He stopped pacing. "Did it ever occur to you to take no for an answer?"

Their gazes were locked. He was being earnest, and

she knew she must be as honest. "At first. Our encounter was so horrendous, I only wished to forget it. I did try to find another smuggler."

His stare was relentless now. "I must confess, no woman has ever described my embrace as horrendous until now."

She swallowed. "But I had no choice," she managed, her heart lurching. "I realize that you do not recall the events of four years ago, but you did save my life, and the lives of my daughter and husband. I trust you, Mr. Greystone. I trust you as I trust no other."

He looked away, his face set. "I do not like that letter. It was a deliberate attempt to bring me to Roselynd, so I could fall under your spell—and do your bidding."

She trembled, hesitating. "I am not certain I like it, either."

His gaze lifted and his eyes blazed. "So you admit it was another devious attempt to make me come to heel? To involve me in your dilemma?"

She bit her lip. "Yes. But the truth is, I wish to make amends. I wish to start over! And, yes, I still need your help!" she cried.

His stare was unwavering now. It was bold, piercing. He said, "I came here to accept your apology, Countess. The truth is, I have no other choice."

She was stunned.

"I may have a rather notorious reputation, but it is not entirely correct. I am a man of honor. Honor requires that I accept such an apology, even if it is not sincere."

She inhaled. "But I will always be in your debt."

A silence had fallen, one thick and heavy. She wondered if he meant to cross the small distance between them—and take her into his arms—in spite of the argument they were having.

But he did not move. Evelyn wet her lips, turned and opened the window. She lifted the collar of her gown. She stared into the gardens below, filled with an absurd disappointment. Clearly, she still yearned for his touch. "If I do not fight for my daughter's future with the utmost determination, who will?"

He did not answer her. She did not turn, but she felt his gaze on her back.

A knock sounded on the door. "Evelyn?" Julianne called.

Evelyn leaped away from the window as Jack whirled to face the door. "Get rid of her." He moved to the far side of the armoire, against the wall—a position that could not be seen from the door.

Evelyn began to breathe, but harshly. She hadn't realized she had been holding her breath.

She rearranged her expression, but she wondered why Jack did not want his sister to be aware of his presence. "Coming," she called brightly. She ran to the door, unlocked and opened it. Julianne stared curiously at her.

"I must have locked it by mistake," Evelyn said quickly. She brushed a trickle of perspiration from her temple.

"That is odd," Julianne responded, entering the room. She handed Evelyn a shawl she was holding. "You left this downstairs," she said, but she suddenly glanced about the room, as if looking for another occupant.

"Thank you," Evelyn said. She could not see Jack from where she stood, but if she went to the bed, she would be able to do so. "I was just about to finish packing." She forced a smile. "Perhaps we can take tea before I leave. I am almost through."

Julianne glanced at her skeptically. "I thought I heard voices," she said.

Evelyn tried to appear innocent. Julianne walked to

the bed and sat down on its end. "I wish you would stay on a bit longer," she said, and then she glanced at the armoire—and saw Jack.

She leaped up, eyes wide. Evelyn slammed the door closed, blushing.

"Hello," Jack said, walking over to his sister and hugging her. But as he did, his gaze met Evelyn's over his sister's shoulders.

Julianne hugged him back, then looked closely at him—and at Evelyn. "I take it I am interrupting?"

"You could never interrupt," Jack said, smiling.

"You are not interrupting," Evelyn said quickly.

Julianne smiled at them. "Are you seducing Evelyn, when she is my houseguest?" she asked Jack. "Once was not enough?"

Evelyn winced, but Jack seemed amused. "How could you possibly suggest such a thing?"

Evelyn knew she was turning red. "Julianne, I am sorry. He simply appeared, and as it isn't safe for him to be seen in public, we decided to have a discussion here."

"I think I understand," Julianne smiled, rather smugly. "And I can suggest such a thing because I know you so well. But try to remember, Jack, Evelyn is a widow and she is in mourning," she told her brother. "She is also a gentlewoman. I expect you to behave, at least for the moment."

"So now I must behave—yet I am to risk my life for her?" Jack bantered.

"Yes, that would sum it up," Julianne said, rather happily.

Her heart lurched hard. Evelyn wondered if she had heard correctly. Had Jack decided to help her after all? He had yet to make any such indication!

Jack's gaze shifted and their eyes locked, before he

turned to face Julianne. "Must you take in every stray, still? Haven't you learned your lesson?" His tone was affectionate. "Must you rally to every injustice? Assist every tragic victim? The countess has many admirers, Julianne, who can fight her causes for her."

"I will take in whom I wish to," she said archly. "And I will certainly continue to fight injustice! I take it the two of you have patched things up? And that you intend to help her retrieve her valuables from France?" Julianne asked, but it wasn't exactly a question.

Evelyn froze as Jack slowly looked at her. They hadn't reached any such understanding.

Jack's stare was relentless. "Yes, I believe I will help her."

Evelyn was in disbelief. She was speechless.

Before Evelyn could answer, Julianne took his arm and kissed his cheek. "I knew you would come around! I knew you could not refuse her for very long." Julianne winked at Evelyn.

Jack wasn't smiling. "Can you give us a moment, please? And, as I cannot linger, I will speak with you quickly before I leave."

Julianne's amusement vanished. She hugged him, hard. "I miss you so much, Jack. I hate this need for secrecy and stealth!" She hurried from the room.

Evelyn wet her lips. "You are going to help me after all?"

"Yes, I am going to help you."

She felt her knees buckle. He reached out and caught her around the waist. Instantly, Evelyn moved into his arms.

For one moment, he held her closely. Evelyn was shocked by the tension she felt coursing in his body— and the answering tremors in her own. "I am running for Roscoff tonight. We will sort out the details when I return," he said harshly. "I will come to Roselynd in a few days."

Her eyes widened. He was going to help her—and in a few more days, he would come to Roselynd.

"I wouldn't have responded to your letter, if I was not planning to go to France for you," he said. And abruptly, he let her go.

Evelyn could barely believe her good fortune. "I can't thank you enough," she whispered.

He studied her. "I'm not sure about that."

CHAPTER SEVEN

EVELYN STARED AT the papers on Henri's desk. She had been home for three days now, having returned in mostly good spirits—Jack Greystone was going to France for her. Unbelievably, they seemed to have resolved their misunderstanding.

She meant to steer a careful course with him now. And that meant she must not think about his opinion of her, or about the attraction that seemed to hang in the air whenever they were in the same room. What did matter was that her financial problems would soon be over and she could give Aimee the childhood she deserved.

Evelyn sighed. The pile of papers on Henri's desk was for accounts owed—and it was shocking. She could not believe how much debt they had accrued in the past few years. They owed local merchants for everything from groceries to kerosene and firewood; but there were even bills dating back several years for clothing and jewelry purchased in London, before they had become so destitute! Evelyn knew she could manage the current accounts, but when she realized how much they had spent, all those years ago when living in town, she was ill. How could they have been so reckless? Hadn't Henri realized that their funds would eventually run out, and that they must maintain an entirely different, and lower, standard of living?

Too late, she wished she had insisted on being involved

in far more than planning menus and caring for Aimee and Henri.

But she had not been involved, she had been entirely ignorant. And it would be so easy to blame Henri for their downfall, but she knew she must not do so. He had been accustomed to living large. The French revolution was to blame, not her deceased husband. He had wanted to keep her in silks and jewels. He had even said so.

Adelaide stepped into the small library, smiling. "Will you come and take luncheon, my lady? I have prepared a very pleasing stew."

Her head ached now, worry filling her heart. When would Jack Greystone call—so they could finalize their plans? A pang of stronger anxiety went through her. He had said he would return to Roselynd shortly, and what he did not yet know was that she intended to go to France with him. Oh, how she hoped to avoid another dispute with him. Clearly, she must walk a fine line.

She did not want to think about having been, briefly, in his arms, in her bedchamber at Bedford House. But every time she thought about Greystone and the impending voyage to France, that was exactly what came to mind. She shuddered. She had to dismiss her feelings, as confused as they were, and her yearnings, which were as perplexing. She had to stop thinking about the one kiss they had shared—and their most recent conversation. But how was she to pretend to herself that she wasn't looking forward to seeing him again? There was so much anticipation, as if she were a young debutante—as if he were a beau.

She stood up. "I think I have lost any appetite I might have had," Evelyn said grimly. She brushed a wrinkle from the skirt of her dove-gray silk gown, which was trimmed in black braid. "We have accumulated so much debt, I am in shock," she said. She may have to try to make the tin mine profitable, even if the gold in France were recovered.

"You will feel better after you eat," Adelaide began. Then she looked past her, out of the window behind the desk. Evelyn turned and saw a handsome carriage in the driveway, halting before the house. Briefly, her heart skittered wildly, but then she realized it had three occupants, not one. Besides, Jack Greystone would not arrive in broad daylight, nor would he knock on her front door.

Another pang went through her. She had seen how fond he was of his sister. She should not feel sorry for him. He was the cause of that bounty on his head, for running the British blockade, and he might very well be a French spy, but she did feel compassion anyway. It could not be easy, being both a gentleman and an outlaw.

Evelyn walked over to the window as Adelaide remarked with some delight that they had visitors, and she would prepare tea. Evelyn watched Trevelyan alight from the carriage's driver's seat. She realized she had begun to smile and that she was pleased to see him. She stood by the window.

He made such a dashing figure as he paused by the horses in the traces. He was undeniably a tall, muscular and handsome man, and she liked the fact that he did not wear a wig. His hair was as dark as hers—it was the color of midnight. There was no mistaking that he was an aristocrat, either, and not just because he wore his dark coat and pale breeches so well. He simply had an air of both elegance and authority about him.

His wife had died ten months ago—he would soon be out of mourning.

She realized that her cousin was with him. John had climbed out of the backseat, and he was helping a young woman she did not know get down. "Do we have anything we can serve with the tea?" she asked Adelaide, with some worry.

"I can make a few small cucumber sandwiches," Adelaide said. "Do not fret about it, my lady. No one will know our cupboards are bare."

But of course she was worried—they had to offer refreshments to their guests, as if all was well. Appearances had to be kept.

"Now that is a handsome man," Adelaide smiled, sending her a knowing look, as she turned and rushed back to the kitchens.

Evelyn certainly agreed. Trev was not only handsome, but wealthy. He was probably the catch of the parish. Even now, she imagined that a great many mothers were scheming about how to best attract his interest in their daughters.

There was a standing mirror in one corner of the room, and she hastily checked her appearance there. She looked well enough—there was a slight flush to her cheeks, a sparkle in her eyes—and she tucked a few escaping tendrils of hair back into the somewhat severe and old-fashioned chignon she wore. But since retreating to the Bodmin Moor, she had no time for fashion, and certainly no inclination to style her long hair. Loose curls styled about the face were the rage, with long hair hanging past one's shoulders, unless one wore a wig, but she had no interest in wigs. Evelyn sighed. She so looked like a country mouse and a widow in mourning.

But she was pleased to have company, never mind that they had little tea to spare. She hurried into the front hall.

The trio of guests was just being ushered inside by Laurent as she came in. Trevelyan smiled at her. "We heard you were back from town and decided to call. I do hope we are not intruding."

His smile was infectious. Evelyn pushed aside her financial worries and smiled back. "I doubt you could ever intrude. You are always welcome here." She gave him her hands and he kissed them properly. But when she pulled away his stare sobered, becoming searching, and Evelyn was flustered. Trev had called on her before she went to London, and they had had tea. She had wondered about his interest then. She found herself wondering about it now.

John swept into the breach, hugging her. "Please meet Matilda, my fiancée. I have been on pins and needles, waiting for the two of you to become acquainted."

Evelyn smiled at the pretty slender blonde. "I am so very happy for you."

"And John speaks so highly of you, Countess," Matilda said, grinning. Freckles splattered her tiny nose. "I have been eager to meet you, too. In fact, I have been counting the days since you returned from town!"

She was certainly not shy, and her smile was wide and infectious. Evelyn liked her immediately. "Why don't we adjourn into the salon? I will serve tea."

Trev smiled at her. "Actually, we have come to invite you on a picnic. Our carriage is laden with roasted chicken and lamb pies."

"It is the middle of March," Evelyn protested. "It is freezing cold outside."

Trev grinned. "Oh, it is not that cold out—and it is perfectly sunny—there isn't a cloud in the sky. Besides, we have furs in the carriage."

Evelyn stared, trying to comprehend why on earth they would have decided to have a picnic when it wasn't even spring yet. John stepped forward. "Maybe it is a bit too early in the season for a picnic. We surely don't want the ladies to be cold."

"You know, you're right. What was I thinking? I cannot think clearly where you are concerned, Evelyn," he said with a wink. "I have a better idea. We will have our picnic right here, and we can pretend we are at the pond, watching the ducks swim by."

She stared at him, eyes wide. He had taken her to the pond one day, when she was fifteen and he was but two years older and they had had a picnic there. She had been overwhelmed with nerves, and she had thought him the most handsome boy she had ever seen.

Lucille had had a fit when he had brought her home, and when Trev had left, Enid had told her she was not allowed to accept him as a caller, not ever again.

Trevelyan wasn't smiling now. She sensed he had never forgotten that day. She hadn't recalled it in years. It was a bit daunting to recall it now.

"Good idea," John agreed. "What do you think, Matilda?"

"I think it excessively clever to have a picnic inside!" Matilda laughed.

"Laurent, my good man, will you help me bring the baskets in?" John asked.

Evelyn's heart skipped as Trev ducked his head and she realized what they were doing. They knew she was in dire financial straits. They had used the excuse of a picnic as a pretext to bring a good meal into her home.

Trev glanced up. Evelyn tried to smile, but she was so moved that she failed, and she felt moisture gathering in her eyes. She should protest—she should have pride. Instead, she simply nodded gratefully. It had been years, but he was still such a good, reliable friend.

And it crossed her mind that he might press a suit, once her period of mourning was over. She tensed. Instantly, she thought of Jack Greystone.

"I think this is even more amusing, to have the picnic indoors," Matilda cried. She looped her arm in Evelyn's. "I saw them stash sherry in one of the baskets. Do you like sherry? My mother says I am too young, but I adore it and I intend to imbibe."

Evelyn fought for her composure. She glanced back at Trev as she and Matilda started into the salon. He gave her a lazy smile.

She was shaken. Was she comparing Trev to Jack? That was the last thing she wished to do! And no comparison could be fair. Jack Greystone was a smuggler—he was an outlaw. Trevelyan was the well-heeled heir to a barony. There was no reason to make comparisons.

But one did leap out at her. She had been in Jack's arms, not once, but twice. Trevelyan knew she was in mourning—and she knew he would remain respectful of the fact.

"You are looking at me as if I have grown horns," he said softly.

She jerked back to reality. "You are being very gallant, Trev."

He smiled slowly. "If I am winning your approval, I am a very happy man."

Evelyn had to smile at him now. If he had intentions, she reminded herself that he would have to delay them—so she need not worry now. "I am trying to recall if you were always so charming."

"You have forgotten? I am stricken," he teased with a laugh.

"Do you have any faults?"

"Oh, I might have a few." He grinned. "Shall we picnic, my lady?"

As Laurent and John brought the wicker baskets in, Matilda began to tell her about the wedding plans that were in progress. Trev left to retrieve a plaid wool blanket and lay it out upon the floor. John rekindled the fire until it roared. Everyone took up plates, and began filling them. Adelaide now brought Aimee downstairs, as Evelyn had asked her to do. She hurried to her daughter.

Aimee was wide-eyed. "Mama, what is this?"

"We are having a picnic, darling, indoors, because it is too cold to do so outside." She took Aimee's hand, watching in some disbelief—the baskets contained roasted chicken, lamb potpies, platters of fruit and cheese, freshly baked breads, and both red and white wines. There was enough food, in fact, to feed the group for several days.

"How are you today, Aimee?" Trev asked. When Aimee blushed he smiled at Evelyn. "She looks exactly like you."

John handed Aimee a heaping plate, and Evelyn smiled gratefully.

Sometime later, everyone was seated on the floor, legs crossed, with glasses of wine and plates piled high. Trev sat on Evelyn's right; Aimee was on her left. "How was town?" he asked with a smile.

She decided instantly that she would never lie to him. "I had a wonderful time, actually. I stayed with Lady Paget."

His smile never changed, but his eyes certainly did. "I see. I had assumed your trip concerned some business affair. I hadn't realized you knew Lady Paget."

She bit her lip. "I didn't. But I called anyway."

"Of course you did—you are so determined." He still smiled, but his gaze was darker now. "I haven't seen Greystone, Evelyn, so I have not been able to speak to him on your behalf."

She hesitated. She hardly needed Trev to solicit Jack for her now.

"Although I am against your having any association with him, and I remain concerned about it, I am your friend, Evelyn, and I only wish to help you if I can."

Evelyn wondered if she flushed. Could he somehow guess that there was tension between her and Jack? "I do appreciate your concern. And I am pleased we are friends again, after so many years have passed."

He studied her. "I truly hope you mean it. I did not expect for us to become reacquainted, but frankly, I am very glad you have returned to Cornwall."

"I do wish we had been reunited under different circumstances."

"Of course you do—and so do I," he said seriously.

She knew he was thinking about his wife's death, just as she was thinking about Henri's passing.

"Did you ever make contact with Greystone?" he asked. "Or, did he ever make contact with you?"

Were her cheeks warming? "Yes, I did. We spoke, rather briefly, at Bedford House."

He wasn't smiling now. "Is the matter now resolved?" His stare was probing.

She set her wineglass down. "I wish I could confide in you, Trev, but it is best that I do not."

"And I would never pry. I take it that the matter is not resolved." He was grim.

"Why are you against our association? Most of the men and women here think so highly of him."

"I know it very well." He took a sip of wine. "He is a great seaman, Evelyn, a great smuggler, and perhaps, a clever spy—for one or both sides." She started, amazed. "And he is a friend, actually. I have known him as long as I have known you. But you are too beautiful to escape his notice, and he is a ladies' man—an unconscionable one."

She wished she were not flushing. His sister had said

very much the same thing, she thought, carefully looking away.

"I am assuming this is about the free trade. I happen to know that your husband was involved in it for some time, but not recently." He hesitated, twirling the red wine in his glass. "He must be eager to help you," he finally said. It was a question.

She took a sip of her sherry. How could she respond? "I do not want to deceive you. I am in need of the services of a smuggler, and, yes, Jack has agreed to help me."

"And now it is Jack? Did Greystone make advances?"

Evelyn stood so abruptly some sherry spilled. "That is a terrible thing to ask," she said, shaken.

Trevelyan also stood. "You are agitated. Yet you are never at a loss for composure. I take it he most definitely made at least one very improper advance. But then, how could he restrain himself?" His eyes were so dark now that they were navy blue.

What did that mean? And what should she say now? She did not want to lie to Trevelyan.

"It is getting late," Evelyn finally said. "It is past Aimee's bedtime. Would you excuse me?" Realizing that he would quickly guess that something illicit had transpired, or worse, that she had some absurd interest in Jack, Evelyn called to Aimee, who was about to fall asleep on the floor. "Come on, *chérie,* let's bid our guests good-night."

But Trevelyan caught her arm. "You did not deny it," he exclaimed.

She bit her lip. "I am a grown woman. I can manage a rogue or two."

"I do not want him treating you callously, Evelyn, and I do not want you getting hurt. You have suffered enough. He will hurt you if you become involved with him!"

She shivered, oddly dismayed. "I am hardly becoming involved—not the way you mean."

His stare became searching. "Don't you remember that once upon a time, I felt far more than kindly toward you?"

"That was a long time ago," she said softly.

"Yes, it was, and we are both older and wiser now—and, I suppose, independent." Trevelyan released her and smiled at Aimee. "Sweet dreams, Aimee."

Aimee yawned. "Good night, my lord."

"I will be right back," Evelyn promised. As she stepped into the hall, holding her daughter's hand, her heart was racing swiftly. She was almost certain that Trevelyan was still interested in her. She was unsure of what to do. She hardly wished to lead him on.

She instantly thought of Jack. Evelyn hurried Aimee upstairs, still able to hear her guests below, softly conversing. Adelaide appeared in the hall, coming forward. "Let me put her to bed, madame, as you still have guests," she said.

Evelyn bent and hugged her daughter. "Did you have a good time?"

Aimee nodded. "That was the best picnic ever, Mama."

Evelyn kissed her. "Then sleep tight. We will certainly have another picnic, soon." She watched Adelaide and her daughter go into the bedroom. It had been a wonderful afternoon. It was comforting to know that she did have family who cared—and a loyal friend in Trevelyan. But she did not know what to do about his interest in her—if it were romantic, as she suspected. Then she reminded herself that she had a year of mourning ahead. No decision had to be made.

She slowly went downstairs, approaching the salon. She could see John gathering up the remaining plates and platters. Matilda was folding up the picnic blanket.

The fire blazed and several kerosene lamps remained on, and the scene remained a cheerful one. "Where is Trev?" she asked.

"He is outside, loading up the carriage," John said.

Evelyn went into the front hall, taking up her shawl as she did so. And then she faltered.

It was twilight now, and from where she stood, she could see outside, through the window next to the front door. Trevelyan stood beside the carriage—alongside Jack Greystone.

HE LEANED AGAINST THE TREE, taking a puff of his cheroot, staring into the brightly lit salon where Evelyn sat with her daughter, John, his fiancée and Ed Trevelyan. Everyone was laughing, smiling, conversing. Everyone was sated and content. It had been a long, pleasant afternoon—for everyone except himself.

He knew he stared at Evelyn and Trevelyan. He had not been able to take his eyes off them—her—for the past hour. They were not only seated closely together, they had been carrying on an intimate conversation for most of the time he had been spying upon them.

Trevelyan could not take his eyes off her.

Jack cursed, but softly. It was impossible, but he was almost jealous.

And the moment he had the thought, he puffed hard on the cheroot and then tossed it to the terrace, grinding it out with his boot heel. Why should he care what transpired between his friend and Evelyn? Trevelyan had once been a rogue, but he was now a marrying man—and the heir to a barony. Evelyn was a widow in need of a wealthy husband. They were perfect for one another.

Jack, on the other hand, was a ladies' man. He was an unconscionable rogue, an unrepentant rake—and he was also a smuggler and a spy. He had no time for romance or relationships, and no inclination for either. He liked it that way. The sea was his mistress, smuggling—and danger—his life.

He was only going to help her get her damned gold out of France because she was a widow with a daughter, irresponsibly left with almost nothing. He was going to help her because it was the damned right thing to do. She was also too beautiful to refuse. He was just going to have to be very careful not to allow himself any genuine interest in her. He was going to have to exercise extraordinary restraint. And he certainly must forget the intimacy they had shared. He must ignore the temptation she posed when they were in the same room.

The cozy afternoon was now breaking up—the sun was setting, and the group would be driving home in the dark. Evelyn had left the room, taking her daughter up to bed, or so he assumed.

He realized that Trevelyan was leaving the salon. Surely his friend wasn't leaving just yet. Surely, he intended to make advances.

Jack started around the terrace, toward the front of the house. As he did, Trevelyan came outside, carrying two wicker baskets. Jack sauntered toward the carriage as Trev set them inside. He turned and saw Jack. Briefly, he was surprised.

Jack smiled, but he did not feel particularly welcoming. "Have you enjoyed your picnic with Lady D'Orsay?"

Trev's smile was slight. "Hello, Jack." He rearranged the baskets in the backseat then stepped away from the carriage. "It has been a very pleasant afternoon, but obviously, you know that. How long have you been lurking about?"

"Just for a moment or two," he lied unabashedly.

Trev stared rather skeptically. "I cannot imagine why you did not join us. John and I are your friends."

He could have joined the little group. The Trevelyan family had been financing local smugglers for generations. The baron had invested in Jack's operations several times, and rather heavily. Trevelyan had actually accompanied him on several runs, some years back—for the sheer adventure. And once in a while Trev directed an operation for Warlock, although Jack had never learned any details. He had transported him to St. Malo nine months ago, leaving him there on some nefarious mission.

"Apparently, I have arrived too late to participate," Jack said with a smile.

"Apparently." Trev leaned on the carriage. "Are you calling on Evelyn?"

He felt his smile vanish. *They were on a first-name basis.* Of course they were. "I'm hardly calling on her servants."

"I cannot imagine any association betwixt the two of you having a proper conclusion."

"Really?" He was amused. "Are you her champion now?"

"I am if that is what I must be."

"And has she told you what she wants?" Trev wasn't a seaman, but he was a capable, courageous man. With his connections, he could easily hire a smuggler to help Evelyn—if she dared to approach him.

"No, she has not. But I imagine she thinks to invest in the trade with you, and while I do not like it, her husband has left her in a poor way, and you are a safe bet."

So she hadn't asked Trevelyan to go to France and retrieve her fortune for her. "You never answered my question. Have you enjoyed your afternoon with the countess?"

"I'm surprised you would even ask. What red-blooded man would not enjoy an afternoon in her company?"

"I remember the days when we raced about this countryside together, about the time when I captained my first ship. We drank and wenched wildly."

"That was a long time ago."

"Are you smitten with her?"

Trev's eyes widened. "Why would you ask me such a question?"

"We are friends. I am curious."

"I have known Evelyn for years. She is going through a difficult time—I intend to do what I can to help her through this patch. Right now, we are friends, and we are catching up."

As Jack absorbed that statement—with some doubt—Trevelyan said, "And you? Are you in pursuit? Or will you respect the fact that she is a widow, grieving for her deceased husband?"

Before Jack could consider how best to respond, he heard the front door open and he turned. Evelyn stood in the doorway, seeming pale, clutching a shawl tightly to her chest. His heart slammed as their gazes locked.

Trev made a harsh sound. "You have a caller," he said, sounding displeased. "And Jack? Whatever you are thinking, you should think differently."

Jack turned and stared at him. "Since when do you tell me what to think?"

Before Trevelyan could answer, Evelyn hurried down the front steps. "Hello, Mr. Greystone." She spoke in a rush, glancing worriedly between them.

"Are you really going to continue calling me Mr. Greystone?" Jack asked, smiling. "I prefer it if you call me Jack."

She bit her lip and looked at Trevelyan.

Jack glanced at his friend, whose expression was taut. He knew without a doubt that Trev did not want to leave now.

"It is a bit late to call," she said uneasily. She looked back and forth between them now. "But we do have some matters to conclude. Would you like to come inside?"

Jack glanced at Trev. "Drive with care," he said with a shrug. "The roads are difficult at night." He started for the steps.

As he did, Evelyn came down them. He faltered, realizing she meant to speak with Trevelyan now. He had no intention of going inside and leaving them alone together. He stared as Trevelyan took both of her hands in his. But as hard as he strained to overhear them, he could not detect a word either one said, not until Trev bowed and Evelyn said, "Good night."

He wondered if a romance was brewing.

And a few moments later, Trevelyan, John and Matilda were driving away.

"HAVE YOU ENJOYED your picnic?"

They were now alone in her salon, where so recently there had been a cheerful indoor picnic.

Evelyn realized that her heart was racing, as indeed, it had been doing since she had first realized that Jack Greystone was at her door. But now they were very much alone and she was acutely aware of it. She was rather breathless. "You have a way," she said slowly, "of arriving very unexpectedly, at the most unusual hour."

He smiled. "It is a habit—one that keeps me from the gallows."

She cringed at such a direct reference to his possible fate.

"What is wrong?" He slowly approached, his gaze

searching. "Does the thought of my swinging from the end of a rope bother you?"

"Of course it does," she cried, unnerved by the graphic remark, which he seemed to relish making. He paused so very close beside her.

"You did not answer my question—but you do not have to. I happened to glance through your window before Trevelyan came outside." He shoved his hands in the pockets of his olive-green wool jacket.

Evelyn rushed to the fire to push at it with the poker. If only she had expected him, she thought, she would not be this nervous. Or was she lying to herself? His presence was so appealing. He simply filled up the room and dominated it. No other man had ever made her so acutely aware of his proximity.

Suddenly she stiffened, poker in hand. Greystone had walked over to her and now stood behind her. "You have had a pleasant afternoon." His breath touched the nape of her neck, the side of her cheek. "I did not realize that you and Trev were such old and dear friends."

She turned, bumped into his chest and leaped away. Why was he crowding her? Was he being mocking? It certainly sounded that way. "We have something in common," she said nervously. "We knew each other as children. How long have you known him?"

"Since I was a boy," he said, continuing to smile and stare relentlessly. "His family is very involved in smuggling, and has been so for generations."

"Then you know he is a good man."

"He will soon court you."

She froze. "I beg your pardon?"

"Do not pretend you do not know that he is swinging upon your hook."

It was hard to think clearly with him regarding her so

intently. "What?" Then, as she realized what he had said, she proclaimed, "He is hardly on my hook!"

"Of course he is. And you know he is smitten with you." Jack turned and paced slowly, restlessly, about the salon.

Evelyn clutched her hands together. Why were they discussing her friendship with Trev? "I sense he is interested," she finally said. "I hope that is not the case."

"Why not? He will eventually remarry. So will you. Or won't you condescend to marry a baron, which is the title he will come into?" He wasn't smiling now. He stopped pacing and faced her directly.

"I am in mourning. I have no plans to remarry."

"Of course you do. It would be odd—extremely so—if you did not."

Is this what he thought? That she planned to remarry, while still in mourning? Did he believe her interested in Trevelyan? She was stunned.

"I take it he has yet to kiss you?"

She gasped. "He is a gentleman."

"So I was right." His smile came and went.

It was so hard to breathe. "Why are you asking me about Trevelyan? Haven't you come to discuss going to France?"

"I was curious," he said with another shrug, "when I realized a flirtation was at hand."

Evelyn knew she had not flirted—she was certain of it. But all ladies flirted, and there was nothing wrong with such behavior. "He played the gallant, coming here as he did, on the pretext of taking me for a picnic, in order to provide us with a meal." She added, "They did not even take the leftovers."

"Yes, he is a hero, certainly—but he is not going to France for you."

She bit her lip. "No. He is not going to France for me."

Their gazes had now locked. He smiled slowly again. "Shall we get to the matters at hand?"

She walked to the sofa and sat down. "I have been afraid that you might change your mind."

He strode indolently to the sofa and sat down, not at its other end, but in the middle, crowding her into the corner where she sat. He stretched out his long, booted legs and leaned indifferently back. "I gave you my word, Evelyn."

Her heart fluttered wildly. His jacket was wide-open, enough so to reveal his broad chest and flat abdomen beneath the cotton shirt he wore. Her glance strayed to the pistol at his hip and the dagger's hilt, peeking out from his jacket.

She glanced aside, abruptly. She was staring. Worse, she had recalled their last encounter—all of it. She had felt his hard, powerful body when they had embraced. How could she ever forget that moment?

Her husband had held her many times. But his embrace had not been memorable.

"I am making the run to France at sunrise," he said harshly.

"You are going to France tomorrow?" she cried. Common sense returned. She intended to go with him, but tomorrow was too soon.

"Yes, I am. You seem…alarmed."

She was very alarmed, because she did not wish to rock this particular boat now. She had little left to sell—the sooner he went to France, the better. "I am surprised." How could she mention that she meant to accompany him, that she feared he would not find the gold if not with her help? "But I am thrilled. Most of my jewels are gone," she said, thinking of Ed Whyte.

"What are you trying to say—exactly?"

She knew she was delaying. "I actually spoke with another smuggler, before you agreed to help me. I spoke with Ed Whyte." She grimaced. "It was an unpleasant encounter, to say the least."

"What?" he exclaimed, his eyes wide with consternation. He sat up.

Was he concerned? "When you refused me, I took matters into my own hands," she said.

"Of course you did—you are stubborn!"

She could not decide what his intense reaction signified. Her mind raced. This was a distraction—when she needed to consider how best to broach her next plea. "I thought we had reached an agreement. I gave him my sapphire ring and ear bobs. He left with the jewels, with no intention of coming back, which I realized far too late."

Jack shook his head. "He robbed you!" It was an incredulous accusation.

"Yes, he did." Was he actually concerned?

"I could have told you to stay away from Whyte," Jack said flatly. "He has no sense of honor, and his character is scurrilous, at best."

"So I have learned," she said slowly.

His gaze narrowed. "Are you about to make a point?"

She inhaled. "I trust you, and I did not trust Whyte." She did not expect him to respond, and he did not, but she trembled, afraid to ask him if she could accompany him to France. He would refuse, she was certain. She wondered if she dared to attempt to steal on board without his knowledge. "Where is your ship?"

He studied her. He shifted position and crossed his legs. "It is actually in the cove below your uncle's house. Why?"

He could be on board in an hour—and so could she.

Faraday Hall was but an hour's ride away. "I hadn't realized that you were berthed so close by."

"I often use that cove," he said, now sitting up straight,
uncrossing his legs. His gray gaze was piercing and it
was also suspicious. "I need maps. You need parchment
and ink."

She knew she was going to have to bring up the subject of her joining him, but just then, she did not have the
courage to do so. She nodded, leaped up and ran into the
small library next door. At the desk, she paused for composure. If she did not ask him if she could join him, her
only other alternative would be to somehow board his
ship without his knowledge.

She looked up.

Jack stood calmly in the doorway but his gaze was
bright with more suspicion now. "There is a plot afoot,"
he said softly. "What is it, Evelyn?"

Her heart slammed at his soft tone and use of her name.
"There is no plot!"

He walked over to the desk, where she had the parchment, quill and inkwell. She tensed but he only pulled out
Henri's chair. Evelyn sat, looking up at him.

He stood behind her, and he laid one large hand on
the desk by the vellum. "Where is your house, exactly?"

She inhaled. The suspicion was gone from his eyes.
He was intent and serious now. "Can you find your way
to the outskirts of the city?" She remained twisted to
look up at him.

He gazed down at her. "Of course."

She turned to the parchment, dipping the quill in the
ink. "The quickest route is to take the main boulevard
halfway through the city and turn south on Rue Lafayette.
That will take you out of town. If you stay on that road,
you will come to several vineyards. At the second one,

you will turn right onto a small dirt lane with no sign. The Chateau D'Orsay is half a mile down the road, surrounded by those vineyards." As she spoke, she rapidly sketched a crude map. He did not move, and he became a distraction, standing so close behind her. She finished and looked up.

He said, very seriously, "You were last there four years ago, correct?" He did not wait for her to respond. "The vineyards may be gone—burned to the ground. The last road may now have a sign. I need another marker."

He was right, she thought with worry. "There is a ruined tower just before the last road, on the north side."

He reached over her arm and took the quill from her and drew an *X* in the spot where the tower was. "Is that correct?"

"Yes." It was difficult to speak.

He laid the quill down by her hand; their hands brushed. "Where are the heirlooms on your property?"

Evelyn hesitated, because his large hand was resting against hers.

"Evelyn."

She wet her lips and opened a drawer, removing a key. Then she leaned down, where a hidden locked drawer was at the very bottom of the desk. "Before he died, Henri gave me the map he made." She unlocked the hidden drawer and opened it, taking out the folded map and handing it to him. "Obviously that shaded square is the house. There were three huge oak trees in the back, just beyond the terrace outside of the ballroom. They are marked by circles. He buried a large chest in the center, between them, and that is the *X* you see."

Jack studied it briefly, then placed it on the desk in front of her, beside the map she had just drawn. "Good."

Staring up at him, she wondered if he felt half of the

tension she did. She wondered if he was at all breathless, disturbed, or thinking illicit, inappropriate thoughts. "You should lock up your husband's map. Destroy the other one." His gaze held hers.

She started. "Don't you need them?"

"I have memorized them," he said softly.

Her heart hammered, hard, in response to his sudden change of tone, and the slight gleam in his eyes. She made no move to do as he had said. He now had all the information he needed to go to France. He was probably going to bid her good-night and go.

And then she realized that they had never discussed his payment—his fair share. Was that why he was hesitating, and standing so motionless? Or was he considering the currents coursing between them, as she was?

She asked, "How am I going to pay you?"

His gray gaze had dropped to her mouth, and now, abruptly, his thick lashes lowered, hiding his eyes. He murmured, "You decide."

She inhaled. Had she mistaken that look? What did that mean? Didn't she know?

Evelyn stared at the maps on the desk, finding it impossible to think clearly. He reached over her arm and took the map she had drawn, this time, his arm brushing over hers, hard. She twisted to face him; he tore up the parchment, his stare unwavering upon her.

Very carefully, she said, "What about the advance payment you insisted upon?"

A long, simmering moment passed. He finally said, "I am waiving it."

She desperately wished to be in his arms—but she was in mourning, she needed him to go to France and she had told herself she would walk a fine line with him now.

"You look very much like a deer, caught in the cross-hairs of my gun," he said. "Except, there is no gun, now is there?"

"You unnerve me."

He leaned over her, laying his hand back on the desk, his chest now against her left shoulder. She felt trapped, seated as she was in the chair, between him and the desk. He had deliberately put her in such a position, she had not a doubt.

Her heart raced madly. Did he mean to kiss her? Why else would he position himself in such a way?

"How do I unnerve you?" he asked.

She shivered. "I think you know."

His gaze was on her mouth. His own lips seemed to curve. But he did not lean closer and brush his mouth over hers. He wasn't going to cross the line, she thought, dismayed.

"I am very grateful," she whispered.

His eyes smoldered. "Really?" He leaned more firmly on the desk, his shoulder pressing down on hers. "If you are going to play with fire, be forewarned, my gallantry has limits."

Evelyn could not even try to comprehend him now. She did not want to think about what was happening. She clasped his hard, taut jaw. But she wanted *him* to kiss *her*.

His eyes blazed. "I swore I would resist all temptation," he said harshly.

She knew he was going to kiss her—and he leaned down, seizing her far arm, and claimed her mouth with his.

She did not move, thrilling, as their mouths wildly fused. Her heart rioted. Her body flamed. Her back pressed into the chair, which was pressed into the desk. She ached desperately, urgently, in every fiber of her being. She was in mourning, but how could something wrong be so right?

He pulled away, breathing hard. "Are you going to send me to France with something to remember you by?"

It was so hard to think, when all she wanted was another moment in his arms. Shaking, she stood, aware of what he had asked, and as she did, he pulled her into his embrace, kissing her hot and hard, openmouthed, again.

Evelyn seized his shoulders and clung to them. His tongue thrust deep. His entire body was stiff with tension. Her own body felt as taut. She had never felt real desire before being in Jack's arms; she knew that now. And this was a raging passion. It was almost frightening, because she was ready to do the unthinkable.

Somehow, she thought about Aimee, who could awaken and walk in on them; she even thought about Henri, so recently deceased. Yet she did not want to think about her husband or her daughter, not now! She simply wanted the kiss to go on and on, endlessly, shamelessly. She wanted to remain on fire, in Jack Greystone's embrace.

But he stepped back from her, breathing hard, loudly. "I want you, Evelyn, I always have. But I am done with games. We are not children."

She fought for air. She had to hold the desk to stand upright. His tone was so thick—she had never heard such a tone before. And she realized exactly what was happening—exactly where she stood. Upon a cliff. One more step and she would fall.

And would it be so terrible?

Their gazes were locked again. His eyes blazed—but there was a question there.

She hesitated, trying to make a choice, when it was impossible to do so with so much urgency raging in her body. But the only man she had ever slept with was her husband. And Henri had died less than five weeks ago. Despite this terrible attraction, she was in mourning.

She felt herself stiffen.

The last time she had made love, she had undressed herself, crawled into bed, the lights out, and waited for her husband to join her. Unlike now, she had been filled with staunch resolution. There had been no wild desire. But Henri had loved her. She had been his wife.

"Are you taking me upstairs?" Jack asked bluntly.

She jerked, meeting his smoldering gaze. Slowly, she hugged herself. "I cannot."

His mouth curled mirthlessly. "So you would lead me on—again?"

"No!" She shook her head. "I want to be in your arms, but…" She stopped. "Henri is dead. I am in mourning. We are not even in love."

His eyes widened. He then made a harsh sound. Incredulous, he slowly said, "This isn't about love. This is better than love and you know it."

What on earth did he mean? "Henri courted me and he married me. He loved me. You don't love me—I can't."

He stared, a long, hard moment passing. "I cannot believe that you are using the excuse of love to deny me." He began to shake his head. "But have no fear. It is better this way. I prefer to avoid your bed, actually. I will see you when I return from France." He started past her, his strides long and hard.

He could not leave this way! "Jack, wait!"

He faltered at the door, turning. "You should count your blessings, Evelyn," he warned.

"I have not been playing games. I do not want you to think so poorly of me!"

He made a disparaging sound. "Haven't you?"

"I am confused," she cried.

He stared, his regard cold. "Well, I am not confused. I am making sail at first tide. Good night, Countess." And with those hard words, he strode from the salon.

CHAPTER EIGHT

THE SUN WAS a flaming orange ball, just emerging over the horizon.

Evelyn hugged her wool cloak close, seated beside Laurent in the front of their carriage, staring at the ship that was at anchor in the cove below her uncle's house. It was a cold morning, with a stiff breeze, and she shivered—but it was perfect for sailing and she knew that.

His ship was larger now, with more cannon, but otherwise, it seemed the same—its sails were black canvas; its hull was also painted black. In the light of day, she seemed ominous.

However, the cove had changed. A dock had been built, a jetty of sorts that ran from the cove to where the ship was anchored, and the vessel's gangplank remained down. Evelyn hadn't been back to the cove in years, not since before her marriage. She had considered how she would get on board his ship, and knowing she would have to ask Jack for a rowboat—and a seaman to row her to the ship—she had worried. But the docks solved that. However, at any moment, that boarding plank would be raised. There was a great deal of activity upon the deck, as sailors rushed about the rigging, preparing to make sail. The sight was a familiar one, recalled from her childhood at Faraday Hall.

She had not been able to sleep at all last night—and not just because of the shocking passion she had shared with Jack—or her cowardly refusal to go through with consummating her desire. She had tossed and turned, torn between desire and regret—and a new fear. Jack Greystone was surely angry with her now. There was so much dread.

But there was so much more. Unless he had changed his mind, he was leaving at sunrise—and she had to go with him. She was more determined now than ever before.

"This is a terrible plan," Laurent said, braking the carriage. "He hasn't seen us yet. Why don't we turn around and go home? You can trust Captain Greystone. He will not steal the gold."

Jack stepped out of his cabin and was walking onto the quarterdeck of his ship. So much tension assailed Evelyn that she could not breathe. For a moment, she could not even speak.

She did not want him to dislike her for her cowardice. She did not want him to think that she had deliberately led him on. Surely, he must understand why she had not been able to consummate their passion.

Evelyn inhaled deliberately and said, "There he is. It is time to make my presence known."

Laurent seized her arm before she could climb out of the carriage. "Why, madame? Why must you go to France, risking your life in doing so?"

She smiled grimly, but she could not take her gaze off the black-hulled ship with its black sails, which were unfurling. She could not take her eyes off Jack.

And he had seen the carriage. Even from the distance between them, she remarked him stiffening. Now she saw him lift a spyglass and train it upon her.

"I am afraid he might not locate the gold and that he will return empty-handed. We cannot afford that." She helped herself out of the carriage, stumbling on the dirt road, picked up a small valise and started across the sand.

Laurent fell into step beside her. "He has a map! Or I can go in your place!"

"I have to go with him, and I trust him to protect me, just as I trust you to care for Aimee while I am gone," she said.

Laurent groaned. "You are not making sense."

She paused. "What if there is trouble? I am sending him into danger."

"That is all the more reason to let him go alone!"

"No, that is all the more reason to accompany him," she said, meaning it. Last night, she had begun to worry about the danger he would face in France. Now that his departure was imminent, she had begun to truly consider the risks he was taking. She was concerned for his welfare, his safety.

Evelyn trudged across the fifty-foot stretch of beach, the sand surprisingly deep, her gaze locked on Jack. He had now crossed his decks and stood at the railing of the *Sea Wolf II,* at the head of the gangplank. His posture was rigid, and his arms were crossed forbiddingly across his chest. His expression was one of vast displeasure. She reached its foot and did not even try to smile. "Good morning."

A dozen feet separated them now. His eyes blazed. "What is this?"

She laid her hand on the plank's rail, and stepped upon it. "Are you sailing for France?"

"Yes."

Her heart slammed. In spite of their altercation, he still meant to help her. "I meant to tell you last night—I must come with you." She could not look at him now as she started up the plank, her pulse racing.

"Like hell!" He leaped over the railing and onto the gangplank, striding down it.

He seized her wrist before Evelyn had crossed even half of the gangplank. Their eyes collided; his gaze continued to burn. Her heart instantly lurched, both from that frightening desire and the fact that he was, so clearly, angry with her.

"I can help you locate the chest," she tried.

"We are at war with France, the Channel is infested with naval ships and France remains torn by revolution! Are you mad? My ship is no place for a woman, and neither is France!"

She wet her lips and managed, "A great many women live in France, as I did, for several years. You are attempting to get to my home. There might be danger. I want to help you in every way that I can."

He hadn't released her. He was incredulous. "You may help me by turning around and going back to Roselynd, where you will be safe!"

Staring directly into his eyes, she said, very softly, "I am sorry about last night."

He inhaled. "That is a low blow."

What did that mean? "I meant to discuss this with you then—but we got off the subject."

He released her. "Yes, we did. You do not have permission to board my ship, Countess."

"I will do so anyway." She started past him, outwardly brave though inwardly frightened.

He grabbed her arm another time, turning her back around. "You would ignore my command?"

She nodded. "Yes. Jack—I can be of help. I know I can. You might have trouble finding the house even with my map. And I speak French fluently, in case you are questioned. There are disguises in the carriage—we can go as a pair of servants. And I know the area well."

He slowly shook his head. "I do not need your help and I would never allow you to disembark in France."

He meant it. Searching his gaze, which was not heated now, she said, "Please. You know that this is really about my daughter. Those valuables are for her future. I must go with you. If there is any problem, we can solve it together."

"You don't trust me."

She trembled. "I do. But as a mother, I cannot bear for you to go without me. I cannot stand to wait for your return at Roselynd, wondering if you could even find the house, or the chest, wondering if there was trouble. And what if you cannot find the house? What if you do need my help? Please." She touched his forearm, careful not to tell him that she would also not be able to bear worrying about him.

He jerked his arm away from her, his gaze hard, meeting hers. "It isn't safe," he warned.

He was crumbling! "I did not even think that you would still go to France today," she whispered. "Not after last night."

He looked away grimly.

What did his silence mean? But she knew his resistance was easing. "I will not be any trouble—I will be helpful, Jack." She wet her lips. "And perhaps, I can explain why I became such a coward last night. I want a chance to explain. You are so angry this morning."

"I am not angry, Evelyn. Not with you—and you do not need to explain while I am crossing the Channel. I would not allow such a distraction."

"I will not be a distraction—I promise. And if that is what you want, I will wait to explain my actions to you another time."

His stare sharpened. "I cannot believe your gumption. We will miss the tide—and the winds are perfect." He cursed again, staring right at her, but she knew she did not blush. "Very well. You may take a berth in my cabin, but be forewarned—I have no time for discussions, no time for distractions and you will not be going ashore with me. If I encounter any problems, we will discuss them on my ship, if I think it necessary." He was grim and she knew he disliked taking her with him.

But she had won somehow. She was jubilant, though she hid it. She turned, to call down the plank and tell Laurent to get the disguises. Jack seized her hand this time. "Do not bother." He leaned close, but only to take her small bag from her. "You will do as I say, Evelyn, while aboard my ship."

"Yes, I will do as you say." She spoke meekly, still fighting to hide her satisfaction.

His gaze moved over her features. Then he gestured to the other sailors. "You will also distract my men, so I suggest you retire to my cabin directly. And do not think I am fooled. You are gloating."

"Thank you," she whispered, biting back a smile.

He ignored her, gesturing at Laurent to leave, then striding past her, calling for the mainsail to be hoisted.

EVELYN STOOD AT THE CABIN'S porthole, staring out into the night. It had been a bright, cloudless night, and the sky overhead had glittered with stars until an hour ago, when it had begun to slowly lighten. The new day would be sunny and bright. These were not the best conditions to be attempting to steal into France.

They were close to land; she could feel it. That would have meant a very swift crossing, but she knew the winds had been exceptionally good for them. And just as she had that thought, a pair of gulls could be seen outside, overhead, wheeling about.

She briefly closed her eyes. She had not been allowed on deck even once, and she probably knew every inch of Jack's cabin. She had made certain not to pry amongst his charts or his personal things, never mind that she was curious, and the cabin's single large chest had attracted her attention, time and again. But she hadn't opened it.

The time had passed with agonizing slowness. She had allowed herself the liberty of looking at his collection of books. Most were histories. He was surprisingly well-read, if those volumes were any indication, and familiar with the history of China, India, Russia, France, the Hapsburg Empire and even the West Indies. But there was also a novel amongst his books. She was not familiar with its author, but it seemed to be a medieval romance of some sort.

He had, once, called on her, to see how she was faring. A seaman had been with him, and she had been given some bread and cheese.

She had managed to sleep for an hour or so in his bed, but restlessly. She kept thinking about the other night, their conversation the previous dawn, and what the fate of her French home might be. She hoped it was still intact. Somehow, she thought that would please Henri.

And it was too unnerving to stay in his bed for very long. His scent was everywhere; she thought she could even feel his presence. And she kept thinking about being in his arms, being overcome with desire and then succumbing to confusion, morality and even fright.

Just then the cabin door opened and Jack stepped into the small chamber.

Evelyn turned fully toward him. He was wearing a dark coat, dark breeches and his riding boots. She knew he was armed. And his expression was dangerous. "We are making land," she said.

"Yes, we are." He left the door open, and he did not come into the cabin. His gaze skidded over her, then he glanced at his bed, with the slightly disturbed sheets. "Did you get some rest?"

"I am worried," she said. "Sleep is impossible."

His gaze flickered. "In the end, it is only some heirlooms."

She hesitated. "I am also worried about you." And she meant it. She was sending him into danger. If anything happened to him, it would be her fault.

His stare slammed to hers. "At the very best, I will be back within three hours. But do not be surprised if I am gone most of the day."

"What could possibly take so long?" she cried, instantly distressed.

"If we alert suspicion, we might have to delay—we might even have to hide. There are troops everywhere. La Vendée is in rebellion. General Hoche has been waging a campaign to bring the Loire valley down. Although he now thinks to end the conflict by allowing the Vendéans to reopen their churches, and he is seeking various agreements throughout the Loire, my sources tell me passersby are suspect."

"I should come with you!" She started forward.

He held up his hand. "I would not allow you on land, under any circumstance."

She halted halfway across the cabin. His face was hard, his regard uncompromising. There was no point in arguing, even if she knew she could help him get to her home more swiftly. He had a gallant streak, she thought, no matter how he might insist otherwise.

She wondered if she should make her own way onto

dry ground and follow him, but instantly dismissed the thought. She was not a fool and she had no wish to cause more problems.

"Do I have your word that you will stay in my cabin? I don't want my men looking at you. They are hardened sailors and you might cause some unrest."

"You have my word."

"Try to get some rest. Even if I return within a few hours, we have to complete the voyage back, and the French navy is at Le Havre."

Le Havre was just north of Nantes. Evelyn finally said, "Then Godspeed."

"There is one more thing. There is a carbine beneath my bed, and a pistol in the desk drawer, with powder. My men have been ordered to guard you—and if they are discovered, they will set sail. Still…you should have a means of defending yourself."

If his ship was remarked, they would sail off without him? She was aghast.

"I can always find passage home." He gave her one last look and turned. He strode out, closing the door behind him.

Evelyn inhaled, the sky outside now the color of shallow waters. She rushed to the porthole, but it clearly faced the channel. Still, there was no mistaking that the ship was slowing. And then she felt it lurch as an anchor was cast overboard.

There was nothing she could do now but wait and pray. She glanced at the gilded clock, glued to his desk. It was almost six in the morning. How was she going to get through the next few hours, much less an entire day?

She was sending Jack Greystone into France, a country torn by revolution and uprisings. And the Loire Val-

ley, where they were, was in the midst of rebellion. As
he had said, there were troops everywhere.

If anyone could succeed in this mission, it was Jack.
But she was afraid for him. She did not want any harm
to befall him, and for the first time, she truly began to
calculate the risks involved in his attempting to retrieve
the gold. Hadn't he insisted, from the very start, that the
mission was simply too dangerous?

And why had he only now confessed that his ship could
return to Britain without him?

Evelyn began to pace wildly. Suddenly she regretted
the entire scheme. Yes, she was destitute, and, yes, she
had to provide for Aimee, but surely, she could have found
another way—or she could have sent someone else to
France, anyone other than Jack. She sat down hard on his
bed, terribly frightened now.

If anything happened to him, it would be her fault.

She was so concerned. First there was the attraction
that raged between them—the kind of attraction she had
never before felt. Now there was her vast concern. Evelyn became still. Could it be that she harbored genuine
feelings of affection for him?

She had been infatuated once. But that had been out
of gratitude, and it had been understandable. Being interested in him—being romantically inclined—was not
sensible now. He found her attractive but he didn't have a
romantic interest in her, didn't love her. Even if she were
not in mourning, he would not be courting her. He was
an adventurer—he would not court any woman.

If she were beginning to care, she might be setting
herself up for more heartbreak.

The hours passed with agonizing slowness. Evelyn
watched the sun rise. At noon, the same sailor brought

her a luncheon—more bread and cheese, this time, with some brandy. She couldn't touch a thing.

She lay down on his bed, staring up at the cabin ceiling, praying he would be all right. She realized she was exhausted, having stayed awake for most of two nights, but she still couldn't sleep. Even when she closed her eyes, her mind raced impossibly. If only the château were whole, and if only Jack found the gold… If only he returned to his ship, alive!

Thud.

Evelyn jerked, realizing she had dozed off, and that her door had been thrown open. Her eyes widened as a chill rushed into the cabin. Outside, it seemed to be late afternoon, one gray and wet with an incoming fog.

She saw his silhouette first. Evelyn sat up as Jack stepped into the doorway, his hair loose and windswept.

The ship was rocking in the wind. And her first reaction was one of wild relief. He was grim, but he was clearly in one piece—he did not even appear tired. Jack had returned—he was all right.

Then she realized he was *very* grim, and her heart lurched, all relief vanishing. "Jack?"

He stepped inside the cabin, closing the door behind him. "We found the house. I am sorry, Evelyn, it has been gutted."

She nodded, clenching the sheets. The château had been destroyed. Poor Henri… "And?"

"We tore up the area between the trees—there was no chest, I am sorry."

She felt herself still. "That is impossible."

"We spent five hours digging up the area. We could not have missed a buried chest." His gaze held hers as he braced against the rocking ship.

There was no gold?

"I am sorry," he repeated more softly.

That gold was her daughter's entire future. "It has to be there," she said harshly, standing.

"It isn't."

She looked at him, reeling, but still in disbelief. Aimee would grow up impoverished? And she would be left penniless? There would be no dowry, no future?

"You will find a way to make ends meet, I am certain," he said, his tone odd—as if he meant to be kind.

She sank back down on the bed, barely having heard him. How could the gold be gone? Henri had left it for them! "I don't believe you," she gasped, panic rearing up. Aimee could not be left with nothing! "It has to be there!"

This time, he regarded her with what could only be compassion.

And his look of sympathy undid her. She began to shake as her sense of panic escalated. She tried to rein it in. She knew she had to be calm, she had to think. If the gold was truly gone, she would find other means!

Oh, God. There was no gold. She was going to leave her daughter with nothing!

"Evelyn?"

Evelyn's father had left her with nothing. As a child, left behind with relations who did not care for her, she had never been able to understand why she was with her aunt and uncle, and not with him. She could not understand why her clothes were used, or why she spent half of her time in the kitchen. Every time he had come to visit, as infrequently as that had been, he had promised her a future—one only a dowry could buy. Every time he had promised her the life of a princess, she had believed him. But he had been killed and his promises had been empty.

How often had she reassured her daughter that all

would be well? How many promises had she made to Aimee?

Evelyn began to shake more fiercely.

Jack was sitting beside her, trying to hand her the brandy she had not taken with her lunch. "You need a drink."

She swatted the glass away, spilling some of the amber liquid. "No!" She looked at him, aware of the tears filling her eyes and blurring her vision. Desperation began. "Henri left us a fortune."

"If he did, it is gone now. Stolen. Here. Take a sip."

She shoved the glass violently away, against his chest, leaping to her feet.

There was no gold. The promises she had made to her daughter were as empty as the ones her father had made to her.

Oh, God.

She was no different than her own father—she was leaving Aimee with nothing.

"Evelyn, you should lie down."

"No!" She looked wildly at him. "My daughter is my life. She means everything to me! Did you know that my own father left me with nothing? That I was a penniless orphan? That if Henri hadn't married me, I would have been a governess, a seamstress, a housemaid?"

He was pale.

"Now I am leaving my daughter the very same way— as if I don't care!" She choked on a harsh sob.

And it was as if her entire life flashed before her eyes, a life in which she had been abandoned and left penniless, not once, but twice. And now her daughter would suffer the same fate….

"Damn him!" she cried, thinking of Henri. She knew

it was wrong to curse him, but she did so again. "How could he do this to us? Damn him, damn him, damn him!"

"You have had a shock," Jack said softly.

"He is exactly like my father," she shouted. And she was furious. Evelyn covered her eyes with her hands. There was no gold—Henri had left his own daughter with nothing. Vaguely, she heard Jack leaving the cabin. She cried harder.

EVELYN OPENED THE CABIN door and shivered, greeted by the silence of the night. The moon was full, and a few stars were scattered in the night sky, but clouds scudded there, too, occasionally crossing the moon. It was so serene. Canvas flapped, rigging rustled, wood groaned. The sea lapped against the ship's great hull. Evelyn trembled and she stared at the ship's helm, where Jack Greystone stood.

He was looking over his shoulder at her.

She didn't even try to smile at him now, acutely aware that she did not wish to be alone. Had he been kind to her, when she had lapsed into hysteria? She seemed to recall so.

She had wept for a long time—for the first time since Henri had died. She hoped that she had been grieving properly, at long last, but she knew better. She had been so furious with her deceased husband.

And then, as the tears had subsided, childhood memories had filled her mind, as had recollections from the past nine years of her marriage. She had begun to genuinely see her husband as a weak man—as someone very much like her own father.

And if she did not know better, she would almost think the bout of tears some kind of pent-up expression of a lifetime's worth of anguish.

She was exhausted, but the need to weep and shout was gone. The panic had dulled, too. She would find a way to provide for her daughter and give her a bright shining future—nothing would stop her now. However, she was aware of being entirely on her own for the first time in her life. It was frightening, but she forced herself to ignore the fear.

The first order of business would be to stop feeling sorry for herself. Henri had failed to provide for them—therefore, she would find a way to do so. The mine was a possible source of revenue for them. She would restore the mine, if it really needed maintenance. She would borrow the funds to make whatever repairs were necessary.

And there was the possibility of remarriage. Of course she would consider that option, not immediately, but when the time was right.

She stared across the deck. Jack had turned back to face the ship's prow, his hands on the huge helm. He was such a powerful man, such a reassuring figure. He had been kind to her, when he had never been kind before. She hoped he did not think badly of her for her inexcusable bout of tears and self-pity.

She hadn't been invited on deck, but she had come up to find him. Maybe it was his recent kindness, or maybe it was that being near him always made her feel safe and protected. He was the kind of man who could weather any crisis, the worst storm. Instinctively she knew he was her safest harbor.

Besides, she had been in that cabin for a day and a half! She closed the cabin door and crossed the deck, pausing beside him. "May I join you?"

His gaze was searching, moving slowly over her face. "Of course."

She did not remind him that she had not been allowed on deck until then. "I must look a fright."

"You could not look poorly." He faced forward again. His profile was stunning, but his expression was solemn. His hair was loose now, a shoulder-length mass of tawny waves.

"You are being gallant."

He glanced at her, almost smiling. "Perhaps."

She smiled ever so slightly back. "I wish to apologize."

His eyes widened. "There is no need."

"There is every need. I exposed you to the worst case of feminine hysteria—I am sorry."

He studied her. "You had every cause to weep. I do not blame you."

"You have never been kind to me before!" she exclaimed, studying him closely. "If you don't think poorly of me, are you feeling sorry for me?"

He seemed to be intrigued with his ship's bow, staring ahead at it now. "I am not allowed to have some sympathy for you?" he finally asked softly.

"I think you told me that I will find a way to make ends meet, and I intend to do just that."

"Are you trying to tell me that you do not need—or want—my sympathy?"

She felt a genuine smile begin. "No. I actually like your sympathy."

He turned to her, his gaze becoming speculative. "You are a strong woman—I see you have bounced back."

She felt her body tighten in response to the light in his eyes. She wondered if it would always be this way, if he would look at her so frankly, and she would desire him in return.

She lifted her face to the night's soft breeze, its scattered stars. "I am not all that strong. I have been dependent on one person or another my entire life. Now, my daughter is dependent on me—and I must depend only on myself."

He looked away again, guiding the ship slightly, as the helm moved in his hands. "As I said, you are strong."

It was so pleasant, to be thought of so highly now. It felt like a miracle, considering that, two nights ago, she had been in his arms, and he had been angry with her. She gazed openly at him. It was enjoyable being with him when he wasn't accusing her of manipulation, when they were not arguing over one thing or another. How had they reached this new ground? she wondered. "Have we finally arrived at a truce?"

His smile was brief. "Were we at war?"

"There were certainly several battles."

"I owe you an apology, Evelyn, for making the wrong assumptions when we first met—for being terribly rude."

She was stunned. "You are forgiven."

"That was too easy, surely, I must redeem myself in a more exemplary manner."

He was serious, she realized. "You risked your life for me," she began.

"I did not bring you the gold."

Her eyes widened at his mention of what was truly inside the chest. "You knew?"

"Yes, your uncle assumed you had told me about it."

"And you do not think that I wished to cheat you?"

"No. I think only a very foolish woman would have told someone she wished to hire for this run that a pot of gold was its objective."

She wondered if she were lucky now. Somehow, she did not think that he would have been so understanding a day or two ago. "I will not be chasing any more pots of gold," she said slowly. "Do you know anything about mining?"

He started. "No. But my brother does."

"My tin mine needs repairs before it can be profitable—or so I have been told. But I was also told that the previous manager was stealing from us. I don't know what to believe, but that mine could be the source of revenue I need for my daughter to have the future she deserves."

"The Greystone estate is a small one, and most consider us an impoverished family, but it isn't true. There is a tin mine and an iron quarry, and both are highly lucrative. Lucas took over the reins of the estate when he was still a boy. He probably knows as much about tin mining as anyone."

"If I could speak to him," she cried in disbelief, "I would be so grateful!"

"I will make certain he helps you," Jack said. "I will see that he visits your mine, speaks with the manager and goes over your books. If that mine can produce revenue, Lucas will determine that."

Evelyn was thrilled. She also realized that Jack thought very highly of his brother. "I will look forward to meeting him," she said, "and not just because he can help me with the mine."

The wind had picked up. She shivered a little as a peaceful silence fell. "Tell me about your father," Jack said softly.

She started, surprised. "That is an odd request." But hadn't he heard her damning her own father?

"Is it?" He smiled. "We may have more in common than you think. My father left my family when I was six. He was a wastrel, and he went off to Europe, preferring its gaming halls and brothels to Greystone Manor. He never returned, not even once, and he never wrote, not a single time. He died of syphilis within a few years."

She was aghast at such a story, but Jack seemed entirely indifferent. "I am sorry! How terrible for you."

He shrugged, without releasing the helm. "I do not remember him, and I do not recall being distraught when he left, probably because he was never at home anyway—he was always in a tavern, or so I am told. I do believe it hurt my brother, who is three years older than me, and my older sister, Amelia. But he wounded my mother the most. She took to her bed, and began to lose her grasp on sanity even then, when she was so young. I remember her thinking he was coming home, when he was already dead. To this day, she confuses the past with the present." He shrugged calmly. "Fortunately, she lives with Amelia and Grenville, and she has her lucid moments."

Evelyn released the rigging to lay her hand on his strong forearm and grasp it comfortingly. He glanced at her hand, and then at her face—very briefly looking at her mouth. "Tell me about your father," he repeated quietly.

Evelyn dropped her hand, her heart skidding. She knew what that direct look meant. And it warmed her entirely. He could not forget kissing her, either.

"He was a rogue, Jack, entirely so—but a dashing one with great charm. I adored him. And when he left me at my uncle's when I was five, I wept and begged and screamed. I did not want to be abandoned! However, I know now that he could not have raised me without my mother. He was correct, sending me to my aunt and uncle after she died." She realized that the hurt was gone. Had she wept it away that afternoon?

"Your uncle is fond of you. He also admires you."

She laughed, a bit mirthlessly. "I realize that now, but he rarely said a word to me when I was a child, not even during meals, when he let my aunt and Lucille direct every conversation."

"Some men do not have the inclination to contest their spouses," Jack pointed out.

"Yes, I understand that now. In any case, my father did write to me, and he did visit me, once or twice a year. I lived for his letters, his visits. And he always came with gifts, tall tales and promises." She had stopped smiling. "His promises were empty ones. He promised me a great future, but he was killed in a duel when I was fifteen, and I learned then that I did not have even the smallest dowry."

"Henri must have stepped into your life shortly thereafter—if you married him at sixteen."

"Yes, he came to stay with us four or five months after my father's death, and he fell in love with me immediately." She regarded Jack carefully now. "I did not expect his attentions. Lucille was being groomed to receive him, not I. Aunt Enid had made it clear that as far as marriage went, I could do no better than a farmer."

Jack stared ahead, into the night. "Of course he fell in love with you," he finally said. "I am beginning to realize how modest you are, but you are unusually attractive. You would catch any man's eye, instantly."

She did not believe him, but that was how she had caught Henri's attention. "A great many have accused me of being a fortune hunter. I am used to the criticism. But because I did not expect his attention, it was some time before I realized that Henri really meant to marry me— that he was not going away."

"Did you fall in love with him?"

She stared. "I loved him—he became my closest friend."

"That isn't what I asked. Falling in love is not the same as loving someone."

She hugged herself. "I was overcome with gratitude, Jack. He gave me everything—a home, a family, respect, love and trust." When he kept staring, she cried, "No, I did not fall in love with him! But I cared, deeply. And he was elegant and dashing, before he became ill." But now, she thought about the revelations she had just had. He had been an irresponsible aristocrat.

"He was ill the night I took you from France. How long was he like that?"

She wondered at his questions. "He seemed entirely healthy until Aimee was born. Gradually there were signs of trouble—mostly, his difficulty breathing, especially after walking or riding. His doctors advised him to take care, to rest, even then."

His gaze was piercing. "So he was ill for most of your marriage."

He was wondering about her relations with Henri, she simply knew it. She glanced away, shivering. "Yes."

"Are you cold?"

She half turned. "The wind has changed."

"Yes, it has picked up. We are now making ten knots. We will be home before dawn."

And he would send Lucas to her, to help her with the mine. But then what?

"Come here," he said softly.

She started as he continued to grasp the helm, which he nodded at. "Surely you do not wish for me to guide the boat?" she asked.

"It is a ship, and, yes, you may steer her briefly." He reached for her and pulled her to stand before the helm, which Evelyn instantly grabbed. And she knew what he intended as he shrugged his jacket off and laid it carefully about her shoulders. His hands lingered there. "Is that better?" he asked.

He stood very close behind her, his hands on her shoulders, his breath on her cheek, and she was enveloped in his body's heat. "Yes."

He slowly took the helm—which had the effect of practically placing her in his embrace, from behind. She was spooned against him. "I doubt we should stand this way for long," he murmured.

She did not want to move. Evelyn leaned back against him, closing her eyes. She had just pressed against him, and she was very much enveloped by his body, his arms around her, and it felt perfectly right.

"Evelyn," he said roughly.

She could not answer, and she did not want to—afraid it would break the magical moment. Her heart thundered now. Surely he could hear it.

He pressed his mouth against her cheek.

She shuddered, with desire, not cold. "Did I catch your eye that way?" He had probably forgotten their discussion, but she hadn't—and she wanted to know if he had wanted her from that first moment of their meeting.

He became still, his mouth on her jaw. "Yes, Evelyn, you did."

Her heart thundered harder. Evelyn released the helm and slowly turned—now standing in his arms as he steered the ship.

She looked at his mouth, overcome with the urge to stand on tiptoe and kiss him wildly, deeply, impossibly....

"I know my ship is quiet," he said, "but there are two watches in the forecastle, and my other four hands are also on deck."

She leaped away, hit the helm and he dropped one arm to let her by. Blushing, she somehow said, "It is just such a beautiful night."

"No. You are the beautiful one."

She had never wanted his attentions more—but she

also wanted his affection—oh, she knew that now. "There is more to beauty than meets the eye."

"Yes, there is." He did not elaborate.

She would leave it alone, she thought, because this was a new beginning—it had to be. She whispered, "I will never forget how we first met. I knew who you were, even though you denied it. I was desperate. And there you were—so calm, when it was such a dangerous night, so confident—when Henri was dying and Aimee's life was at stake. It was as if I knew you would save us."

His gaze locked with hers. A long moment passed, and Evelyn wondered why he didn't respond. And then the watch cried out, loud and shrill, his meaning inde-cipherable to her ears. But she knew it was a warning. "Jack?" she cried.

He had seized a spyglass and was training it over the port railing. Suddenly he shouted, "Hoist the topsail, furl the gallant! Evelyn! Go below!"

She was in absolute shock as his men appeared in the rigging, as one sail was dropped, another opening with a huge whoosh. And the ship lurched hard, changing course. "What is it? What has happened?"

His gray eyes flashed. "There is a French destroyer on our portside, and she has the wind at her back."

Her eyes widened. Her mind raced. But the French navy allowed him to pass, did it not?

Impatiently, he cried, "She is in hot pursuit. Being as you are on board, I will not exchange fire—therefore, we must tuck our tail between our legs and run."

Evelyn took one look at his fierce expression and rushed below.

CHAPTER NINE

"Evelyn."

She started, her eyes opening—she had fallen asleep—and instantly, her gaze met Jack's.

She was curled up in his bed, atop the sheets; he sat beside her hip, his hand on her shoulder. He smiled a little and released her, standing. But his gray gaze skidded over her from head to toe, before he glanced away.

Too late, she had seen the appreciation in his eyes. She had also seen the speculation. She sat up, glancing past him at the portholes. Her tension was replaced by surprise. It had to be close to noon! "I fell asleep," she cried. "What happened?"

Last night, before dawn, she had actually heard a cannon being fired, but in the distance. She hadn't known if they were being fired upon, but it had seemed likely. There had been no response from Jack's ship, and eventually, she had sat down on the bed, only to doze off.

"We had to run south, as far south as Penzance, but they are long gone." He smiled, as if cheerful. He wasn't wearing his jacket, just his ruffled shirt, which was open at the neck. He wore his pistol and his dagger, of course. His hair was now entirely loose. He hadn't shaved in two days—and the effect was that he appeared entirely disreputable.

"It was a French destroyer, and had you not been on board, I would have loved to engage her."

There was actually a wistful look in his eyes. He would have enjoyed a battle, she realized, not certain if she should admire him, or be appalled.

"I am pleased you got some sleep," he said.

"I did not know what was happening." Evelyn stood up, her legs feeling terribly weak. She was exhausted. She had been at sea for two entire days—actually, if it were close to noon, for more than forty-eight hours—and she doubted she had slept more than a few hours, if that. She hadn't eaten much, either. In fact, just then, she realized that she was hungry—when she rarely had any appetite.

Jack did not look tired. To the contrary, he was smiling, as if jovial, and his eyes were bright. Clearly, he was in high spirits.

He loved the sea, but mostly he loved the danger of his activities.

But the French navy had been chasing them. Comprehension suddenly claimed her. She was now entirely awake. Didn't that mean that he was not a French spy? "Jack, I am bewildered. Everyone claims you run the British blockade. Why would the French navy pursue you?"

He slowly smiled and shrugged. Then, he said, "We are at my island home, but I have yet to drop anchor. If you wish to go home directly, it will take us less than an hour to reach Fowey. But I was wondering if you would care to come ashore and share some supper with me. I realize you are exhausted, and I can offer you a night's accommodations, and then take you to Roselynd tomorrow." His expression never changed, remaining bland.

Evelyn realized she was holding her breath. Under normal circumstances, such an invitation should have been refused, but these were hardly normal circumstances—they were allies of sorts, if not partners in crime, and they were both exhausted. Of course she needed to return to her daughter, as soon as was possible. But was it fair to ask him to sail on, when he hadn't closed his eyes for forty-eight hours—or not that she knew of? And she was so exhausted—she thought she could sleep for a solid twelve hours, if given a proper bed.

And they were at his secret island home. She was so curious to see it!

Their relationship had changed last night. They had truly put their past misunderstandings and differences aside. So much tension remained between them, but the run to France had changed everything. A friendship had begun. She was fiercely glad.

How could she go home now?

In that moment, her decision was made. "You do not appear fatigued, not in the least, but I am frankly exhausted. I am even hungry! I would love to take supper with you, and if it truly isn't trouble, I would accept your offer of a night's accommodations, too." She felt her cheeks warm as she spoke. She was going to spend the night as his guest. She so hoped they would have another frank and prolonged conversation. She so wanted to continue down this new path.

He finally looked at her. "Good. You will stay the night, then."

Evelyn hesitated. Her heart was racing. His glance had been direct and masculine. They might be on a new path, but that did not mean that the smoldering attraction they shared had changed. She meant to dine with him, and share an enjoyable evening, before getting some sorely needed rest. She was not going to think past that. She did not think he was, either. Somehow, she was certain she had gained his respect.

He glanced at her again, but in a sidelong manner. "You

will like my chef…. He is French." With that, he strode from the cabin. "Furl the aft sail," he ordered.

Evelyn shivered, and not because it was a chilly afternoon.

She followed him on deck and stopped suddenly, surprised. A small island was within two stone's throws of the ship. The island was mostly dark rock, a small white beach facing them, a grassy ridge in its center. The ridge was high enough that it might take a good hour to climb it. She could also see a part of a large country house, its pale stone making a stark contrast to the island's black rocks.

She studied the view. The island was treeless, windswept, barren—so stark and desolate. She wondered how he could live there. It had to be lonely—wasn't it an exile, of sorts?

Jack was standing by the railing. He swept her a bow. "Welcome to Looe Island, Countess."

EVELYN STARED OUT OF HER bedchamber's window. Her room was on the second floor, and she gazed down upon a dark stone tower that was on lower ground. The island had an interesting history. Her host had told her that the tower was all that remained of the island's original Elizabethan home. It had been gutted, Jack had said, by a series of attacks and fires. Looe Island had been used as a home and safe haven for pirates and smugglers for centuries.

They had arrived a few hours ago. They had taken a small dinghy from the ship to the beach, and then had walked, on foot, up a sandy path to a rocky road that led to the house. Because the island was so barren, its location so remote—although Britain's shoreline could be seen from the cove—she had not known what to expect. And then the handsome country house built from pale stone had appeared, as if rising up out of the island's sand and rocks.

And the moment she had stepped through the heavy ebony front doors, she had found herself in an entry hall with stone floors, fine furniture and oil paintings in gilded frames.

As a pair of servants had rushed to greet them, Evelyn had looked around—at a home as luxuriously furnished as the toniest residence in London. She had been amazed.

Her bedroom was no exception. The walls were covered in a blue-and-white fabric, as was the four-poster bed. The mantel over the fireplace was white plaster, sculpted with vines and flowers, and a blue-and-white silk sofa faced it. A sterling tray was on the table before the couch, laden with small sandwiches and tea.

Evelyn now glanced at the small garden, which lay between the tower and the house. It was mid-April, and a gardener was tending new pink and purple blooms.

Just then, she felt as if she were the guest in a gentleman's country home.

Evelyn turned from the window, aware of her heart racing. She had been on edge ever since accepting Jack's invitation. She had taken a long hot bath, and a maid had helped her dress. The gray gown she now wore was lighter in color than the dress she'd worn previously, with a slightly lower neckline, enough to reveal her pearls. It made her feel dressed for supper—and as if she were not in mourning.

Evelyn went to the mirror and pinched herself—because she was very much in mourning, and she meant to stay that way. She did not know why she felt as if she were young and pretty, indefatigable, really, and about to attend a supper party—with a handsome beau.

And while Jack might not be a suitor, she did look young and pretty. In spite of not having slept for most of two days, her eyes sparkled. Her cheeks were pink.

Her complexion was flawless. She no longer appeared haggard, and as if she bore the world's weight upon her shoulders. There was almost no explanation as to why she should appear so animated and so bright.

But there was a reason—her host. He was consuming her thoughts. In another moment, she would go downstairs to dine with him—and she could not wait. She felt like a debutante of sixteen, not a widow of almost twenty-five.

Had she ever been this excited to share supper with Henri? There had been anticipation, of course there had—he had been such a skilled suitor—but it simply hadn't been like this.

The maid, Alice, had helped Evelyn put up her hair loosely, but now, Evelyn tugged a few long strands down.

"Is there anything else that you need, madame?"

Evelyn faced the middle-aged woman. "I am fine, Alice, and thank you for your help."

"You are beautiful," she said, beaming. "And you will certainly turn the captain's head."

"I am in mourning," Evelyn said, but it sounded like a question to her own ears.

"Yes, I heard. But you will still turn his head.... And we do not follow any rules here."

Last night, Evelyn had been on board's Jack's ship, while the French navy had pursued them. What if they had been caught? Or, what if there had been a violent gun battle? Jack was in France every week, or so she believed. The British navy wished to capture him, and apparently, so did the French. He risked his life on a near-daily basis. Of course they did not adhere to the social graces on Looe Island.

She had always felt it terribly important to attempt to maintain decorum, to live with self-respect and dignity, to adhere to society's dictums. Yet she had witnessed the violence of the French Revolution; she had been a prisoner of the people while in Paris; she was lucky to be out of France—she was lucky to be alive. And what about all the years she had spent being a nursemaid to her ill husband? In that moment, it crossed her mind that she wouldn't mind bending the rules—or even ignoring them—for a while.

She straightened. Having such thoughts was dangerous, especially now. And she wondered what Jack was thinking, as he waited for her to join him.

His invitation had been a casual one. Or had it?

He might have the reputation of being a ladies' man, but Evelyn dismissed it. In truth, he had treated her with respect, even when they had gotten off to a very rocky start. He was not half as notorious as the gossips claimed. Therefore, he probably wasn't wondering about this evening at all. His invitation had probably been as casual and straightforward as it had seemed—which was perfect, as she had no wish to repeat the other evening's disastrous encounter. She wished to avoid rocking the boat.

"Alice? How long have you been employed by the captain?" Evelyn asked as Alice started to leave.

She paused, her eyes widening. "I have been here for the past two and a half years, madame."

"You must know him well, then."

The maid replied with some surprise, "He is a good employer."

"And he is a very brave and skilled seaman."

"Yes, he is."

"This house is so beautiful. Is he here often?"

"Often enough."

"I would be lonely if I lived here, so far removed from

everything and everyone," she said. "It must be lonely, living here alone, on an island."

Alice shrugged. "*Madame,* my husband is the gardener, and our children live in Looe," she said, referring to the mainland village. "So we are not lonely—we feel fortunate to have this employment."

"Yes, but that isn't quite what I meant. I am not sure how Mr. Greystone manages, living here, by himself." Evelyn now smiled, as she waited for Alice's answer.

Alice hesitated. "You will have to ask him, madame."

Evelyn smiled again, realizing that the maid would not gossip about Jack. She supposed she had all evening to find out how he felt about living on the island—among other things. She wondered how he felt about *her* now, being as they had formed a truce.

She gave herself a last glance in the mirror.

"He will think you very beautiful, my lady, and in the firelight, the gown looks silver," Alice said softly. "It is a wonderful color for you. You look like a princess."

"Am I terribly obvious?" Evelyn asked, blushing.

"Yes, but he is very handsome and we all think so." She smiled, and Evelyn thought she was referring to women in general. "Have no fear. I do not know of his having entertained any ladies here." Alice nodded and left.

Evelyn followed, lost in her own thoughts. Did that mean that he didn't entertain? Or that the only women he had brought to Looe Island were of a different ilk? She was almost certain the latter was the case.

Evelyn went downstairs, faltering as she passed the closed door to the suite of rooms that belonged to him. She was very curious as to what his private apartments were like, but she was not going to find that out.

She found her host in the salon, a glass of red wine in

hand. Evelyn faltered as she saw him. Her heart slammed, and she lost her breath.

Jack was dressed formally for evening, with the single exception that he was not wearing a wig. Still, he had shaven, and his hair was pulled back into a perfectly arranged queue, and tied with a black ribbon. He was clad in a chocolate-brown velvet coat, with a great deal of black-and-gold embroidery. Lace frothed from the collar of his shirt and cascaded from the sleeves. His breeches were almost as dark, but his stockings were pale white. His black patent shoes were buckled, and a dark red ring, perhaps a ruby, glinted from one finger.

He did not look like a smuggler or an outlaw now. He appeared to be an elegant aristocrat, and a very handsome one at that. Just then, it was terribly easy to recall how wonderful and maddening it was to be in his arms.

"You are staring," he said softly. "I hope you do not mind. I have helped myself to a drink before your joining me."

"Of course I do not mind."

His gaze moved slowly down her silvery gray dress. "I approve. You have never looked lovelier."

She felt her heart slam. "And I did not realize you meant to attire so formally tonight." But that wasn't what she wanted to say—she wanted to ask him if he was dressing up for her. He was dressed like a suitor, and he was as beautiful as a mythological Greek god. "Dressing up suits you." She managed a composed smile.

"I have attended the occasional London supper party." He smiled in return. "Red or white?"

She entered the gold-and-white salon, a large room with a great many oversize windows that looked out onto his gardens. All the furniture was gilded, as were the two chandeliers overhead. "I will have whatever you are having."

He walked over to a magnificent sideboard and poured a glass of red wine, which he then handed to her. "I hope I haven't rushed you."

She took the wineglass, but did not sip. She was seeing such a different side of him, she thought. "Where is the captain of the *Sea Wolf?*" she asked.

He laughed. "Right here. I am capable of good manners, Countess." His smile faded as he took her arm and they strolled from the salon. "But of course, you would not realize that, considering how I have acted since we first met."

She halted, as did he. "You have been the perfect gentleman!" She realized she sounded fierce.

"I have behaved horribly—and we both know it. But I am appreciative of the fact that I am somehow forgiven. Shall we?"

His smile was the male equivalent of a sea siren's, she thought, as her insides lurched in response. It was charming and seductive—impossible to resist. Had she been fooling herself to think that this invitation was casual and innocent?

"Do my accommodations satisfy you? Is there anything you need?" he asked, now speaking softly.

She shivered in response to his tone. "Your home is beautiful. I do not think I am lacking for anything."

"I like beauty," he said softly but firmly. "But that, of course, you know."

She met his gaze, stumbling; he caught her around her waist, smiling. Her heart pounding, Evelyn slowly detached herself from his embrace. "You flatter me far too much."

"That is not possible." As he spoke, his unwavering

attention intensified. "But I am beginning to believe that you do not have a clue as to your effect upon the male gender."

Evelyn wet her lips, but could not reply. He gestured at the dining room.

The two doors to the room were open. Evelyn faced a table that could seat twelve, set with gold-rimmed plates, gold dinnerware and sparkling crystal. Several tall gold candlesticks held burning golden tapers. The beautifully adorned table was set for two.

She walked inside, Jack following. The two place settings were kitty-corner, his at the head of the table. He held her chair out for her. Evelyn thanked him and sat down.

As he took his seat adjacent hers, she said, "You have gone to a great deal of trouble, furnishing this house." Her tone was husky and she cleared her throat.

"Yes, I have. I prefer to live in a privileged manner, now that I can."

"I do not understand."

"Greystone Manor is barely furnished. It is not the impoverished estate everyone thinks, but it is hardly a wealthy one. And Lucas is a very frugal and serious man. His decision has been to put as much of the family fortune away as is possible—until recently, he did not know that Julianne or Amelia would ever marry, much less well. He was determined to set aside what wealth he could for their futures, and that is exactly what he did. I like the finer things in life, Evelyn, but I grew up with only the bare necessities. I enjoy having all of this." He gestured at the room.

Servants in livery appeared. Plates filled with salmon were set down before them. "Is that why you have chosen the life of a smuggler?"

He smiled with amusement. "The sea is my true love, Evelyn."

"The sea—or adventure?"

He laughed. "Both. I could never live as my brother does. Boredom would destroy me. And I do like reaping the rewards of the free trade."

He would never be a gentleman farmer, a landlord or some such expected thing, she thought. "I do not blame you. Everyone prefers luxury to subsistence."

His gaze sobered. "In a way, our lives have taken opposite courses, have they not?"

She thought about how much she and Henri had had before the revolution. "I was fortunate to marry Henri. Now I have been returned to less fortunate circumstances." She shrugged, as if indifferent. "You, however, have earned a life of luxury."

"And you are not looking down your nose at me." Then he became serious. "One never knows what life has in store. You might have another change of fortune—I should rather expect it." He gestured at the cold poached salmon salad. "Please."

She wondered at his comment. He was so optimistic about her future, and not for the first time. Evelyn smiled, now ravenous, and took a bite. The salmon was delicious and for a moment, they both ate, rather determinedly, in silence. When she had devoured half of her plate, she sighed, set her utensils down and took a sip of wine. "That might be the best salmon I have ever had."

"I told you," he said, "my chef is exceptional."

He resumed eating and she studied him, wondering at his tone, his searching looks. Did he think to seduce her after supper? Or was she the one consumed with illicit thoughts? Hadn't he told her how beautiful he thought her—time and again? There was tension between them, she thought, and it was too much to ignore.

And if he did make advances, could she really refuse? Did she even wish to?

When he had finished his portion, and she declined finishing hers, their plates were removed.

"A penny for your thoughts," he said.

She felt herself flush. "You seem to have every luxury here, when the island seems so desolate."

He stared at her, and she suspected he knew those had hardly been her thoughts. "It is desolate. And that is why so many pirates and smugglers have used the island as their home."

"Why is this island safe for them—for you?" she asked. "I would think it dangerous. You are isolated and so close to shore."

He leaned back in his chair, one large hand on the table, his fingers sprawled out casually there. "When a ship is approaching, we can see it. And we can run." He smiled at her, now lounging very informally in his chair. He had finished his wine, and a servant promptly poured him another glass.

In that moment, even so well dressed, he reminded her of a big panther sunning itself. His demeanor was changing, too. He was becoming more than relaxed, and his gaze was now trained steadily upon her.

"I always have two lookouts on watch. No one can land here without my knowing it."

"Surely the authorities know you are here?"

"The deed is not in my name."

Of course the deed was recorded to a friend or an alias. Otherwise the authorities would come looking for him. She thought about their recent voyage, taking a sip of her wine. "You hate running away."

"Yes, I do."

"You would have loved to have a gun battle with the French."

He slowly smiled. "I would have loved nothing more." Then his stare became direct. His smile vanished. "Almost."

She met his gaze. Did that comment mean what she thought it did? And he was so serious now.

He glanced away, suddenly drumming his fingers on the table, as if restless. "I do not mean to be rude," he finally said. "I am appreciative of your being my guest. I am enjoying your company."

"You are not being rude." But she was certain he had been thinking about the passion they had shared—and could still share. And because the silence was so tense now, she said, "Jack? I cannot understand why the French navy would purse you."

He toyed with his wineglass, and for a moment, she thought he would not answer her, just as he had avoided doing so on board his ship. "This is a time of war," he finally said. "Everyone is suspect. There are places in France where I can pass easily enough, but at other times, I am scrutinized as all passersby who are not the French navy are."

She supposed that made some sense. "If you are risking your life to run the British blockade, that isn't fair."

He laughed without mirth. "Nothing is fair in a time of war, and when it suits me, I outrun the French blockades. Their navy is pitiful—and it is easy enough to do."

She suddenly recalled a remark made by Trevelyan— that he was a spy, perhaps for both sides. She lowered her eyes from his scrutiny, quickly picked up her wineglass and took a sip.

"What is it?" he asked softly.

She was not going to ruin the evening, she thought fiercely, by accusing him of being a spy. "Will this war ever end?"

He gave her an odd look, clearly aware that she was changing the subject. "All wars end, sooner or later," he said. "But the question is, who will triumph and who will be defeated?"

More plates were set down in front of them, this time containing lamb shanks, potatoes and vegetables. Mouthwatering aromas of lamb roasted with thyme filled the room. The timing was perfect, as talk of war could ruin the evening. This time, they ate in silence for quite a while.

When she was finished, incapable of taking another bite, she watched him. He finally set his utensils down and sighed. Then he looked at her and smiled.

Her heart turned over, hard. Would she ever be immune to his smile? "Do you like living here?"

"Is that a loaded question?"

"Am I prying?" she asked. "I am curious. This house is lovely. But it reminds me of Roselynd, as there are no neighbors nearby, and the island is so barren—just like the Bodmin Moor."

"It is the perfect haven."

He hadn't answered her question. "I would be lonely if I lived here," she said. "It is lonely living at Roselynd, even with Aimee, Bette, Laurent and Adelaide."

He took a sip of wine. "I am not lonely, Evelyn." His tone almost seemed warning. Then he smiled. "You do not like your wine? You have not even finished one glass."

He was changing the topic, she thought. "I love it, but I will become foxed on one glass, after all that has transpired, if I am not careful."

He lifted his glass and regarded her over the rim, leaning back in his chair again. "And then? Will you tell me all of your secrets?"

"You know most of my secrets," she said, suddenly realizing that was true. He knew more about her than anyone, other than her deceased husband.

His stare was piercing.

She found it hard to breathe. Slowly she said, "And you? If you become foxed—will you tell me your secrets?"

"No." And then his hard expression softened. "I have no secrets. I am an open book."

THE TABLE WAS BEING cleared; supper was over. Evelyn looked down at her place mat, her heart skidding. It was getting late. The evening was about to end. They were going to leave the table, go upstairs and say good-night. But then what would happen?

She slowly looked up. Her heart was racing, as it had throughout the evening, and her cheeks felt hot.

Jack said softly, "I do not think I have ever passed such an enjoyable evening."

She met his probing regard. She realized she felt the same way. Jack had asked her more questions about her childhood. She hadn't minded sharing her memories with him of life at Faraday Hall. She had then learned a bit about his boyhood. Somehow, she had not been surprised to find out that he had been fascinated with smugglers from a very young age, especially in their battles with the revenue men. She had been surprised, though, to learn that he had helped unload cargoes and keep watch from the time he was a small boy of five; he had been a first mate when he was a boy of thirteen. No wonder he was so skilled and successful now.

"I am so glad you asked me to supper," she said.

Jack lounged in his chair, his stare unrelenting. Its intensity was at odds with his posture, which was entirely relaxed now. But then, he had had a great many glasses of wine; she had had one. He did not seem inebriated, but one could not consume as much wine as he had and remain sober.

"I suppose there is no getting past the fact that supper is over," he said. "Thank you for joining me, Evelyn." He stood up, his actions unrushed, and slowly came around to the back of her chair. Briefly, she felt his hands brush her as she stood, but he then stepped back from her. "Can you find your way back to your chamber?" he asked, his gray gaze intent.

She was adamant. "Of course I can. It is at the end of the hall on the second floor."

He gestured, and she preceded him from the room. "Good," he said.

Evelyn was disbelieving. Did his question mean that he would not see her to her bedroom? They passed the salon, the stairs ahead. She suddenly realized that she expected a kiss good-night—and not a formal one.

Surely his heart was hammering as incessantly as hers was. Surely he was as stiff with the same tension.

She started up the stairs, holding the banister, Jack behind her. Her heart was now thundering, with both alarm and anticipation. They reached his suite of rooms and she turned abruptly. He sidestepped her, avoiding a collision. He did not reach out to steady her, as he had done earlier in the evening.

She wet her lips and smiled. "I suppose this is good-night, then."

"I suppose so." His gray gaze skidded past her shoulder. "Thank you again, Evelyn, and good night."

Had he just bid her good-night? Why wasn't he looking

at her intently, as he had done all evening? She breathed and said, "I would not mind an escort down the hallway." Had she really just said such a thing? "It is rather dark."

He glanced at her once, and then glanced away. "There are sconces…you will be fine. Good night."

Was his tone *firm?* Had he just *dismissed* her?

He stepped into his suite. She stared after him, glimpsing a large sitting room with red walls and burgundy appointments, accented with gold. He left the door ajar, crossing it and disappearing into what must be his bedchamber.

Jack had not tried to take her into his arms. He had not tried to kiss her.

And she was beyond disappointment.

She hurried down the hall and into her own bedchamber. Alice was waiting for her there, and a fire was roaring in her hearth.

What had just happened? she wondered.

"Can I help you disrobe, madame?" The maid smiled.

As she changed into her cotton-and-lace nightgown, took her hair down and braided it into a single tail, Evelyn reminded herself that he was exhausted, probably far more so than she was. And he had drunk a great deal of wine.

But he had decided to become the perfect gentleman, and she simply could not understand why!

Now she realized that she had been expecting his advances all along, and that she had probably decided to stay on the island that evening because she wanted to be in his arms. She sat down on the sofa and stared unseeingly at the hearth. She should not be so disappointed, she decided. Jack respected her now. He was treating her the way she should be treated—as a lady in mourning.

But she was not calmed or convinced. Henri had never made her feel so tense and so desperate, so explosive.

But Henri wasn't young and handsome, and he could not outrace a navy, and he would never wish to engage in a gun battle with his enemies! Her heart turned over hard, Jack's golden, handsome image filling her mind. Maybe it was time to admit that she was entirely infatuated with him, and the attraction was far greater than a physical one.

But why not? He had saved her life, and her daughter's, and he wasn't just a handsome and intelligent man, he was skilled and courageous, and he even came from a good family. Was she falling in love? That would be so dangerous, wouldn't it? Even though he thought her beautiful, and they were becoming friends, he was a smuggler and an outlaw. Men like that did not court and marry women like her.

Did she want him to court her? And if he did, what would she do? Wasn't she in mourning? Evelyn was amazed at her train of thoughts. This was the second time in as many days that she had considered his character in relationship to the prospect of a courtship.

She suddenly realized that she didn't care about mourning Henri. She had nursed him for almost eight years—she had done enough! If Jack became serious about her, she would welcome his suit. And he was becoming interested in her. Why else would they have shared that supper, and so much conversation? She had not mistaken all of those heavy, lingering looks!

She sat very still, breathing hard. She had never been interested in any man as she was in Jack. She had never been attracted to any man the way she was to him. And she had never admired anyone as much.

If she was falling in love, as dangerous as it was, she had to do something about it.

After all, there were no rules on Looe Island.

She stood up. She had spent eight years nursing an old man. Now, she wanted to live her own life.

Evelyn began taking out her braid, her hands shaking in some shock over what she meant to do—uncertain whether she merely meant to seek Jack out for his kisses or for far more. It just didn't matter. Suddenly she felt as if she were escaping prison. Evelyn shook out her waist-length hair and stared at her flushed reflection in the mirror. Her eyes glittered almost wildly. She did not recognize herself.

She had been following rules her entire life. Yet she was a grown woman, a mother and a widow. If she wanted to be in Jack's arms, she had every right.

Evelyn fanned out her hair, donned her cotton wrapper and hurried from her room.

His door remained entirely open. She looked across the gold-and-red sitting room, and into his bedchamber, for that door was also wide-open. However, it was barely lit and cast in shadow. She could not see anyone.

"What are you doing?"

She started, and realized Jack stood in the sitting room after all, but by the hearth—he had one hand on the marble mantel. And he wore only his pale wool, knee-length knickers.

"What are you doing?" he demanded again as harshly as the first time. His expression was hard but incredulous.

She had not expected him to be undressed, and she had never seen such a man in a naked state before. She stared. His hair was unbound. It brushed his broad shoulders. His chest was wide and hard, two massive slabs of muscle. His nipples were erect. His abdomen was tight and flat. She did not dare look lower, although she wanted to. She slowly lifted her gaze up to his.

His eyes widened.

"May I come in?" She smiled, even though her mouth was entirely dry.

"No."

She swallowed. "There are no rules on Looe Island."

His eyes widened even more. He stepped toward the sofa, but not past it, his face hard, his eyes smoldering. He did not seem inebriated now. "What is wrong with you?"

"I am tired of living like a widow."

He began shaking his head, incredulously. "Go back to your bedchamber—if you know what is good for you."

"I can't," she whispered, starting forward.

"If you come in here, you will not be leaving."

"Good," she said. She halted, two steps within his room, barely able to breathe. "That is what I want!"

"You are a moral woman. I am not a moral man. Go back to your room—before I show my true colors."

She inhaled. "You have shown, and are showing, your true colors. You are a very moral man—and you are proving it, right now. Meanwhile, I have decided to be the amoral one."

"You are not amoral…. You could not be amoral." And he shuddered. "I am an instant from seizing you and taking you to bed," he warned. "But I am trying to play the gentleman."

"You can play the gentleman tomorrow—and tomorrow, I can play the widow." She bit her lip, so hard, she tasted blood. Very aware of what she was doing, she unbelted the wrapper and slid it from her shoulders. It fell onto the floor by her feet.

He breathed hard—she saw his muscular chest rising and falling. "I am not going to allow you to turn tail on me this time," he ground out.

"I won't," she managed, feeling faint with need. "I won't, Jack. I love you."

He began shaking his head. "This isn't love, Evelyn, this is lust."

"No. I am falling in love with you."

"Then I will break your heart, sooner or later, because this is not about love, not for me." His eyes did not meet hers as he said this, and his expression was fierce.

She did not believe him. No two people could feel such desire and not be falling in love. Evelyn turned and shut his bedroom door. Then she faced him and shrugged off her nightgown. She was naked beneath.

His eyes blazed. He strode to her. Before she could think or react, Evelyn was swept into his arms, and up his body. Somehow she was astride his waist, her legs around his hips, clutching his shoulders, and he was pressing her into the door. And his mouth was on hers, in a frenzy.

Evelyn kissed him back, clawing his shoulders, thrusting her tongue past his teeth. She heard him gasp. Their tongues mated. His palm grasped one buttock, shifting her. Something massive and hard pushed up against her sex. She cried out, thrilled, beyond excitement.

He pressed her harder against the wall, and without breaking the kiss, he reached down and pulled at the drawstring of his knickers. The undergarment slid down and he kicked it aside. "Evelyn."

Evelyn could not think. He was throbbing dangerously against her and desire consumed her.

He caught her face with both hands, framing it. She met his blazing regard. "Last chance. I will let you go if you tell me now that you have changed your mind."

"Make love to me," she gasped, clawing his shoulders and wriggling lower.

He groaned, lifting her into his arms and carrying her into the bedroom. He laid her down on the bed, and for one instant they stared at one another.

"I have never had a lover," she said softly.

His eyes widened. "You were married to an old man!"

She could not smile. "But I have never wanted anyone before. I never considered an affair—until I met you."

He stared, his eyes blazing. "You are an extraordinary woman," he said roughly. "And I do not want to hurt you."

And just when she thought he meant that he did not want to break her heart, she glimpsed his entire muscular, hard, proud body, hovering over hers. She had become so hollow, so faint, that she went still. She could not bear the anticipation any longer. "Hurry," she whispered. "Make love to me."

He moved over her, smiling. And in moments, Evelyn was weeping in ecstasy and pleasure.

CHAPTER TEN

EVELYN AWOKE IN Jack Greystone's bed.

She grinned, stretching like a cat, recalling bits and pieces of his lovemaking last night. She had never felt so wonderful, so delicious, so replete and so loved. And she was shameless, wasn't she? For she was stark naked beneath his sheets, relishing it!

She wondered where he was as she sat up. His half of the bed was cold, indicating he had arisen some time ago. She slid her hand over the silky sheets where he had slept, her heart turning over hard. If she hadn't been falling in love with him before, she was most certainly falling in love now.

She wished he hadn't gotten up! So easily she could slip into his arms another time.

Evelyn rose from the bed, pleased to see that he had left her nightgown and wrapper draped over a big burgundy chair, and she donned both. Then she opened the heavy damask draperies, allowing bright sunlight to fill the room.

Outside, the sun was high—it was close to noon. The sky was a bright blue, filled with puffy white cumulus clouds—it was a beautiful spring day. She glimpsed the gardens below, and just past the hedges, the blue-gray sea. White horses frothed merrily upon it.

Evelyn turned, crossed the room and carefully opened the door to his sitting room. It was empty she saw with relief. She hurried through it and then peeked into the hall. When she did not see anyone, she ran up the corridor to her room, and slammed that door closed.

Panting, she laughed. Hopefully no one knew she had spent the night in Jack's bed, but if they did, who cared? She wondered if she had ever felt as buoyant, as happy, as carefree and as young. Now she truly felt like a debutante, and she did not care if she was being foolish. Except no debutante would have taken a lover last night. And she was thrilled she had decided to break the rules!

Suddenly she thought of Henri and she sobered. How had she ever endured his touch? She had never allowed herself to fault him at the time, but now she knew the difference between tolerating a man and wildly wanting someone.

She felt sorry for the child bride she had once been, but she hadn't known better, and Henri had given her Aimee. For that, she would always be grateful. However, gratitude was not love.

A knock sounded on her door. *Jack.* Evelyn whirled, thrilled and opened it. Her smile vanished as she faced Alice, carrying a breakfast tray.

"Good morning," Alice said cheerfully, walking past her and placing the tray on the small dining table beside one window. "Did you sleep well?"

"Yes." Evelyn wondered if Alice knew about her affair, but could see no sign that she did. "I slept wonderfully—it is so late!"

"It is half past eleven, my lady. Can I help you dress?"

"That would be wonderful." She stared, smiling fixedly now. Where was Jack? Was he in as good spirits as she was?

She felt her smile falter.

This is not about love, not for me. This is about lust.

Why had she recalled that terrible statement? She rubbed her arms, suddenly worried. But he had subsequently called her an extraordinary woman, and he had made love to her many, many times.

Alice handed her a cup of hot chocolate. Evelyn thanked her. "Is Mr. Greystone up? I cannot imagine him sleeping in."

Alice looked away. "He is walking on the beach."

Evelyn set her cup down, surprised.

"He walks this entire island every morning when he is at home. He never sleeps past six or so."

She could not wait to encounter him now. She wanted to rush back into his arms, have him hold her—and reassure her. Surely, he was as thrilled with their affair as she was—and surely, he had some affection for her now. She could not simply be just one of his many lovers! "Alice, help me dress. I am going to join the captain."

IT WAS A BEAUTIFUL DAY, bright and sunny, but with a strong breeze, and Evelyn left the house, inhaling the salt tang in the air. Her heart was racing with anticipation as she glanced at the fork in the road just ahead. The island had two beaches, and the servants hadn't known which beach Jack was on, so her guess was as good as any. She decided to head toward the cove where his ship was anchored, and she turned left, taking the same road as when she had first arrived.

Although rocky, the road leaving the house was well used, and Evelyn hurried down it, in spite of her small heels. She imagined Jack's surprise when he saw her, and then she imagined a lover's warm embrace. She smiled. Suddenly she wondered if she had ever been this happy. The only instance that could compare was her joy when Aimee was born.

She slowed, the end of the road ahead. She had been so intent on getting dressed as rapidly as possible that she hadn't paused to consider the fact that she was supposed to return to Roselynd that afternoon. And she had to return—she was a mother, with a mother's duties and responsibilities, and she missed Aimee. Still, she didn't want to leave, not just yet. She wondered if she could rationalize staying for another day or two.

She had reached the sandy path that led to the beach and she lifted her skirts, trudging through the deep white sand now. The island's central ridge was on her left, and ahead she saw the small, pale beach and the cove where they had disembarked yesterday. Jack's black ship floated at anchor. In the distance, she could just glimpse the hazy British shore. But no one was on the beach, and she halted abruptly, disappointment claiming her.

He had to be on the island's only other beach, which was on the south side of the house—facing the open waters of the Channel. She sighed, lifted her skirts and began trudging back the way she had come. She was now warm, and she took off her cloak, sliding it over her arm. Her shoes were not meant for walking on sandy paths and rocky roads. Her feet were starting to hurt.

Sometime later—she wasn't walking quite as sprightly now—she had returned to the house. She briefly considered giving up her quest and waiting for Jack at the house, but she was afraid he might be gone for hours. She continued past the gardens and hedges. And when she passed the last hedge, she faced nothing but the black rocks which formed the perimeter of that side of the island.

Evelyn hesitated, for this side of the island was so inhospitable. The road led up that hill into those rocks, and it was a much rougher path than the previous one. She frankly did not know if she could navigate it, but she had been told that once she reached the top of the knoll, the road descended almost directly to the beach. How far could the beach be?

Evelyn folded up her cloak and laid it on a boulder that was twice her size. Then she started grimly up the road, tripping now and then on the rocks and ruts. She was quickly out of breath. She would surely break a heel. She was probably getting blisters. She debated turning around.

But she was almost at the top of the hill. Evelyn increased her pace, panting, and finally arrived at the crest of the black rock knoll.

And she stared ahead. The view was magnificent, the ocean seeming to stretch out into infinity, sparkling silver in the sunlight. She even thought she saw specks in the distance, which she assumed where ships crossing Channel.

glanced down at the beach below the hill and froze. tood a hundred feet below her—speaking to an-

s widened as she saw the small dinghy lying on the beach in the ocean's shallow water. A larger ship, perhaps a cutter, sat anchored not far from the shore.

Who was Jack meeting? Her heart slammed. He must be engaged with another smuggler. There was no other sensible explanation!

She thought about turning around. Then she dismissed the notion—she knew he was a smuggler, so there was nothing to hide.

Evelyn started down. The road had become a narrow, steep, winding path, very much like a gorge, between the rocks and cliffs. It was treacherous, commandeering all of her attention, and the cliffs quickly obfuscated her view. She could not see the beach, the two men or the ocean.

Black rock formed walls on either side of her, but above her head, the sky was bright.

Evelyn finally reached the very foot of the path, perhaps a half an hour later. She paused, panting hard, and partially collapsed against a boulder. She realized that she had been a fool to go down such a route. From where she stood, she could glimpse a part of the sandy beach, and just a bit of the tide. Inhaling, she stepped past the boulder.

And she saw Jack and the other man. They hadn't seen her yet, and while she could hear their muted voices, she could not make out any of the conversation. She was surprised—the other man was most definitely not a smuggler—unless he also came from a good family. For the stranger wore the clothing of a gentleman. He was clad in a tan coat and pale breeches, his dark hair tied in a queue.

As she looked at the stranger, she was alarmed seemed familiar. But that was impossible, wasn'

Both men had their backs to her, as they ocean. Suddenly the wind shifted, blowing har elyn's skirts flew up. She caught them as she h Jack say, "I told you. I do not know when it will take place."

"That is hardly helpful!" the stranger replied.

Evelyn froze—she knew that voice!

The stranger continued, his French accent thick, "How many men will D'Hervilly muster?"

"Three or four thousand," Jack said promptly. "But your problem will come from the Chouans. Cadoudal will have as many as ten thousand rebels, if not more."

The stranger cursed in French. Evelyn stared widely at the two men now. She did not know who Cadoudal was, but were they speaking of the infamous Comte D'Hervilly? He was a well-known émigré, one constantly begging the British government for its support against the

French government in the French countryside, where re-
bellions were taking place. Had she heard correctly? But
what were they talking about?

"A rebel army of fifteen thousand will be easily defeated." The Frenchman shrugged. "But we must know
when the damned invasion will take place. Gossip has
it they will invade Brittany—find out." It was an order.

She began to shake. They were talking about a Chouan
rebel army—which the French would defeat. She knew
who the Chouans were—they were the peasants and noblemen who continued to wage a rebellion against the
French republic in La Vendée, from its hills and valleys,
its farms and villages. Recently the French government
had begun to seriously suppress them.

She could not breathe adequately now. She tried to
comprehend what she had heard—when she was afraid
of what she might think. They had also been talking of
an invasion of Brittany. D'Hervilly would have three or
four thousand men—that sounded like an émigré army!

Were they discussing an invasion of Britanny by émigré and British forces?

And had Jack been ordered to discover—and divulge—
British military plans?

Surely, she had misheard! Surely, she did not understand! She could not think clearly now!

"Has my contact changed?"

"No, it has not," the Frenchman said. Too late, Evelyn
realized that she had cried out the moment Jack had made
his last comment. And the stranger whirled, facing her—
instantly seeing her.

And now, Evelyn realized that she was staring at Victor
LaSalle, the Vicomte LeClerc, who had been her neighbor
in Paris in the summer of 1791—who had been impris-

oned that summer, as an enemy of the state, just before she had fled Paris with her family. In shock, she stared.

As shocked, he stared back.

And real comprehension began. Why was LeClerc asking Jack about an invasion of France—if that was what he was doing? And how was it that he had survived the charges leveled against him? How had he survived a French prison?

"Evelyn!" Jack started up the beach, toward her, smiling. She did not move, because his smile was entirely false—it did not reach his eyes.

Somehow, she smiled back. "Hello! I heard you were walking on the beach and I had hoped to join you!"

He took her hand and kissed it. "Did you sleep well?"

"Very." What had she interrupted? What was she to think?

There was only one conclusion. *LeClerc was a Republican now. Jack was a French spy. They had been discussing a British invasion of France!*

Their gazes met, but she could not see into his gray depths. They were flat and cold. His expression was tight and hard, in spite of the fixed smile. "Have I disturbed your...meeting?" She continued to smile, her heart racing with fear. Jack could not be a spy!

"You could never disturb me," Jack said lightly. "May I introduce you to an old friend?"

Evelyn trembled. She had been using LeClerc's name when she had fled France four years ago, and surely Jack recalled that. But she could have picked his name out of a hat. He would not know that they were acquainted, would he? She finally met the Vicomte LeClerc's eyes, which were even colder than Jack's. She wet her lips nervously.

"Do not bother," he said. "I am well acquainted with the comtesse. Bonjour, Evelyn. *Ça va bien?*"

They had never been on a first-name basis—they had socialized once or twice. "Monsieur le Vicomte. Thank God you escaped prison. We fled France, shortly after your incarceration. I never expected to see you again. This is a…wonderful…surprise."

"I imagine not. And I certainly never expected to see you again, Comtesse." He took her hand and kissed it. "I heard about Henri. I am so sorry for your loss."

She was afraid to ask him about his wife and children. He smiled and said, "They did not survive. My wife was arrested several days after I was, and she was taken to the guillotine. My sons eventually suffered the same fate."

She inhaled. "I am sorry."

LeClerc said, "I cannot imagine how you found your way to this island. Or should I even ask?"

Jack said, his odd smile fixed in place, "The countess is my guest."

"Obviously. Well, I do hope you are enjoying the amenities my friend is offering." He seemed amused. "I am off, Greystone."

Jack gave her a look. "Wait here."

Evelyn nodded stiffly. She had no intention of moving—not unless she was told to do so.

Jack and LeClerc walked toward the dinghy, neither one speaking. The vicomte got into the rowboat, lifting the oars, while Jack pushed it into the water. When it was rocking on the waves, and Jack was knee-deep in the surf, they spoke briefly. Of course, Evelyn could not hear a word they were saying.

Tears abruptly filled her eyes and blurred her vision. LeClerc was alive—and she was glad. But if she had understood correctly, Jack had been betraying his country. Oh, God. She had to be wrong. This could not be happening.

She hugged herself, watching as Jack turned the din-ghy so it faced the waiting ship and then gave it a shove. LeClerc began to row. Jack turned, wading through the water toward her. Surely he would begin to smile, surely he would embrace her, tell her he loved her—and explain what she had heard.

He waded out of the water, onto the beach, his face hard and set. She closed her eyes in dread.

"How much did you overhear?"

Her eyes flew open. "So much for a lover's reunion."

His face tightened. His gray gaze heated. "I haven't for-gotten last night, Evelyn. Are you trying to distract me?"

She shook her head, and she felt a tear spilling down her cheek. "I woke up so happy."

He began shaking his head. His eyes flashed. "Yes, I imagine you were happy, and do not attempt to dissuade me! How long were you standing there—listening to us?"

Through her tears, she stared at him. "Why were you discussing le Comte D'Hervilly? Why were you discuss-ing the Chouans? Who is Cadoudal?" She was breath-ing hard.

He cursed, not once, but several times.

"How did LeClerc escape Le Razor? It took the rest of his family!" she cried.

"How do you think?" he roared.

She cringed. She knew how he had escaped execution! "He is a republican, isn't he? He turned on his friends, his family, swore his loyalty to la Patrie… He is not the first to do so!" She was sobbing now. She had not met his sons, but she had met his lovely wife. She could not recall the pretty blonde vicomtesse clearly, but she was now dead, so did it even matter?

"You shouldn't have come down to this beach," he cried. "And when you saw LeClerc, you should have left!"

"We made love last night! Are you a spy?" How was this happening? How? She clenched her fists.

His eyes continued to blaze. He finally said, "We did not make love, Evelyn."

She hit him, hard, across the face. "You are a French spy!"

He stepped back, as if reeling from her blow. Red blossomed on his cheek. "I suggest that you forget what you saw and heard today. Let's go back to the house. And I will take you home." He gestured angrily at the rocky path.

She refused to move. "Oh! You haven't denied it! But you deny making love!" Was she about to weep? Of course she was—a knife was stabbing through her heart, and he was the one wielding it!

"I told you," he said softly, his anger now tightly reined, "that I would break your heart. I just did not realize it would be the morning after!"

She wanted to strike him again. "How can you betray your country? My co _____ She _____?"

His stare sharpened. _____ know, Evelyn. I have no conscience. I am _____ ercenary. Let's go." He seized her elbow an _____ dragged her to the road.

She pulled her arm free. She did not want to believe him, but she had not misheard. Jack Greystone was a goddamned French spy. "Damn you."

His eyes widened and she thought he flinched. "Well said. Now let's go."

She rushed past him; he followed.

SHE HARDLY HAD ANYTHING to pack.

In tears, Evelyn folded her underclothes from the previous day and stuffed them into her valise. Her used stockings followed. Then she folded her dark gray dress and added that to the small bag, too. She had already packed her nightgown and robe, though she felt like burning both garments.

Jack was a French spy. She had worried that that might be the case, but now, it was like ice water thrown in her face. No, it was like gunpowder exploding in her heart.

She had been falling in love. She had woken up that morning, delirious with joy. She had believed, from the bottom of her heart, that Jack was a great man—a hero. He was intelligent, ambitious, powerful. He was strong and brave. He could outrun any navy. He was a smuggler, but it was a way of life for a man like him. And he had saved her life, and her daughter's, four years ago in France. Of course he was a hero, a man she could admire and depend on.

But she had been wrong, hadn't she? And it was as if she had viewed him in a bubble, and that bubble had now burst. He was aiding her enemies, Henri's enemies and Aimee's enemies. He wasn't a great man—he was a *traitor.*

She was so sick now and not just in her heart, but in her stomach. She was going to have to reconcile her view of the Jack she had believed in—the man she had taken as a lover—and the one she had overheard on the beach. But how, exactly, was she going to do that, when a part of her was protesting furiously? A part of her wanted an explanation—one that would make that afternoon go away—as if it had never happened!

But she knew what she had heard. He had told the French about a British invasion of Britanny. He had peddled military secrets. Had he been well paid? Justly rewarded? His services were expensive!

She sank onto the foot of the bed, more tears arising. How could this be happening? Last night, they had made love. This morning, she had gone down to the beach to find him and leap into his arms. She began to laugh, bitterly. But her lover was a spy—he was actually her enemy!

Of course he was. After all, she had no experience when it came to taking lovers, otherwise, she would have sensed something amiss; she would have known better! She surely would have considered the fact that everyone in Britain knew he ran the British blockade, and was wanted for treason!

Her heart should not be broken and she should not be surprised.

It was so hard to think clearly, when she was in such anguish. Would D'Hervilly and the British troops accompanying him be massacred because of what Jack was doing? She did not know much about war, but only a fool would think that the count and the British would land in France safely now. French troops would probably be waiting for them.

Shouldn't she tell someone, anyone, what she knew? Shouldn't she go to the authorities?

"Are you ready?" Jack asked coldly.

She slowly turned and stared at him as he stood in the doorway of her bedchamber. His face was taut, his eyes dark and flat. He was clad for travel in his dark brown wool jacket. She slowly stood up. "I was falling in love with you."

His expression tightened. "I never wanted your love, Evelyn, and I never expected it."

How his words hurt! "My God, you meant it, didn't you? When you said our desire was just lust."

His eyes blazed and he did not answer her.

"I don't understand," she said, sickened. And she was not referring to what she had just said. "I will accept that you are a cad, a rogue, a man who takes lovers unconscionably—" and his face hardened "—but you have an entire family whom you adore, and they are all British. Dear God, Julianne's husband was in France, fighting the revolution! When you give state secrets to the French, you are not only betraying your country, you are betraying them."

"You are leaping to conclusions," he warned.

"I know what I heard. Comte D'Hervilly has amassed an émigré army, and he will be meeting a Chouan army—after invading France." She wiped at fresh tears as they arose. "And you will soon tell LeClerc precisely when they will invade—won't you?"

He moved. His strides were like pistons as he approached, his face enraged. Evelyn cringed as he seized her arm. "You have one choice, Evelyn, and I mean it. You are to forget every damned word you heard."

Was he threatening her? "And if I cannot?" she cried. "If I go to the authorities?"

"Then you are placing your life in jeopardy!" he exclaimed shaking her. "Swear to me now that you will forget this day. Swear it!"

She shook her head, crying. "You mean, I am placing *your* life in jeopardy?"

He lifted her chin. "No, I meant exactly what I said. My life is already in jeopardy, Evelyn. If you tell anyone about this, you are placing your life in danger. I am looking after you, damn it. I do not want you hurt by any of this."

"I don't believe you," she managed. "I just don't know what to believe!" Was he now, absurdly, incredibly, trying to protect her? Or was he trying to protect himself?

"You might believe in me," he said harshly.

She froze. "Deny it, then. Explain it away."

He stared. And when he spoke, he was calmer. "I am not a French spy. You misheard—because you did not hear the entire conversation. I am asking you to give me the benefit of the doubt—because you care about me."

She stared incredulously. Was she supposed to believe him? She knew what she had heard—what she had seen! Was she supposed to trust him? Because she wanted to trust him! And he was now using the fact that she cared— that she was falling in love with him—to gain her compliance. "That's not fair," she whispered.

He stared, hard. "Nothing is fair."

Nothing is fair in a time of war, she thought. He had said so last night.

"I can see that you have doubts. What if you are wrong, Evelyn? How will you feel if you go to the authorities, accusing me of treason, if I am innocent—when I am the man you love?"

"Don't play me!"

"Then don't play war games!"

She stood, shaking. "And what if I am right? What if you are giving the republicans our military secrets? What then? British soldiers—and émigrés—will die!"

"Since when did you become such a patriot?" he shouted.

"Others believe you a traitor—there is a bounty on your head!" she shouted back. And that was the final coup de grâce, she thought, the proof that she had not misunderstood. For wasn't he running the British blockade? How could any Englishman do such a thing?

"Yes, there is. And at times, I run the British blockade— which is why there is a bounty. But I told you last night, I run the French blockade lines, too. If you care for me, you will forget everything that happened today. If you truly care, you will make the decision to trust me."

"You are using my feelings against me!"

"Then let your heart decide!"

"Damn it!" Evelyn cried. Her heart would lead her astray, as it was protesting wildly now. And she was almost ready to forget that entire, horrid afternoon. "What if D'Hervilly leads his men into a massacre?"

"What if you are wrong?" he shot back. He stared for a long moment. "And what about Aimee?"

She gasped, not because his tone was so dire, his stare so frightening, but because he was involving her daughter now. "How dare you bring Aimee into this!"

"This is war, damn it, and this is a war game, Evelyn, one you will be playing if you tell anyone what you have heard. I don't think you understand that the stakes are life and death."

She whispered, "Life and death for whom? D'Hervilly and his men—or you?"

His eyes flashed with impatience. "Life and death for him, them, me…and you."

She gasped. Now she truly did not understand. Now she felt as if she were drowning, she was so far out of her depth. "Are you protecting or threatening me?"

His eyes widened. "I would never threaten you—I am not a monster! Good men—and good women—die every single day because of this war and the games we play. I do not want you to be another damned victim of this war. I am trying to protect you in spite of your accusations."

"If you are trying to frighten me, you are succeeding."

"Good. Hopefully I have frightened you into a memory lapse." He seized her valise. "Aimee just lost her father. She cannot afford to lose you, too." He left the room.

Evelyn cried out. She did not know what to do, or even what to believe. She did not know why he might wish to protect her, for if he were a scurrilous spy, he had no conscience. And she was also afraid he was using her feelings to gain her silence.

But what if she was mistaken, what if he was innocent? With more tears arising, she slowly followed.

HER UNCLE'S CARRIAGE halted in the driveway at Roselynd, Evelyn having spent the past hour in the backseat fighting tears. It was truly over, she kept thinking, as she could hardly continue a love affair with Jack Greystone now— and he undoubtedly did not even want one. He seemed so hateful now. It had been lust, anyway, not love.

Her grief was consuming.

But she also kept recalling the night he had helped her and her family flee from France. And as much as she fought it, she recalled their voyage to France and his lovemaking last night.

It was as if she had memories of two entirely different men.

The first was not real, she reminded herself. The French spy was the genuine Jack Greystone.

Except, he wanted her to give him the benefit of the doubt—he wanted her to trust him. A part of her wished to do just that!

But she would not be that foolish, she thought grimly. She would be strong. She had a daughter to protect. She must stay out of these war games.

As she alighted, the front door of the house opened and Aimee ran out. "Mama! Mama!"

Evelyn turned, holding out her arms, thrilled to see her child now, no matter the staggering heartbreak. Aimee flew into her embrace. Evelyn knelt and rocked her, as much to find comfort as to greet and hold her daughter.

"Mama! You are crying!" Aimee accused.

She was crying—when she had hardly shed a single tear over her husband's death. In the past few hours since her discovery on the beach at Looe Island, she had shed a thousand tears. It amazed her that Jack Greystone could hurt her this way.

And there had not been even the briefest, or most cordial, of goodbyes. Jack had sailed her to the cove below her uncle's house, the short voyage taking a bit more than an hour. He had stood stiffly at the ship's helm the entire time, while she had stood at the railing, her back to him. He had been angry; she had been engulfed in her own anguish.

He had not escorted her ashore. One of his men had done that. Evelyn had wanted to look over her shoulder at him, one last time, but she hadn't. She had forced herself not to look back.

"I am still sad, about your father." Oh, how she hated lying to Aimee now! "But I am so happy to see you, *chérie*."

"I'm sad, too, Mama, but Laurent took me to the inn and look, we have a puppy!" Aimee beamed.

Evelyn rose as she saw Laurent coming out of the house, a chubby tan puppy with small floppy ears bounding ahead of him, its tail wagging. The pup was as large as a full-grown Labrador. "Is that a mastiff?"

Laurent gave her a sheepish smile. "Mr. Trim's bitch had a litter, and we went to see the puppies. Aimee insisted, madame." His smile vanished, alarm in his eyes. "Are you all right?"

In that instant, she forgot about the new and soon-to-be very large addition to their household. Jack had asked her to believe in him, but not convincingly. In that moment she also knew that she could not betray him to Laurent. And she knew her motives were not related to the jeopardy such a revelation might put her in. Was she giving him some benefit of the doubt, even though she should know better?

"Our journey was not successful," she replied.

His eyes widened.

She met his regard briefly, and then knelt to pet the puppy, which was jumping on her skirts. "Get down," she said. "What is his name?"

"*Her* name is Jolie," Aimee said. "We are keeping her, aren't we? Please! She already sleeps in my bed!"

How would they feed that dog? Evelyn sighed. "Yes, we will keep Jolie, but you will have to make certain she doesn't chew the furniture we have left."

Aimee promised, and ran sideways back into the house, the pup leaping after her.

Watching them, Evelyn had to smile. The sight of her daughter playing happily with the puppy was a beautiful one. "A smaller dog would have been so much easier to feed," she said softly.

Laurent took her hand. "There is no gold?"

"Apparently it was stolen, for Jack dug up the entire area." Laurent followed her as she went into the house. *"Mon Dieu,"* he said. "And now it is Jack?"

She started, handing him her small valise. Her pulse was racing. She was almost ready to confide in Laurent, at least partly, and tell him that she had had a brief affair. "Yes, it is now Jack."

"You have been crying. Somehow, I do not imagine that you have been crying over the gold."

"Actually, I cried for a great many hours, on board his ship, but not because there was no gold. Henri should have made certain we had something for our future." She was firm as she turned to the flowers on the only table in the entry hall. She began to rearrange them. "He left us penniless, Laurent. It is inexcusable."

For once, Laurent did not rush to his beloved master's defense. "I do not know how he did such a thing," he confessed.

She paused, a rose in hand. "I am no longer in mourning." As she spoke, she realized she would never wear black or gray again, or not for a very long time. "Ask Adelaide to press my burgundy gown."

He straightened. "I think you are making the right decision, madame, as Henri was ill for so long!"

She took his arm, forestalling him. "I had an affair with Jack." Oh, how calm she sounded.

His eyes grew as large as saucers.

She smiled grimly. "I believe I fell in love."

"Madame!" He began to smile in delight.

"No." She shook her head. "He warned me he would break my heart Laurent, sooner or later, and in a single day, he did just that." Before he could speak, she said, "I cannot supply details. But I was a fool, and it is over."

He took her hand and squeezed it. "Madame, how can it be over? When you are still so deeply in love?"

"I am not in love," she said, and the moment she had spoken, she knew that Laurent was right. She was still in love, no matter the extent of his perfidy. She was in love with a traitor.

Unless he was innocent and, somehow, she was wrong.

Laurent put his arm around her. "You have had a lover's quarrel, madame, and you are just too inexperienced to realize it. Have no fear. Monsieur Greystone will be at this house in no time at all—and he will have flowers in his hands."

Evelyn knew her smile was a frozen one. Jack Greystone was not going to appear at Roselynd, and especially not with flowers. On that point, she had not a single doubt.

CHAPTER ELEVEN

THE PUPPY WAS growing, Evelyn thought with a frown, as she watched Aimee and the mastiff frolicking about the front lawns through a window in the entry hall. A week had passed since she had returned from Looe Island, and the pup had already grown significantly in size.

She could not regret allowing her daughter to keep the dog, because they were constant companions. But it ate a great deal, and she was afraid she would simply not be able to afford it for much longer. She had also banished it to the kitchens at night; it did not need to share her daughter's bed!

Her heart lurched. Tomorrow she was driving out to the tin mine. Her visit would not be a surprise, for she had sent a letter to the new manager earlier in the week, informing him of her plans. She had also spoken with two banks, one in Fowey, the other in Falmouth, to find out if it was even possible for a woman in her straits to borrow funds, and if so, how much credit might be available to her. She had not been reassured. Her application would not be considered until she could prove ownership of Henri's estate! And once she managed to do that, she had been warned that the outcome was not promising. Apparently Henri had used up all his credit long ago, and impoverished widows were considered unworthy of loans.

She had tried to explain that, with the price of tin as high as it was, she would have enough revenue from the mines, once the repairs were made, to pay back the loan. But neither clerk had seemed interested in her assessment.

She sighed, wishing the heavy feeling in her heart would go away.

Laurent kept telling her that it was a lover's quarrel, and Jack would soon call. She had finally shouted at him that it was far more than a lover's quarrel, shocking him to no end. He had been grossly insulted, and she had had to apologize. Her grief was making her the worst of shrews. Even Aimee looked at her with worry now.

She had to move on. But it was extremely hard to do, considering that she had spent an entire night in his arms. And even if she could forget that evening, how could she forget the conversation she had overheard on the beach, or the conversation they had had afterward?

She had given that conversation a great deal of thought—it was almost all she could think of. She could not allow a British-led émigré army to invade Brittany and face a certain massacre. She had since decided she was going to have to speak with the authorities—soon. It was her patriotic duty.

The idea made her feel violently ill. She was not certain that she could actually betray Jack. She wondered if she could claim to have overheard a pair of men she did not know. And if she did that, she would be lying for him—when he did not love her as she loved him.

She hugged herself, impossibly saddened. Then she saw a carriage coming up the drive. She stared, unsmiling. It was still too far away for her to make it or its occupants out, but she was certain it was Trevelyan.

She had sent him a note requesting his call. She was boxed in now. Therefore, she would do what she had to do—she intended to ask him to advance her the funds she might need for the mine's repairs.

She had no pride left; she was that desperate. But what was worse was that she knew he was fond of her, and that his affection would make him inclined to help. Didn't that make her as unprincipled as Jack? Abruptly, Evelyn shoved her misgivings aside. She walked into the kitchens to ask Adelaide to bring tea—and only tea—with some sugar cubes and lemon. Trev would understand.

She went back to the front door and opened it, making certain to smile. Trev was standing with Aimee, his hand on her back, and the puppy. Then he bent, picked up a stick, and threw it for the dog. Jolie raced after it happily, barking.

Aimee clapped her hands as the mastiff sniffed about the stick. It decided to grasp it, and Trev instantly praised her. "Now, Aimee, go to her and pet her, then toss it again and say fetch," he said. "Soon you will be able to play fetch with her, anytime you like."

Warmth stole through Evelyn as Aimee ran up to the dog, telling her how good she was. Aimee took the stick and Jolie began leaping about in excitement. Her daughter threw it, shouting, "Fetch!" Instead of chasing the stick, Jolie began jumping up and down around Aimee.

Evelyn felt like crying. She decided then and there that she would never give the dog away. And one day, Trevelyan would make a wonderful father. It was so obvious.

Then she realized that Trev was watching her. She reminded herself to smile. "Hello."

Unsmiling, he approached. "What has happened? You look so sad!"

She inhaled. She hadn't wanted him to realize the state she was in. "I was enjoying watching you with Aimee," she said, meaning it. He was so kind, she thought, and he was handsome and honorable; why couldn't he make her heart race?

"You seem stricken, Evelyn, but I won't pry. I was thrilled to get your note." He took her hand and kissed it, but his gaze remained worried.

"Thank you for coming," she said. "And thank you for teaching Aimee how to play with her dog."

"That is a large dog for a little girl." He smiled, following her inside.

"I was away for a few days, and when I came home, it was a fait accompli."

"Really? Where did you go?"

She hesitated before the salon, wishing she hadn't brought up the subject of her brief voyage.

"You look as if you were caught stealing from a cookie jar," he said softly.

She couldn't quite smile. "Henri left some valuables behind in France. I went to retrieve them, but they were gone—stolen, perhaps."

He choked. "You went to France?" He was incredulous, and as she hurried into the salon, he followed, his eyes now wide with growing comprehension. "Wait a moment. Let me guess. This is why you were seeking out Jack? Did he take you to France, Evelyn?"

She smiled tightly at him. "Yes, he did, and it was a brief trip." She was final.

He stared at her in absolute disbelief. "I cannot believe," he finally said, "that my friend would actually transport you to a country we are at war with. In war-infested waters!" he added. "Why didn't you come to me? I have a great many connections. And I would have gone to France for you!"

She sat down hard on the nearest chair, trying not to cry. "I meant to reward him well," she said.

He was skeptical. "Greystone did not take you across the Channel for a few pounds—or a thousand pounds!"

He now stared very closely. "Something has happened, it is obvious. Why are you upset?"

She stared back at him. Should she confide in Trevelyan? Should she tell him, not about the affair, but about the conversation she overheard on the beach? She so needed a confidant, and she so needed advice. But she felt ill again; she could not do it. "I was counting on those valuables, Trev. Now, instead, I must investigate my mine, and find a way to make it profitable."

"I wish to help," he said immediately. He sat down beside her and seized her hands. "You have a child to feed—not to mention a very large dog that will grow for some time." He finally smiled.

His gaze was searching hers now. In that moment, Evelyn knew he harbored a romantic interest in her. She could not mislead him. "You are so kind," she cried. "I do need a loan. I have already gone to two banks, but I must prove I have inherited Henri's estate. They also indicated they would probably refuse me."

"I would never refuse you," he said, releasing her hands and standing.

She stood, as well. "I do not want to manipulate you, not in any way."

"That is an odd statement."

"Not really. I asked you here today so I could ask you for a loan. I was told that I need to make repairs to the mine before it can be profitable. Obviously I don't have the means to make any repairs. But once those repairs are made, I can repay you." She swallowed. "So you see, this is not a social call."

He shook his head grimly. "I did not think it was, actually—as you are in mourning."

She tensed, instantly thinking of the shameful night

she had spent in Jack's bed. She hoped she was not blushing.

"Why are you afraid to ask me for a loan? You are my friend, Evelyn, and you are a beautiful, gracious, kind woman—one in dire straits. I wish to be the gallant dashing to your rescue." He smiled, clearly trying to ease her mind.

"You are a heroic man. I treasure our friendship."

His smile vanished. "But?"

"I cannot return any romantic affection," she said harshly. "Not now, not yet—and maybe, not ever."

He stared, lowered his gaze and slowly paced. Evelyn stood very still, watching him. Then he faced her. "I understand. I wasn't asking for romantic affection—but I must admit you have captured some of my interest."

She could not meet his gaze. What should she do now? She did not want to mislead him—and even broken, her heart seemed to be already taken.

"But I am not in love with you, Evelyn. I am intrigued, and perhaps I could fall in love with you, but that day has not yet come."

Her relief was boundless. "I am so glad we have our old friendship back."

"You have my friendship, Evelyn, whether you want it or not. However, I do have one question for you."

She knew what was coming and she froze.

Trev stared. "He has turned your head, hasn't he?"

Evelyn simply stared.

"You do not have to answer—that is answer enough."

She clasped her hands. "We aren't even friends!"

"Of course you are not. I suggest prudence, Evelyn. Greystone is a rake, he is interested in you and little good will come of your association with him." He was firm. "Besides, infatuation is only that."

Evelyn was at a loss. She wanted to deny any interest on her part, including infatuation, but that would be a terrible deception to make. And it felt good, in a way, to have a confession out in the open, even if she had not made it—even if he was so astute that he had guessed some of the truth.

"How much do you need?" he asked softly. Tears of relief and gratitude arose.

"I don't know yet." Then she realized that Laurent had come to the door. They both turned to him.

"You have another caller," Laurent said. "Lucas Greystone."

It took her a moment to comprehend him. Jack's brother was at her door? Her heart skipped wildly as she realized what his arrival meant. Jack had sent Lucas to help her, in spite of what had happened.

Trevelyan came to stand beside her. "You are acquainted with Lucas Greystone?"

"He is here to help me with the mine," she whispered. Why would Jack send his brother to her aid now?

"That is an excellent idea," Trev said. "Lucas knows more about mining than anyone else I know. And he will certainly decide what repairs the mine needs, and how much you will need to finance those repairs."

Evelyn regarded him, thinking about all she had learned. "Do you know him well?"

Trev nodded. "Yes, I do."

She hesitated. "Can I trust him?"

"Lucas is a gentleman, if that is what you are asking."

She flushed. Jack was a spy—but hadn't he said that his brother managed the family estate? And wasn't Julianne married to a renowned Tory? There was no reason to believe that Lucas was involved in the war.

"I think I will go and leave you to your discussion."

Evelyn looked up at him, impulsively taking his hand. "Thank you so much."

He bowed. "Anytime, Evelyn—you need only ask."

They walked together into the front hall, where Lucas Greystone stood. "Lady D'Orsay?" He bowed briefly. He was tall and golden, broad-shouldered and nearly a twin version of his brother. "I am Lucas Greystone, and my brother has insisted that I must help you with your tin mine, at all costs."

EVELYN SLOWLY PREPARED for bed, now braiding her long dark hair. As she did so, she stared at her reflection in the mirror.

Jack had sent Lucas to help her. Why?

Lucas had spent a single hour with her after greeting Trevelyan, who had then left. He had taken a cup of tea and asked a dozen questions, none of which she could answer. Then he had asked for permission to visit the mine, which he wanted to do that afternoon, on his way back to London. She had given it instantly, writing a new note to her manager. And when he had left, he had had all of her mine ledgers in his possession. He wanted some time to go over the accounts, and when he was done, he would return them to her.

She had thanked him profusely.

"Of course, it is my pleasure. But do not thank me," he had said. "Thank Jack. He made it abundantly clear that I had no choice but to rush to your side. You must have made a great impression upon him." And with that, he had left.

Why would Jack wish to help her? Did that mean that he had some feelings for her, still?

What other reason could there be?

Evelyn realized that she wished, desperately, that he

still cared, even though he was a damned spy. Tears arose. God, what was wrong with her?

And as she wondered that, a man appeared in the mirror behind her, smiling with malicious intent.

He was slim and dark, elegantly dressed, but with a missing front tooth—and he was holding a knife.

Before Evelyn could scream, she was seized from behind, the knife placed hard against her throat. She cried out in pain as the blade nipped at the sensitive skin of her throat.

A paralyzing fear consumed her. *He was going to slit her throat.*

Her heart slammed. Was Aimee all right?

"Vous devriez fermer vos portes la nuit, Comtesse." You should lock your door at night, Countess.

"Aimee?" she gasped, struggling. And as she seized his forearms and writhed to free herself, she felt a pinprick on her throat—and then she felt blood trickling down her neck. "Please!" she gasped. "My daughter!"

"I would not speak if I were you!" He jerked hard on her.

She choked in fear, but she went still. *Dear God, was Aimee all right?*

"I have a message for you," he said softly, his mouth on her ear.

She whimpered, afraid the knife would cut deeper into her throat. But the feeling of his lips made her want to retch, as did the feeling of his body against hers.

"If LeClerc is betrayed, you and your daughter are the ones who will pay. *Comprenez-vous?*"

She was pressed even more tightly against his body now. Evelyn was afraid to nod. She whimpered.

"Comprenez-vous?" he demanded, jerking on her. "Betray us and you both die!"

"Yes," she sobbed, "Yes!"

She was released and Evelyn fell, clutching her moist throat. She heard him running out of her bedroom and down the hall. Downstairs, she heard a door slam closed. Jolie began to bark.

She gasped, struggling to stand, and then she staggered across her bedchamber and into the hall. She was ready to scream for her daughter, but if Aimee was asleep, she did not want to awaken and frighten her. She rushed into her bedroom, which was entirely in darkness. Aimee was soundly asleep in her bed.

She sagged against the bed, then fell to her knees on the floor, choking on fresh sobs. Aimee was all right. She thanked God.

And Jolie had stopped barking. Did that mean the intruder was gone?

She now touched her throat. How much blood was there? If Aimee awoke now and saw her this way, she would be terrified.

And as she had that thought, she heard footsteps in the hall. She rushed from the chamber, closing the door behind her, and almost collided with Laurent, who held a taper high.

He turned white. *"Mon Dieu! Qu'est-ce que c'est passé? Evelyn! Vous êtes d'accord?"*

"Shh! I have been attacked, but I am fine." She collapsed against the wall.

"You are hardly fine!" he gasped. He shoved his arm around her and dragged her into her bedroom. There, she sank down on the bed. He set the candle down, found a handkerchief, and quickly inspected her throat. "It is only a cut! Who did this?"

Evelyn stared at him, dazed. How had that intruder

gotten in? He must have broken a lock. The lock would have to be fixed. "I don't know," she whispered.

"You don't know?" he cried. "Who would do this? What did he want? Was he a thief?"

Evelyn hardly heard him. The man had broken into her home, cut her and threatened her and Aimee. He could come back at any time, and he had implied that he would do so. She did not know what to do. Change the locks, get another dog, start guarding the house... And what if, dear God, LeClerc was betrayed—not by her, but by someone else? Would she and Aimee be hunted down anyway? Would the intruder come back? Would he kill her? Kill Aimee?

This is war, damn it, and this is a war game.... The stakes are life and death.

I do not want you to be another damned victim of this war—I am trying to protect you.

Jack had tried to warn her—and he had been trying to protect her! He might be a spy, but he had known what she had not, that she was in danger the moment she had overheard that conversation between him and LeClerc. God, that was so clear now.

"Yes, it was a thief," she lied to Laurent. She had to, for his own protection. "He wanted jewels."

Evelyn reached for a pillow and hugged it. What should she do now? Because she had to protect Aimee, and she was involved in these war games, when she did not want to be!

They could go to London—except, they had no funds to spare for a room!

Evelyn trembled. It felt too dangerous, to stay at the house now. But she had nowhere else to go.

She wanted to ask Jack what she should do. He might

be a spy, but she believed he wanted to protect her and
Aimee—now she believed it with all of her heart.

"I am getting my pistol and locking the house," Laurent cried. "Will you be all right?"

Evelyn did not know if she would ever be all right
again, but she managed to nod. He left, determinedly.
Evelyn took a few deep, calming breaths, got up and took
out her own pistol from beneath the bed. It was loaded,
of course, but she checked it anyway. Then she took up
a taper and went downstairs to help Laurent secure the
house.

JACK HALTED HIS gray stallion abruptly. It was late afternoon in early May, and spring had finally arrived in Cornwall. The sky was blue, the clouds white, the sun bright.
A few wildflowers and gorse had begun to bloom, turning the moors purple. And for the past hour or so, since
leaving the outskirts of Bodmin, he had been the only
traveler on the road.

The Black Briar Inn was ahead. He stared, aware of
his tension, and too late, annoyed with himself for choosing Trim's tavern for his meeting. He had already run to
Roscoff and delivered an entire shipload of fine Chinese
silks. He had decided to make another run for more of it,
and he was meeting an investor. He hadn't thought about
it when he had sent Thomas Godfrey a note, suggesting
Trim's establishment as the place to meet.

He was thinking about it now.

He nudged his stallion forward, but at a walk. Unlike
the road, the inn was busy—a dozen horses and carriages
were parked outside. He preferred a crowded establishment; it was easier to escape notice. Just as he preferred
an isolated, untraveled road—it was impossible for any-

one to follow him without his being noticed, not once he left the vicinity of the city.

And Roselyn was about a half an hour's ride away.

He was grim. Evelyn had been haunting his thoughts—and not happily. He was angry every time he thought about making love to her. Not because he regretted it, but because he hadn't been able to control his urgency, because his passion had been frantic and frenzied, as never before. He did not want to have experienced such desire, not then—and not now.

For he remained heavily in lust; his damned desire had not abated.

He could manage unrequited desire. However, he was furious when he recalled her accusations against him.

Of course, he was a spy—for both sides. So in a way, she was right. But damn it, she was also very wrong. For in the end, he would put his country first, above even his own life.

How ironic it was, he managed to think sourly. Jack Greystone, the mercenary, was a patriot at heart!

He had no intention of explaining himself to her or telling her about his role in the war. He would not tell her about his activities because he did not want her involved.

I love you.

This is not about love. It is about lust.

His dark mood had never been worse. She could not love him. She did not even know him. But if she *did* love him, she would believe in him, never mind the rumors, the gossips, his notoriety and the damned bounty that was on his head.

Like the whole damned country, she thought him an outlaw.

He had to stop thinking about Evelyn. In a way, he was her first lover. She was a mother and a widow, but as inexperienced and naive as a debutante. The one night they had spent together had proved how innocent she was. He had been savagely thrilled to be the one to show her true passion.

He remained in lust—not love, he insisted to himself—as never before, and why not? She was also gentle and kind, determined and intelligent, and brave. He cursed again. She was, most definitely, a very beautiful and very extraordinary woman. The affair they had begun should have been full-blown by now. Instead, it was over, just like that, and he could hardly stand it. The attraction raged, disturbing him to no end. But there was more.

She did not deserve to be a part of this goddamned bloody war. No one did. He wanted her out of it. He would even admit he had the frank urge to protect her now—but, then, hadn't he always had that instinct, since first meeting her in France? So much for his lack of a conscience or a soul. The gallant lived within him, still.

He truly hoped she had forgotten the conversation she had overheard. He had meant every word when he had told her that if she spoke of it to anyone, she could be putting her life and her daughter's in the gravest jeopardy. Since leaving Bodmin, he had begun to consider calling on her—to make certain she was keeping his secrets.

He trotted his stallion into the inn's courtyard and dismounted, tying him to the porch railing, some distance from the other horses. Jack strode up the front steps, pushed open the tavern door and paused, quickly scanning the entire public room.

A dozen tables were occupied. He saw Godfrey, seated alone at a table, not far from the counter behind which Trim and a tavern wench were pulling ale. There were no red uniforms present; he had discerned that instantly, and now, more carefully, he looked for suspicious patrons—officers in plain clothes and other spies.

His glance slammed onto Ed Whyte, who sat with two men, who seemed equally scurrilous, and they were playing cards. Whyte was not in the British armed forces, but once in a while he ferried information about the British navy and British fortifications to the French. As a French agent, he was at the lowest end of the scale, and insignificant.

But Jack thought of Evelyn, who had been robbed, and his heart began a slow, dangerous thudding.

Smiling to himself, Jack walked over to Trim. "Good afternoon, John. You are doing a good business today."

Trim beamed at him. "I am so pleased to see you! It has been some time. What can I get you?"

"Is there any news out of Roselynd?" He had not premeditated the question, and he could barely believe he was asking.

"The countess's servant was in a couple of weeks ago with her daughter. They took one of my mastiff pups." He was proud.

Jack kept smiling. "That is a pretty child," he said. "She looks so much like her mother."

"Yes, she does. My wife has been meaning to call on the countess. Perhaps I will send her to do so. Oh, I did hear some odd gossip—that she was at several banks, seeking credit."

Evelyn would find a way, Jack thought, to get through her dire financial situation. Hopefully Lucas would be able to turn the tin mine into a profitable enterprise. "It is too bad that her husband failed to provide for her and their daughter."

"Yes, and I heard the banks might not advance her any funds, but Lord Trevelyan was in the other day. He told me to advance her credit if she ever comes in here, and he will pick up the bills."

Jack remained impassive, though inwardly enraged. But of course Trevelyan was pursuing Evelyn, and he would make such a handsome, noble gesture. "He will probably advance her whatever she needs," he said grimly.

"I am hoping he will court her, when she is out of mourning," Trim said. "She needs a husband and he is a fine gentleman."

Jack turned away. "How right you are," he said, his back now to Trim. And John Trim was right. He knew it—but he couldn't be happy for her or them. "Excuse me, Trim."

Jack walked toward Godfrey's table. He was a short, portly man, in a curly white wig and a teal satin coat. "My God," Godfrey said. "What a place!"

Jack glanced past him at Whyte, aware of being even more annoyed now than when he had first walked into the inn. "It suits my purposes," he said. Pulling out a chair he swung it around backward and straddled it. "How are you?"

Godfrey slammed down the dark amber contents of a glass. "Eager to hear what you plan next."

Eyeing Whyte again, Jack told Godfrey about the Chinese silk. "I would have to run for Roscoff immediately, otherwise, the silk will have been sold. I am offering you a 50 percent share, Tom. My profits from the last run were thirty-five hundred pounds—and I had the silk sold before it ever reached our shores." As he spoke he thought of Evelyn.

I am offering you a fair share. How am I going to pay you?

You decide....

"I am in. How much do you need?" Godfrey's question interrupted his thoughts.

Jack was relieved. He told him, and Godfrey assured him he would leave a check at the bank in Fowey, where Jack had his accounts, in the same name as the deed to Looe Island. Godfrey then said, "Are you having a drink? If so, I will join you, otherwise, I am getting back to London." He grinned. "I have a new mistress, Jack. An opera singer from Venice. And she is only twenty!"

Jack laughed. "I would go back to London if I were you," he said, thinking again of Evelyn. Was he ever going to forget how she looked at him with such passion, when she lay beneath him in bed?

Godfrey agreed, pumped his hand and left.

Jack did not move, still straddling the turned-around chair. He stared across the crowd at Whyte.

That bastard had robbed Evelyn.... Evelyn, who claimed to love him but had no faith.... Evelyn, whom he could not stop thinking about, whom he still wanted—and whom he was worried about.

He seethed, staring.

Whyte looked, saw him and started.

Jack felt a savage pleasure begin. Oh, how he meant to pick a fight! He stood, kicking his chair aside. It fell over.

The tavern became silent.

Paling, Whyte stared as Jack sauntered over. "Hello, Ed."

Whyte leaped to his feet. "What is wrong? Greystone, if I have crossed you, it was a mistake!" There was alarm in his high tone.

Jack laughed without mirth, and slammed his fist into Whyte's face.

The man crashed backward into an adjacent table, the patrons there leaping up and rushing away.

Jack seized him before he could get up and landed another blow to the other side of his face. Whyte choked in pain.

Then Jack pushed him down on the table and straddled him, his dagger now pressed fully, sharp edge of the blade first, to his throat. "I want the Countess D'Orsay's sapphires."

Whyte sputtered. "Don't."

"Don't what? Don't do this?" He drew a fine line across the jugular, only nicking the skin.

Whyte shouted. "All right! All right!"

"Like hell it is all right. You stole from the countess. That is not all right, Whyte." He took his knee and placed it on Whyte's groin.

Whyte turned red, choking on the pain, his eyes bulging. Jack released his knee, bent close, and still holding the dagger to his throat, whispered, "Where are the jewels?"

Whyte managed, "In my saddlebags!"

Triumph seized him. Jack slid his arm around him and let him stand, still holding the blade to his throat, Whyte now in a viselike grip. "Trim," Jack called. "Get his saddlebags."

John Trim rushed from behind the counter, holding a musket. He ran outside. A moment later, he reappeared with a pair of dusty, cracked saddlebags. Jack jerked his head at an adjacent and empty table. Trim laid them down and went through them. He produced a small cloth bundle.

"Open it," Jack said.

Trim did, exposing a large sapphire ring and a pair of earrings. "The countess's sapphires!" Trim exclaimed.

Jack smiled at Whyte. "I will tell her you have seen God, my good fellow. And God works in mysterious ways." He released him, hard.

Whyte clutched his crotch, groaning, as the men in the crowd chuckled and laughed. Chairs scraped back. Seats were retaken. Jack bundled up the sapphires and put them in his pocket as Whyte and his two friends hurried outside. Watching them through a window, Jack said, "I am sorry, John, for causing an uproar."

"The poor countess! You were right to take back her jewels," Trim said. "If I had known that Whyte was robbing her, I would have stepped in. I was here that day. I warned her not to seek him out!"

Whyte had finally mounted, with help, and he and his cronies left. "She doesn't listen," Jack said softly. How was he going to return the jewels without seeing her? But didn't he have to speak to her to make certain she had understood that she must forget everything she had overheard on Looe Island?

Trim was staring in some surprise.

Quickly, Jack smiled—blandly. Had he just sounded like a love-struck idiot? "What can I give you for any damages?"

Trim looked at the single broken chair. "Probably a shilling or two."

Jack gave him a pound, patted his back and walked through the tables toward the door. A few of the men seated there turned to greet him and cheer. "Well done, Greystone," someone said.

Clearly, the countess was well liked.

And why wouldn't she be? Everyone could see that she had had a difficult life.

Jack went to his stallion, suddenly realizing that he wanted to see Evelyn, terribly, and for that very reason, he should not go near her just yet. He could send Trevelyan to check up on her. Trevelyan could return the sapphires. He was a caller anyway. He might even confide in his friend, partially, and use Trevelyan to keep her out of danger.

And he was so involved in his musings that when he realized that someone had come up to stand behind him, it was too late.

Jack started to turn, instantly sensing danger, and he just glimpsed a huge, dark object before it struck the side of his head. He gasped from the stunning pain. Stars exploded before his eyes. As he staggered, trying to reach for his dagger, another blow followed, directly across his kidneys, this one from behind, from another man, and he fell. And then the blows rained down on him as he was hit with the butt of a gun, repeatedly, and as he was kicked, many times, in the back, the chest, the ribs.

He had been taken by surprise. He was going to die.

Bright lights filled his vision. He swam in pain. And then, through the horrific haze of pain, he realized that the beating had stopped. He tasted blood.

Had Ed Whyte done this?

"Do you know where your loyalties lie?"

His mind blazed to life; he knew that thick French accent. Jack tried to blink away the exploding stars; he tried to see. A face with a dark complexion and dark eyes swam before him now—a very familiar face.

"You had better not be deceiving us, *mon ami,*" Victor LaSalle said softly. "We will not tolerate treachery."

LeClerc suspected the truth, Jack realized. Now the stars faded, and their gazes met. He suspected Jack spied for both sides.

LeClerc smiled coldly at him. "Make certain you are with us, *mon ami,* and not against us," he said very softly. "Can you hear me?"

Jack nodded. Instantly pain stabbed through the side of his head. Someone moaned—he realized it was him.

"Good. Know this. If you betray us, those you love the most will pay a terrible price for your treachery."

Jack tried desperately to comprehend him. What the hell was he saying?

LeClerc leaned so close now, Jack could feel his breath. "Your pretty mistress will not be pretty anymore, and I will enjoy every moment I spend with her."

Jack gasped—and groaned.

LeClerc stood and nodded at the man standing with him. The fellow kicked Jack hard in the ribs another time. Jack screamed.

"That is to make certain you understand the consequences of all your actions…*mon ami*."

Jack heard him perfectly now. He understood him. LeClerc would hurt Evelyn, rape her and then destroy her. He had to warn her. He had to protect her.

Jack heard horses galloping off. LeClerc and the other man were gone. He tried to push himself to sit. As he began to do so, pain exploded in his rib cage, his head. With the explosion of pain, there was blinding light. And then there was only darkness.

CHAPTER TWELVE

EVELYN SAT BOLT upright, awakened from a deep sleep, the dog barking madly. Someone was banging on the front door. Fear seized her—it was the middle of the night! She leaped from her bed as the barking and knocking continued, lighting a taper quickly and then grabbing the pistol she now kept on her bedside table—and it was loaded. Fully awake, she ran barefoot across the room and encountered Laurent rushing down the corridor, holding a carbine and a candle. He was also barefoot.

"Who could be at the door?" she cried.

His eyes were wide and wild, his nightcap askew. "Thieves do not knock."

No, thieves did not knock; this was an emergency, then! They both hurried down the stairs, Evelyn's heart thundering with alarm and fear. They did not have close neighbors. Was a stranger at her front door?

Laurent called loudly, "Who is it? Who is there?"

The frantic pounding ceased, although Jolie kept barking. "Madame! It is John Trim! Hurry!"

Evelyn stumbled in surprise as they reached the front hall, sharing a confused glance with Laurent. What on earth had happened? Trim's inn was an hour away! Then as Laurent started to lower the carbine, she seized his arm. "It could be a trap."

He blinked in shock at her.

She could not believe she had become so suspicious, so

wary—but she was not about to forget being threatened by LeClerc's crony the other night. They had changed the locks on the house already. Trim could be outside with anyone, including another armed intruder with malicious intent.

Evelyn set the taper down on the hall's single table, while Laurent kept his held high. She hurried to the door, holding her pistol tightly. She did not think her heart had ever pounded with so much force. She cocked the trigger and aimed the gun in the direction of whoever was standing outside. She nodded at Laurent to go and open it.

He opened the door, revealing John Trim. The innkeeper was huddled in a heavy coat, his hat pulled low, and in the dark, all she saw were the whites of his eyes and his pale, frightened face. "My lady! Forgive me! It is Greystone—he insisted!"

Evelyn now saw a wagon in her driveway, another man standing beside it. In the dark, she thought she recognized the fellow, but wasn't sure who it was. "What is wrong?" she cried. She could not imagine what had happened to bring Trim to her door this way, or how Jack was involved.

"Greystone is badly injured! I found him outside the inn, and we wished to tend him, but he insisted, very strongly, that we take him here instead!"

Evelyn had frozen. Jack was hurt? Jack was in that wagon? She could see no one there!

"He has been unconscious for the past hour!" He turned and ran back to the wagon.

Jack was hurt—so hurt that he was prone.

Realizing what was happening, Evelyn rushed to the edge of the front steps, ready to run down to them, even barefoot and without a robe. She shivered, her gaze locked on the wagon as both men lowered the back and reached within it.

In real fear, Evelyn watched as Trim and the man she now recognized as Will Lacey, one of the villagers, dragged Jack to the edge of the wagon's bed. She bit her lip hard to keep from crying out, as they then maneuvered Jack into a sitting position. Evelyn gasped as his head rolled back, as he slumped between them. He was unconscious, as Trim had said.

Laurent ran past her. "You will catch an ague," he warned as he went to help the two men.

Evelyn could not go inside, not now, as Trim and Will started forward, dragging Jack from the wagon and taking him with them. He moaned, stumbling.

"Help us if you can, Jack-O," Trim said. "We are at Roselynd."

Jack now attempted to walk with the men, staggering as they both dragged and carried him toward her. He groaned again. "Evelyn?"

If only she could help—but there was nothing she could do. If only he would be all right!

She stepped aside as they approached, Laurent with them and holding his taper high to light the dark way. She finally glimpsed his battered face and covered her mouth with her hands, to prevent her frightened cry from escaping.

Blood had dried on one side of his face.

And now, she saw the blood on his white shirt.

Oh, God, what had they done to him?

Who had done this to him?

They reached the top of the front steps, both Trim and Will panting from the exertion of carrying such a large man. Jack remained slumped in their arms between them, but their gazes met. His was glazed with pain. "Where do you want us to put him?" Trim asked.

"We will put him upstairs. He needs a proper bed,"

she heard herself say briskly. Was that her speaking, so calmly, so sensibly, when she was sick with fear now? "It will be difficult, but he will recover better there than on the couch."

He whispered, "Evelyn."

"Hush." She managed a smile. "You must help them get you upstairs. It will be an effort, I know, but once you are in bed, you will be much happier." How much blood had he lost?

He smiled at her, the pain clouding his eyes. "I am always happier…in bed." And he turned ghastly white.

"Jack!" But it was too late…. He slumped over; he had fainted.

"It is for the best," Laurent cried.

Her heart pounding, Evelyn followed the men inside as they half dragged and half carried Jack across the hall, and then, with great difficulty and agonizing slowness, up the stairs. He remained unconscious through the ordeal. Finally they reached the second floor.

Evelyn now ran ahead. She hurried into a small, unused chamber and quickly laid her pistol down—she hadn't realized she still held it. Laurent rushed in, as well, and together they turned down the bed. Laurent began lighting tapers. Adelaide appeared, her face ashen. Trim and Will now dragged Jack to the bed. "On three," Trim said.

Evelyn now clamped her hand over her mouth. The bedchamber was mostly lit and she could finally see how badly Jack was injured. The bloody side of his head was frightening. He had clearly been struck above his left ear, and blood had dried on his cheek and temple and in his hair.

He wasn't wearing a jacket, and there were also numerous bloodstains on his shirt and even on his breeches. It was as if he had been kicked and punched repeatedly.

Had he also been struck with a heavy or sharp object? Or, dear God, had he been shot? She was sick.

And now Trim counted to three and they heaved Jack onto the bed. He woke and cried out and cursed.

Evelyn ran to him, taking his hand in both of hers, gripping it firmly. "You are safe now."

His lashes lifted. His pain-filled gaze met hers, but without recognition.

She was only vaguely aware of the audience they had. "You will be fine," she said softly. "I am going to take care of you now."

His eyes brightened with the light of recognition. His mouth softened and for one moment, their gazes held. Then he fainted again.

Evelyn's insides roiled. "What happened?" She began to unbutton his shirt. "Was he shot?"

"We don't know what happened—but he has been badly beaten," Trim said. "And, no, he was not shot. When I saw the blood, that was my first thought, too."

She was shaking like a leaf, but Jack needed her now. She almost lifted his hand and kissed it, but managed to refrain. She pulled aside his shirt and managed not to cry out when she saw the bruises and abrasions covering his chest. She was so sick now. "Who did this?"

"We don't know. Maybe it was Ed Whyte."

"Whyte?" she gasped, turning to stare at Trim and Will.

"Jack was at my inn, my lady, and he and Whyte had a row. Whyte left, then Jack did. A customer found him out front. Clearly he was attacked when he left the inn. Mrs. Trim thinks he has broken several ribs. Broken ribs are painful, Lady D'Orsay, and that would explain why he cannot stay conscious. But he did not give us a chance to tend him, so I do not know the extent of his injuries.

He insisted, very strongly, that we take him here, just before passing out."

She inhaled. Had Whyte done this? Oddly, she did not think so! She was looking at his head wound now, but it was hard to see, as dried blood and hair obscured her vision. "I need a basin of water, and some cloths—as well as soap and brandy."

"I will get everything, my lady," Adelaide said, rushing away.

Laurent stood beside her. He murmured, "That head wound might need stitches."

"A blow to the head can cause a lot of damage, my lady. He needs a physician and he needs rest," Trim commented.

Of course he did—the closest doctor was in Bodmin. But Jack needed attention now. She opened his shirt completely—his ribs were mottled with bruises, too. She managed not to let tears arise. "Mr. Trim, I cannot thank you and Will enough for bringing him here. Please, let me give you a chamber for the night." She prayed for Adelaide to hurry.

"Can we help tend him?" Trim asked. "After you clean him up, I could wrap his ribs."

Evelyn did not know the first thing about nursing, much less bandaging a man's broken or bruised ribs. She intended to wash away all the blood, in order to see exactly what his injuries were. But she was hopeful now, and she looked at John Trim. "Do you know how to bandage his ribs?"

Trim smiled briefly. "This is the Bodmin Moor, my lady. Of course I do."

She realized she was still holding Jack's hand. She released it and stood up. "Then I accept your offer."

EVELYN HAD TAKEN a small wooden chair from the corner of the room and pulled it up to Jack's bed. She had been seated there for hours; dawn was staining the sky outside mauve. Jack remained unmoving in the bed. But he was sleeping, and for that she was grateful.

Laurent had helped her remove all of his clothing, except his knickers, and had stayed with her while she bathed away the blood, mostly because she was so shaken and she needed his encouragement, reassurance and support. A number of abrasions had caused the blood, and his most serious wound seemed to be the hole in his head, above his ear, but it did not appear to need stitches.

Trim and Will had remained downstairs, eating a small meal left over from supper, which Adelaide had served them. Once Jack had been bathed, she had called Trim up. Trim had begun to bandage his ribs, causing Jack to awaken. They had given him two excessively large glasses of brandy—for the pain. He had somehow, stoically, endured the bandaging, gritting his teeth, not uttering a word. And the moment Trim was done, he had looked at her, closed his eyes and fallen asleep. He had been sleeping ever since.

Evelyn had not moved since taking her chair by his bed, even though everyone else in the house had gone to bed. She had been battling tears for hours.

In order not to cry, she reassured herself. Jack was not going to die—broken ribs would hardly kill a man. And while an infection could, they had doused his wounds with brandy smuggled from France—the clear, undiluted alcohol that was so strong it would kill a man if drunk.

She wiped at her tears, and then continued to hold his hand. She wanted to know what had happened, and why— she wanted to know who was responsible for such a brutal beating. She did not know why he had been arguing with

Whyte, but the smuggler was a coward, and she did not believe he would attack Jack, not in such a manner. And she also thought she must send a letter to Lucas, which she would do in another hour or so. She would not tell his sisters what had happened, however—she did not want to worry them, and she would leave such a decision to Lucas.

Was this assault related to his spying? Hadn't she been assaulted and threatened ten days ago?

"Why…are you crying?"

His hoarse, broken words jerked her attention back to him. Evelyn met his weary, searching gaze and cried out, "You are awake!"

He moaned softly and asked, "What…happened?"

She kissed his hand. "You were beaten. Who did this, Jack?"

He was startled. "Where…am I?"

He did not remember? "You are at Roselynd. Trim found you outside of the inn. You had been beaten—savagely! He wanted to attend you there, but you insisted on coming here." She could not hold back the tears. They trickled down her face.

He had been staring steadily at her, but now, as if exhausted, his eyes closed.

Still holding his hand, she stroked his brow with her other one. His gray gaze flew open. "You are so concerned."

She trembled. "I am very concerned."

"Why?"

She was disbelieving. And she began to flush. "I believe you know why." She felt her color increase.

"No…I don't." He lifted his hand toward her face, and suddenly dropped it, groaning.

Not for the first time, she wished she had laudanum in the house. "Do you want some brandy?"

He was pale now; clearly, a simple movement was intolerable. When he did not answer, she realized he was struggling not to faint. Evelyn leaped up to bring him a glass, which she had ready. Trim had suggested he would need the liquor when he awoke. She was using the fine French brandy that Henri had kept, both for their own use and for entertaining guests.

She sat on the bed now, by his hip. He was lying prone, and she hesitated. He would not be able to sip unless he sat up. Yet she knew that moving him would hurt.

"Help me…to sit."

Evelyn set the glass down on the bedside table and put her arm beneath him, under his shoulders. He cried out.

She was dismayed and afraid—as she hadn't even moved him, yet. His eyes were tightly closed now, and sweat shone on his brow. He was panting.

A long moment passed. Jack inhaled and looked at her, his face hard with determination. "Help me sit, Evelyn," he said, and it was an order.

Afraid to hurt him, Evelyn began to lift him. He grunted, biting off a groan, now sweating, leveraging himself up. He finally cried out, seated upright, and very abruptly, she jammed two pillows behind him.

"Bloody damn hell." Jack sat there panting, his eyes closed, fighting the pain. Evelyn wiped away her tears and then picked up a damp cloth and wiped the sweat from his brow and temples. His lashes lifted and their gazes locked.

It was inappropriate, she thought, to be seated so closely on the bed beside him, but Trim would never walk in on them, and Laurent knew the truth. She smiled slightly and slid the washcloth over his upper chest. Then she laid it aside and put the glass to his lips. She helped him take a sip.

And when she began to remove the glass, he said, "I need a great deal more...than one sip."

"Of course you do." Evelyn helped him drink the entire glass.

When it was empty, she set it down. Jack remained seated against the pillows, his eyes closed again, sweat upon his temples and forehead. Sipping the brandy was an act of exertion for him. She wanted to question him, but talking would tire him, too.

She took up a damp cloth and laid it on his brow. After a moment, she removed it, and returned to her chair.

He opened his eyes and looked directly at her. "Thank you."

"Did the brandy help?"

"I'd like another glass."

She helped him drink another glass, in silence. When he was done, she finally saw the brandy taking effect. His mouth softened for the first time. The glazed look that had been filling his eyes faded. "Is that better?" she whispered.

He smiled slightly, his gaze going over her features, one by one. He stared at her mouth for a moment. "Did Trim bring me here?"

"Yes." She set the mostly empty glass down and clasped her hands in her lap. "What happened, Jack?" she asked, wondering if she was insane now. Had she imagined a new tension? Because Jack was injured, and surely, he was not thinking of kissing her now.

His gaze shifted past her, as if he was fascinated by the small room's bland decor. "I was attacked when I left Trim's inn."

Evelyn sat down in the small wooden chair. "Who did this?"

His gaze returned to hers. "I don't know."

She gaped. "You didn't see your attackers?"

"No, I did not. I was struck from behind, Evelyn."

She shuddered, staring. Jack was the most intelligent man she had ever met. She did not believe that he did not know who his attackers were—even if he hadn't seen them. "Trim said you argued with Whyte."

"Yes, I did. But Whyte would not have the courage to do this." His stare was so familiar now—unwavering, relentless. "Have you been caring for me by yourself?"

"Trim bandaged your ribs. They are probably broken. I did not know how to wrap them, but otherwise, I have been here with you since just before midnight."

He stared back. "My ribs aren't broken."

"You can't know that."

"They aren't broken." He was firm. He then said softly, "You seem frightened. Are you frightened for me?"

She nodded slowly, the urge to cry arising yet again. "Of course I am frightened for you."

"Do not cry for me," he said softly. "I am fine."

She swatted at her tears. "You are hardly fine! You have broken ribs! Your head was bashed in. You could have been killed!"

"I will soon be fine," he said firmly. "Gashes heal—so do ribs."

She wiped away more tears. "I must know the truth, damn it. If you know who did this, I must know!"

His eyes widened slightly. "I do not know who did this, Evelyn, and why would you want to know? Haven't you learned enough of my secrets?"

She thought about his greatest secret—his being a French spy. And how she wished she did not know that secret. But it was too late. She was involved in his war games. She thought about being assaulted and threatened in her own home. She could hardly tell Jack about the incident now. "Was this savagery related to your war activities?"

His smile was amused, but it was also affected, Evelyn was certain. "I am a smuggler, Evelyn, and I live dangerously. Even without the war—even before it—I have had my life threatened a great many times. There is no reason to think this is related to the war."

She thought about LeClerc. "There is every reason to think so!"

"I have made many enemies over the years." He was final.

She was breathing hard. Their gazes were locked. "What if the British have learned about you?"

"They would hang me, not beat me."

She sat upright, hugging herself. "That is very reassuring!"

He reached out, wincing, took her hand and tugged it away from her body. He lifted it to his mouth and said, "You are so concerned about me." He kissed it. Softly, he said, "I thought you hated me."

She could not believe the shocking desire that burned through her. She stared. Jack could have been killed last night. He lived so dangerously. He could be killed on any given day. "I could never hate you." Just then, she had nothing to hide. She leaned close, clasping his jaw gently. "My feelings haven't changed. I am afraid for you… because I love you."

He stared, his eyes darkening. "Bastard that I am, I am glad."

Evelyn searched his eyes, wishing he would give her some sign that he cared—that his feelings for her were far greater than a raging physical attraction. But he only smiled, and as he did, he murmured, "Come sit by me again."

She knew she should refuse. But he tugged slightly on her hand and she slid onto the bed. Her pads and bustles pressed against his hip. His slight grasp deepened. She found herself leaning over him, her silk-clad bosom against his bare arm.

"I have missed you," he said.

Her heart slammed. "I have missed you, too. But, Jack—"

"No. I am too tired to discuss this anymore." He turned his face and pressed a kiss against the side of her breast, in lieu of being able to rise up and kiss her properly. And then he sank back into the pillows, his eyes closed, his hand still closed on her wrist.

Her heart thundered with frightening force. He was weak, injured and exhausted, and she was overcome—with fear, with desire, with profound love. And as he finally began to breathe deeply and evenly, now asleep, she leaned close and kissed his unblemished temple. "I am afraid, Jack," she whispered. "I am so afraid, for us both."

"CAN I TAKE THAT FOR YOU?" Laurent grinned.

It was the next day, and Evelyn held a luncheon tray, and was about to go up the stairs. Jack had been sleeping for the past day and a half, and she imagined he would awaken soon. "I do not mind."

Laurent laughed at her. "You haven't left his side, madame, except to attend Aimee!"

"He will be hungry when he awakens!" she tried, flushing.

"You are smitten, and I approve," he said. But his smile faded. "But you refuse to discuss the real matter. You have been acting oddly—nervously—ever since that thief got into the house. I know when you are dissembling, if you beg my pardon, Countess."

She smiled grimly. "First a thief in the night, then John Trim—why wouldn't I be nervous?" She started past him, tray in both hands.

"I only wish to be of help!" he called after her.

On the stairs, Evelyn turned. "Laurent, I would tell you everything if I could—but I cannot." With that, ignoring his dismay, she hurried upstairs.

She had begun the habit of leaving Jack's chamber door open, so if he awoke when she was not with him and called for her, she would be able to hear him. She glanced into the small room as she approached and instantly saw that his bed was empty. Her heart slammed and she faltered, her gaze veering to the window where he stood.

He was awake; he was even standing. She was thrilled, as he shifted slightly to glance at her.

Her pleasure faded. He wore only his tan wool knickers, and his back remained bruised, with several large purple spots. Seeing those bruises hurt her terribly. But his gold-streaked hair was disheveled and hanging just past his shoulders. His gray gaze was lucid, sharp. He was tall, broad-shouldered, impossibly muscular—impossibly masculine—he was the epitome of a beautiful man.

For a few seconds she watched him with appreciation. "You are awake!" she finally cried softly. But her heart was racing uncontrollably. Her mouth was even dry.

"I am most definitely awake," he said very softly, not smiling.

"And you must be feeling better, to be up and about." His stare was so direct. He had looked at her that way so many times, the night they had shared supper—the night they had become lovers.

He turned to face her fully, his gray gaze sliding from the tray she held down to her toes, and then back up to her face. "You are staring—as if you have never seen me without my clothes."

She flushed. She came into the room, placing the tray on the chair she had been using. She would not respond to his entire remark! "I did not know you would be up. You have been sleeping so soundly. It is three o'clock." Had his tone been seductive? It had certainly been intimate! And she was babbling. Why was she nervous now?

But it almost felt as if they were still lovers.

Jack took one last glance out of the window. "From this window, one can see for miles." He left the window, moving slowly, with care, clearly trying to avoid jostling his ribs. He walked to the bed and grasped the footboard, as if for support. He winced. "How long have I been here?" he asked, the foot of the bed between them.

She now became aware of the fact his powerful presence filled the tiny room. "John Trim brought you here the day before yesterday, just before midnight."

His gaze was searching. "I vaguely recall being outside his inn, after having been attacked."

"He said you fainted almost immediately after demanding to be brought here. Do you recall the carriage ride?"

"No." His gaze sharpened; his stare intensified. "Are you all right, Evelyn?"

She started. "Why on earth would you ask after me? You were beaten, Jack, and the attack was ruthless, I might add."

His gaze had narrowed. "I take it all is well, then?"

Uncertain of his meaning, she slowly said, "Yes, all is well." She thought about the intruder who had threatened her—LeClerc's crony. She would tell Jack about that incident when he was stronger. "You should not be out of bed!" she cried.

"I was testing myself," he returned grimly. "Where is my gun? My knife?"

She was taken aback. Clearly, the slightest movement hurt. But he was worried that, if his attacker returned, he could not defend himself. "Downstairs."

"Could you retrieve them, please?" Then he smiled, as if to soften his words.

"Are you still in danger?"

"I am always in danger. There is a bounty on my head."

She could not decide whether to believe him or not. Did he think he might be attacked again? "I will be right back." She ran from the room, her mind racing, and took up the gun, the powder and his knife from where the items had been left in the front hall. She hurried back upstairs. Jack had returned to the window and was staring outside to the south. Of course, the coast was not visible from the moors there.

Evelyn set the arms and powder down on the bedside table as he came back slowly to the bed. "Thank you."

"You are worrying me," she said. Was he staring outside—in case someone might be approaching?

"That is not my intention." He suddenly sagged, as if his knee had buckled, and he reached for the bedpost. He had paled.

Her alarm was immediate—he was still gravely injured. "You need to rest! Can I help you back into bed?" She hurried over to him and took his arm, determined.

"You can always help me to bed, Evelyn."

She flushed. "Jack."

He finally began to smile. "I'm sorry—I could not resist." He allowed her to guide him slowly around the bed. When he sat, he cursed, but indecipherably and under his breath.

"Can I help you eat? You must be ravenous."

He shook his head, his face hard, not even looking at the tray. "How many people know that I am here?"

She started. "My servants, Trim, Will Lacey, the Bodmin blacksmith." But now she realized the trouble he could be in—no one should know he was at Roselynd. "However, Trim and Lacey know better than to discuss your whereabouts."

"Everyone gossips. Hopefully, they will refrain." He studied her. "You know Evelyn, we have never discussed it, but you are a widow, living alone with a single manservant—in a time of war."

She was even more alarmed now. "The war is hundreds of miles away."

"Last year French deserters landed at Land's End—and they took a farmer and his wife hostage."

She hugged herself. "I am hardly on the coast."

"There are food riots everywhere."

She had not heard of any food riots in Cornwall, but she decided not to rebut. "What are you trying to say?"

"I am not sure a widow with a small child should live alone on the moors, as you are doing."

She was very grim, thinking about LeClerc's threats. "This is my home! We have nowhere else to go."

"You should think about returning to your uncle's—at least temporarily."

She cried out. "You have never said such a thing before! Do you want me to move away because of the attack upon you?"

His gaze flickered. "I want you to move for the reasons I have stated, Evelyn." He now looked at the luncheon tray. "Actually, I am very hungry."

She remained very alarmed—he was obviously changing the subject. But she managed a smile that felt grim and said, "Can you use a fork and spoon?" She placed the tray by his hip, on the bed.

He eyed her. "I am not an infant. I have had bruises and gashes before."

She sat down on the chair, folding her arms, even more determined now to find out what had happened and why—and if they might be in more jeopardy than she knew. She let him eat for a moment. "Do you recall the beating?" She hoped that today, as he was far more lucid and in far less pain, he would remember the assault—and who his attacker had been.

"No." He did not look up.

"Do you have any idea who would do this—and why?"

"No." He set his fork aside, having finished half of a bowl of beef stew. "But I vaguely recall your having already asked me these questions. Did you?"

"Yes, you awoke briefly yesterday morning. I don't believe you, Jack."

He slowly smiled. "Really?"

She hadn't meant to issue such a challenge, but she pressed on. "I think you know who attacked you."

He studied her, his eyes watchful, but not hard. "Evelyn, even if I did know, I wouldn't tell you. When we were on my island, I said that I did not want you involved in the war, and what I meant is that I don't want you involved in any aspect of my life that might be dangerous."

She thought about how he had insisted she was in danger after having overheard him speaking with LeClerc, and she thought about the threats issued by LeClerc's crony. And now there was this beating—which was not related to his smuggling activity. She was already very, very involved in dangerous affairs, she thought uneasily.

"Why do you seem alarmed?"

She jerked. "I am very alarmed, Jack—you were

brought here in the worst of conditions! Two weeks ago, I overheard that terrible conversation! Yesterday you tried to tell me that the beating was related to the free trade. But it was not, was it? This has something to do with your wartime activities."

"What a conclusion to draw!" he exclaimed, eyes wide with feigned innocence.

"You do not deny it?"

"You are too stubborn. I deny it, Evelyn." He did not bat an eye.

Yet she knew—she just knew—he was lying boldly to her now! "I wrote Lucas. I told him you had been assaulted and badly beaten."

He shrugged. "And did you tell him I am alive and well, anyway?"

"Of course!"

"He will probably show up at your door. As an older brother, he can be annoying. Sometimes, I think he has forgotten that I am a grown man."

"If he does come, I intend to ask him the same questions I am asking you."

"He will undoubtedly answer as I have." Jack shrugged and paled.

Evelyn leaped to her feet, then realized there was nothing she could do to ease his discomfort. She clasped her hands, when she wanted to clasp his. "Why did you send him here? I did not think you would, not after we had such an argument on the island."

He glanced away, instantly. "He could be of help. Just because we argued—just because you think me a traitor—doesn't mean I am indifferent to your plight."

She bit her lip. He had just referenced the terrible deception—the terrible betrayal—that stood between them.

He now looked directly at her. His gaze became piercing. "I am beginning to recall something, Evelyn, a vague memory. Or perhaps, it was a dream. Did you sit beside me, and were you crying?"

She froze. Yesterday she had been crying, and she had told him that she loved him, still. Carefully, she said, "Yes."

"You have been caring for me—you could have turned me away. Another woman would have done just that."

"I am not another woman. I would never do such a thing."

"No, you would not, no matter our differences. But tears? Why would you cry over a French spy—a traitor?" He did not add the words, *a lover,* nor did he have to, as they hung in the air between them.

She inhaled. "Stop. You are not being fair."

"I have no intention of being fair now. In fact, I am having some very odd memories." His eyes glittered.

"Of the beating?" She was hopeful.

He ignored that. "Did you help me drink brandy? Did you help me sit up?"

She frowned. How much did he recall? Had he recalled that she had declared her love? Should she make such a confession again? But he was the one who needed to admit to some genuine affection!

"I am furious that you were assaulted—whatever the reason. I was crying. Of course I would be upset to see you so badly hurt." She inhaled. "We are friends."

"I am beginning to think that you still care about me, and we were more than friends."

Was she red? Oh, how she must ignore that! "I want you to get well. And you are certainly welcome to stay here until you have recuperated."

"I know an evasion when I am given one…Evelyn." His voice hardened. "I thought we agreed—Roselynd is too isolated, too remote, for a widow living alone with her child."

They had not come to such a consensus—but he was so very right. "I cannot ask my uncle to take us in." But what else could she really do?

"I can." He was calm.

She started, immediately imagining being under her aunt's roof again. Then, she heard the dog barking downstairs. Alarm began.

"You have a dog?" He threw his legs over the bed, preparing to stand, clearly ignoring the immediate pain.

"Aimee has a puppy," she said. "Do not get up!" She rushed to the window and looked out. A carriage was coming up the drive, and she recognized it immediately.

"Who is it?" He was alert, pistol in hand.

"It is Trevelyan," she cried, relieved.

He sank back down on the bed, breathing hard and with an effort. "You told him I am here?" He was incredulous.

"Of course not!" She suddenly wondered what to do—but Jack was hurt, and Trevelyan could surely help them.

"Evelyn, send him up. I wish to speak with him—privately."

She tried to imagine why Jack wished a word, and was alarmed at the notion that he meant to discuss her.

"I am not asking," he said so softly she shivered. "I have matters I must discuss with him. And, Evelyn? Do not even think to eavesdrop."

She had intended to do just that. Somehow, she smiled tightly at him.

He smiled coolly back.

CHAPTER THIRTEEN

LAURENT HAD JUST let Trevelyan into the house when Evelyn came downstairs. Removing his bicorn hat, Trevelyan hurried to her. "I just heard," he said grimly. "How is he?"

Evelyn gasped. "You know that Jack is here?"

"Yes. There is gossip, Evelyn, and it might not be wise for him to linger here much longer." He studied her closely. "My butler told me that he was beaten and he is now recovering from his injuries here."

"He was badly beaten, Trev, outside the Black Briar Inn. But he is doing a bit better today. However, he can hardly move to another location." She could not imagine his enduring a carriage ride. "He just awoke, and he is asking for you."

Trevelyan started for the stairs. "May I?"

She seized his arm from behind. "Why is he asking for you? Do you know who did this—and why?" she asked quickly. If Jack would not tell her, perhaps Trev would.

"I do not know why he wishes to speak with me, but I have known Jack for years and I hope to help him out of any trouble that he is in." He smiled reassuringly at her. "And how would I know anything about the beating?"

She stared closely at him. "I have begun to wonder if you are involved in the war, too."

He laughed. "Evelyn, I have a very large estate to run. I have no time for wars and revolutions."

She smiled grimly at him, certain now that he was

very much involved, although she could not guess how. "He wants to speak privately. Go on up."

JACK WOULD HAVE PACED if he were capable of doing so without pain constantly stabbing through him. Instead, he sat on the edge of the bed, now holding his throbbing ribs, his thoughts racing, his head aching. While he did not remember much of the carriage ride to Roselynd, he recalled every single detail of the beating—and the threats LeClerc had made against Evelyn.

And now that she was gone from the room, he could blanch openly. Thank God she was all right!

But she could not continue to live alone at Roselynd. He would not allow it. Clearly, his enemies thought to use her to make him behave as they wished.

He was still in disbelief, as well as some shock. Now he knew that his interest in her was putting her in danger. If he hadn't invited her to Looe Island, if he hadn't made love to her, LeClerc would not have ever thought to threaten Evelyn. And the worst part was that he knew LeClerc would follow through on his threats.

He finally stood up, wincing, because he had to pace. His ribs hurt more now, but he knew they were not broken. LeClerc needed him in action, not in a sick bed.

The throbbing in his head also intensified as he slowly paced. He had to protect Evelyn—he simply had to. He should not be at Roselynd, but he had only come to find out if she had been hurt. He also must not resume any relations with her.

His heart lurched in an unfamiliar manner. Had she told him that she loved him? Had he dreamed her declaration—or was he, in fact, remembering it?

No good could come of her caring for him, and he

should not be glad because he suspected her confession had been real.

His mind was made up.

Jack turned as he heard Trevelyan's heavy and rapid footsteps. The baron's heir paused on the threshold of the room, his gaze sharp. He glanced back into the hall, and then entered, not closing the door. "Will you survive?" He wasn't smiling. But Trev undoubtedly guessed a great deal of the truth and being beaten up by the fanatics who would die for la Patrie was not a laughing matter.

Jack's expression was neutral. "Undoubtedly. Make certain no one eavesdrops."

Trev glanced into the hall again. "I suppose we are going to get to the gist of the matter that we have both, deliberately, made certain to never discuss."

"Yes," Jack said, thinking of Warlock now, and his circle of spies, "I suppose so."

Trev walked over to the room's single window and looked outside briefly. He turned. "This is a godforsaken place. Are there spies in this house?"

"I believe Evelyn's staff is loyal."

Trevelyan stared out the single window another time. "No one should have to live here."

Jack happened to agree. And clearly, Trevelyan remained fond of Evelyn. Jack despised the fact, but Trevelyan did not have a bounty on his head and more importantly, he hadn't been beaten up by rabid revolutionaries. However, that didn't mean he didn't have his own secrets. "What do you do—for Warlock?" Jack asked. He happened to know that Trevelyan had been to London a dozen times in the past two years—when he usually went to town no more than once or twice. He was obviously in the damned club.

"Whatever I can—when I can," Trev said sounding

vague. He smiled slightly, with a shrug. "My involvement in the circle is on an 'as needed' basis. I prefer it that way." Trev circled the bed. "And which of your 'friends' did this?"

Jack looked at him. "I have been playing both sides, Trev, for a long time."

"I suspected as much," Trev said. "So, can I assume a republican agent assaulted you? Being as Captain Barrow and his ilk wish for you to hang, and they would hardly bother with a pummeling when they could have the satisfaction—and the reward—of watching you hang. And Warlock would never jeopardize his own asset. He has better ways to bring recalcitrant spies to heel."

Jack wondered at the comment. Had Trev been forced into service? "My French comrades suspect me of treachery," Jack said softly. He had to sit. It hurt like hell to change positions and he grimaced.

"But they are right, aren't they?" He poured brandy into the single glass on the table and handed it to him. "You can pretend to the entire country that you are a reckless mercenary, available to the highest bidder, and that this is a thrilling game, but we both know that isn't true."

Jack sipped. "I am a mercenary. I enjoy every profit I make. I have, in fact, become very accustomed to luxury. I am enjoying my wealth."

Trev snorted. "You enjoy being hunted. You enjoy being a hunter. You enjoy the danger, and you would be up to your neck in this game, even if it did not afford you a single penny! I can think of no one better suited to being a double agent than you, Jack."

Jack decided not to argue, because Trev knew him too well. "I have been warned to reassess my loyalties," Jack said, now thinking of the threats against Evelyn. His insides curdled with fear for her. And he might try to deny it, but his feelings for her hadn't changed. They seemed stronger than ever, in fact.

LeClerc wanted to know when the Quiberon Bay invasion would take place. How would he withhold that information now? Yet he could hardly jeopardize the mission.

"That is a problem, is it not?" Trev was saying. "Because you can pretend to be indifferent to each cause, and you can claim to be playing both sides for your own self-aggrandizement, but I happen to know you cannot reassess your loyalty because in the end, you are as much a patriot as I am." Trev took up the bottle of brandy. "May I?"

Jack nodded and watched him take a sip from the bottle. Warlock would put Britain first, always. Jack had thought he would, too, but just then, he knew he would put Evelyn first.

He shuddered, afraid of what such determination meant. "Before we discuss this any further, I must know that everything we say here will be held in the strictest confidence."

Trev took another draught of brandy and put the bottle down. "And who are you afraid I will speak to? I am hardly playing the French spy, as you are," he said, referring to the fact that he would not be divulging privileged information to the enemy.

He did not want Warlock to know that Evelyn D'Orsay was now dangerously involved in this one war game—or that he meant to protect her. "You can speak of this to no one," he said firmly. "Not even to Lucas."

No slouch, Trev's eyes slowly widened. "You do not want me telling your secrets to Warlock!"

"I hardly said that," Jack lied easily, his face never changing expression, "but he should not be apprised, either."

Trev stared intently for a long moment. Jack knew he was trying to decide why Jack wished to keep the spymaster in the dark. "Go on. You have my word."

"I am in the middle of an operation," Jack said slowly. "I have to convince my French masters I am sincere, at least until the end of the summer."

"Spare me the details—I don't want to know what you are doing. Can you possibly convince them you are loyal? And if you can, what happens when this mission is over? What happens if it succeeds? Will the French then know you are the enemy?"

Jack's head was aching more insistently now, for he was wondering the exact same thing. "Until now, I have never doubted my ability to slither through this game. However, it is possible that in the fall, the truth will be out—and I will have two bounties on my head."

"How perfect." But Trev's blue eyes flashed with anger. "Looe Island will not remain a safe haven forever, Jack."

"You are worried about me?" Jack pretended amusement.

"We are friends."

He sobered. Candidly, he said, "I have never contemplated how this double-sided game might eventually end. I have been too busy, playing first the French spy, then the British one, while trying to avoid both our navy and the few revenue men who, from time to time, dare to appear in Cornwall." And it was true. At first, he had simply helped Lucas extract an émigré or two. Then Warlock had suggested he ferry information back from France. That had been easy enough to do, until he had decided to retrieve the information himself—and become a veritable spy. He had never before regretted his deepening involvement. He was simply too preoccupied with eluding one navy or another, avoiding the British authorities when on British soil, and eluding the French authorities when in France.

Now he thought about both of his brothers-in-law. Paget and Grenville had been spies in France and they had both managed to end their activities—and stay alive.

And now they were both husbands and fathers....

"You had better think about it now," Trev said. "I wish to help. This is my suggestion. You can either wriggle out of this current mission—and out of all involvement with the republicans. Return in fact to your life as a simple smuggler. Claim you are done with the war, as so many smugglers have done."

Jack hesitated. Trevelyan made it sound so easy. Warlock would not let him walk away, he was certain, and the rebels in La Vendée were so desperate for British aid now. Having met Cadoudal a number of times, he did not feel that he could simply turn his back on him and his cause.

And even after the Quiberon Bay invasion, was he truly ready to retire from these war games? He was only twenty-six years old! What would he do without the hunt, without the pursuit, the danger?

An image flashed in his mind's eye, of Evelyn, living alone with her daughter at Roselynd, when she needed protection, when she needed a husband and a family....

"I cannot get out now," he said softly. But he felt oddly uncomfortable as he spoke.

"I did not think so," Trev said. "Will you try to get out after this operation, in the fall?"

He was endangering Evelyn. She needed someone solid in her life, someone very much like Trevelyan, who spied only upon occasion, was not a double agent and hadn't been beaten to a pulp, or had his loved ones threatened. "I doubt it. I have always intended to see this war through."

"I am not surprised. What about Evelyn?"

Jack flinched as their gazes met and held.

Trev added, "You may be putting Evelyn in danger."

Jack set his glass down and stared grimly. "That is the last thing I want. How intrigued are you with her?"

His brows lifted. His smile was mirthless. "I am not in love, if that is what you are asking."

He was frankly relieved, when he should not be. "Why not?"

"I am only recently out of mourning," Trev said. "And she is most definitely still in mourning. Besides, we are old friends."

"When she is out of mourning, would you consider courting her? Would you consider marriage? One cannot help but notice that the two of you would make a good match."

Trevelyan was wry. "In case you have not noticed, she thinks of me as a friend, not a suitor. You are her knight in shining armor—or should I say, in rusted iron?" His stare hardened. "I think she is infatuated with you."

He wondered if Trev really thought her infatuated, and he knew he should not be pleased to hear his remark. "Has she spoken to you—about me?"

"If she has, I would not betray her confidence."

"Since when did you become such a damned gentleman?"

"Since my wife died," he snapped. "I have learned a lesson or two," he added more calmly. "Why did you come here? You could have gone to any number of places to hide and recuperate."

"I am worried about Evelyn, too. She may be in more danger than I am in." Jack's tone was grave.

"What the hell does that mean?" Trev cried.

"My French masters seem to think that I am fond of her. They have threatened her."

Trevelyan seemed to pale. "When?"

"At the Black Briar," he said.

Trevelyan's eyes widened. "They threatened her when they beat you? So they will use her against you?"

"They think to use her to gain my complete loyalty, but it is even worse than that. Evelyn overheard a conversation fit only for my ears and those of the republican I was with. She was discovered. And unfortunately, my French friend happened to recognize her from when she lived in Paris."

Trev cursed. "So they will threaten her—to encourage you to do their bidding—and she has knowledge she should not have?"

"Precisely," he said.

"You should not be here," Trev said, impassioned. "You should not see her again—not until you have gotten completely out of these war games."

Jack realized he was right. He also realized that Trevelyan did care about Evelyn, perhaps more than he was admitting. "I think I might be able to endure a carriage ride tomorrow. But I am also trying to convince her to return to Faraday Hall. In any case, I want you to look after her." He could not force a smile. He hated asking Trevelyan to play champion and protector now. Surely Evelyn would soon realize that her interests should be directed at the baron's heir, not at a disreputable smuggler and a notorious outlaw.

Trevelyan was quiet for a few seconds.. "That is magnanimous of you," he finally said. "This isn't casual, is it? She isn't a passing fancy. You have finally been ensnared."

Jack flushed. "I am not ensnared. I simply don't want her hurt. She is an innocent in all of this—I am sick and tired of seeing the innocent pay with their lives, when they have done nothing wrong."

"You will not be able to leave tomorrow," Trevelyan said after a long pause. "I imagine you need two or three more days before you can withstand a carriage ride. However, Evelyn can leave, with Aimee."

Jack clenched his fists, aware of his dismay—which he had to ignore. "That is an excellent idea."

EVELYN PACED BACK and forth repeatedly in the front hall, wondering at the conversation that was taking place upstairs. Oh, how she wished she had eavesdropped! She desperately wanted to know what they were discussing, and she felt certain it was the reason for the attack upon Jack.

She finally heard a movement on the stairs, and she saw Trevelyan coming down—his face set and grim. He paused. "Evelyn? Could you come up to Jack's room? There is something we wish to discuss with you."

Her alarm knew no bounds. *Both* men wished to speak to her now? What could they possibly want?

Somehow, she smiled. "Of course." She hurried to the stairs. "Has something happened?" she asked carefully as he stepped back so she could precede him up. "Your expression is so dire."

He smiled blandly at her. "Jack wants to speak with you, and I will leave shortly after."

Evelyn paused to look searchingly at him, but his casual expression never changed. Her alarm increased. She lifted the hem of her burgundy skirt and hurried upstairs, Trev following.

Jack sat on the edge of the bed, now wearing a pair of ill-fitting breeches and an equally shapeless shirt. He held a glass of brandy, but his gray gaze instantly locked with hers. He smiled.

And Evelyn knew a conspiracy was afoot. "Are you all right?"

Jack slowly stood up. "Trevelyan is going to take you and Aimee to your uncle's."

She jerked, confused. "I beg your pardon?"

"Trevelyan is leaving, Evelyn. It will soon be dark." Jack walked over to her and stared down at her. "I want him to take you and Aimee to Robert's—tonight."

She gasped, shocked.

"Laurent can bring your bags tomorrow," Jack added. "So you can leave immediately."

She was incredulous now. Behind her, Trevelyan said, "I am happy to do so, Evelyn."

She whirled to look at Trevelyan, who smiled at her. Becoming outraged, she turned back to Jack. "Are you coming with us?"

"No."

She began to shake, she was so angry. "I did not think so! As you cannot stand up without turning white from the pain! So I am to leave you here, alone, after you were savagely beaten?"

He seized her arm and bit off a gasp. "Evelyn." Pale now, he continued to hold her. "You cannot live here alone like this. It is simply too dangerous."

She would have flung him off, except that doing so would hurt him. "I am not leaving you here, alone, which would simply be too dangerous!" She finally turned to face Trev, and Jack let her go. "Why would you agree to this preposterous scheme? Jack is hurt. He can barely defend himself…. He was almost killed."

Trevelyan regarded her seriously for a long moment. Sorrow flitted through his eyes. "There is always a danger by association, Evelyn. Jack is an outlaw. He has many enemies. They gave him a warning. Next time,

they might think to do more—and you would be caught
in the middle."

She was shaking again. "If there is a next time, I mean
to be caught in the middle—so I can help him!" she cried
fiercely. "Do you both think there is more danger?"

Trevelyan stared, seeming dismayed and saddened.
"One never knows," he said. "Caution is usually a wise
course."

Evelyn hugged herself. She was certain Trev had just
realized that she was deeply in love with Jack, and she
wished he hadn't found out as he had, but she was too
upset to really care. She finally turned to Jack. "Why
do you want me to run away now—are you in danger at
the moment? This is my home…. My daughter is here.
I must know!"

He hesitated. "I am always in trouble, Evelyn. Danger
follows me everywhere—and it found me at the Black
Briar. Do I think that tonight, my enemies might appear
here? No, I do not. But Trev is right. There is danger by
association with me. I should not be here. I should not
have come here. And you should not be here, living alone
as you do, and that is regardless of what happened to me
the other day."

"I cannot even contemplate returning to my uncle's
while you are here. And before you protest, I am not leaving you alone in this house, not today and not tomorrow."

His stare was hard, but it was also searching. "Does
that mean you would consider leaving Roselynd once I
can go, as well?"

She inhaled. What kind of danger was he in? And what
about the fact that there was danger for her and Aimee
at Roselynd? LeClerc had threatened them! She wished
she had told Jack, but if she did so now, she would lose

the argument. "Yes, I would consider it—if you went to a safer place, as well."

Trevelyan broke the silence. "You are very much like a pair of lovers," he said quietly.

Evelyn tensed, but she did not look at him, her attention unwavering upon Jack. "Would you please go back to bed? You are supposed to be resting," she finally said.

His gaze was probing, holding hers. He handed her the glass of brandy and moved slowly to the bed. Evelyn rushed to his side, took his arm and helped ease him as he sat. He instantly held his bandaged midsection, his expression somber but steady.

Evelyn stared back as soberly.

"I do not deserve your loyalty," Jack said slowly. "Evelyn, you should reconsider—for Aimee's sake."

God, how he frightened her. "I cannot leave you alone when you are injured," she whispered. "I just can't. And you have my loyalty, Jack, deserved or not." She heard Trevelyan leave, but she did not turn. Jack remained unmoving, too.

She finally folded her arms and forced a smile.

Jack did not smile back.

EVELYN SAT DOWN HARD on the edge of her bed, a hairbrush in hand, absolutely exhausted. Trevelyan had left well before dark, several hours ago, and she had been able to rush downstairs in order to thank him for his concern and say goodbye. He had been so solemn, and he had advised her to leave Roselynd as soon as was possible. Then he had left.

Well, he now knew she was in love with Jack, and he might even have guessed that they had been lovers—she had not mistaken his comment. She was so sorry if she had hurt him. However, his concern aggravated her anxiety.

And she remained amazed that the two men had conspired against her as they had, even if they both thought to protect her.

Jack had gone to sleep in the late afternoon much to her relief. She had looked in on him several times, but he had been unmoving. Rest would help him heal all the more quickly.

She had finally taken a light supper with Aimee and the staff in the kitchens, before the kitchen's large hearth. And while Bette got Aimee ready for bed, she and Laurent had locked every door and every window, securing the house the best that they could.

It was late now—it was almost eleven. But she was restless and she could not sleep. Were she and Aimee in imminent danger? Was Jack? If only she knew why Jack had been attacked. If only she knew what kind of danger he was in.

He and Trevelyan were right. She should not be living alone with Aimee and three servants on the Bodmin Moor, not now that Henri was dead. Even if she hadn't overheard that conversation on the island, no widow should live alone this way. She dreaded returning to her uncle's, but she doubted she had another recourse. Even if she borrowed the funds, rooms in London would be prohibitive.

A footstep sounded in the hallway outside of her door; a floorboard creaked.

Evelyn seized her pistol and leaped up, training it on the open doorway, her heart slamming. Her hand shook and she cursed inwardly, because she could not hold it steady.

Jack moved onto the threshold and froze there.

Her eyes widened; so did his.

"Put the gun down," he said swiftly.

She did, her knees buckling. "You frightened me!"

"That was not my intention." His gray eyes flashed. And then he looked directly at her cotton-and-lace nightgown, at her loose flowing hair.

She sank onto the edge of the bed, suddenly filled with tension. Jack was in her *bedroom*.

And it was so very late, they were alone and he was clad in those baggy breeches, the borrowed shirt hanging completely open. His abdomen beneath the bandages was flat and hard. She did not dare look lower. "Why aren't you asleep?" she managed, her mouth dry.

He leaned against the doorjamb, his dark, indolent gaze holding hers. "Why aren't you?" And his gray eyes moved slowly over her face, over her nightgown, the appraisal so clearly sexual.

Desire arose instantly. It slammed through her like a cyclone. Evelyn slowly stood, breathlessly. "How can I sleep?"

"How can I?" His lashes lowered, hiding the heat in his eyes.

Did he mean to make love to her? He could hardly walk! But why else would he have come? "I cannot sleep because I am so worried about you." She wet her lips, nervous.

His lashes lifted. "I don't want you to worry about me," he said softly. "I don't want you to have to sleep with a gun."

She hesitated. "I began sleeping with a gun before you were attacked, Jack. I have always been aware of how isolated this house is." Of course, she was distorting the truth. She now slept with a pistol because of LeClerc and the threats his crony had made against her.

"I am going to leave tomorrow," Jack said abruptly. "And you are going to go to your uncle's."

"That sounded like a command, one you might give your sailors."

"Damn it," he said, soft and harsh at once. "You are an independent thinker—so much like Julianne and Amelia! But this one time can you not take an order and simply obey it?"

She quickly evaded his tangent. "You have not recovered from being beaten. You cannot recover in three days! You can hardly travel anywhere tomorrow!"

He said, "You are in danger now—because of me."

She became alarmed. "What do you mean to say?"

"I should have never brought you to my island. I should have never taken you to my bed. I have too many enemies, Evelyn. And look at what happened. You overheard my conversation with LeClerc, putting you in a terrible position. And then my enemies attacked me, and I came here—possibly attracting them to Roselynd."

She stood up, stunned. "You regret the time we spent on Looe Island?'

"Don't you?"

"No," she cried, her heart thundering. "No, I do not!"

He slowly shook his head. "I am a selfish bastard, but not as selfish as I appear. I can't continue to put you and your daughter in danger. I just can't."

She was disbelieving. Was he saying goodbye? Did he really mean to travel tomorrow? "We are hardly in any more danger," she began, and then she stopped. Oh, he was right, wasn't he? On that single point, he was right, and she could not deny it. She was in danger because she had been on his island, and his enemies might think to follow him to Roselynd.

"I see that you have finally realized that I am right."

She stiffened. "You cannot possibly travel tomorrow."

"I can, and I will." He was final.

If he left tomorrow, he would suffer terribly—and surely set back his recovery. And then what? And how would she survive when she did not know the extent of the danger he was in? She would worry each and every day! "Jack! What did they want? Why did they attack you? Please! I must know!"

"It was only a warning." He smiled without mirth. "If they wanted me dead, I would be dead now, Evelyn. They took me by surprise and I could not defend myself."

She cringed. "Then I am grateful it was a warning!"

He studied her very seriously now. "And I am grateful that you have not been harmed. I could not live with myself if you suffered more than you have, and on my account."

She tensed, thinking of the intruder who had threatened her.

"Evelyn?"

Had he come to genuinely care for her? He certainly acted like a man who cared. And she could not tell him about the intruder now—it would only upset him further. "If it was only a warning, why do you feel that you must rush off tomorrow—when you can barely walk?"

"Because I have so many enemies," he said flatly. "Any one of whom could decide to pursue me. Our association jeopardizes you."

She felt her heart lurch with dismay, with fear. "You are worrying me," she finally said. "We have every right to be friends. It almost sounds as if you wish to completely end our relationship."

His gaze smoldered. "It wasn't a dream. You told me that you love me—didn't you?"

She froze.

He started walking into the room and he did not stop until he had taken her shoulders in his hands. "Will you deny it?" he asked softly.

She slowly shook her head. "No."

He pulled her close and slid his arms around her. "I am an outlaw, Evelyn. I am a spy. This country is at war—and this war will not end tomorrow. I don't deserve your loyalty—and I certainly do not deserve your love."

She began shaking her head in protest. Tears welled. "I don't care that you are an outlaw—I don't care that you have been spying for the French!" Except, she did care, she cared greatly. And when he was silent, she realized what was missing—he had not declared any genuine affection for her. She wet her lips and breathed hard. "You asked me why I was so concerned about you. Now, I must ask you the same question."

"Don't," he said as he slid his hands from her shoulders up her neck to her face. "Don't ask me for what I cannot give."

She gasped. He refused to admit to any feelings, but surely he had them?

His mouth moved very close to hers. "I will go mad, if I do not make love to you one more time before I go," he said roughly. "Evelyn, I need you tonight."

She cried out, tears finally falling. Should she resist? But why? She loved him, even if he did not love her back—and her body was screaming for his now. And he meant to leave tomorrow. He meant to end their relationship.

She managed to meet his gaze through her tears. "I do love you—and I am not afraid to say so."

His arms tightened, immobilizing her with his embrace, as Jack kissed her, deeply, heatedly, wildly.

Evelyn had one coherent thought—this might be the last time they ever made love. And she seized his shoulders and kissed him back.

CHAPTER FOURTEEN

EVELYN LAY IN Jack's arms, breathless, her heart thundering. Her cheek was on his chest, their legs entwined. She could not believe the explosion of passion they had just shared, not once, but twice.

He clasped her hand tightly, then lifted it and kissed it. She felt him tense with pain as he did so.

Evelyn rose up on an elbow, still beneath the sheets. "Are you all right?" As she spoke, she began to blush. Jack had not made love to her entirely; she had made love to him!

He slowly smiled at her. "I am more than all right, Evelyn." His eyes gleamed and narrowed. "You are such a quick study."

She knew her color increased. "I am shameless." He had just shown her several ways to make love, none of which involved his being elevated above her, as he could hardly maintain such a position. She could barely believe what they had done.

"You are very shameless," he said with suppressed laughter, kissing her hand again. This time, he grimaced and lay back down carefully.

And now, as her mind cleared, as her heart rate dulled, she began to worry about his injuries. "Oh, dear, we have probably just set your recovery back."

"You have probably just helped my recovery," he said. "I do not think I have ever felt better." But then he began to sit up, with difficulty, his smile vanishing, an expression of determination replacing it.

Evelyn quickly slid her arm around him, now worrying about his decision to leave in the morning. She knew he would suffer terribly if he traveled. He needed bed rest—and they should not have made love. But he had said he wished to make love to her one last time.

She sobered, doused with reality now. Surely, he did not have the discipline to end their affair now. Surely, he cared about her, and their affair was only just beginning. She was convinced that he had some genuine affection for her.

"Do your ribs hurt?" she asked, the thrill of their passion now entirely gone. It was replaced by worry and fear. She did not want him leaving and facing any new danger alone. She did not want to be at Roselynd without him, either—it felt so much safer with him there. And she could hardly contemplate their parting and her taking Aimee to her uncle's.

Leaning into the pillows, he looked seriously at her. "Yes, they do. And they will bother me for another week or so, but they are bruised, Evelyn, not broken. I cannot regret being with you just now."

She wanted to touch his face, tenderly, but she refrained. "I have no regrets, either."

A wicked grin formed on his face. "I imagine you do not."

Was she blushing another time? She glanced at the door to his bedroom, which was open, and into the sitting room. "I hope everyone is asleep." Had she been as unrestrained as she was now recalling? Oh, she hoped not!

"You have awoken the entire house, undoubtedly."

She flinched in alarm, and realized he was teasing her.

She softened. "I already confided in Laurent. I told him we became lovers on your island."

His eyes widened. "I am glad you have a confidant, Evelyn, but are you certain that was wise?"

"He would never gossip about me."

He studied her for a moment. "I should go. We may have escaped notice for now, but we will not remain undetected if I spend the night with you."

She bit her lip, almost ready to ask him to stay, anyway. And what about the previous conversation they had had? "I dread going to my uncle's, and you remain injured and we both know it. You said that you did not think there would be any immediate danger. Why can't you rest for another few days?"

He eyed her. "Are we going to have the exact same argument of a moment ago? I think not." He reached for her, but as he did, she saw him deliberately fight the urge to wince. "And you know as well as I do, if I stay here with you, I will not be getting a great deal of rest."

She pulled away. "So you are leaving in the morning?"

"We will both leave." He was firm. "I know that you are reluctant to return to your uncle's because of your aunt. But it is so much safer for you. I cannot leave, not if you remain here."

She studied him and he stared back. Of course she should not remain at Roselynd alone. She knew she had to tell him about the intruder; she could hardly keep such a secret, and it might even affect him, as a spy. With tension, she turned, slid to the floor, and with her back to him, she quickly shrugged on her nightgown. When she turned, he wore a soft smile. "You are so impossibly alluring," he said.

She refused to be distracted. "You are right about

one thing. I should not be living here at Roselynd with Aimee."

"Good, then we are agreed." And as if he knew there was more, his eyes narrowed. "Evelyn?"

She hugged herself. "I haven't told you everything, Jack."

His stare hardened. "What does that mean?"

"About two weeks ago, the day Lucas called, we had an intruder break into this house."

"What?" he exclaimed, his eyes darkening.

"I was preparing for bed when I realized an intruder was in my chamber. He seized me. And he had a knife," she said.

Jack leaped from the bed, grunting. "You are telling me this now?" He was incredulous.

She flushed, but he pulled a sheet from the bed and wrapped it around his waist. "I could hardly worry you when you arrived at my door bloody and unconscious!"

He loomed over her. "What happened, Evelyn?"

She trembled, as his tone was so dangerous. "He held a knife to my throat and told me that if LeClerc was betrayed, I would pay, and so would Aimee."

He blanched.

"He then left," she added, her voice tremulous.

He inhaled harshly. "I cannot believe you are telling me this now! Were you hurt?"

"No. But I was very frightened."

"And this was two weeks ago? Why the hell didn't you send word?"

"We were hardly on good terms," she cried.

"So what?" He suddenly seized her arm and pulled her closer. "Don't you know I would always come to you when you are in danger or trouble?"

She shook her head. "No. I didn't know."

"Then know it now!" He released her and paced angrily. "Forget Faraday Hall. You are going to London. Amelia is about to have a child, so you can stay with Julianne and Paget."

Evelyn gasped. "I can hardly impose!"

"But I can—and I will. Robert cannot keep you safe, not if something happens to LeClerc. Paget keeps guards. The authorities often watch the house, as well. And because of his past as Pitt's spy, I can tell Dominic everything. I can, in fact, think of no safer, better place for you."

"What about Looe Island?" She could not believe she had been so bold, but she realized she wished to stay with him then.

"I am not always there, Evelyn. When can your household be ready to depart?"

Evelyn was amazed by the rapidity of events. "Jack, it would take days to ready my entire household to leave."

"Be ready tomorrow," he said. "I am giving you one more day."

THE HOUSE WAS IN AN UPROAR, with everyone, herself included, packing up their belongings frantically now. It was the following morning, and Evelyn thought they would be ready to depart in the midafternoon. Packing up clothing had been the easiest task, but for an extended stay, there were personal possessions, books and ledgers, which had to be boxed, too. And with prices so dear, she would not leave behind any perishable items, either.

Laurent had gone to town and Trim had lent them his wagon, so they had two vehicles instead of one.

Now Laurent appeared on the threshold of Aimee's room. "This is madness," he said, scowling. "But if you must know, the pantries are almost bare, and my wagon does not have any space left in it."

She smiled, avoiding eye contact. "That is wonderful."

He folded his arms and stared. "Why are we in such haste? What has happened? Why won't you look me in the eye?"

She flushed. She could not tell Laurent that Jack was a spy, and that she had been threatened by his French allies. Nor could she declare that Jack's enemies might simply seek him out at Roselynd, putting her and Aimee in harm's way. She had deceived Laurent deliberately, telling him that Julianne had invited them to spend the summer with them in London. Laurent had been thrilled—he loved town—but then he had become suspicious. After all, most of the ton left town for their country estates in the summer. "I just think it's best for Aimee, to live with some luxury. I could not refuse Lady Paget."

He harrumphed. "You spent the night with him."

She tensed. Jack had come to her bedchamber again last night, but she had not been surprised—she had been waiting for him. Without saying a word, he had taken her in his arms, and this time, he had not left her until dawn. "Yes, I did."

"This is about Greystone, I am certain. For some reason, he is sending you to London. As he was badly beaten, can I assume he is afraid of his enemies? But why, why on earth would his enemies be a threat to you?"

She sat down hard on the edge of her bed. "Oh, Laurent. If I could tell you his secrets, I would. Can't we please leave it at that?"

He sat down beside her. "I have never seen you happier— and I have never seen you as frightened."

"A widow should not live alone as I am doing, not on this desolate moor, not with a child—not in a time of war."

He took her hand. "There are so many rumors about him. But I think I know what is happening. He is one of our spies—and the French think to hurt him—or even kill him. And now you are his lover. So you could be in danger, too." He was pale. "We could all be in danger if he stays here with us."

Evelyn was relieved that he thought Jack a British agent, but before she could respond and reassure him, there was a firm knocking on the front door. She stood up, wondering who could be calling—perhaps it was Trev.

Jack came striding into the bedroom from his own chamber, where he had been resting. She smiled but he did not smile back, instead hurrying past her to one of her bedchamber windows, as Jolie began barking and the knocking resumed. In that moment, the banging became demanding and urgent. Evelyn knew it was not Trevelyan at her front door.

Her room faced north, and the driveway and the garden in front of the house was below the window. Jack stiffened as he looked outside. "Soldiers," he said.

Evelyn felt her heart lurch with alarm. She ran to the window and saw five mounted cavalry in red uniforms and black helmets, muskets strapped to their shoulders, swords at their sides. Their bay horses were lathered and blowing. The determined knocking sounded again. Jolie barked more insistently now.

"Is anyone home?" someone shouted. "Open up!"

She looked up at Jack, aghast. He said, "They are here for me."

He was going to be arrested, she thought in panic. But he laid his hand on her arm, smiled briefly and faced Laurent. "Delay them," he said. "Give me five minutes, if not ten."

"Where are you going?" Evelyn cried, but he was already rushing across the room. "How can you possibly hide?"

He did not answer, now in the hall. Evelyn took up her gun, meeting Laurent's eyes. He said, very low, "He found tunnels, madame, his first day here."

She was stunned. "He was barely conscious!"

"He knew where to look, and he sent me to find them. One leads to the stables. The rest, I do not know."

The tunnels had been used for smuggling by the house's previous owners. And clearly Jack had known where to find them—he had made certain to locate an exit for himself, should the need for a hasty escape ever arise. "You will show me later," Evelyn managed.

His gaze dark, Laurent nodded. Evelyn hurried out of her bedroom, her pistol in hand, Laurent following.

In the corridor, she glanced back at Jack's room. It was already empty. He had taken the back stairs.

They ran downstairs, just as the officer opened the front door. "Sir! You have scared me witless," Evelyn cried.

Standing outside, the door wide-open, he glanced at the gun she held, and at Laurent, and then past her into the entry hall. Evelyn heard footsteps and turned. Adelaide and Bette stood there, Aimee between them. Jolie was on a leash, now wagging her tail.

"Mama?" Aimee cried, frightened.

Evelyn gave the officer a fierce, warning look. She then rushed to her daughter and knelt, somehow smiling. "It is all right, darling, these are British officers—good men, who will protect us from bad people like the French soldiers in Paris."

Aimee was trembling and near tears. "Tell them to go away!"

"I intend to do just that." She kissed her cheek. "Adelaide, take her into the kitchens. And take Jolie." Dismayed, she heard how sharp and nervous she sounded.

Adelaide gave her a worried look, hurrying Aimee and the mastiff puppy off, Bette following. Evelyn waited till they were gone before she turned to face the officer. "You are scaring my daughter, sir."

"I wonder why." He bowed formally. He was about her own age, and rather good-looking, with brown hair and green eyes and a wide, flat nose. "Captain Richard Barrow, of the Royal Horse Guards. I presume you are the Countess D'Orsay?"

Had he just challenged her? She was taken aback. "Yes, I am Lady D'Orsay, Captain, and my daughter is frightened because she has not forgotten what it was like, living in Paris under Robespierre. She is afraid of all soldiers, and with good cause."

His smile was cool. "And I am sorry to have frightened a child, so I must apologize. Have I interrupted, Madam Countess?"

"Of course not," Evelyn returned.

"I was knocking on your door for a great many moments," he rejoined, his gaze on hers.

Evelyn gestured around her. "As you can see, I am quite preoccupied today."

"Yes, you are obviously vacating the premises. May I ask why?"

"We are going to London, sir." She inhaled. "Not that it is your concern."

"I will decide that," he said.

He was most definitely hostile, she thought. "How can I help you, Captain?"

That cool smile reappeared. "I have learned that you are harboring an enemy of the state, madam, a man wanted for treason. Where is Jack Greystone?"

She felt paralyzed, but with an effort, she said, "You

have misheard, sir. I would hardly harbor an enemy of this country."

"I have it from an excellent source—and the gossip is all about the countryside."

"I never heed gossip, nor should you. As for your source, he or she is wrong."

He smiled slowly at her. "If you do not mind, we will search the house and the grounds." He turned and signaled his men.

Alarm flooded her. Was Jack in the tunnels? Would he attempt to hide in the stables? Or would he try to leave the estate? In any case, she had been told to delay, and delay she would.

"I am sorry, Captain, but as you can see, we are very busy today as we are about to leave for town. This is a highly inconvenient time for you to turn my household upside down. Hopefully, my word will suffice. Mr. Greystone is not here."

He stared. "I would also remind you, Countess, that if you are aiding and abetting him, that is also a very grave crime, punishable by imprisonment or transportation."

She stiffened. "He is not here, sir."

"I am afraid, then, that your word is insufficient. For I have also been told, on good authority, that you are friendly with Greystone. We are going to search the house, the stables and the grounds."

"Do you have papers, documents, if you will, or even some kind of warrant? Otherwise, I do not think you can simply barge into my home!"

"Of course I can search this house—and I do not need a warrant or any unusual authority to do so." His cool smile returned. "This is war, Countess." He turned and waved his five men, now dismounted, inside.

Evelyn was horrified. She could be arrested. Of course,

she would always help Jack, but how had she gotten into such a position? It would be different if her daughter did not need her so.

And she prayed the captain would not find Jack.

As his men entered the house, Barrow turned to her. "Why don't you take a seat, madame? In the salon, if you please."

Evelyn realized it was not a request. She shared a worried glance with Laurent, as Barrow added, "And you, as well, my good fellow. Please take seats and remain there until I tell you otherwise."

Evelyn inhaled and walked into the salon with Laurent. She sat on the sofa, as he did, and then he took her hand. They exchanged another look but said nothing, listening to the booted steps of the soldiers as they went through every room on the ground floor, then went upstairs.

No more than a quarter of an hour had passed when Barrow appeared on the threshold of the salon, his gaze cool. "My men have found five used beds, not four. So you have had a guest?"

Evelyn stood up.

"Do not deny it, Countess. For we have also found a bloody shirt in the garbage."

Laurent got to his feet. "The shirt is my cousin's, Captain. He was in a fight two nights ago and I put him up without the countess's knowledge. He left this morning, in borrowed clothes, and my wife threw out his shirt."

Barrow stared. "I will repeat what I told the Countess D'Orsay. Greystone is a traitor. If you are hiding him from us, you will be charged as an accomplice to his treason."

Laurent turned white.

The captain turned to Evelyn. "Where is he? He could not have escaped, not unless he left before we arrived."

Evelyn swallowed. "He was not here, Captain."

He smiled dangerously at her. "I wish to speak with your daughter."

Evelyn froze, and then her heart thundered. "Absolutely not!" Aimee had met Jack, and she would innocently reveal that he had been in the house!

"I am not asking your permission!" He whirled, striding out.

Evelyn ran after him. "You will not distress my daughter, not any more than she is already distressed!"

He ignored her, hurrying with hard strides through the house and into the kitchen. Evelyn remained at his heels, panting. "Sir, I beg you!" she cried. Aimee would be so frightened!

And Aimee was sitting happily at the center table with Adelaide and Bette, with three small pots of paint, a brush and parchment. She had been painting a brown pony in the midst of pink flowers. As they entered the room, her smile vanished and everyone at the table became silent.

"What is her name?" Barrow demanded coldly.

His back was to her as he faced the table and Aimee; Evelyn walked around him and barred his way. "You will not torment my daughter!"

He stepped past her. "Child, I wish a word with you."

Tears filled Aimee's eyes and she looked at her mother. Evelyn rushed to her and swept her into her arms. "Get out," she screamed. "Get out now!"

Barrow stared, frustrated. "This is inexcusable!" he exploded. "You are an émigré, my lady, and my country has welcomed you with open arms in a time of war and revolution. Now I seek a traitor—a villain who betrays us both! Jack Greystone is your enemy, madam, not just mine!"

Aimee was crying now. Evelyn held her and spat,

"Then do your duty and find him—but leave me and my child out of this!"

Barrow trembled with anger. "We will search the stables and the grounds. If he is here, I am arresting you, madam." With that, he spun on his heel and left.

Holding Aimee, Evelyn collapsed into the closest chair. "It's all right," she whispered to her daughter, but she knew it wasn't true.

She and Aimee were in more danger than before, but not from LeClerc and his fanatics—from the British authorities, because she was Jack's lover. And even as she now understood fully why he wished to end their relationship, even as she now agreed that it must end, she prayed he had escaped.

IT HAD TAKEN AN HOUR to calm and distract Aimee, but now she was in her room, practicing her handwriting, with the puppy soundly asleep by her feet. "Darling." Evelyn smiled brightly. "Can I leave you with Bette? I still have some packing to do. Remember, we are going to town shortly!"

Aimee smiled at her. "So you like my letters?" She showed her the page filled with a carefully scripted alphabet.

"Your handwriting is beautiful," Evelyn said, meaning it. She suddenly kissed her cheek, hard. Inwardly, she felt nauseous. How dare Captain Barrow think to question her daughter!

Evelyn quickly left the bedchamber, and the moment she was in the hall, her smile vanished and she was ready to collapse. She did not want Aimee involved in these frightening and dangerous war games! But she was Jack's lover, so she had put her own daughter in terrible danger. It was one thing to endanger herself, another to endanger Aimee.

And Jack remained injured. Was he even now in the tunnels, hiding? Or had he somehow fled the property? And how could he do that, when he was hurt and on foot? At least he had his carbine and dagger with him. His weapons were not in his room.

As she turned toward the stairs, Laurent came hurrying up them. "How is she?" he asked.

"She has forgotten the ugliness of the afternoon. He left a soldier here, Laurent. I can see one outside my bedroom window!" She trembled with outrage. She had been in disbelief when she had seen the soldier earlier, seated outside beneath a tree, his horse hobbled and grazing. Clearly, they meant to watch the house and arrest Jack if he dared return.

He could hang if he were ever arrested. She was sick with even more fear.

Laurent touched her arm. "He left another soldier out back. How will Jack return for us?" He spoke in a rushed whisper. "They are watching this house, hoping to capture him, and if they do, they will arrest us, too!"

Evelyn inhaled. She did not think Barrow's threats idle ones. Who would take care of Aimee if she were ever arrested? "The British have watched his sisters' homes and his uncle's, yet they have failed to catch him. Jack is very clever, when it comes to eluding the authorities."

Laurent grimaced. "Do you think he will dare come back here? And if he does, we can hardly leave with him now, not with two soldiers outside."

Evelyn suddenly realized why she was feeling so ill. Once, she had been afraid to leave her home in Paris, where she had been watched and guarded by the people and the gendarmerie. Suddenly it felt like déjà vu. She was a prisoner in her own home, afraid to leave, and incapable of doing so.

"If he does come back, we cannot simply walk outside, climb into our carriage and leave." She took a deep breath, aware of being both highly alert and exhausted at the very same time. "I do not think Jack has left the tunnels. Not in his condition."

"What do you wish to do, madame?"

She realized she did not know. "We must wait a bit and see if Jack is still here. If he is, he will probably slip into the house after dark. If he doesn't do so tonight, it means he is gone. In which case, we should travel to London without him."

"It is a three-day trip—if we can change horses, which we cannot. And I am not up to the task of driving us for three entire days."

"I know you are not." Should they simply remain at Roselynd? Should they go to her uncle and plead with him for his hospitality and help? Jack did not think her safe at Faraday Hall. "If I leave you behind, I can afford tickets for Aimee and myself to take a coach." Oh, how she wished she did not have to make such frightening decisions now.

"That is what you should do," Laurent said unhappily. "We will be fine here."

Evelyn's head suddenly ached. She rubbed her temple. "I would send for you when I can."

"Madame—why don't you lie down?" Laurent said. "You are exhausted. After a nap, we can finish this discussion. Besides, you will be better able to think after you rest."

He was right. She hugged him impulsively. "I am so sorry I have endangered you." She turned and went into her bedchamber, closing her door. She walked right over to the window, and stared at the soldier outside. It pleased her to realize he was sleeping under the elm tree where he sat. It made her feel savagely satisfied—as if, somehow, she had won a small victory.

Her head hurt more now. Had the British authorities become her enemy now, too? Oh, it was a horrible thought. She lay down on the bed, not even taking off her shoes. Then she pulled up the throw at the foot of the bed. And she fell instantly asleep.

Jack's voice awoke her, as did his hand on her shoulder as he gently shook her. "Evelyn. Wake up."

She blinked and saw him sitting by her side, a single taper lit. Otherwise, her chamber was in darkness—it was evening now.

She sat bolt upright, throwing her arms around him. "Are you all right?"

He held her for a moment, before releasing her. "I am fine." He tilted up her chin and stared at her. "So you have met Captain Barrow." His tone was hard, but not as hard as his eyes.

She recoiled. "He knows you have been here. It isn't safe for you to be here now."

"I am not staying." He stood up. She instantly saw he had his pistol and knife, as she had thought. "He is now watching your home."

She slipped to her feet, alarmed by his set, determined and closed expression. "Were you hiding in the tunnels?"

"Yes. What did he say to you, Evelyn, exactly?"

She inhaled. "He told me that if I was hiding you here, then I am an accomplice to your crimes."

Jack nodded, his gray eyes flashing. "Go on."

She hesitated. "He has threatened to arrest me."

"I am not surprised. And?"

She felt tears arising. She fought them. "He wished to

question Aimee. She would have told him that you were here. Obviously I would not let him speak to her, and he left. However, I believe he will be back."

"Welcome to my world, Evelyn." His tone was thick with disgust and anger.

She hugged herself. "I am worried."

"You should be worried—there is no habeas corpus now, and you could be thrown in prison, without ever being charged."

She gasped. "Are you trying to frighten me?"

"You need to know the facts. I am leaving, Evelyn. I intend to elude those two guards and make it to my ship. Once there, I can elude anyone. Meanwhile, I want you to go to Trevelyan. Tell him I am financing your trip to London. He can advance you the tickets, and I will repay him within the week. Take the next coach—there should be one departing Fowey tomorrow afternoon."

"Julianne?"

"I will send her a letter, and I will call on her and Dom as soon as I can. However, you may explain everything to Paget—and I do mean everything."

She hated the idea of simply showing up on Julianne's doorstep, begging for her charity.

He knew. He said softly, "My sister is an angel of mercy. She will love taking you in. I know you think it an imposition, and that you are being terribly bold—when do not have a rude, self-serving bone in your body. Evelyn, it is what is best for you and what is best for Aimee. Promise me you will go to Julianne."

He was so right—she hated being so bold—but it was best for Aimee.

Evelyn met his gaze, which remained frighteningly hard. How had her love for Jack come down to this moment?

"I am sorry I have put you and your daughter in so much danger," he said harshly. "I regret being so selfish."

Tears finally filled her eyes. "I have no regrets! I love you!"

He flinched. "You would hardly say such a thing if Aimee had been questioned by Barrow, or if you were now separated from your daughter and in a cold prison cell."

"I did not realize it would come to this."

"No good could have come of our association." He was final. Then, he said, "I have something for you."

Her heart cracked. "Will I see you when you are in London?"

His expression hardened. "No." He reached into his pocket and produced a very small cloth bundle, which fit into her palm as he placed it there.

She looked at it briefly, confused. Tears wet her cheeks as she opened the cloth. Evelyn gasped when she saw her sapphires there.

She glanced up at Jack, stunned. He had retrieved the jewels stolen by Whyte. What did the gesture mean?

"I could not let him get away with the theft," he said flatly.

Pain stabbed through her now. The gesture meant that he cared. "This is goodbye, isn't it?"

"This is goodbye," Jack Greystone said.

CHAPTER FIFTEEN

"HAVE NO FEAR," Trevelyan said. "You will not be turned away."

Evelyn smiled grimly at him. They had just arrived at Bedford House, but had yet to get out from their carriage. She had gone to Trevelyan as Jack had directed her to do, and when she had showed up on his doorstep, at once brokenhearted and afraid, he had taken one look at her white face and red eyes and demanded to know what had happened. She had told him most of the truth—she had told him what pertained to their flight from the Bodmin Moor now. Trevelyan knew that Captain Barrow had come to Roselynd to arrest Jack, and that he had almost questioned Aimee, frightening her terribly in the process.

And once he had been apprised of the situation, Trevelyan had insisted on escorting her, Aimee and her staff to London. As it turned out, he knew Julianne almost as well as he knew Jack; he had known her since she was a small child. He was, he had explained, a rather frequent visitor at Bedford House now, and in the past few years he had become good friends with Dominic Paget.

Of course he had—they were all spies and ex-spies, they were all in that same secret circle playing terrible war games. They were all the spymaster's men.

He had been terribly kind from the moment she had appeared at Blackmoor, and throughout the entire three-day trip to town. But what she had refused to do was discuss her personal relationship with Jack. While he had never asked why she was so aggrieved, she knew he realized something was terribly wrong. He surely guessed that the affair was finally over.

Evelyn allowed Trev to help her out of the carriage, meeting his gaze. "We are being so bold, inviting ourselves to stay with Lady Paget," she said. She was anxious. She hated being so forward. She disliked being an imposition. And what if Julianne turned her away?

"She will welcome you with open arms when you explain to her and Dom what you have explained to me." He now smiled, reaching for Aimee and taking her down from the coach with a grand flourish. Aimee laughed as he swung her about before setting her down. Her daughter had become very fond of Trevelyan.

"Look, darling, have you ever seen such a grand home?" Evelyn cried, smiling and taking her daughter's hand.

Aimee's eyes widened. "Oh, Mama, is this a palace? Will we really stay here?"

With its imposing facade, its magnificent grounds and the stunning water fountain in the center of the drive, Bedford House most definitely resembled a royal palace, not an earl's city home. She squeezed Aimee's hand. "Mr. Greystone seems to think so, and we will soon find out."

Laurent, Adelaide and Bette were now alighting with a happy Jolie. They had come in one hired coach, changing horses every half day, so in the end, they had left everything behind, except for their clothing. Trev took her arm in his and they approached the house, going up pale, wide stone steps. A pair of liveried doormen stood there, as still as statues, until one came to life and opened the door instantly for them.

Trev handed the fellow his card. "I must see Bedford, or Lady Paget. Are either the earl or the countess in?"

The doorman blinked at him, perfectly coiffed in a white wig, his livery royal-blue and gold. "They are both in, my lord," he said, bowing.

Evelyn knew the request was an informal one, but considering his relationship with Julianne and her husband, she suspected they did not stand on formality often. Footsteps sounded and the butler, Gerard, appeared. "Good day, my lord, my lady," he said, smiling.

"Gerard, my good man, please rouse Bedford. We have had a difficult trip and the countess is exhausted, as is her daughter."

Evelyn was grateful. Trev had been taking care of them for days, which allowed her to worry about her relationship with Jack and his escape from Roselynd. The heartbreak rose up again, its force threatening to consume her. As if he knew, Trev caught her elbow and steadied her.

It was Julianne who appeared first, before Gerard had even left the front hall. Her eyes widened as she took in the sight of them. "Trevelyan!" She smiled, but her eyes remained wide, and they were on Evelyn now, a huge question there. She went to Trev and gave him her hands; he kissed both at once. "We are imposing, Julianne. The countess is in need of your hospitality."

She stared at him for a moment, as if trying to discern what was happening by gazing into his eyes, and then she turned to Evelyn and hugged her warmly. Relief began. Julianne was happy to see her!

"Darling, I am so glad to see you, and of course you are welcome here—at any time." But her gaze was searching. She then turned to Aimee. "You must be Aimee! Hello! I am Lady Paget, and I have heard so much about you!"

Aimee smiled shyly. "Good day, my lady," she whispered.

"I have a daughter, too, but she is much younger than you. However, she loves older children. She is playing in the nursery. Would you like to meet her?" Julianne smiled.

Aimee glanced at Evelyn, who nodded. "I think you should meet Jacquelyn. Bette can take you up."

"What about Jolie?" Aimee asked.

Evelyn turned to Julianne. "Aimee has a dog."

"How wonderful—we love dogs. I have three! Why doesn't Jolie take a walk in the back gardens, and then she can go up to the nursery, too."

As Bette took Aimee's hand, Dominic Paget, the Earl of Bedford, strode into the hall.

He was a tall, muscular, handsome man with dark hair and an unmistakable air of power and authority. He was elegantly dressed in a sapphire-blue satin coat, a lace shirt, pale breeches and stockings. He did not wear a wig, and his unpowdered hair was pulled back into a queue. Rings glinted from his hands.

He was smiling, but his eyes were hard. He exchanged a quick look with Trevelyan, before greeting everyone. "I am pleased to see you again, Countess," he said.

"Thank you, my lord," she returned nervously.

"Why don't we adjourn to the salon?" Julianne said. "Gerard? I imagine our visitors would like some refreshments sent up to their rooms." She turned to Trev. "You will stay for the night?"

"I will stay until Evelyn is safely settled," he returned, directing his gaze to her.

Evelyn smiled gratefully. She truly could not have a more loyal friend—or a better champion.

Then she thought of Jack and it simply hurt so much. How could it be over? And where was he now? Had he made it safely back to his ship? She hadn't heard and she was so worried!

Julianne had turned and was looking at Evelyn, and Evelyn suspected she was wondering about her relationship with Trev. Then she gestured everyone inside, and closed both doors behind them.

"I cannot thank you enough for taking me and my daughter in," Evelyn began, looking at Bedford.

Julianne went to stand beside him, no longer smiling. Dom said, "What has happened?"

Trevelyan stood beside her, but Evelyn did not look at him. Aimee wasn't present so her fear and grief surfaced, causing her to speak thickly. "Jack was beaten by his enemies. I was taking care of him at Roselynd," she said.

Julianne cried out. "Is he all right?"

"I don't know," Evelyn said. "He survived the beating, with bruised or even broken ribs, and a gash on his head, so he was on his way to recovering fully. But Captain Barrow learned he was at Roselynd. Four days ago, Barrow surprised us. Jack hid in the tunnels below the house while Barrow and his men searched everywhere for him. They did not find him, and Jack returned later that night, telling me he planned to evade the guards Barrow left behind and get to his ship. He instructed me to come here, my lord, my lady." She trembled. "I have not heard a word from him, so I do not know if he escaped the soldiers, if he made it to his ship or where he now is."

Evelyn was so distraught that she had to sit down. Julianne came to sit beside her, putting her arm around her.

"We will hear from Jack, sooner or later," Dominic said. "And if he had been caught and apprehended, I would have heard such news by now."

"I am very worried," Evelyn managed. "He was hardly in full health when he left."

"Jack is clever," Julianne said. "He has been outwitting the British authorities for most of his life. Once he reaches his ship, he will be able to escape all pursuit." She took Evelyn's hand and held it. But her gaze was searching. Evelyn had to avoid it.

"Lady D'Orsay," Dominic said. "Why did Jack insist that you come here? Once he had left Roselynd, what made your home unsafe?"

She inhaled. "I overheard Jack speaking with a Frenchman, discussing a British military plan."

Julianne stared, and so did her husband. Both were stone-faced. If surprised, they did not show it. Obviously they knew Jack ran the British blockade, but did they also know that he was spying for the French?

Trevelyan explained, "She has heard information that she should not have heard. And the French republicans know it."

Dominic said, "But why would Jack think you in danger—so much so that he has sent you here, to us? Have you been threatened? Were you discovered?"

She so did not want to tell them the entire truth! But Julianne squeezed her hand. "It is all right. Dominic was once a spy. He can help you, Evelyn."

She brushed a seeping tear. "Jack was giving away our plans to invade France and aid the rebels there. Yes, I was discovered. And I was also threatened—in my own home."

Julianne stared grimly at Dominic.

Evelyn was taken aback. Didn't they care that Jack was a French spy? For, if they had not realized it before, they certainly did now!

"Who threatened you? Whom was Jack speaking to?" Dominic asked.

"Jack's French ally is Victor LaSalle, the Viscount

LeClerc. Unbelievably, he was once a friend and neighbor of ours, of Henri's and mine, in Paris. And he not only saw me, he recognized me, too. Two weeks ago he sent someone to threaten me—and my daughter—at Roselynd." She tried to breathe slowly, her heart lurching.

Julianne paled.

"You were told to keep silent?" Dominic asked.

Evelyn whispered, "I was told that if LeClerc were betrayed, I would pay—and so would Aimee."

Julianne held her tightly. "You are safe here."

"I am so worried," Evelyn whispered. But why hadn't anyone reacted to what she had said—and to the fact that Jack had been betraying Britain to her enemies? It seemed that no one was surprised.

Yet everyone in the salon was a patriot. Indifference was impossible.

"You will be safe here," Dominic said firmly. "I do not want you to worry, Lady D'Orsay, and you are welcome to stay as our guest, until the danger passes. Trev, will you join me for a drink? I have a fine scotch whiskey in my library, and we can give the ladies a moment alone."

Trev nodded, but he paused before Evelyn. "Are you all right? Surely, you feel better now?"

She smiled up at him. "Thank you...for being kind, for helping us get to London...for everything." She took both of his hands and held them, hard.

He studied her. "I will always come to your rescue, Evelyn, if you are in need of rescuing," he said. Then he whirled and left with Dominic.

Julianne took her hand and asked quietly, "Is Trev courting you now?"

"He can't court me—I am in love with your brother." And she felt more tears falling.

"You are in love!" Julianne hugged her again. But then

she gazed at her with worry. "Has he broken your heart already?"

"Of course he has! Because we cannot be together, not now, not ever—I cannot put Aimee in this kind of danger!"

Julianne studied her. "If I had taken the safe course, I would not be with Dominic now. He was a Tory, an aristocrat and a spy, while I was a poor gentlewoman from Cornwall, who sympathized with the Jacobins in France. But I fell in love with him anyway. And then I fought for that love. And as I did, I began to know him—and understand him. And my love only became stronger. It was worth the pain, the fear."

"How can I put Aimee in any more danger? I did not tell Lord Paget, but when LeClerc's crony broke into our house, he held a knife to my throat. What if Aimee had seen that? What if, next time, he puts a knife to her throat? And Captain Barrow terrified her. He wished to interrogate her! Not to mention that, if they had found Jack at Roselynd, I would now be in prison, arrested for being his accomplice!"

"You are in a terrible bind," Julianne agreed.

"And I am so worried about him. Julianne, we have to find out if he is safely aboard his ship."

"That may not be that hard to do." She smiled. "Does he love you, too?"

Evelyn froze.

"Does he love you?" Julianne repeated patiently.

"He has never said so."

Julianne stood. "He is such a ladies' man, but I knew when I first met you that you were somehow special…he must care greatly, Evelyn, otherwise, he would not have sent you here!"

Evelyn regarded her. "But?"

She sighed. "But he is a man of danger, and he has always lived life on the edge. I wonder if Jack could ever settle down."

Her heart slammed. She wished that there was no war, no revolution, that Jack was not a spy for Britain's enemies—and that he wished to live with her and Aimee at Roselynd.

"If he hurts you, I will never speak with him again," Julianne finally said firmly.

"He knows we cannot be together. He knows he has put Aimee and me in danger," Evelyn said. "He was very final about it. I cannot be with him, not now, not like this." Pain stabbed through her chest again. "But I will always love him, always! No matter what he does...."

Julianne sat back down beside her. "There was a time when I thought I would never see Dom again...and I was wrong. There was a time when I thought he would be one of Pitt's spies until he died, if the war went on that long! This is a terrible time, but you cannot predict what tomorrow will bring."

"Lord Paget was a great man, a hero in this war." She thought of his spying for the French. Why didn't Julianne care about that? Why didn't Paget? "Did you not understand what I said earlier? Jack was giving a Frenchman our military secrets!"

Julianne seemed bewildered. "I heard your every word."

Perhaps Julianne loved her brother too much to have comprehended her. "He is a French spy, Julianne."

A stunned silence greeted her words. Julianne stood up, eyes flashing. "You are wrong."

Evelyn shook her head miserably. "I wish I was wrong but I know what I heard."

"I cannot believe you think him a French spy!" Julianne cried.

Evelyn finally stood up, as well. Was she now alienating her friend and hostess? "No one is sorrier than I am! I know what I heard. Jack is selling out this country to our enemies! I begged him to deny it. He did deny it—but so poorly, as a genuine denial was impossible to make!"

"No, he is not a French spy. He would never do such a thing." Julianne's eyes flashed, but she was pale. "You do not know Jack the way that I do. He appears to be a French spy, but appearances are only that! I cannot believe that you love him as you say you do, but you do not trust him."

Evelyn hugged herself. Hadn't Jack asked her to have faith? "I pray you are right."

"I am right. My brother is a patriot," Julianne said. "And one day, you will realize it." She walked to the door and opened it, then turned, found a bell and rang it. "You must be tired. Gerard will show you to your room."

ANOTHER NIGHT, ANOTHER inn, another clandestine meeting, Jack thought grimly, pausing on the threshold of a dark, crowded public room. It was raining, and as he shook the rain from his broad shoulders, he gazed through the smoke and shadows at the crowd.

He saw no one unusual—just ordinary farmers and tradesmen, busy imbibing rum and ale, smoking tobacco and playing cards. The conversation was loud and raucous.

Lucas stood up, gesturing, in a dark corner of the room. Jack nodded and pushed his way through the men seated at the tables, now raking the rain from his damp hair.

Lucas remained standing, looking terribly elegant and out of place in his dark brown velvet jacket and white lace shirt. Warlock was seated, and because this corner of the room did not receive any illumination from either the unlit tapers on the table or the central fireplace, and he was clad entirely in black, he could barely be distinguished.

Lucas threw his arm around him briefly. "You are late." There was a question in his eyes.

Jack winced—his injuries still hurt. "There was a British frigate leaving Dover. I had to lie low until she passed."

"Are you hurt?"

Lucas never missed a trick, Jack thought. He parted the neckline of his shirt and lowered it, revealing the top of the bandages he continued to wear. Without the support, his ribs hurt more. Then he took his own seat, his back to the crowd. Normally he would not sit so indifferently, but he knew he could trust the spymaster and his brother to watch out for British soldiers and French spies. And with his back to the crowd, he could not be recognized.

Finally, with some tension arising, he met Warlock's dark, burning gaze.

"What happened?" Warlock asked almost casually.

"I was given a warning by LeClerc," Jack said, smiling as if indifferent. He shrugged. "I was told to make certain my loyalties are not compromised."

Lucas's expression tightened as he poured Jack a glass of red wine. "*Are* you compromised?"

Jack now stared at Warlock. "For some odd reason, they have decided to become suspicious of me." He had no intention of involving Evelyn any more than he had already. Warlock did not need to know that she was his lover, or that the British had sought him out at her home. But he would want an explanation, and Jack had devised one.

Almost an entire week had passed since he had last seen her—and told her that they could not continue any association. By now, she was at Julianne's, surely. And there, she would be safe from the repercussions of the war games he played.

His heart ached as he thought of her. He doubted he would ever forget the last time they had made love—or her eyes and expression when he had said that this was goodbye. He despised himself for so recklessly putting her directly in the path of danger. He could not believe he had been so selfish. But then, he had not cared so much about her when they had first met—desire was not affection.

Warlock's dark gaze was intent. "I cannot have you under suspicion, not now. You must prove your loyalty to them, within the next few weeks."

"I beg to differ!" Lucas shot back with anger. "So it is acceptable if he is under suspicion after Quiberon Bay?"

"I hardly said such a thing." Warlock was calm. "So why don't we begin with the facts? Something—or someone—must have caused LeClerc to doubt your integrity."

Jack took a sip of the wine, which was too sweet, too weak bodied and inadequate. Warlock would eventually hear that Evelyn was at Julianne's, but Jack would make certain he believed Lucas responsible for that. In fact, he did not trust Warlock, not as far as Evelyn was concerned. Warlock would always put Britain first, above anyone and everyone. He might help protect her at first, but in the end, he would not think twice about sacrificing her if he had to.

Every liar knew that telling a part of the truth deflected suspicion. So did every spy. "I helped a French émigré retrieve valuables from her home in France. The task required of me was too easy, the compensation too great, for me not to undertake it. As it turns out, LeClerc discovered the association. He did not believe I was simply being well paid to help a beautiful damsel in distress. He has chosen to think I was on some secret mission. And unfortunately for me, I was taken by surprise and then warned, and I have the battered ribs to prove it."

Warlock regarded him, as did Lucas. It was his brother who said, "Had you not slept with her, you might not have raised doubt in LeClerc's mind!"

Jack smirked. "Well, as I said, she was beautiful—and the compensation was simply too great to refuse."

Warlock drummed his fingers on the table. "Stay away from her. You should not be associated with a French émigré now."

"I believe I have learned my lesson." But he thought of Evelyn, and his heart ached, making it hard to maintain a smug facade.

Lucas was staring, as if he knew the story was just that, and incomplete. But then, his brother knew him better than anyone. "I have never liked this double game for you. I like it even less now." He turned to Warlock. "Jack is under suspicion, and the timing could not be worse. We should reverse places. I can take over Jack's intrigues, and no one will think anything of it, as I am his brother. Jack can return to his life as a smuggler outwitting the revenue men."

Warlock's dark brows lifted. "I cannot simply switch you and Jack and you know it—even if I were inclined to do so, which I am not. Jack has been brilliant slipping in and out of France as he does, and his ship thus far has never been beaten in battle, or defeated in a race."

Jack stared at them both. He had been supporting Cadoudal for almost an entire year now. Their relationship had become a personal one. No one knew as well as he did how desperate the rebels were for arms and supplies, how they lived in constant hiding, on the run, when they were not engaging the French troops. No one knew as he did how deeply they hated the republicans, and how determined they were to liberate the Loire Valley—even if it meant death.

"I don't know if I could turn my back on the rebels now, even if Warlock ordered me to," he said to Lucas. And he thought of Evelyn again, who had been left widowed, without any means, and who had been, until recently, living alone at Roselynd. She needed a protector and a champion, but that could not be him.

Warlock looked pleased. "Do not let anyone else hear you speak like such a patriot."

Lucas shook his head. He said to Warlock, "How will Jack survive his perfidy if all goes well?" Then he glanced hard at Jack. "A date has been set."

Jack tensed, surprised. A date for the invasion of Quiberon Bay, led by the Comte D'Hervilly, had been chosen. This game was now rapidly being played—and would soon have winners and losers. He had never doubted his ability to survive these war games until now. But he had to consider how he would be one of those to triumph—and survive. Now he understood why his brother was so concerned about him. One misstep and he would be uncovered....

Warlock ignored the question. He said, "Cadoudal must meet our force on June 25 with his entire army."

They would be on land on the peninsula on June 25. "I need details—he will want them," Jack said swiftly. And in spite of the reservations he had so recently begun to have, excitement began. The invasion had been a year in the planning! Finally, it would come!

"D'Hervilly will command thirty-five hundred troops—two-thirds of them are French prisoners of war. The naval squadron will disembark from Plymouth on June 23.

There will be three warships and six supply ships, with enough supplies for forty thousand troops." Warlock had been leaning forward, and speaking in a near whisper. Now, he sat back, appearing savagely satisfied.

Jack's pulse was racing. Cadoudal would be thrilled to hear this news! Finally, they could drive General Hoche and the rest of the French army from the Loire Valley!

But so much luck was involved in an operation like this one. Other French spies might discover what Warlock had just relayed; the squadron could be espied approaching France, warning the enemy of the impending invasion; Cadoudal might be thwarted in his efforts to join the invading forces....

His heart thrummed. An entire year of secret meetings, debates and planning had gone into the invasion of Quiberon Bay. He intended to be a part of the liberation of Le Loire. Evelyn needed a hero, but he could not be that hero, not now and probably not ever.

He should not feel dismayed—he should be pleased. His life was the sea—his life was danger. Now his life was the war. He had never wanted anything else or anything more.

"When can you meet with Cadoudal?" Warlock asked.

"I will set it up for some time in the next week," Jack said. His mind raced. He usually used a network of couriers to arrange meetings like this. Now he realized it was too dangerous. He would go to France directly, and use his own resources to contact Cadoudal, even if it meant he would have to drift about the Brittany coast for several days, hiding from both the British and French navies, until contact could be made. The fewer people who knew about this meeting, the better.

"We need to feed LeClerc misinformation," Warlock said, interrupting his racing thoughts. "Give him a date in July for the invasion—also tell him we will land at St Malo."

"You will be dead by the time July comes," Lucas said harshly.

Jack looked at him. "I have no intention of dying in July—or at any other time." But now alarm began.

If he betrayed LeClerc as he had been instructed to do, the Frenchman would seek vengeance upon Evelyn and her daughter.

"He will have his every suspicion confirmed," Lucas said, his gray eyes flashing. He turned to Warlock. "You cannot mean to sacrifice my brother to your cause, not after all I have done for you!"

"Why would I wish to sacrifice one of my best agents?" Warlock was bemused. "Jack can talk a good game. No one is as swaggering or has as much bravado. I have every confidence in him. He will talk his way out of a noose if he has to. However, after the invasion, Jack can remain in Britain for a few months, even a year, if need be, until any danger has passed."

Jack did not hear Warlock. LeClerc would know he had been used and betrayed, and no amount of talking or hiding would convince him otherwise. And LeClerc had threatened Evelyn.

But the liberation of the Loire Valley was at stake—as were the lives of thousands of British and French émigré troops.

Jack realized both men were staring at him. Was he wearing a ghastly expression? "You may have confidence in my powers of persuasion, but I am going to have to kill LeClerc," he said very softly. He could think of no other solution—no other way to protect Evelyn and Aimee. If he fed LeClerc such misinformation now, LeClerc would have to die.

Lucas started, his eyes wide. Then they narrowed—and now Jack knew he was entirely suspicious of him. "LeClerc hardly operates alone."

"He is a great conduit to the French Republicans for us," Warlock said, hard. "Killing him is a last resort, Jack, and you cannot do so before we triumph in Brittany."

Jack quickly smiled but all he could think of was that by midnight of June 25, he would be uncovered, and Evelyn would be in danger. "Fine. It is a last resort." He realized he was sweating now. "I will tell him the invasion is set for St Malo, on July 15."

"And LeClerc will know before midnight on the twenty-fifth that he has been betrayed," Lucas said.

Jack kept smiling. "Probably...unless I have played a very good game."

Lucas's gaze was narrow and hard with continued suspicion.

"I will find a tidbit for you to toss to LeClerc soon, to convince him of your loyalty now." Warlock stood, clearly about to leave. "By the way, why did Captain Barrow think to find you at Roselynd—the home of the deceased Comte D'Orsay?"

Jack froze inwardly; outwardly, he reached for his glass of wine. "I don't know. But as you know, I am a good friend of Robert Faraday. His widow is Robert's niece."

Warlock smiled congenially. "I have heard she is a stunner." He nodded and left.

Jack began to sip his wine but Lucas seized his wrist, causing the glass to tilt and the wine to spill all over the table. "I would like a dose of the truth," Lucas snapped.

Jack shook the wine from his hand and faced his brother grimly. "Evelyn is in danger."

Lucas's eyes widened. "Evelyn? Are you speaking of the widow D'Orsay?"

He trusted his brother completely—with his life, with her life. "I have sent her to Julianne's. And I have a letter for Dom, if you do not mind." He reached into his interior pocket and handed the folded parchment to Lucas. It was sealed with wax.

Lucas moved his chair closer. "What the hell is going on?"

Jack did not hesitate. "I did not take a Frenchwoman to France. I took Evelyn. Unfortunately, I was foolish enough—and selfish enough—to bring her to Looe Island. She stumbled across a meeting I had with LeClerc and he happens to know her well, from when she lived in Paris. She is the reason LeClerc suspects me now, and he has threatened her and her daughter. If he is betrayed, he will seek vengeance upon them, and he made himself very clear." He clenched his fists. "That is why I am going to have to kill him, sooner, not later."

Lucas cursed. "The last thing you need is a personal involvement now! LeClerc will manipulate you thoroughly, Jack, through her. Damn it."

"I have ended the association."

Lucas laughed harshly. "Really? And that is why you sent her to Julianne and Paget? To end the affair? I have no doubt you will be knocking on her bedroom door before the week is out!"

Jack flushed, because he had had just such treacherous urges, a great many times. "I am the reason she is in danger and I cannot—I will not—allow anything ill to befall her."

Lucas stiffened, staring. "You are in love?"

Jack felt his cheeks warm. Was he in love with Evelyn D'Orsay? "She has no one to protect her."

His eyes widened. "You are truly in love!"

Jack stood. "I will kill LeClerc just before or just after midnight of June 25."

Lucas leaped up. "Even if you were reckless enough to seek out LeClerc in the heart of France, you are not a killer!"

"What else am I to do?" Jack said, fighting to remain quiet in the crowded room. "God willing, we will liberate Le Loire, but I am going to betray him. He will seek revenge on Evelyn and her daughter! I am in too deep to bow out now, and even if I could, I cannot turn my back on the Chouans! But I cannot turn my back on Evelyn, either!"

He stared at his brother, who stared back, their expressions of dismay and fear undoubtedly identical. And Jack knew it was true. "Yes," he said softly. "To answer your question—I am in love."

CHAPTER SIXTEEN

THERE HAD BEEN no word. It was truly over.

Evelyn paused before the open door of the library. She had been in London for three days, and the time felt like an eternity. Even though the earl had told her that Jack was safely aboard his ship the day after her arrival in town, there had been no other details—not a single one. She did not know if he was better, or where he was—or what he was doing. And maybe that was best. But Evelyn had been waiting for a message from him. She could not believe that Jack would not contact her, even if they had ended things.

But his failure to do so sent such a strong signal. He meant to keep his distance. She knew it was for the best. She could hardly remain his lover now. But it was one thing to have decided upon a wise course of action, another to accept it with one's heart.

How could she stop loving him?

It was so difficult, being strong. No matter how she tried to tell herself that she must move forward with her life—without him—it seemed impossible. No matter how she told herself that she must stop loving him, that also seemed hopeless.

Yet that was exactly what she must now do—she must focus on her life in town, on Aimee's upbringing, on her daughter's future.

And Aimee was thrilled with their new life. She loved

living in town. She was taking her lessons with Amelia's three stepchildren at Lambert Hall, and after classes, there were rides on the ponies Grenville kept for his children and picnics in the gardens behind the house. Grenville's oldest son was Aimee's age, and they had become fast friends. Indeed, the children were all getting along famously. And Amelia had welcomed Aimee into her home with open arms—as if she were a blood relation. But then, Amelia loved nothing more than being a mother hen with a large brood.

Still, Evelyn had not slept well since she had left Roselynd—since they had decided it was over. She was tormented by her heartbreak, her love and her worry for him. Surely, ending their affair did not exclude some communication. For, in spite of everything that had happened, they were friends now. They might not be lovers, but they cared for one another and respected one another. He had a responsibility to contact her, to let her know that he was all right! Surely Jack knew just how worried she was.

She could not help wondering if he had healed. Was he capable of defending himself, if he were ever brutally attacked again?

Was he in France? Was he in French waters? Had he followed LeClerc's orders? Had he uncovered the date for the invasion of Quiberon Bay, and passed that information over? Were the British and émigré troops in jeopardy? Would their invasion be met by an ambush—a massacre?

Whenever she thought of his betraying her and their country and countrymen, she was sickened. But at the very same time, her heart would scream in protest at her—somehow, a part of her did not believe he was capable of ever committing such an act of treason. But it had begun to truly sink in. She had information that might affect the course of the war....

Dominic Paget was at his massive desk at the far end of the library. As always, he was such an imposing figure, and a bit intimidating. He had noticed her, and he set aside the papers he was reading. "Lady D'Orsay?" His smile was brief.

She had never sought him out for a private word before. She wished she did not have to do so now. But she could not keep this secret. The authorities had to know what Jack meant to do—what he was doing. She could not allow thousands of lives to be endangered.

"My lord, I hope I am not interrupting," she said nervously. She felt heartsick as she spoke.

He stood, smiling. "Come in, Countess. Clearly, you wish a word."

She shut the door and turned, aware of the enormity of what she meant to do. Yet she had no choice. "Is there any more news of Jack?" she asked carefully, because she so wished to know.

"I am afraid not, but that is hardly unusual. He is rarely in one place for very long."

Evelyn clasped her hands. "I am very concerned about him, but I am also very concerned about the conversation I overheard when I was on his island."

Paget turned, gesturing at the chair in front of his desk. Evelyn took it, thanking him. Her heart was pounding. She had decided to reveal what she knew to Dominic, because he was both a great patriot and Jack's brother-in-law. She felt certain the earl would protect Jack, yet she also felt as certain that he would never allow the French invasion to be jeopardized.

"Jack has lived in the eye of danger for most of his life. I understand that you have become fond of him—he is my wife's brother, and I am fond of him, too. But I am also confident that if anyone can survive the intrigues of this war, it is Jack."

How she wished she could have a drop of the earl's confidence! "He is wanted for treason," she cried. "How will he ever survive such charges? Even if the war ends, he is an outlaw."

"Charges can be dropped." He was matter-of-fact.

Evelyn stiffened in her seat, wondering if he truly meant it.

"I know that I cannot stop you from worrying about Jack, but I wish you would try. You are clearly exhausting yourself—and you have Aimee to think of."

"She has always come first, and that is why I am here," Evelyn said. Was it possible that one day, Jack could be a free man? She had to rein in her hope. He was a spy, in a time of war. So much could befall him.

She thought about the beating he had endured; she thought about LeClerc and his threats, and the frenzy of accusations and executions in France during Le Razor.

"I take it you wish to discuss another matter with me?" Paget's soft tone cut into her anxious thoughts.

"Sir, no one seemed disturbed when I revealed the nature of the conversation I overheard on Looe Island."

His mouth curled. "As you know—as the world knows—I was one of Pitt's agents, once upon a time. My wife and I have been involved in a great many intrigues, Lady D'Orsay, so perhaps we are a bit desensitized now."

"An invasion of Quiberon Bay is planned, my lord, one with both British and émigré troops. Jack told LeClerc as much, but what he did not reveal was the date of the invasion. LeClerc ordered him to uncover that date."

Paget stared. "And what is your point?"

She inhaled. "If Jack reveals the date of that invasion, it

could fail. Or worse, thousands of fine British soldiers—and émigrés—could die!"

"Yes, if Jack betrayed us, the invasion would surely fail and a great many Englishmen and émigrés would die. I take it you believe he will betray us?"

How could Dominic be so calm? Surely, he understood the implications of what she had said! "I know what I witnessed and what I heard. Jack is a French spy. I could not keep such a secret. Someone in authority had to know. I decided to come to you."

He studied her for an interminable moment, his bland expression never changing. "You are very brave. Lady D'Orsay, you should forget that you ever heard what you did. Recalling it only keeps you in danger. I will take care of the matter."

She was amazed. "What will you do with the information I have given you?"

"The less you know the better." He was final.

And she realized that Paget did not believe that Jack was a spy for their enemies. Like Julianne, he believed in Jack. There was no other explanation for his calm reaction to what she had revealed. But was it at all possible that they were right?

"I wish I knew nothing," she cried. She realized she was standing. "I love Jack, even if I should not. I feel like an absolute traitor, having told you what I have."

He got to his feet and came out from behind his desk, and he actually put his arm around her. "My dear, you did the right thing, coming to me. You know, in many ways Jack is like my wife—they are both impulsive and passionate, determinedly so. I am not surprised that you have come to care for him. You could do worse, Lady D'Orsay."

She had no more doubt—Dominic Paget did not believe Jack a traitor, not for a single second!

"But now, you must forget what you know—what you have heard," he said.

She had never been as confused! Evelyn met his green gaze, which was direct and commanding. "That is probably impossible." She hesitated. "Will you protect him?"

"He is my family. Of course I will protect him."

She nodded, near tears, relieved.

"But I must add one more piece of advice. Listen closely." He dropped his arm. "If you are ever questioned about Jack, and you cannot plead ignorance, then you must reveal what you have told me today—you believe Jack a traitor and a French spy."

Evelyn was taken aback. "Why?"

"Because his life will depend upon it," Dominic Paget said. "You should not be involved in these games, but unfortunately, it is too late."

"I UNDERSTAND THAT you have been residing in Cornwall, Lady D'Orsay. How is London treating you?"

Evelyn smiled at the Comte D'Archand. Julianne had given a dinner party, and she had met the émigré and his eldest daughter, Nadine, before supper, for the first time. Apparently they had just returned to town.

She had been seated between two gentlemen, and it had been a pleasant affair, with a great deal of meandering conversation, some of it related to the comings and goings of the ton, recent affairs and announcements, and some of it related to the war. A part of her had truly enjoyed the gay evening—just as a part of her had enjoyed the past weeks spent in town. But if she allowed her thoughts to wander, she would not feel quite as content. Until she heard from Jack or heard news of him, she lived in a state of constant worry. Not a day went by that she did not recall LeClerc and his threats or the pending invasion of Quiberon Bay and the danger surrounding Jack.

Supper had just ended and Julianne had ushered everyone out, the gentlemen to their cigars and brandies, the ladies to their sherry and port. Evelyn was tired—she continued to sleep fitfully—and she had lagged behind the women, debating retiring for the evening, if she could politely do so. The comte had caught her in the corridor, outside the salon where the ladies had assembled.

They had been briefly introduced before supper. The comte was in his early forties, she thought, but he was tall, broad-shouldered, dark-haired and very handsome. She was already aware that he found her attractive—she had caught him casting glances at her throughout the meal. But then, she had teased and curled her hair, and her headdress matched her gold-and-burgundy evening gown exactly. She did not look like a widow in mourning; she looked like a fashionable and elegant noblewoman.

"Sir." Evelyn smiled politely. "London has treated me very well. I believe that Julianne and Amelia have made it their life's mission to entertain and amuse me, when Amelia should not even be out and about." Amelia was due to give birth next week, but no one could convince her to stay home, not even her husband.

He laughed, flashing bright, even teeth. "She is very bold to be out in society in her condition. Grenville seems beyond anxious. So…have they succeeded?"

She had to smile back. "There have been teas and luncheons and carriage rides. The past week or so has passed in a veritable whirl." She was speaking the truth. She had been introduced to a dozen peers. Everyone had, in fact, been kind, curious and friendly. Amelia was the most determined—she was the leader of this social effort, Evelyn had quickly realized. It was as if introducing Evelyn

to the ton was a task she must accomplish before she had
her first child. "They have become such good friends—
I almost feel as if they are my sisters."

"Nadine feels the same way—no two women could be
more generous in spirit," D'Archand said. "And do you
prefer town to the country?"

"Sometimes I do. But sometimes I miss Cornwall,
with its stark moors and rocky beaches, its inclement
weather!" She smiled. "Did I hear that you also have a
home in Cornwall?"

"Yes, we do, but far south, in the St Just parish. Actually, we are not far from St Just Hall and Greystone
Manor." Evelyn tensed at the mention of Greystone
Manor, which she knew was Jack's family home. "Lady
D'Orsay," the comte continued, "would I be overstep-
ping my bounds, as we have only just been introduced,
if I asked you if I might show you some of London's
brighter attractions?"

She froze. A tall, tawny-haired man in a brown satin
coat and pale breeches and stockings was entering the
front hall. *Jack.*

Evelyn's heart slammed. It had been almost three
weeks since their parting at Roselynd.

He turned, and their glances collided.

Dismay flooded her. Evelyn realized she was staring
at his brother, Lucas. They were so alike—tall, broad-
shouldered, powerfully built, with that same tawny, sun-
streaked hair.

From across the great hall, Lucas smiled at her.

"Do you know Lucas Greystone?" D'Archand asked.

Evelyn inhaled, facing him—while summoning up a
smile. "Yes, I do. He has been kind enough to look into
the operations of a mine on my estate."

D'Archand's stare was speculative. "Greystone is a

great patriot and a good friend of mine. As is his brother. I must say, you look as if you have seen a ghost."

She flushed. What could she say to such a comment—when he was staring so closely at her? And now she realized she was faced with a good friend of Jack's. It was such a small world. "I think we both know that these are difficult times."

"Yes." He was grim. "I am sorry, Countess, I am aware that you fled France with your family a few years ago—as I did. May I offer you condolences for the passing of your husband?"

"Thank you." She hesitated. "I have not answered your question." From the corner of her eye, she watched Lucas enter the salon. Amelia hugged him instantly. With her due date so near, she was huge for a tiny woman. Several women rushed up to him then, the younger ladies clearly eager to flirt with him.

"No, you have not."

She focused on the gentleman standing before her. How could she lead him on? "As you can see, I am not in mourning, yet Henri died two months ago. I loved him, monsieur, but he was ill for a very long time."

His eyes flickered. "I have heard the story. I do not condemn you."

"I have a daughter to raise." She held her head proudly. "These are very difficult times. Henri left us in rather strained circumstances. I simply have no inclination—and no time—to mourn now. Instead, I must find the means with which to raise my daughter and launch her successfully." She shrugged. Now she saw Lucas leaving the salon. He was on his way to the library, but he glanced directly at her.

Did he know where Jack was?

She smiled at D'Archand. "I also have no time or inclination for romance."

His eyes widened. "You are brutal, madame." But he spoke softly, without condemnation.

"I do not mean to be. But Julianne and Amelia speak so highly of you—I do not wish to mislead you. However—" and she smiled briefly "—I do have the time and inclination to make new friends."

He slowly smiled. "And they have spoken highly of you, madame. I believe I understand you. I would still like to show you London—as a friend, of course."

She smiled then, with relief. "I hope I have not offended you."

He returned the smile. "I am rather intrigued with your candor. It is not usual, here in town." He bowed and walked off.

Evelyn inhaled. He might wish to be friends, but his admiration was obvious. She realized her temples throbbed, but as she reached up to rub them, she realized Lucas remained in the corridor, staring at her.

Evelyn turned breathlessly to face him.

He strode swiftly to her then, and bowed. "Lady D'Orsay, it is good to see you again, although I do wish we were meeting under different circumstances."

Her heart lurched with pain. God, she was still so heartbroken, she thought. Lucas looked so much like Jack and it hurt. "Hello, Mr. Greystone." She held out her hand.

He took it briefly, his gaze searching. "Are my sisters taking proper care of you and your daughter?"

"Amelia is about to have a child—yet she is rushing about town, for my sake! And no one is kinder than Julianne." She stopped, aware of tears arising.

"Yes, Amelia is unstoppable and no one is kinder than

Julianne." He reached into an interior breast pocket and handed her an ivory linen handkerchief.

Evelyn did not use it. She asked low, "Where is Jack? Is he all right?"

"He is healed, Countess, having fully recovered from his recent ordeal."

She bit her lip, tears forming. "So you have seen him recently?"

"He is my brother," Lucas said. "Of course I have seen him."

Evelyn had spent the past two weeks in London, trying so hard to enjoy being Julianne's guest—trying so hard to recover from her affair with Jack. But no amount of pretense could make her life in London right. "You did not tell me where he is."

"I can only tell you not to worry. He is safe."

She knew she should not say another word. "I want to see him! Can you help me—please?"

"Right now, it is best if you stay away from one another."

The tears rose up again, more swiftly, with more heat. Evelyn dabbed her eyes. Why would Lucas say such a thing? Did he know about her involvement with Jack, as the rest of the family did? "What has Jack said?"

"Does it matter? I know my brother, and when he speaks of you, I can read between the lines. Your relationship is rather obvious—to me, at least." He studied her. "Do you love him?"

"I am trying to forget him."

He slowly smiled. "Seeing him will hardly accomplish that."

She hugged herself. "I realize that. This has been so hard, Mr. Greystone. I must speak with Jack—one final time."

His brows rose, incredulous. Then he said, "Call me Lucas, Lady D'Orsay. But I must overstep myself now. Jack cares for you and your daughter—and his enemies know it. You are his Achilles' heel."

Evelyn bit back a cry. "Believe me, sir, I know so well that we must not be together!"

"Then find resolve." His gray eyes flashed. "Because he has enough troubles now, and if you are used against him, it could be his death."

Evelyn gasped.

"I do not wish to frighten you any more than you are already frightened—I know what you have been through." He leaned close. His gaze was hard, but not hostile. "I actually came here tonight to meet you. Maybe the day will come when I can take you to Jack, but that day is not now."

She almost felt like asking him when that day would be—if it would be before or after the Quiberon Bay invasion. She knew better than to say such things.

"I realize you have a pair of protectors in Grenville and Paget. But you may also come to me, at any time of the night or day." With that, he nodded in parting. "I am sorry you are distressed. I am even sorrier if I have caused you distress."

"It is not your fault," she whispered. He bowed and turned toward the library. Evelyn sank against the wall. At least Jack was all right.

"Evelyn."

At the sound of Amelia's brisk tone, Evelyn turned and forced a smile. The Countess of St Just was a petite woman with dark blond hair and classic features. Amelia looped their arms. "They look like twins, don't they?" She was sympathetic. "Until one gets to know them—as they could not be more different."

"I thought he was Jack at first…. I was so shaken," Evelyn managed.

Amelia patted her hand. "I wish I could help you through this terrible time, but I know it will pass!" She shook her head then with disparagement. "I must sound like Julianne, who is an eternal romantic. Evelyn, you seem tired. I will give your regards to everyone, if you wish to retire."

Evelyn was relieved. "Would you please tell Julianne it has been a lovely evening? But after speaking with Lucas, I am undone. I do not think I can converse sensibly now."

"How often must we insist that Jack is fine and you must stop worrying?"

Evelyn had heard all about Amelia's relationship with Grenville—who had courted her when she was sixteen, only to vanish without a word and marry someone else. Ten years later he had reappeared in Cornwall for his wife's funeral—and Amelia had felt obligated to come to his aid and help with his children. Of course, eventually the love affair had been renewed.

But for a time, Grenville had fled the country, wanted for treason. Grenville had actually been spying for both the French and British governments. "Did you ever cease worrying about St Just," she asked, "when he was an outlaw?"

"Of course not," Amelia acquiesced. "I did what you are doing—I took refuge in my duties, taking care of the children and his home, until he returned. Aimee is doing wonderfully now. You must concentrate on that." And then she smiled and hugged her. "Be patient, Evelyn. That is the best advice I can give you, other than to have faith."

Evelyn hugged her in return, then slowly went upstairs. She remained shaken. Seeing Lucas had reopened every wound she had—her heart ached terribly, as if she and

Jack had parted a moment ago, not three weeks earlier. As much to comfort herself as to check upon her daughter, Evelyn went up to the room Aimee shared with Bette. They were both soundly asleep. Jolie was in bed with her daughter.

Evelyn kissed her daughter's cheek as Jolie wagged her tail. "Naughty dog," she said softly, but she did not order it to leave the bed. Then she backed out of the room.

A small fire glowed in the hearth of the sitting room attached to her bedchamber. Every night a maid started it, and that night was no exception. Evelyn slipped inside, closed the door and leaning against it, stared at the dancing flames. She thought about Lucas, and she thought about Jack.

Then she realized she was being watched.

She stiffened, and slowly turned only her head, searching for the gaze that was upon her.

Most of the sitting room was in shadow. And in the far, dark corner, a man was seated in a chair.

He moved, lighting a taper on the table there.

Evelyn cried out, her heart slamming as the candle illuminated the corner and Jack stood up.

Evelyn looked at every inch of him—his burning gaze, his loose hair, his navy blue coat, his spotless lawn shirt, his dagger and pistol, his doeskin breeches, his polished Hessian boots. Her gaze flew back to his. "Jack!" He was whole, he was alive, he was there!

"Hello, Evelyn," he said roughly.

She realized she was running to him. He started for her and she leaped into his arms.

They encircled her as their mouths fused. Evelyn returned his kiss ferociously, her hands in his hair as he lifted her up. She wrapped her legs around his waist, as they kissed with frightening hunger and alarming force.

And Evelyn realized that he had missed her as strongly as she had missed him. He carried her across the room and into the bedchamber....

EVELYN LAY IN Jack's arms, breathing hard, their legs entwined. Her cheek was against his chest, and she could hear the rapid and furious pounding of his heart. She wondered if it was possible that his heart beat faster than hers; she did not think so.

Their lovemaking had been stunning—frantic, furious, frenzied. But as coherent thought returned, tears arose. They had just made love, but they could not be together.

As he held her, his grip tightened. "How are you, Evelyn?"

She blinked back the tears, smiled and looked up at him. Only a fire burned in the bedchamber hearth, so the room was mostly in shadow. "Your sisters have been wonderful to me and to Aimee. Jack, I have missed you."

He kissed her temple briefly, but hard. "I cannot stay."

She trembled. She wanted him to declare his love and confess that he had missed her, too, and she wanted to discuss the terrible dilemma they were in. "Are you going to the island?"

His gray gaze moved over her face. "I do not want to lie to you, and I am not going to answer that," he finally said.

She nodded, more tears rising. He was going to France. Maybe he was going to Quiberon Bay! "What about LeClerc?"

He released her, sitting up. He glanced around—their clothes were strewn about the room. "What about him?" He stood, his muscular body rippling, and reached for and stepped into his drawers.

Evelyn sat up, holding a sheet to her chest, aware of

how instantaneously her desire arose again. "Have you given him the answers he seeks?"

His glance slammed to hers. "I cannot believe you would ask me such a question. Do you really want to know?"

"Neither Julianne or Paget think you a spy for the French, Jack."

His face hardened, but his eyes moved to her fist, as she held the sheet to her chest. "They are loyal—they are my family."

"I am afraid for you."

He sat back down on the bed, taking her hand in his and kissing it. The sheet dropped to her waist. "I know. I do not want you worrying about me. I want you enjoying town." He kissed her hand again. Evelyn closed her eyes, her heart thrumming, her body aching with a familiar vibrancy. He touched her chin and she opened her eyes, their gazes meeting. "I want you attending tea, dancing at balls...perhaps with D'Archand."

She lifted an eyebrow.

"I have put you and Aimee in danger. He is taken with you.... Like Trev, he is a good man." He was unsmiling and terribly serious.

"Were you spying on us tonight?"

"I could hardly invite myself to supper."

Evelyn felt more tears well. Jack should have been at that table with them—and he should have been at her side. Instead, he was in hiding, an outlaw, with a bounty on his head. "I am not interested in D'Archand."

"You should be," he said roughly. But even as he said it, he seized her shoulder, pulling her close, claiming her mouth with his.

Evelyn wrapped her arms around him and kissed him back, kicking the sheets aside.

SEVERAL DAYS HAD passed, and Evelyn was curled up on a chaise, embroidery in her hand, carefully stitching the pillowcase she was making. The pattern was of red roses, and she meant to give it to Julianne, as a thank-you gift for all she had done. Julianne, meanwhile, was curled up on the sofa, engrossed in a political treatise on the rights of man. Amelia lay on the sofa, dozing. Her tiny hands were splayed on her large belly, and as she slept, she smiled. Evelyn thought she was dreaming of her unborn child.

The two women had become like sisters. If Evelyn did not miss Jack so much, she would be entirely enjoying her time in town.

But she did miss him. Jack had not even stayed the night. They had made love another time and then he had left, but not before asking her to keep his visit a secret. Being with him again had only rekindled the fierce nature of her love, and it had been so hard to act in an ordinary manner—when she wanted to tell his sisters how madly she was in love.

But they had not discussed the future. And Evelyn had been afraid to ask him if she would see him again.

For nothing had changed. He was a source of danger for her and her daughter, and apparently, she was a source of danger for him. They did not seem to have a future, yet that fact did not quiet her raging, insistent heart.

Gerard came to the open doors. Julianne did not notice, as she was so absorbed, but Amelia awoke, yawning, as he intoned, "Madam?"

Evelyn wondered at his odd expression—and then realized he was looking at her. "Gerard?" Evelyn responded.

"I am so sorry to interrupt, madam, but Captain Barrow is in the foyer, asking for you."

Evelyn felt her heart slam. "The captain is here? Asking for me?" How her voice sounded like a squeak!

Julianne shoved her treatise aside. She turned to look at Evelyn sharply. "Wasn't Barrow the captain who came to Roselynd—looking for Jack?"

Evelyn was alarmed. "Yes."

"He is asking for Lady D'Orsay, madam," Gerard said to Julianne. "Should I send him away?"

Amelia stood up, using the arms of the sofa to do so. The three women exchanged looks. "Did he say what he wants?" she asked briskly.

"He said he wishes to speak with the Countess D'Orsay."

"Should we send him away?" Julianne asked low.

"I think we should find out what he wants," Amelia said, already starting for the door.

Evelyn was filled with dread. She could not imagine what the captain wanted. Perhaps he was hunting Jack. Perhaps Jack had been remarked, either coming or going the other night. If Barrow had remained in Cornwall, it would take him about three days to get to town in response to such information. "Wait," she said to both women.

Julianne turned to Gerard. "Please tell him we will be right there." She shut the door behind him.

"Jack was here, three nights ago," Evelyn whispered.

Amelia and Julianne exchanged brief glances. "Why didn't you tell us?" Julianne cried, but she kept her voice low.

Evelyn knew she flushed. "Because he told me not to do so."

"You think Barrow has come here to arrest him?" Amelia asked.

"Why else would he come?" Suddenly Evelyn felt her heart lurch with dread. "Oh, God. What if Jack has stayed in London?"

"He never stays in town. It is too dangerous." Julianne

was firm. "We had better greet the captain. She opened the doors and strode out. Evelyn and Amelia followed.

Evelyn saw Barrow the moment she left the salon. He was standing impatiently beside the front door, along with two of his men and the two liveried doormen. Through the window that was behind him, Evelyn now saw two more mounted soldiers, holding the three officers' chargers. Her dread intensified, but she managed a smile as she lifted her head and squared her shoulders. "Good afternoon, Captain. I did not realize your jurisdiction included town."

"Countess." He bowed slightly, and then nodded at Julianne and Amelia. He stepped briskly forward, extending a tied and rolled parchment at Evelyn. "I am afraid I have a warrant for your arrest, Lady D'Orsay."

Evelyn reeled, shocked. "I beg your pardon?"

"You might wish to read it, but I have been instructed to take you into custody," he said.

He was going to arrest her? What had she done? Evelyn succumbed to panic.

Amelia barreled forward. "There must be a mistake, Captain." Her tone was hard, and filled with authority. She planted herself between the captain and Evelyn, hands on her hips. "I am Lady Grenville, Captain, the Countess of St Just."

"There is no mistake." His smile was cold.

Evelyn had begun to think. There could be no charges—what had she done wrong? She realized Julianne now stood beside her, quite protectively.

"And what are the charges?" Amelia demanded.

"I have an arrest warrant, Countess, and I do not need charges in order to arrest Lady D'Orsay. However, I will tell you this—it is a criminal act to harbor a fugitive of the Crown in a time of war."

Evelyn did not know the law well. But she did know that anyone could be arrested for anything, without charges being leveled. "You searched the house. Jack Greystone wasn't there," she cried.

Barrow whirled to face her, his green eyes flashing. "But since then, I have sworn testimony that he was indeed in hiding in your home—and that you were, most definitely, aiding and abetting the enemy."

Evelyn gasped. None of her servants would ever betray her in such a manner! "That is impossible!"

"Your maid has signed an affidavit, Lady D'Orsay, indicting you for harboring a fugitive of the crown—an enemy of the state, a traitor."

Adelaide would never betray her this way. Evelyn felt her knees give way. Julianne caught her arm. "Bette did this? Why?"

"I imagine she is a patriot." His implication was clear, even if left unspoken—unlike her. And Barrow stepped aggressively toward Evelyn, clearly meaning to seize her.

As bulky and unwieldy as she was, Amelia moved with the agility of a cat, stepping in front of Evelyn yet again. "You are not taking the Countess from this house. That would be a terrible mistake on your part, Captain. Clearly, this is a misunderstanding. Or perhaps, Bette was forced into making such an erroneous indictment. In any case, my husband, St Just, will repair this matter."

"There is no mistake," Barrow said harshly.

"I am warning you, sir, there is a staff here of two dozen—do not attempt to remove Lady D'Orsay from these premises!" Amelia was furious now. Her gray eyes flashed. "And you do not wish to get on the count's wrong side."

"You intend to physically obstruct me?" He was incredulous. "You even threaten me?"

"We will most definitely physically obstruct you and your men. I suggest you return to your superiors and check your facts. In the interim, I have no doubt you will find the arrest warrant to have been mistakenly and illegally issued." She smiled coldly. "Good day, Captain."

Barrow trembled in anger, but he was hesitant now. "Fine," he snapped, turning to Evelyn. "You are not to leave this house, Countess, and I will be back after I discuss this matter with my superiors." He gestured at his men and flung open the front door himself. The trio pounded down the front steps, toward the waiting soldiers and horses.

Julianne leaped past Amelia, slamming the door shut. "Bolt it," she cried to the two doormen.

Evelyn staggered to the closest chair. Amazingly, Amelia did not move, her hands still on her hips. "Are you all right, Evelyn?"

Evelyn could not find her voice. Julianne hugged her. "We would never let you be arrested."

"Never," Amelia confirmed. She finally sighed and walked over to an adjacent chair and sat down. "The babe is kicking." She patted her belly, but looked up. "If Bette has betrayed you, and I imagine she has, then you cannot stay here."

Evelyn hugged herself. "She would never voluntarily do such a thing!"

Julianne clasped her shoulder. "Barrow has been after Jack for the past year. He is obsessed, clearly. I will gamble my favorite necklace that he coerced Bette."

"He is going to come back," Evelyn managed, still stunned by her narrow escape from imprisonment.

"Yes, I imagine he will—which is why you must leave—immediately—as soon as it is dark."

And Evelyn realized what was happening. She was

about to be arrested—and if she did not flee—she would go to prison. "Aimee is at Lambert Hall."

Amelia patted her hand. "It will be all right, Evelyn. Simon will correct this, and if he does not, Dominic will. I am certain."

"But we are going to have to hide until they do," Evelyn cried. "My God, where will we go?"

"I know exactly where you and Aimee can hide, Evelyn." Julianne smiled. "Looe Island."

CHAPTER SEVENTEEN

EVELYN SHIVERED, her arm around Aimee. She could hardly breathe. It was a dark cloudy night, with no stars, no moon and a sharp breeze. She huddled in a wool cloak, as did her daughter. The small dinghy they were in raced toward the nearby cove. In the cloudy night, Looe Island loomed blackly before them.

She felt as if she were in a dream. Just that afternoon, Captain Barrow had tried to arrest her. It remained stunning, unbelievable. Five hours ago, at midnight, she and Aimee had stolen out of Bedford House, led by Paget. That was as incredible. The earl had taken them by a hired coach to the docks at Southwark. There, Lucas had escorted them onto a small cutter, and they had set sail immediately.

Aimee looked up at her now with wide eyes. Evelyn had convinced her that they were on an adventure—that they were sneaking away in the middle of the night, in order to surprise Jack. She had told her daughter that they were going to visit him for a while, and she had extolled the virtues of his island home, until Aimee had become eager to leave town. For the moment, Laurent, Adelaide and Bette would stay at Bedford house with Jolie.

Lucas and another sailor were rowing them to shore. No one spoke, which made the dark, windy night more eerie. The surf was choppy, and they were being sprayed.

She smiled at Aimee though her heart felt as if it was lodged in her throat.

She had no choice but to flee London—and the authorities—now. She was a fugitive, a warrant out for her arrest, and Aimee could not afford to lose her mother. Somehow, like Jack, Evelyn was an outlaw.

She did not want this for her daughter, and she should have regrets. Yet she had none. Instead, she was acutely aware of the fact that in a few more moments, she would see Jack again.

It would be bittersweet.

Lucas leaped out of the dinghy, onto the wet sand, deftly avoiding the small waves. The other sailor followed suit, and they dragged the dinghy onto the beach. Lucas then lifted Aimee out, before helping Evelyn climb out.

He smiled briefly at her, taking a lantern from the dinghy. He gave it to the sailor. "It's a bit of a walk, Aimee," he said quietly, taking her hand. He glanced at Evelyn.

"I'm fine," she assured him. She could not imagine Jack's reaction to what had transpired—other than that he wouldn't be very pleased. On the other hand, she could imagine exactly the nature of their reunion, once he had recovered from her arrival.

They trudged across the deeper sand and reached the rocky path that led to the house. They had not taken more than a few steps when Lucas halted abruptly. Suddenly they were surrounded by a group of men holding lanterns that blazed—and muskets. Half a dozen muskets were aimed at them.

Lucas set Aimee down, and the little girl dashed to Evelyn. "Jack!" he called out.

Evelyn held Aimee's hand, her heart lurching, as Jack suddenly stepped through the circle of men, holding up a lantern, his hair loose, wearing a lawn shirt and his breeches. Clearly, he had just leaped out of his bed.

His eyes widened in alarm when he saw her. He paled. "What happened?"

"I will tell you when we get to the house. It has been a long and cold night," Lucas said.

Jack nodded at his men, who lowered their arms, as he stepped over to Evelyn. She wanted to leap into his arms. Instead, she managed a frail smile. "We are fine."

His expression hardened. "Somehow, I doubt that." And he smiled. "Aimee! Come, let me give you a ride on my shoulders. It is far better than walking—you may trust me on that."

Evelyn watched her daughter smile shyly and give her hand to Jack. He heaved her up, piggyback style, and glanced unsmiling at Evelyn. Her own smile vanished.

They turned and started up the path to the house.

AIMEE YAWNED, FIGHTING to keep her eyes open. Alice had shown them to their rooms, while Lucas and Jack had vanished into the library downstairs. While Alice made a fire, Evelyn had helped Aimee change out of her damp clothes, and then she had tucked her into bed. Aimee had not slept on the cutter. She was about to fall asleep now. "Good night," she finally murmured, eyes closed.

Alice laid her hand on Evelyn's shoulder. "I can sit with her if you want," she said.

Evelyn wanted to go downstairs and learn what was being said—and planned. But she did not want to leave her daughter alone, in a strange bed, in a strange house. Not after their flight through the night. "But it is so late."

Alice smiled. "My lady, it is almost dawn."

Evelyn jerked and got up. She went to the draperies

and parted them. The sky was just beginning to lighten. "I can't thank you enough," she said, meaning it.

"She is such a lovely child," Alice said.

Evelyn warmed, well aware that Alice was not referring to her daughter's appearance. Aimee hadn't complained, and she had been polite. "Yes, she is," she said.

She left the room, faltering as she passed the open door to Jack's bedchamber. They had made love for the very first time in that room—and she would never forget it.

Her heart was racing. Of course it was. No matter the circumstance, no matter the danger, she would always be thrilled to see him.

As Evelyn went downstairs, she heard soft, low tones coming from the library. She paused on the threshold there.

Both men were seated on the sofa, Lucas somewhat sprawled out, with a glass of red wine in his hand. Jack appeared tense. The moment she appeared in the doorway, he jumped to his feet and strode over to her. "How is Aimee?"

"She is fast asleep," Evelyn said, grateful that he had asked.

He stared for a moment. "So my nemesis has decided to hunt you now."

She was chilled. "Bette was coerced into making her confession. She has admitted it."

"Of course she was. But does it matter?" His gray eyes flashed. "There is a warrant for your arrest, Evelyn. Because of me you are a fugitive—an outlaw."

"I am hardly an outlaw." But hadn't she just thought the very same thing?

"If there is a difference between being wanted by the law, and fleeing from it, then you are splitting hairs." He was harsh.

"You are blaming yourself!" she cried.

"Who else is to blame?" he demanded. "I do not want you and your daughter having to live this way!"

"I know you don't," she said. "And I don't want to live this way, either. But that will not change the past, nor will it change my feelings for you."

His eyes flickered. "You should hate me now."

"I could never hate you."

He turned away with frustration. "I sent you to Julianne to keep you safe. Damn it!"

She touched his back. "We are safe now."

He whirled and their gazes met. Evelyn managed to smile. He finally softened. Grudgingly, he said, "Perhaps. But for how long?"

"Dominic and Simon mean to use their connections to have that warrant rescinded. Apparently one has the ear of Pitt, the other, the King."

"Good." He gave her a wild look. "And the moment they do, you can return to Julianne's!" He gave her another look, this one dark, and he paced.

Evelyn now met Lucas's wide, rapt gaze. She began to blush. If he hadn't realized they were lovers before, he certainly did so now.

And not for the first time, she thought about residing on Looe Island, with Jack. They had decided that continuing their affair was too dangerous, but that hadn't stopped them from making love the other night at Bedford House. She could not imagine living with him now, day in and day out, and not sharing his bed come nightfall. Frankly, it did not even make sense.

Lucas finished his wine and stood. "I am going," he said. "Is there anything else that you need, Evelyn?"

She walked over to him. "I cannot thank you enough for all you have done."

Lucas smiled. "You are like another sister." He gave his brother a wry glance. "I will always help, if I can." He sent Jack a salute. "I will send word the moment I hear anything."

Jack stood by the window, his hands clenched by his side. Outside, the sky was pale and stained with streaks of pink and mauve as the sun rose. He did not answer.

Evelyn looked carefully back and forth between them with some alarm. Just then, she was certain Lucas was not referring to her predicament, but to the war—and perhaps, to the Quiberon Bay invasion.

Lucas picked up his jacket and walked out. Evelyn turned to Jack. "You were not discussing me—you were discussing the war," she said softly, without accusation.

"We did discuss you, Evelyn, at some length."

She felt her heart slam. "Should I be concerned?"

"No. I only had the kindest words." His gray gaze was heating. "If I could think of another place to hide you, I would do so. We agreed it is better if we stay away from one another."

She thought about their brief rendezvous, four days earlier. They had made love in a frenzy, with urgency, but they hadn't had a chance to discuss his spying, the war, or anything else—including their feelings for one another. "Maybe I do not mind being here."

"You should mind, Evelyn. You should mind very much."

"No one knows I am here, other than your family."

He started walking slowly toward her. "The sailors know."

"They do not know who I am." Her body was stiff with tension now. "We did not have a chance to speak at all…the other night."

He paused before her. "I don't want to talk about the war, Evelyn, or how it affects us."

"That isn't fair," she said softly. "Maybe I can change your mind." She clasped his shoulders and stood on tiptoe. "I hardly wished to be pursued by Captain Barrow, but there is a benefit to my being here now."

"Thinking so makes you a very foolish woman," he said, leaning close. He brushed his lips against hers. "You are right. No one knows you are here." And this time, he pulled her close and kissed her, hard.

And Evelyn thought, *I am not a foolish woman—I am a woman in love.*

EVELYN LAUGHED. She was seated on the beach and dug her bare feet into the sand as Aimee skipped through the wet shoreline, dodging the incoming and outgoing tide, a pail in her hand. "Look!" Aimee cried, bending and holding up a gleaming white shell.

"It is lovely," Evelyn called, leaning back on her hands. It was lovely—just as the early June day was lovely. The sun was bright and warm, the sky blue, gulls soared overhead, and they had now been at the island for five days.

She flushed as her heart beat wildly and her body tightened with so much love and desire. She was almost living openly with Jack now. She had not a doubt that everyone in the house knew they spent each and every night together, even if he always awoke before her in the morning and stole out of her rooms.

It almost felt as if they were man and wife—as if they were all a family. Jack did not join them for breakfast, but he had joined them for all but two luncheons, and every night, she took supper with him alone. He spent a great deal of his time in the library, where she imagined he was going over various accounts and planning his projects—

both smuggling runs and the war games he still played. He went to the mainland every day, sometimes for just an hour. She guessed he had meetings to attend. She was afraid he was meeting French agents. When she asked, he refused to answer and her alarm knew no bounds.

But she found the respite wonderful. She spent hours reading, embroidering or walking the beaches with Aimee. She had begun to help with the management of Jack's household. She now planned their menus and supervised the house's cleaning. Every day a servant went ashore to shop, so she lacked for nothing. The days did not feel too long and the island did not feel isolated. To the contrary, Evelyn felt as if she were in a wonderful dream, and almost as if she were a newlywed.

She wondered if she were even more deeply in love than before.

"A penny for your thoughts." Jack sat down beside her.

Evelyn thrilled. "I thought you had gone ashore."

"I did. I am back." He gave her a long look, smiling slightly. Then he glanced at Aimee, who was now jumping small waves, having put her pail aside. "She is so happy."

"What child isn't happy spending her days on the beach?"

He looked at Evelyn now, glancing at her bare feet. "This idyll will soon end, Evelyn."

She felt her heart sink. "I know it is only an interlude, Jack. Has there been any word about the warrant for my arrest?"

He studied her. "No. You haven't even been here a week."

"No, I have not." She thought about his lovemaking, which remained heated and passionate, and how adept he was at avoiding serious discussion afterward and throughout the day. "You sound as if you know precisely when this idyll will end."

He now leaned back on his hands in the sand, as well. He sighed. "Will you ever cease attempting to be a sleuth?'

"It was an innocent question."

"Was it?" Impulsively, he took her hand and kissed it. "I want you to know that, even though I was horrified when you arrived here, considering the circumstances, I also feel as if this is a sweet, yet impossible, idyll."

Jack was never affectionate out of bed, and Evelyn felt her heart race with happiness. "You are becoming romantic," she said softly.

"How can I not be romantic where you are concerned?" he said ruefully, unsmiling.

Evelyn waited. Was he about to confess his feelings for her—at long last?

"A part of me, the selfish part of me, is fiercely glad to have you here," he said softly. "And I am not even ashamed to admit it."

She clasped his cheek. "Thank you for telling me that."

He studied her. "But we must both be realistic—we must both anticipate the end." He now sat up and crossed his legs.

She sat up straighter, too. Dismay accompanied the surge of dread. "You have a plan to leave," she cried. And where would he go? France? Quiberon Bay?

"Even if I had a plan to leave the island, I would not tell you, and you know why."

"Jack!" She seized his hands, startling them both. She hated being so afraid for him! "Has it ever occurred to you to simply get out of this war—completely? And spend the rest of your days in such an idyllic life?"

"I cannot simply quit what I am doing, Evelyn."

"Why not? I love you—as you know. I do not want you to die for some damned war. Why can't you quit? I am so happy—you seem happy, too." Her heart now thundered. She knew exactly what she was asking, and how monumental such a question was. But she loved him too much to be afraid to push him to get out of the war.

"Even if I wanted to, my enemies would manipulate me back into the game," he said.

She bit her lip. "Not if they could not find you."

"You want me to run away? To hide?" He was incredulous.

She began to nod. "If it meant saving your life, yes…. I would even go with you."

He jumped to his feet, his eyes wide. "I have friends who are dependent upon me now, and their lives and their freedom depend on me, as well."

Evelyn got up more slowly. She searched his gaze, and he did not flinch or look away. "Julianne thinks you are a patriot. She has said so. Paget also believes you innocent of the charge of treason. Jack! The people of France have already shed the yoke of tyranny, so whose freedom are you speaking of?"

"Oh, you are so clever!" His shoved his hands in his breeches' pockets. "You know that if you have more information, you will be in more danger!"

"We are so close now. You can trust me!" she cried. "Are you spying for the French?"

"Yes." He was final.

She was shaken, and now, in disbelief. She realized she no longer believed him capable of committing treason. It was impossible. She would never love him as she did if he were a spy for her enemies.

"Evelyn, you have proof—and lots of it."

"Grenville was once a spy—for both sides."

"He was genuinely spying for both France and England—he had genuinely cast his patriotism aside."

She found herself defending Amelia's husband. "He was protecting those he loved. Is that what you are doing, Jack?"

His eyes widened. "Are you interrogating me now?"

"I have a right to know the truth."

"No! Your sharing my bed gives you no such right!"

She flinched. "Your French friends have threatened me. They have threatened Aimee. If you are really one of them, then I am in love with someone who does not exist—then I am in love with a man I have created in my imagination!" she cried.

"Stop pushing me," he chided.

Her mind raced frantically. "Have you told LeClerc when we will invade Quiberon Bay? I do not believe that you could send our troops into the jaws of a trap."

He stared, jaw tight, eyes ablaze.

"Have you told him? Could you be so callous, so heartless? So mercenary?"

"I am going back to the house," he flashed.

"Oh, so now you run away from me?"

He whirled.

"I want to know if I am sleeping with a patriot—or a traitor! A hero—or a mercenary! I have every right to know!"

He was red. "You already know. Damn it, Evelyn, fine! I am playing LeClerc for my country, damn it, like Paget, like Grenville, like Lucas, I dance to Warlock's tune!"

Evelyn almost collapsed in relief.

"I have been put in place to play both sides, but only so we will win in the end!" He spoke now in a harsh whisper. "And I have hated misleading you—I have hated your thinking the worst of me!"

She began to shake. Evelyn glanced at Aimee, but she was now building some small hills in the sand. "In my heart, I never believed that you were a French spy, not even for a moment."

He was also trembling. Now a look of disbelief crossed his hard face. "You are a witch to have extracted such a confession from me!"

She walked into his arms. "I am so relieved."

He held her at arm's length. "Why? Nothing has changed. I am in a dangerous game, and so are you."

She put her arms around him. "I want you to get out."

He held her. "I know you do. I cannot, Evelyn. The rebels need me."

"Then after Quiberon Bay?"

His face hardened and he did not answer her.

EVELYN HELD HER DAUGHTER'S hand as they made their way down the rocky path to the beach for their daily outing. She thought that this was the part of the day that she liked best—other than the evenings that she spent with Jack.

The path abruptly turned to deep white sand. Evelyn paused to remove her shoes, as did her daughter. "Can I go ahead?" Aimee asked.

"Of course," Evelyn replied.

Aimee raced through the deep sand toward the water. Evelyn smiled, lifting her skirts and following more slowly.

A hand touched her shoulder from behind.

Evelyn turned, smiling, expecting to see Jack, who intended to go ashore that day, but had yet to leave. The Viscount LeClerc smiled at her. "Good morning, Countess."

Her heart seemed to drop through her entire body. She froze, paralyzed with alarm.

"You seem frightened, Countess. But why would you be frightened of me?" He continued to smile.

Jack was not a French spy; Jack was betraying the French and LeClerc; LeClerc would kill her if he knew it.

She glanced past him at Aimee, who ran along the water's edge, away from them. Horrified, she turned her gaze back to the slim man facing her. "You have frightened me. I did not hear you approach."

"I did not mean to terrify you," he said.

"What do you want? Does Jack know you are here?"

"Actually, I wish to speak to Greystone, but to answer your question, no, he does not know I am here. Your daughter is growing up."

Dread consumed her. "If you ever touch my daughter, I will kill you."

He chuckled. "And how will you do that? Instead, you might wish to keep your lover on a leash, Countess, making certain he understands his priorities."

She could not breathe. "Are you threatening me?" But her mind was trying to function now. Did LeClerc know that he was being betrayed by Jack?

"I am reminding you of your priorities," he said amiably. "Now, won't you introduce me to your daughter?"

Evelyn felt her fists ball up. "Stay away from her," she warned.

He shrugged. "Fine. I am going up to the house." He turned and started toward the rocky path.

Evelyn lifted her skirts and ran down to the water's edge, catching up to her daughter. Aimee turned and showed her a snail. Evelyn tried to smile. It felt impossible.

LeClerc knew where she was. How could she remain on the island now?

For when he found out that Jack was not his spy, he would come after her and Aimee.

"Mama? What is wrong?" Aimee cried, lowering her hand.

"My stomach is bothering me. I feel ill," she said swiftly. "Darling, would you mind? I think we must go back to the house."

Aimee nodded, somber now. Evelyn took her hand and reminded herself not to hurry. Why hadn't Jack's men, who kept a twenty-four-hour watch for intruders, spotted LeClerc? She assumed his ship was anchored on the island's eastern beach.

The walk back to the house, which took ten minutes or so, felt as if it took ten hours. Evelyn steered her daughter into the gardens behind the house and then into the kitchens through a back door. Alice and her daughter were preparing their lunch. Both women started upon seeing them. Evelyn smiled tightly. "Alice, would you please take Aimee upstairs for a moment?"

Alice looked carefully at her, clearly aware of her agitation, and took Aimee from the kitchens. Her heart still pounding, Evelyn hurried into the central part of the house. It was frighteningly silent. She did not hear any voices at all.

She hurried toward the library, afraid of what the silence might mean. Its dark wood door was open. Evelyn cried out.

Jack had LeClerc in a viselike grip, one arm around his throat, choking him. The Frenchman was red. "I do not care to be waylaid by your men, LeClerc, but I like it even less when you threaten Evelyn and her daughter," Jack snarled. His expression was frightening and vicious.

This would not help anything, she thought wildly. "Jack! Stop!"

He started, espying her. "Go away, Evelyn." He did not release LeClerc.

"No, Evelyn, stay," LeClerc choked out, "and tell him about our friendly chat on the beach."

Evelyn knew she blanched. "Jack, please! You are not thinking clearly!"

"Did he threaten you again?" Jack cried.

"No!" she lied frantically.

Jack released LeClerc, pushing him away hard as he did so. LeClerc stumbled but righted himself by catching an edge of Jack's desk. Then he straightened, smiling coldly as he did so. "Are you now declaring your loyalties, Greystone?" His jacket was askew, and Evelyn now saw the pistol holstered on his belt.

Jack glared. "I have not given you permission to call, LeClerc. The next time you appear here without notice, my men will undoubtedly shoot first and ask questions later."

"So now you threaten me?" He was amused.

"I am telling you that this is my island. Here, I am king. And if you wish to meet with me, you will arrange it beforehand." Jack's eyes blazed. But he glanced quickly at Evelyn.

She knew he wanted to see if she was really all right— if she had been telling the truth. She nodded at him, aware that she wasn't all right, not at all.

"I want to speak with you, and there wasn't time to arrange a meeting in advance."

"There is always time."

"Really? Maybe, Greystone, you are becoming too complacent in your duties."

Jack stared as coldly back. "I am never complacent, and especially not about war."

"A naval squadron is sailing toward Plymouth, where three supply ships are in the harbor."

Jack's expression never changed. His eyes did not flicker. He slowly looked at Evelyn. "Would you please leave us? And close the door."

Evelyn stared, wanting to know what they meant to discuss. Obviously they would speak of the war, and perhaps the invasion of France. She finally nodded and rushed from the room, shutting the door behind her. Then, shamelessly, she put her ear to it. It was so hard to hear, because her heart was hammering so loudly.

"There is gossip that the invasion of Quiberon Bay is imminent. You told me it was planned for mid-July. Has the date been changed?" LeClerc asked briskly.

Evelyn felt her heart pound as she listened.

"I do not know if the date was changed. My sources claim the invasion will take place on July 15."

"Then I hope, for your sake, that your sources are right."

"And if my sources are wrong?" Jack's tone was challenging. "I would think twice about making more threats, Victor."

"You need me, Greystone, and your country—Britain—needs me. You are better off with men like myself in power and you know it. So make certain your sources are right."

Evelyn strained to hear, but there was a silence now.

"I will check," Jack finally said. "But I cannot believe there would be changes without my knowing it."

"Ah, yes. You betray even your own brother now." LeClerc's tone was mocking, and maybe skeptical.

"What else do you want to discuss?" Jack asked sharply. "Because if you are done, I suggest you take your leave."

"You are a fool, Greystone, to allow a woman to unravel you as she has done."

Booted footsteps sounded, approaching. Evelyn leaped away from the door as it opened. LeClerc saw her a moment before Jack did, and he laughed. He turned to Jack. "You know, we can always use another agent, especially a beautiful female one." He hurried past her, his smile gone, his expression hard and frightening.

Evelyn collapsed against the wall as Jack seized her arm.

"You were eavesdropping!" he accused.

"Yes, and I heard every word!" she cried.

He pulled her into the library, slamming the door angrily closed. "Damn it, Evelyn, it is as if you wish to become so deeply involved that you have but one certain fate!"

Evelyn stared in dismay at him, then turned, opened the door and glanced out. LeClerc was gone. "There will not be an invasion July 15, will there?"

"I am not answering that!"

"Is that naval squadron a part of the invasion forces? Is it? Jack! Will there be an invasion soon? It is mid-June, not mid July!"

"If you think I am telling you war secrets, you are mad! But I will tell you this—our idyll here has just ended."

Evelyn stumbled to the couch and sat down. Jack was misleading LeClerc. LeClerc thought the invasion imminent, and he was probably right. And when it came— when it came before July 15—he would know Jack was truly a British agent.

He sat down beside her and pulled her close. "You can't stay here now, Evelyn, not after LeClerc has realized you are here. It isn't safe."

He was right. "I have nowhere to go."

"You are wrong. You can return to London." He smiled grimly. "The warrant for your arrest was rescinded ten days ago."

She started. "You didn't tell me?"

He seemed to blush. And he pulled her closer. "No, I didn't tell you. Pitt quickly agreed to its dismissal, once Paget had a chance to speak with him." He paused, watching her. "I didn't want you to leave, not yet. I did not want this to end."

Evelyn felt tears arise. "Our idyll is truly over."

He wiped a stray tear away from her cheek, then tucked some hair behind her ears. "Yes. I'm afraid it is."

It was as if her heart was breaking another time! "So I will go back to London. And you? Where will you go, Jack?"

His lashes lowered. "What makes you think I will go anywhere?"

Oh, she felt like smacking him silly! "There is a naval squadron approaching Plymouth. Will it then go on to France? To Britanny? To Quiberon Bay?"

He stared directly at her now.

"Where will you be, Jack, when they invade Britanny?"

He studied her in silence. His expression was so somber now.

"Oh, let me guess! You are going to France—to Quiberon Bay!" she cried. She seized his shoulders. "Don't go, Jack. Please. For me, and for my daughter. You have done enough to help the rebels. You have done enough to help Britain!"

Jack was calm. "You know I cannot—will not—reveal my plans to you. But most of all, you know I am not a coward."

She simply stared, her insides curdling. He was going to France. She was certain.

"Evelyn, there is no point in delaying. Pack your bags. I will take you and Aimee to Julianne's this afternoon." He stood up.

She stood, as well. "When are you going to France? I have to know."

"There is only one thing you have to know." He embraced her. "I am in love with you, Evelyn."

CHAPTER EIGHTEEN

London
June 23, 1795

EVELYN STOOD BY the front door, waving at Aimee as she got into the Bedford coach with Bette. Aimee grinned back at her as Jolie jumped into the carriage before the liveried footman closed the door. She was on her way to Lambert Hall for her lessons, which she was continuing to take with Grenville's children—never mind that Amelia had just had her first child, a boy.

Evelyn stepped back from the door as the doorman closed it. Her smile faded as the queasy feeling which had been plaguing her the entire week she had been in London suddenly returned, inexplicably. In fact the nausea was so powerful, she had the urge to retch.

Evelyn thought about Amelia and her newborn, whom she had visited daily since the little boy's birth four days ago. As she envisioned the pair, Amelia in bed, the infant in her arms, both mother and child content as only a mother and her infant can be, her heart turned over, hard.

Could she be with child herself?

She had become Jack's lover exactly thirteen weeks ago. She hadn't paid attention to the fact, but she hadn't had a single monthly, not since mid-March—two and a half weeks after Henri's funeral.

She had never expected to be blessed with another

child, because Henri had been too ill to father another one. But she loved being a mother, and now, faced with the possibility that she might be pregnant, she was over-joyed. She knew she should probably care that she was unwed, and that it would be considered scandalous for her to have taken a lover on the heels of her husband's death, but she couldn't care less about the impropriety of her condition—if she was even in a condition.

However, she could not imagine what Jack might do or think if she was carrying his child.

She was so afraid for him now. She was certain he was on his way to France—or even already there. Every day she slipped into the chapel on Fox Lane, praying that he would survive his intrigues and the war.

And he had finally told her that he loved her. It felt like a miracle. Cornwall's most notorious smuggler—its most notorious rogue—had come to love her in return.

She did not have to even think about it to know he was not a marrying man. He loved smuggling, the sea and danger. Britain was at war, and contrary to popular belief, he wasn't a traitor—he was a patriot who refused to abandon his country, his cause and his friends in this darkest, most dangerous of times.

And even if the war ended, she could not imagine Jack sitting at home, going over estate ledgers and the accounts from her tin mine. He loved adventure, and he would never give up the free trade.

But he would probably marry her, if she allowed it, if he knew she was with child. The world might think him conscienceless, but she knew better. He was a great and noble man, and his sense of honor and justice would pro-pel him into matrimony, if even for all the wrong reasons.

But didn't this child deserve two lawfully wedded par-ents and the legitimacy that entailed?

And if she were pregnant, she would now have two mouths to feed, not one. She would have two futures to secure. Suddenly Evelyn was overwhelmed. She had yet to discuss the mine with Lucas, and maybe she needed to do so immediately. And Jack would never allow his child to lack, whether they married or not—she was certain.

"You are lost in thought!" Julianne exclaimed, sailing into the front hall, beaming.

Evelyn smiled back. She had quickly realized that Julianne was delighted to have another nephew. She had been singing and humming throughout the days, ever since her sister had successfully delivered little Hal, who had been named in honor of his deceased French cousin Henri Jourdan.

"Aimee has just left for Lambert Hall," Evelyn said. "I still cannot believe Amelia wishes for such a noisy and busy household, when her baby is only four days old!"

"My sister is relentless, and she loves children—the more the merrier." Julianne approached with a sigh. "Your smile has changed, Evelyn. When you used to smile, your eyes would light up. But since returning here, you are so sad."

"You know how worried I am about Jack," Evelyn said softly. She almost wished she could tell Julianne that she suspected she was pregnant. But Jack should be the first to know, not his sister.

"I know, and I have told you repeatedly, my brother is very, very clever, and he has a very, very swift ship, and if anyone can outrun an enemy ship, it is Jack." Julianne patted her shoulder. "Besides, he has never been beaten at sea, not in a race or a battle."

Evelyn decided not to point out that there could always be a first time. She decided not to point out that an invasion would take place on land. She asked Julianne a now-familiar, often repeated question. "Have you heard anything from him—or about him?"

"No, I have not. What aren't you telling me? Why are you so worried?"

Jack had told her, very definitively, not to discuss his war-related intrigues with anyone, not even his sisters. "I am worried because the day may come where he has to face his enemies on land." Her heart filled with dread. Where was he? Was he in France? So far, there hadn't been a peep of gossip or a word in the news about a British naval squadron sailing for France. She did not know whether to be relieved or dismayed. She hated being kept in the dark. If only she knew his plans, and if he meant to take place in the invasion of Quiberon Bay—and when the damned invasion would occur!

"Somehow I do not think you mean on British soil. Now I am becoming worried. What haven't you told us? Evelyn—he is my brother! If he is in danger, I would like to know."

Evelyn bit her lip. "He made me promise to keep his secrets, Julianne, and I am afraid I must do just that."

Julianne studied her. "Fine. But now I am worried, so I will seek out Lucas and find out what he knows—and I will get to the bottom of this!"

Evelyn hoped she would do just that—because then she would have a confidante, without breaking her word to Jack.

Quiberon Bay, France
June 25, 1795

JACK MOVED HARD AND FAST, propelling his strides, his carbine in his hand. The road leading down to the beach was rutted and rocky, making it easier to traverse on foot than on horse or by wagon. It was late afternoon, the day filled with clouds, so the visibility wasn't very good, either. But he did not decrease his pace. So far, so good—but the sooner he got out of there, the better.

He was breathing hard. It was always dangerous, being on French soil, and more so this time. But he was not being followed, and the enemy had yet to remark him. Still, there was no time to waste. The sooner he was back on board his ship, the better.

He was almost running. He had just left Georges Cadoudal and six of his men. The rebel army would be making its rendezvous with the British and émigré army as planned, after the British troops landed that night. Of course, General Hoche was racing across Britanny toward the peninsula and Cadoudal had told him so—yesterday, the French navy had spotted the British naval squadron in the Channel. But Admiral Hood's fleet had prevented the French warships from intercepting and engaging the British squadron. The fleet was now just off the peninsula, awaiting its final orders before landing its troops.

And the rebels were armed and ready to unite with Comte D'Hervilly's troops once they made land, and would then seize and occupy the peninsula, before marching across Britanny to liberate it.

His mission was, finally, complete.

Images flashed in his mind now—of Evelyn, of Aimee and the memories they had so recently made on his island. God, he wanted to get home. But returning to Britain would not solve the predicament he would soon find himself in. He thought about LeClerc. By tomorrow, the vicomte would surely realize the extent of Jack's treachery.

He did not know where LeClerc was. But he would find out.

He had one ambition now—to get on board his ship,

where he could flee France if need be. He wished he could do just that. He realized that he would not mind if he never returned.

But he could not return to Britain just yet. The hunt had just begun—and only when he found LeClerc would he be able to go home to Evelyn.

The beach was just ahead. In the growing twilight, he could just make out his black ship on the iron-colored sea. His glance moved to the shoreline, where he had left the dinghy with three of his men.

Jack stumbled.

There were six men there—his sailors were bound, and held at gunpoint.

He heard an assailant coming from behind and whirled, raising his carbine, pulling the trigger. But he faced three men, and each man had his musket leveled at his face.

And LeClerc was behind them, his eyes blazing. "*Bonjour,* Jack. I did not realize you had a penchant for our beautiful countryside."

"LeClerc," he said tersely, his mind racing. He had found LeClerc! But the tables had been turned. He had to talk his way out of this—otherwise, he was the dead man walking, and LeClerc could exact his vengeance upon Evelyn. "Fancy meeting you here."

"There is nothing fancy about it," LeClerc said, stepping past his men. "May I?" He reached for Jack's gun.

Jack tensed, instantly realizing he would have little choice but to hand his weapon over. "I have been trying to make contact with you, LeClerc. You can be a hard man to find." He spoke calmly—as if he were not about to be seized, and maybe murdered, on the spot. "There is a British naval squadron offshore. They are about to land their troops. You must get word to the French at Fort Penthievre."

"Liar!" LeClerc struck him hard, across the cheek, with the butt of his gun. "Royalist!"

Jack had seen the blow coming, and he had jerked back, so the gun did not strike him squarely. Still, pain exploded in his head and he stumbled. However, he still held his carbine.

"You are wrong," he said as calmly. "Or have you forgotten that I am wanted for treason in Britain? I can hardly be a traitor in two warring countries."

LeClerc nodded at whomever stood behind Jack.

Jack whirled to deflect the blow, but he was too late, as a musket was used to slam his legs out from under him and another musket slammed down on his chest. Jack rolled away, firing; the Frenchman he had aimed at, who had hit him last, fell back, his chest exploding bright red.

From behind, someone wrenched the carbine from him.

Someone else kicked him hard in the ribs.

Another savage beating ensued, as he was kicked and beaten with the guns. And finally, when his body was a mass of blazing pain, the cloud of darkness descended. Almost miraculously, the kicking, the punches, the blows from the guns, stopped.

LeClerc bent over him and whispered, "We still execute enemies of the revolution, *mon ami*. You have made a terrible mistake, and now, you will pay…with your head."

LAURENT CRIED OUT, his eyes wide, and then he swept Evelyn into his arms, embracing her happily.

Evelyn hugged him in return. She had not been able to keep her suspicions to herself; she had just told him that she believed she was three months pregnant.

"You are going to have another child! *Mon Dieu!*" Tears now filled his eyes.

"I am praying it is true," Evelyn said as she sat down on the sofa in her sitting room. She touched her still-flat belly. "Of course, I do not know what Jack will do."

"He loves you, madame. It is obvious—so of course he will marry you!"

Evelyn simply smiled, her hand still on her abdomen. The door to her sitting room was ajar, and Julianne suddenly stepped onto the threshold. She prepared to politely knock on the open door. Instead, her gaze shot to Evelyn's hand as it rested on her belly in a gesture as old as time.

Evelyn stood up, smiling. But inwardly, she was dismayed. If she wasn't careful, Julianne would guess that she was with child. Her hostess was astute and clever.

"Am I intruding?" Julianne asked.

"You could never intrude," Evelyn said meaning it. But Julianne's bearing was a bit sober. "Julianne?"

"I have war news and I know you will want to be the first to hear it." She hurried into the parlor and put her arm around Evelyn.

"You're frightening me! Is it Jack? Have you heard from him? Is he all right?" she cried, her heart lurching horrifically.

"I haven't heard from Jack, and we haven't heard anything about him. But, Evelyn, a British force comprised of our troops and émigrés, led by the Comte D'Hervilly, has invaded the peninsula of Quiberon Bay."

Evelyn had to sit down.

"You are as white as a ghost!" Julianne cried, sitting beside her. "Why does this news strike you so?"

"Jack could be with them," Evelyn managed, filled with fear.

Julianne's eyes widened. "When you came here in April, you told us you had overheard Jack speaking about an invasion of France. He was speaking about this invasion?"

Evelyn nodded. "I begged him to tell me if he would be a part of it—he refused to even answer!"

Julianne was now pale, too. She took Evelyn's hand and gripped it tightly. She finally said, "Well, my brother may be reckless, but he is a dangerous man in his own right. If he is there, he will survive whatever intrigues he is up to. I have no doubt." She was firm.

"There is more," Evelyn whispered.

Julianne started, stiff with dread.

"He told the French that the invasion would take place next month. Now they know he is not their spy. Now they know he has deliberately misled them—and betrayed them."

Julianne was on her feet in an instant. "Lucas must know about this. Damn it, why did he keep this from me? I want to know everything!" She started for the door, and then turned. "Evelyn? I love you as much as I would if you were truly my own sister."

Evelyn didn't know where that had come from. "And I you."

"Good. Then you must tell me the truth. Are you with child?"

Fort Penthievre, Quiberon Bay, France
June 30, 1795

IT HURT TO SIT UP.

Jack somehow did so, gasping and holding his ribs—which were broken this time. His head also hurt, as did various other body parts. He had been savagely beaten for his treachery, but he was still alive.

However, he would not fool himself. He was going to

be executed for his crimes against the republic, for even if there was a trial, it would be a mockery. LeClerc had been very clear on that point.

And now he was in a prison in France.

His heart shuddered with real fear—a feeling he was not accustomed to. He was a prisoner of the French, and unless he escaped, soon, he would be beheaded as a spy.

He knew better than to hope that he would be rescued. If his crew had decided to set sail without him, Lucas and Warlock would probably already know that he had been captured, and the obvious place of imprisonment was at this fort. On the other hand it was unlikely that his ship had disembarked; his ship and crew were probably being held by the French. If that were the case, it might be days or even weeks before his brother and the spymaster realized he was a prisoner of war—and one destined for the guillotine. He did not think he had a great deal of time— only that morning, a prison guard had leered at him and told him that his days were numbered.

Jack limped over to the small, barred window of his cell. From it, he looked out over the beach and the bay. That afternoon was bright and sunny, gulls wheeled overhead, and the bay was unblemished. The British naval squadron was not in sight, not from his cell window, at least.

He did not think rescue likely.

And he had already tried to bribe two of his captors with the promise of a fortune in gold, but to no avail. He had approached each individually, in a hoarse whisper, at suppertime. The first guard had spit in his face and laughed at him; the second had begun to sing "La Marseillaise."

Attempting bribery was dangerous—he could be reported to the warden. Therefore, he had begun to think of escape.

And there was only one way out of this prison—from his cell door. Every day, two guards came in the morning and at night, to bring a piece of bread and some bug-infested gruel. The guards were armed, and they used a trap door to slide the trays into the prisoners. Thus far, in the five days he had been a prisoner, he had identified six different guards.

He had already decided which pair was the most vulnerable. The boy in that pair was clearly unnerved by the nearby fighting; he was thin, weak in appearance and even somewhat effeminate. Jack had heard him speaking. He had come from a good family, and by some bad luck, he had wound up in the republican army, as a prison guard.

His partner was middle-aged and overweight. He moved slowly, and Jack was certain his restricted movements were caused by arthritis or an injury, as much as they were by his obesity.

Jack thought it would be easy to seize the boy from behind, after he slid his tray into his cell and turned away—and put a knife to his throat. A successful escape would then depend upon good fortune—whether the second guard would hand over his weapons to save his comrade's life.

Jack was well aware that he was desperate. But if the second guard could be coerced into dropping his arms, Jack knew he could get the boy to open up his cell. Last night, Jack had spoken to the man in the cell beside his. The prisoner—a slim, dark Frenchman who was a captured Chouan rebel—was eager to help.

The plan was simple. After the overweight guard surrendered his weapons and opened up the cell, Jack would knock both guards out, then release every prisoner on his row. In the ensuing chaos, he would don his captor's uniform and find a way to escape.

There was no point in delaying their attempt at escape beyond tonight. Because he was damned if he wasn't going to see Evelyn again.

Jack continued to stare out at the serene waters of the bay. But he was worried. He prayed that LeClerc had given up his thoughts of revenge against Evelyn, now that Jack was his prisoner. Hopefully he was preoccupied with the rebel invasion.

But he had to get home to her, and not just to protect her. There was no more denying the extent of his feelings for her. It hadn't been easy, telling her how he felt, just before he had taken her from Looe Island back to London. But he had been compelled to declare his love. It was that consuming.

He now knew he had fallen in love with her at first sight, that night in Brest, when she had appeared in the middle of the night at the docks, seeking a way out of France. She had been so strong and so brave then. She was as strong and as brave now.

And she deserved a life of happiness, after all that she had endured. If he ever got out of that prison—if he ever got out of France—he wanted to be the man to give her that life. And he wondered at himself. He could hardly believe his own thoughts. He was an adventurer, a smuggler, a spy. But in the darkness of his prison cell, he did not feel the call of danger as he was used to. Instead, he could only think of Evelyn, and of Aimee, and how they needed a champion and a protector....

A war like this one could go on for ten or even twenty years. He knew that. Wars like this were always fought in the name of freedom, but they brought destruction

and tyranny instead. He suddenly gripped the bars of his
window. He was most definitely imprisoned by this war
now. But even if he escaped the French, would he really
be free, if he continued to work for Warlock? Did he really want to spend the next few years outracing two navies
and outwitting both the French and his English spymas-
ters? When Evelyn needed him?

When he needed her?

And suddenly he stiffened, as he heard footsteps in
the corridor outside his cell. He was disbelieving. Were
they coming to execute him *now?* When he planned to
escape that night?

Jack slowly turned—and saw LeClerc standing outside his cell. "*Bonjour, mon ami.* I have a few questions
for you."

A guard was with him, holding a ring of keys. Jack
looked from the key ring to LeClerc, his heart racing. He
did not think he would be politely questioned; he thought
he would be brutally tortured. And that guard had the
keys to his cell....

Cannon boomed.

In the quiet of the afternoon, the sound was shocking. It was very close by. Jack started—as did LeClerc.

And then more cannon boomed, again and again, and
there were the screams and shouts of an invading army
and the sound of muskets firing.

Within the prison, bells began to toll, rapidly, warningly—
a sound even a child would know....

"The fort is being attacked!" LeClerc cried, blanching.

Jack saw fear in his eyes.

"I have to get out of here!" LeClerc whirled, and as
he did, the guard turned to look at him—and Jack seized
him through the bars of his cell, both of his hands on his
neck. The guard gasped and began to choke.

LeClerc looked at them in terror, and ran away, down the corridor.

"Pierre!" Jack ordered his neighbor, because he had had the good fortune to have seized the guard at the edge of his cell.

Pierre reached forward, laughing, and took the gun from the guard's belt. He then placed it against the guard's temple.

"Open my door," Jack ordered, as more cannons boomed, as muskets fired, as horses screamed and men shouted. The battle seemed to be just below his window, which meant that the fort was being besieged.

The guard jammed his key into Jack's cell door, unlocking it.

Jack stepped through, took his musket from him and hit him over the head with it. He crumpled. Jack then opened Pierre's cell, and the one across from them. "Finish this," he said, handing him the keys, he ran into the opposite cell and looked out of the window.

He saw the British troops below the fort walls, a sea of invading red, fighting the French in blue. And in the center of the battle, waving high, was the red cross of St George, atop the white cross of St Andrew. His gaze slammed to the officer on the black charger, who was beneath the British tricolor, and in the midst of the battle— at once fighting his way forward and rallying his men.

"It is D'Hervilly," he said. "And if I do not miss my guess, they are about to take the fort."

CHAPTER NINETEEN

London
July 10, 1795

EVERY PASSING DAY felt like an eternity now. Émigré troops, led by the Comte D'Hervilly, had invaded Quiberon Bay. All of London waited with bated breath for the daily war news, as the British forces took the fort there, and then, as the fighting swung back and forth between both armies, with the rebels advancing, and then the French. But in the past two weeks, there had been no word from Jack and no news about him.

Evelyn sat in the salon downstairs, alone, curled up on a sofa. She could not embroider or read. She was so sick at heart—afraid that Jack was dead. What other explanation could there be for this terrible sound of silence?

"Hello, Evelyn."

And even though she now knew the timbre of Lucas's voice, he sounded so much like Jack that as she glanced up, her heart slammed. He stood in the doorway, bicorn hat in hand, golden and handsome, smiling slightly at her. Julianne was with him.

Evelyn slowly got up. She was most definitely pregnant—she was probably four months along, or close to it. "Lucas!" Her gaze searched his. He was not an expressive man and it was hard to tell if he was disturbed or simply solemn.

He strode into the room, taking her hands warmly in his. "How are you?" he asked softly.

By now, the entire family and both households knew of her condition; she instantly knew Julianne had either written him, or mentioned it to him after he had just walked in the door. "As far as this child goes, I am fine. But I am terribly worried about Jack."

He put his arm around her. "Jack is very much alive."

She cried out, beyond relief, then turned into his arms, her face against his chest. She fought her tears, quite unsuccessfully. Her condition was making her temperamental now. She looked up. "Are you certain?"

"I received word indirectly, Evelyn. But I am certain." His smile was brief but reassuring. However, he sent Julianne an odd, inquiring glance.

"What is wrong?" Evelyn cried as Julianne came forward. "What happened and where is Jack?"

"We do not know where he is now," Julianne soothed. "Evelyn, he was captured during the invasion. He was, briefly, in prison."

Evelyn had to sit down. Jack had been captured by the French—if he had been in prison, they knew he was not their agent.

LeClerc would know it, too.

Were they both in danger now?

"He spent five days in the prison at Fort Penthievre," Lucas said, sitting down beside her. "The fort was liberated by our troops and the rebels—Jack got out then."

"Thank God," she breathed. "Was he hurt?"

"We don't know," Lucas said. "But I have some good news. Victor LaSalle, the Vicomte LeClerc, was badly wounded when we took the fort. He died there a few days ago."

She shuddered. She could not wish death on anyone,

but he had been intent on using her and Aimee against Jack, and she had believed his threats. "I cannot be sorry," she whispered.

Julianne put her arm around her. "No one expects you to be sorry, Evelyn. At least we do not have to worry about LeClerc now."

Evelyn's mind raced. Did Jack know LeClerc was dead? God, she hoped so! And Jack was, at least, freed. "Could he still be in France? There is so much fighting going on now—I can't even follow the news! One day, the rebels seem to have won, the next, we hear of a French victory. Would he stay to help the rebels, who are his friends?"

Lucas hesitated. "He might. But he could have returned to Looe Island."

"No." She shook her head, standing. "He would come to me, I am certain."

Julianne took her arm. "But he doesn't know about the child. His men have families in Looe."

"Can we send word?"

Lucas patted her shoulder. "I am on my way to Quiberon Bay now. I intend to stop at the island briefly. If you wish to compose a note, why don't you do so now? If he is there, I will give it to him."

"And if he isn't there?"

"Then I will surely see him in France," Lucas said.

And suddenly Evelyn knew he was still in France— he would never abandon the émigré troops and the rebels now. He would be in the midst of combat, fighting alongside them for their freedom. He would be there not just because he was so reckless with his life, and so enamored with danger, but because he was a man of honor, a patriot, a hero.

Evelyn closed her eyes. If he came home alive, it would

be enough, and she would not ask him for anything more. Then she looked at Lucas. "When you find him, tell him that I love him," she said.

Lucas smiled. "I will…but I am sure he already knows."

THE DAYS PASSED WITH excruciating slowness. Evelyn stared grimly out of a salon window at Lambert House. Outside, in the gardens, Aimee was playing tag with William and John, Grenville's sons, with Jolie racing madly about them. In a moment, they would all troop over to the stables to ride Grenville's ponies.

She could not smile. Her heart felt frozen over with fear, with dread. Lucas had sent a brief message to them, a week ago—Jack was not at Looe Island. In fact, he hadn't been in residence since the third week of June. Evelyn was not surprised. Of course he hadn't been there—he was at Quiberon Bay.

If she did not have a child to care for, she would shout and scream, rant and rave, and allow herself to become a madwoman. But Aimee must never suspect how frightened she was. And there was her unborn child to care for.

And of course, neither Amelia nor Julianne would leave her alone for very long. Both sisters recalled the time in their lives when they had been separated from their husbands during the war, and what it was like to live with the fear of the unknown. Amelia and Julianne were determined to preoccupy and distract her with the family's many affairs. Every day she went with Julianne, Jacquelyn and Aimee to Lambert House, and every evening there was a family supper. If she dared retire to her chamber for a moment of privacy, a knock would sound on her door and either Amelia or Julianne would inquire after her to make certain she was well.

And Evelyn did not mind. They had all grown so close. She knew that Amelia and Julianne merely wished to comfort and reassure her—even if that task was an impossible one.

Because the invasion had failed.

The French had recaptured Fort Penthievre the other day, shocking London with the news. And to make matters worse, the British émigrés and Chouan rebels had been routed. Thousands had died or had been captured, while thousands more had been pushed from the beaches into the sea. And gale winds had prevented the British navy from rescuing the troops.

She hated the damned war!

And she was sick, because she knew Jack had been among the rebels. Now, she did not know if he was one of those captured, or if he was even alive.

Looe Island
August 3, 1795

JACK LIMPED SLOWLY INTO his bedchamber, ripping off his bloody and dirty shirt. He was so exhausted, he could barely stand, and he collapsed into a chair to take off his riding boots.

He threw them aside. Then he slumped in the chair, eyes closed, sitting motionless.

Images from the various land battles he had been in assailed him yet again—men in red and blue slashing at one another with their bayonets, human blood spurting, spraying, men screaming, as cannons boomed, as smoke filled the air, as horses whinnied in terror....

Would he ever forget those battles on the peninsula?

He dreamed of the wounded and the dying at night, and in the day, the ghastly images haunted him, too.

He opened his eyes and stared across the bedchamber, but he did not see the four-poster bed he slept in, or any other accoutrement.

Help! Help!
Aidez-moi! Aidez-moi!

They bobbed in the gale-driven ocean, waving frantically, screaming for help. Dozens of heads and dozens of arms were all that could be seen of the drowning troops, begging to be rescued. It was a horrific sight, one he would never forget.

Abruptly, Jack flinched and forced his vision to clear. He made himself identify the furnishings of his bedroom. And while he stared at the dark four-poster bed with its gold-and-red coverings, he still saw those bobbing heads and flailing arms.... He thought he might live with the gruesome memory until he died.

Hot tears filled his eyes.

He had been setting sail for Britain, having stayed along the French coast to help with the invasion. As it turned out, the delay had been timely; he was just in time to rescue one hundred and three of the drowning men, mostly émigrés, but a few had been former French prisoners of war. He wished he had been able to save more of them, but by the time he had dragged the last survivor aboard his ship, the ocean had been silent, the cries for help having ceased, and when he had looked out over the water, there had been no one left....

He had the terrible urge to weep.

God, he was so sick and tired of war and death!

He stood, cursed at the pain in his knee and limped over to the bureau and poured a stiff drink. He had been in other battles, but never had he planned for and fought in a cause like this. He had truly believed they could liberate Britanny from the French. Instead, thousands were dead, as many were captured and General Hoche was rampaging across the countryside, exacting vengeance upon anyone and everyone associated with the Chouans.

He slammed down the entire glass of brandy. At least LeClerc was dead. His French master had died from the wounds inflicted during the first attack upon Fort Penthievre. Jack had run past him, too, as he was leaving the fort. He had taken one look at LeClerc, who lay bleeding upon the ground, shot in the chest, and he had known he would not survive.

He hadn't felt satisfaction, and he hadn't felt remorse. He hadn't felt anything at all, but now he was grateful that he had been spared the ugly task of murdering his enemy.

Evelyn's enemy.

His hand shaking, Jack poured another drink. Not a day had gone by in this past month of hell that he hadn't thought of Evelyn and Aimee, that he hadn't been aware of the depth of his yearning and love for them. Just then, he would give his soul to have her in his arms, so he could hold her tight.

He continued to tremble. The dreams about the battles and the drowning men were bad enough, but he had other dreams, as well: of being in prison. Almost nightly, he was trapped behind stone walls and iron bars, the sound of cannons booming, exploding. In those nightmares he knew he would never escape the French prison and the French wars. LeClerc came to leer at him. So did Warlock.

He was furious, he was frustrated and he was desperate. He would beg to be set free—so he could return to Evelyn. But no one ever answered his pleas. Instead, he would awaken, aware that even though he was not behind bars now, he was still a prisoner of the war, and shaken to the core because of it.

It was said that war changed a man. So did prison. One was bad enough—both were sheer madness.

He wasn't sure how it had happened, but he was done—with the war, with Warlock, with spy games. He would never take his life or his liberty for granted again. And he never intended to be a prisoner of war again, either. Not due to incarceration, and not due to these war games.

He had given Britain everything he had—he had almost given her his life. And for what? He, Jack Greystone, could not save Europe from the French Revolution. He had done his best to play his part in the effort; let someone else save Britain and her Allies from the French now. Everyone who was anyone in the world of intrigue knew he had been playing the French, so he was useless to Warlock in continuing to play both sides. There could be no better time to get out.

And even if it were a bad time to stop spying, he didn't care.

He cared about Evelyn and her daughter.

Jack turned slowly. He almost cringed when he faced his reflection in the mirror. He was unshaven, bruised, battered and shirtless. He looked as disreputable as a fifteenth-century pirate. He did not appear to be a gentleman, or at all good enough for the Countess D'Orsay.

She was a great lady. He was just a smuggler and a rogue.

But he was a soon-to-be-free smuggling rogue; Admiral Hood thought him a hero. He had invited him to dine aboard the Channel fleet's flagship after the rescue of the drowning men. Jack had accepted.

And it was probably the most fortunate invitation he had ever received. They had drunk a great deal of wine and shared a great many stories and secrets. Jack had told Hood almost everything about the spy games he had been playing. He had also pointed out that his government had a price on his head. Hood had been furious.

And he had promised him that he would be a free man again—before the summer was over. He had stated it was his personal mission.

Jack stared at his dirty, battered reflection. He had never cared about that bounty, until recently. For a long time, he had enjoyed the notoriety of being wanted by not just one government, but two. It had been an amusing game, avoiding the authorities on both sides of the Channel.

And he knew exactly when he had grown tired of the game; he knew exactly when it had begun to hamper and hinder him, when it had become frustrating. When Captain Barrow had come looking for him at Roselynd, something within him had snapped. Every urge he had—and had always had—was to protect Evelyn, not to put her in more danger.

The truth was, he wanted to be a free man again—he wanted that damned bounty gone. He wanted to go to London and visit his sisters and their children whenever he felt like it. He wanted to come and go at Cavendish Square, where his brother so often resided, as anybody else could. He even wanted to return to Greystone Manor, his family's home, so he could restore it to the glory it had once enjoyed centuries ago.

Generations of Greystone men and women had been smugglers, of course. The manor had been built above Sennen Cove long ago, because it was the perfect location from which to smuggle goods between Britain and France. It remained an ideal haven now.

He might be done with spying, but smuggling was his life. He could no more give up the free trade and his life at sea than he could give up Evelyn. If he became a free man, would Evelyn really wish to remain with him? Would she be willing to embark upon a future together? Would she consider becoming a smuggler's wife?

His heart was thundering. He missed her desperately and had a terrible need to be with her now, to hold her, make love to her and forget the hell of war. Jack walked over to the small wood box that was on top of the bedroom bureau. He flipped open the lid. The ruby necklace Evelyn had given him to pay for her passage from France, four years earlier, was inside.

He had never sold it. He had buried it along with some other valuables in one of the caves used by generations of Greystone smugglers behind the cliffs at Greystone Manor. At the time, he hadn't thought much about it, he had simply stashed the valuable necklace away. Now, in hindsight, he knew he hadn't sold the necklace because he had been so smitten with Evelyn from the very start.

It had taken him an extra day to sail to Sennen Cove to retrieve it, another day to return to Looe Island. He hoped Evelyn would comprehend the gesture when he returned the necklace to her. He hoped she would be thrilled when he brought it to her—when she realized he hadn't ever been able to part with it.

Jack slowly closed the lid. Evelyn was a very intelligent woman. She knew she could do far better than him. And she had Aimee to think of. She loved him, but he did not know if she would accept his suit.

He intended to do whatever he had to in order to convince her to become his wife.

EVELYN PAUSED BEFORE climbing into the Bedford coach, with Aimee, Julianne and Jacquelyn, and the two children's maids behind her. Today, Julianne had decided they would take the children for a picnic in the park, skipping their reading and arithmetic lessons. Amelia was meeting them in Hyde Park with Will, John, her tiny stepdaughter, Lucille, and baby Hal.

It promised to be a wonderful afternoon. But Evelyn did not want to go. She did not think she could feign another moment of happiness. A list of survivors had been posted at the Admiralty, and she happened to know that Jack's name was not on that list. Now, she was waiting for her brothers-in-law to obtain highly classified information—a list of the British prisoners languishing in France.

She realized a small carriage drawn by a single bay horse had turned into the drive. It was obviously a hired hansom.

"Dom must have a caller," Julianne said brightly. "Aimee, Jackie, do get in, or we will be starting our picnic at suppertime!"

Evelyn realized she was paralyzed, staring at the approaching vehicle. It was an open carriage, and a gentleman sat in the back, in a dark jacket and hat. She could not take her eyes off of him.

The gentleman was tall, dark, elegantly clothed, but as he stood to get out, she saw his golden hair beneath the black felt bicorn hat. And he was staring intently—relentlessly—at her.

It was Jack.

And Evelyn knew there had to be a mistake. She must be staring at Lucas. Jack would not drive through town in an open vehicle, or so casually appear at the house in the broad light of day!

He jumped down from the carriage, never taking his gaze from her.

She was not mistaken! "Jack!" she gasped.

He strode to her with long, hard, determined strides

and pulled her into his arms, kissing her fully on the mouth, deeply, with heat.

Evelyn began to cry. She held on to him, hard, as he kissed her again and again.

And finally, he ended the kiss. "Hello, Evelyn." He was hoarse—and his eyes glistened.

She clasped his face in her hands. "You are alive! You are home!" But her vision was blurred with tears.

"I am alive…." He smiled now. "I am home." He put his arm around her and pulled her to his side and smiled at his sister.

Julianne ran to him and hugged him, then cried, "Why are you standing in my driveway like this?"

"Surely we must rush inside?" Evelyn asked. But as she met his gray gaze, as she saw the softness in his eyes, so much hope began. What was happening? Jack would never be standing outside like this as an outlaw!

"We do not have to rush anywhere." He now turned and smiled at Aimee. "Hello, Aimee. Have you been enjoying your stay in town?"

Aimee smiled bashfully, nodding.

Julianne stepped forward. "Why don't you go inside with Evelyn, Jack, and I will take the children to the park, as planned." Then her gaze became direct. "I am so glad you are safe—and home."

He smiled at her. "So am I."

Evelyn realized she was shocked and dazed, her heart thundering, her mind nearly shut down. She hurried to Aimee. "Would you mind if I stayed behind today? Aimee, I have so much to discuss with Mr. Greystone."

Aimee was solemn. "I don't mind, Mama. I know you love him."

Evelyn started, genuinely surprised. "Have I been so obvious?"

Aimee smiled. "He is so handsome…and I like him, too."

Evelyn hugged her, and then helped her into the carriage. She was acutely aware of Jack standing behind her, and now, she had a hundred questions! The driver carried his baggage past them, as Julianne was the last to get into the coach.

Evelyn seized her hand, suddenly near tears. "He is home."

Julianne was also misty-eyed. She smiled and kissed her cheek. "He is home and I am so happy for you both!"

Evelyn stepped back as the footman closed the door. Instantly, Jack took her hand.

She turned and behind them, the Bedford coach pulled away. "Is this a dream?"

"No, it is not."

"Jack! What has happened? You never use the front door!"

He began to smile, a smile she had never before seen. "The bounty has been removed, Evelyn. I am a free man."

She cried out, thrilled. Putting his arm around her, he walked her into the house. "You are free," Evelyn whispered. "Oh, God, I had hoped that one day you might be a free man—but I never dreamed it would happen so soon—like this!"

"We have Admiral Hood to thank," Jack said softly as the doormen closed the front door behind them. "There is more. He has recommended a medal of honor for me. Next month, I am to be knighted."

Evelyn realized she held both of his hands in hers. "You are to be recognized as the hero you truly are!"

"Yes." He swept her suddenly into his arms, holding her tightly against his strong body. "I have missed you terribly." He was rough. "When I was in prison, my greatest fear was that I would never hold you again."

Tears came. "Jack, I have missed you, too. I have been living in a state of terror—I was afraid you were dead!"

"I had no plan to die—because that would mean leaving you."

She basked in his burning gaze. And Evelyn had no doubt then about the depth of his love for her. No words could be as romantic. "We have so much to discuss," she began, thinking of his child, which she carried.

"Later!" He lifted her into his arms—both doormen gaping—and started for the stairs. Evelyn touched his beautiful face, having no desire to protest. Upstairs, he kicked open the door to her bedroom, closed it, carried her to the bed and laid her down on it. And as he shrugged off his jacket, Evelyn saw dark, terrible shadows flitting through his eyes. Jack was so adept at hiding his feelings, but then, his expression was utterly ravaged.

She knew the war had scarred him.

And a moment later he was joining her in that bed. "I need you," he said thickly. "But I love you—so do not think I am a terrible cad."

She touched his face, exhilarated—he had finally declared himself! "I would never think such a thing."

He did not answer, claiming her mouth, his kiss so hard and deep, it was almost hurtful. Evelyn barely knew what happened next. She threw her arms around him, realizing that he was terribly wounded by his adventures in France, as never before, while he kicked off his breeches and lifted her skirts. "I love you," he said again, his tone thick and desperate.

Evelyn held him hard, as he kissed her and touched her, fanning not just her desire, but also her love. A moment later, they were joined.

And she looked up at him as they made love and realized he was crying. "Don't," she gasped.

He smiled through his tears. "Don't what? Don't do... this?"

She gasped, and suddenly she was shattering, and she could not stand it—the love, the desire and the ecstasy were simply too powerful—and she wept, as well. He cried out, holding her tightly, his cheeks damp with tears.

And as Evelyn floated back to reality, she began to caress him. She kissed his temple. "What happened in France, Jack?"

He studied her. "You do not want to know."

She hugged him. "I am sorry." She could not imagine the horrors he had been through, but she would help him heal from the wounds of war now. "Maybe, one day, you will tell me what happened. But if you do not, I will respect that choice. No matter what, I will always be here for you."

He sat up, looked around and found his breeches at the bottom of the bed. As he put them on, Evelyn rearranged her skirts and underclothes. She finished and found Jack standing by the bed, staring intently at her. "Always?" he said.

Her heart hammered. "Yes, always." What was he thinking?

"Let's go back downstairs. I have something for you."

Evelyn was puzzled, but she gave him her hand and got up. While she fixed her hair, he finished dressing. He then took her hand again, smiling, and did not let her go as they went back downstairs. Jack went to his valise and opened it, removing a small, gleaming wood box.

It was the kind of box a lady used to store jewelry. She looked at Jack, and he handed her the small box. "This is for you, Evelyn."

Her heart thundered. She could not imagine what was inside, as it was not a velvet gift box. She opened it and gasped as her ruby-and-diamond necklace winked up at her. "What is this?"

"I hope you are pleased," he murmured.

Evelyn bit back another gasp. Jack had never sold the ruby necklace she had given him for her passage from France!

"I could not part with the jewels."

She began shaking her head wildly. "Oh, how you pretended to be so indifferent to me! Oh, how you claimed to be a cold mercenary!"

He took her hand again. "I am somewhat mercenary. But I was never indifferent to you."

Her heart turned over, hard. "Jack, are you saying that you were taken with me from the moment we first met?"

"Yes, that is what I am saying."

She inhaled. "You hid it so well!"

"I fought my every feeling for you. I was a fool, Evelyn." He tugged her into his arms. "I buried it at Greystone Manor, otherwise, I would have returned it to you sooner."

She felt like blurting out that she loved him—insanely. "Jack, we are even. I was smitten, too, from that very first night."

He slowly smiled, pleased. "Were you?"

"I think I fell in love with you then."

His smile grew. "You are giving me hope!"

What did that mean? she wondered. "I have begged God a thousand times to keep you safe and out of all harm, Jack. That is all I care about. I am so glad you are home. And you are free!"

He cupped her shoulders, his expression so solemn and serious. "I have had a great deal of time to think. I have few regrets in my life, but I do regret resisting my feelings for you—and I regret making you my mistress."

Evelyn started. "Surely you do not regret the time we have spent together?'

"Selfishly, I do not. But then, you do know I am a selfish man?" His gaze pierced hers.

"You are the most selfless man I know!"

"I am a smuggler, Evelyn, a rogue. I am a man who is accustomed to getting what he wants."

"You are a hero! And you are being knighted—which proves it!" she cried. "Sir Jack Greystone," she added.

"Evelyn, I want you."

She froze. Excitement began. "I do not comprehend you, Jack. You have me already."

"You deserve so much more than life as a smuggler's mistress."

Was he going to propose? No, it was impossible; Jack was an adventurer, not a marrying man!

He gave her an odd look, and then paced around her slowly. She had to turn to watch him. "You are young and beautiful, and you can have more children—and I imagine you want more children. You deserve to be someone's wife." He paused, facing her. "You could have a queue of suitors lined up, Evelyn, beginning with Trevelyan and D'Archand."

She was confused, but not alarmed. And what should she say? She wanted to be his wife! And they would soon have a child together! "Of course I would like more children. But I do not want a queue of suitors. I do not want Trev or the count!"

He hesitated. Suddenly he appeared uncertain. "Evelyn. I am trying to ask you if you will condescend to be my wife." But his gaze was stunning in its intensity.

She cried out as her heart slammed. "Did I hear you correctly? Did you just propose?"

He reached into the pocket of his bronze jacket and pulled out a large yellow diamond stone. "I obtained this in France. It isn't set yet, obviously. But it suits you perfectly. It is yours, whether you accept my proposal or not."

She barely looked at the stone, reeling. Jack was not a marrying man! He did not even know about her pregnancy! Yet he was proposing! "You love danger," she managed. "You are an adventurer!"

"I enjoy danger, but it is you that I love." He smiled briefly. "Before you answer, I must tell you I have given up these war games, Evelyn. I am done spying." His gaze searched hers. "But I cannot give up my life at sea. The sea will always be my mistress—she will always be my *second* love. I intend to return to Greystone Manor and restore it to its former glory. I will continue to engage in the free trade, as my grandfather and great-grandfather have done. If you refuse me, I will not be hurt. Obviously you belong with a gentleman—not a smuggler."

Evelyn realized she was crying. She could not speak.

"And if you refuse me," he said hoarsely, "I want you to know, you are not alone. I will always be there for you. I will always be your champion and protector, even if you choose to marry someone else."

She reached for his hands and took them. She looked at him, crying. "I have told you a great many times how much I love you! So, yes, I will become your wife!"

He stared, eyes wide. "Are you certain?"

"I have never been as certain of anything," she began. She knew she must tell him about the child now.

He swept her into his arms and off the floor, and whirled her, laughing. It was a free, light, joyous sound.

"Jack!" she cried. "I have news. I pray you are going to be pleased. Jack, I am close to five months along—I am carrying our child."

His eyes widened again, bigger than before.

She felt his confusion then. "We were reckless," she said. "Is it really such a surprise?"

He began to smile. "You are having my child?" And he laughed, loud. "Now you have no choice, Evelyn, but to marry me—as soon as is possible. We must elope!" He laughed again.

Evelyn realized he was absurdly pleased. "Are you happy because you think I am obligated to marry you? Or because we are about to bring a beautiful child into this world?"

"Both," he said adamantly. "Both." He swept her close. "Have I told you just how much I love you?"

"Maybe," she whispered, in his arms, smiling. "But I do not mind if you tell me again."

"Then I am going to do just that," he said. "But first, I think we should assemble the family—and call the clos-est parson. Evelyn, if you do not mind, I will make an honest woman of you tonight."

"How could I mind? I cannot wait to be your wife," she whispered, her heart ballooning with love. "I almost feel as if we are in a magical dream."

He smiled tenderly then. "As do I. But we are not dreaming. We have survived the war, and we are together. You are having my child—and I am never leaving you again."

Evelyn went into his embrace and he held her tight. And it was so right. But then, hadn't she known that Jack Greystone was her destiny from the moment they had first met, when he had stood so proudly upon the deck of his black ship, when he had taken her rubies to transport her from France? And she didn't care that the sea was his mistress. Because she knew she was his first love—his love for all time.

* * * * *

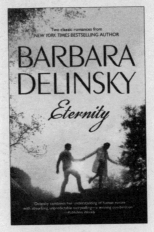

Meet the Redgraves—four siblings celebrated for
their legacy of scandal and seduction....

A delicious new series from *USA TODAY*
bestselling author

KASEY MICHAELS

In stores now.

REQUEST YOUR FREE BOOKS!

2 FREE NOVELS
FROM THE ROMANCE COLLECTION
PLUS 2 FREE GIFTS!

YES! Please send me 2 FREE novels from the Romance Collection and my 2 FREE gifts (gifts are worth about $10). After receiving them, if I don't wish to receive any more books, I can return the shipping statement marked "cancel." If I don't cancel, I will receive 4 brand-new novels every month and be billed just $5.99 per book in the U.S. or $6.49 per book in Canada. That's a saving of at least 25% off the cover price. It's quite a bargain! Shipping and handling is just 50¢ per book in the U.S. and 75¢ per book in Canada.* I understand that accepting the 2 free books and gifts places me under no obligation to buy anything. I can always return a shipment and cancel at any time. Even if I never buy another book, the two free books and gifts are mine to keep forever.

194/394 MDN FELQ

Name	(PLEASE PRINT)	
Address		Apt. #
City	State/Prov.	Zip/Postal Code

Signature (if under 18, a parent or guardian must sign)

Mail to the **Reader Service:**
IN U.S.A.: P.O. Box 1867, Buffalo, NY 14240-1867
IN CANADA: P.O. Box 609, Fort Erie, Ontario L2A 5X3

Not valid for current subscribers to the Romance Collection
or the Romance/Suspense Collection.

Want to try two free books from another line?
Call 1-800-873-8635 or visit www.ReaderService.com.

* Terms and prices subject to change without notice. Prices do not include applicable taxes. Sales tax applicable in N.Y. Canadian residents will be charged applicable taxes. Offer not valid in Quebec. This offer is limited to one order per household. All orders subject to credit approval. Credit or debit balances in a customer's account(s) may be offset by any other outstanding balance owed by or to the customer. Please allow 4 to 6 weeks for delivery. Offer available while quantities last.

Your Privacy—The Reader Service is committed to protecting your privacy. Our Privacy Policy is available online at www.ReaderService.com or upon request from the Reader Service.

We make a portion of our mailing list available to reputable third parties that offer products we believe may interest you. If you prefer that we not exchange your name with third parties, or if you wish to clarify or modify your communication preferences, please visit us at www.ReaderService.com/consumerschoice or write to us at Reader Service Preference Service, P.O. Box 9062, Buffalo, NY 14269. Include your complete name and address.

BRENDA JOYCE

77692	PERSUASION	___ $7.99 U.S.	___ $9.99 CAN.
77655	SEDUCTION	___ $7.99 U.S.	___ $9.99 CAN.
77551	DEADLY VOWS	___ $7.99 U.S.	___ $9.99 CAN.
77547	DEADLY KISSES	___ $7.99 U.S.	___ $9.99 CAN.
77541	DEADLY ILLUSIONS	___ $7.99 U.S.	___ $9.99 CAN.
77507	THE MASQUERADE	___ $7.99 U.S.	___ $9.99 CAN.
77460	AN IMPOSSIBLE ATTRACTION	___ $7.99 U.S.	___ $9.99 CAN.
77442	THE PROMISE	___ $7.99 U.S.	___ $9.99 CAN.
77346	DARK VICTORY	___ $7.99 U.S.	___ $7.99 CAN.
77334	DARK EMBRACE	___ $7.99 U.S.	___ $7.99 CAN.
77275	A DANGEROUS LOVE	___ $7.99 U.S.	___ $7.99 CAN.
77219	DARK RIVAL	___ $7.99 U.S.	___ $9.50 CAN.

(limited quantities available)

TOTAL AMOUNT	$ _____
POSTAGE & HANDLING	$ _____
($1.00 FOR 1 BOOK, 50¢ for each additional)	
APPLICABLE TAXES*	$ _____
TOTAL PAYABLE	$ _____

(check or money order—please do not send cash)

To order, complete this form and send it, along with a check or money order for the total above, payable to Harlequin HQN, to: **In the U.S.:** 3010 Walden Avenue, P.O. Box 9077, Buffalo, NY 14269-9077; **In Canada:** P.O. Box 636, Fort Erie, Ontario, L2A 5X3.

Name: _____
Address: _____ City: _____
State/Prov.: _____ Zip/Postal Code: _____
Account Number (if applicable): _____

075 CSAS

*New York residents remit applicable sales taxes.
*Canadian residents remit applicable GST and provincial taxes.

HARLEQUIN® HQN™
www.Harlequin.com

PHBJ1212BL